DEMON IN THE BONES

SEQUEL TO *ARD MAGISTER*

Laura J. Underwood

Demon in the Bones
Laura J. Underwood
Second Electronic Edition Copyright © Laura J. Underwood,
2016
First Print Edition Copyright © Laura J. Underwood, 2016

Published by Yard Dog Press at Create Space

Print Version ISBN 978-1-937105-92-1
Demon in the Bones
First Print Edition Copyright © Laura J. Underwood, 2016

Yard Dog Press
710 W. Redbud Lane
Alma, AR 72921-7247

http://www.yarddogpress.com

Edited by Selina Rosen
Copy Editor & Technical Editor Lynn Rosen
Cover art by Mitchell Bentley

First Print Edition July 1, 2016
Printed in the United States of America
0 9 8 7 6 5 4 3 2 1

Dedication

Dedicated to all the fans who have waited patiently for me
to continue the story.

PROLOGUE

"There's one..."

"Too old."

"And that one?"

"Too young."

"How about..."

"Too inebriated. They would only hire him out of desperation."

The long sigh of resignation filled the Demon-Bound with its resonance.

"I'm only trying to help," his internal companion said.

"I know," the Demon-Bound thought back and smiled. *"But I have to pick the right one this time. That last one turned out to be something of a coward. His fear made him hard to control, and he nearly gave me away more than once."*

"What about the tall man over in the corner talking to the merchant? He doesn't look like he sort of man who would be afraid of anything."

The Demon-Bound studied the man in question. Tall was putting it mildly, since even sitting the fellow was a head taller than the merchant. He had coppery red hair, intelligent green eyes, and was wrapped in a length of blue tartan wool with bits of black and white woven through it. That one was a mercenary and a former militiaman too, for he wore his weapons in the manner of a man used to battle. *A Keltoran.*

That one just might do, he thought to himself. A good muckle fellow like that would carry more than enough essence to hide behind.

But when the Demon-Bound stretched senses to test the man's mind, the big man bristled and turned to glance over the crowd. Those green eyes narrowed briefly on *his* corner, then flashed elsewhere as though seeking someone or something.

Horns, he felt that!

"Mage blood," his internal companion said and chuckled. *"I guess he won't do after all."*

"*Too risky,* the Demon-Bound agreed and sighed. One of mage blood would resist any efforts to guide him. *"I'll have to find someone else, then."*

"*Well you had better make up your mind soon. They're going to be here within a few hours. It would not do for you to be using demon magic while their leader is close."*

"*Not to mention in the presence of the Other."*

It was the Other—one of the Elderkin—who worried him more. The whole reason the Demon-Bound had been tracking and working the caravan in various guises all the way from the ranges was that when they left, he sensed the Other in their midst. Not good. If their precious cargo were to fall into the wrong hands now, all would be lost. But he could not let them know he had come with them. That was just as risky. If they knew he was in their company, they would panic—give themselves away—and increase the danger tenfold.

After all these years, the Demon-Bound had come to accept that he had that effect on mortal men and mageborn alike.

They just didn't understand, and even those he called friend were always hesitant to rile him. He could not help himself sometimes, especially when he lost his temper. That was why he needed the essence of an ordinary mortal man to hide his own behind. To keep the more astute among mageborn from learning what he really was. Granted, only Elderkin and Youngerkin could see what he carried within, but as time passed, he had found that some mageborn had just enough sensitivity to his companion to *see*. But then, bound as he was to his internal companion for eternity, he was starting to learn to live with his *affliction*. He just needed to be careful.

But then, I don't really have a lot of choice, do I?

He sighed once more and pulled his hood back a little more to allow him to see the rest of the room without moving much. Over in the corner, the Demon-Bound spied a man with dark hair who nursed a small mug of ale, and looked like he had lost his best friend. Stretching senses carefully—so as not to draw the attention of the Keltoran again—the Demon-Bound scried the man. No magic. Not a whit of mage blood in this one. And his essence was strong, so the man was healthy.

The Demon-Bound probed deeper, filtering his own essence into the man's thoughts to test them.

Bloody sod, four more weeks! I can't wait four weeks for

another job. If I can't get the money honestly, I'll have to go back to thieving for it...

He pulled his senses back. So this man's scruples were not the best. Still, one could not be so choosey. Besides, once he had control of the man—once he was using the mortalborn's essence to disguise his own—it would be easier to keep him honest.

He hoped.

He left his corner to make for the bar, ordering two large ales. Then he threaded his way across the tavern. The man looked up, surly at first, so he set one of the ales before him and offered a friendly smile.

"You look like a man who is looking for a friend," he said.

The man took one look at the ale then glanced up at him. "Got a name?"

"As a matter of fact," the Demon-Bound said, sliding into the bench beside the dark-haired man, "I was about to ask you for yours."

He offered his hand in friendship, whispered his new name, and as the stranger clasped his hand, the Demon-Bound slipped into the man's mind and carefully began to weave the spell that would make this mortalborn his slave.

ONE

Well, that was a trip fae *naught,* Conor Mac Manahan thought as he walked back to the inn at the gate of Torlea, a small township along the southern borders of Elenthorn. A hard ride north through the snowy mountains rising along the border between Loughan and Tamnagh, and now it came to this. Caperton passed away last autumn, and his son had no desire to run a caravan before the final thaw. *Which 'twill no be before the spring moon rises.* That was two fortnights away, far longer than Conor wanted to wait. While he had coin enough to spare, he could not afford to sit idle until spring.

He sighed and pushed his way into the inn. Warm air surrounded him as he climbed the stairs to the tiny garret room he shared with his wife and his adopted son. He rapped lightly on the door before pushing it open. Eithne was sitting on the pallet with Rhoyd, showing the lad how to roll bandage strips, but at Conor's entrance, Rhoyd dropped the linen and charged towards the door with an enthusiastic shout. Smiling, Conor opened his arms and caught the lad, lifting him. It was hard to believe that three years had passed, and still Rhoyd showed no sign of getting taller or older.

"Been behaving yourself?" Conor asked, not quite as cheerfully as he would have any other time.

"Of course," Rhoyd said then frowned. "Is something wrong?"

"Are ye reading minds now lad?" Conor asked. He set Rhoyd down and shuffled a hand through his thick black hair.

"You feel...unhappy," Rhoyd said.

Conor sighed as Eithne looked up at him in a questioning manner. "You do look a bit disappointed about something," she agreed.

"There's no caravan," Conor said. "Caperton's gone to the Summerland. His son is holding off another moon to leave for Caer Elenthorn."

"Oh, dear," Eithne said. "What shall we do?"

"Well, we could ride south again, get back across the river and maybe hope to catch one in Caer Tamnagh," Conor said. "Otherwise, we have to wait here and hope another caravan comes through that we can ride out with—or wait for Caperton's son to give the order."

"If we must, I suppose we must," Eithne agreed and shook her head. "I suspect we'll have to select a less private room."

Conor knew what she was thinking. Seven days on the road, and only a hope that he might be fortunate enough to get across the river in time to catch a caravan. Or waste fourteen days here sitting around with little to do. It was not that he didn't have enough coin to support them for the time, but he hated not having a definite job when they now had an extra mouth to feed and were so far from the place they called home.

"I've got silver," Rhoyd said quite suddenly.

Conor set a firm parental scowl on the lad. "I thought you left the coin yer auntie gave ye with Mistress Meg?"

Rhoyd shrugged, showing no fear of the look, which pleased Conor though he would not show it. "I brought ten silvers just in case. Aunt Genna said I should always have coin."

"Well, we've got more than enough coin," Conor said. "So you keep those sgillinns well hid, aye? Don't want ye tempting some light-fingered rogue with a dagger."

Eithne gave Conor a hard look.

"We'll manage," Conor said. "We'll take to the road tomorrow. I'm certain we'll find another caravan in Caer Tamnagh."

She sighed and nodded.

"So who's for a meal?" Conor asked.

"And a story?" Rhoyd added.

"Well, there might be a story, yes," Conor said and smiled. "Come on."

He started back for the door. An ale to make him forget. A story for the lad. Tomorrow, they could head for Caer Tamnagh and hope that their luck was better.

"Do you feel it?"

Noreen Lothorsdotter paused from loosening the traces on the team that pulled her cook's wagon and turned towards the speaker. She stood head and shoulders taller than the man beside her who glanced out at the rest of the caravan and frowned. One would call him nondescript at the moment, the sort of fellow who did not stick in your memory. But of course, she knew that was not entirely true.

"Feel what?" she asked.

"I'm not sure," he said. "I was scrying the place and there was something there—I thought, but then it vanished."

"I thought we weren't supposed to go scrying places," she said and turned back to finish the task of unhitching Bellow and Brawny. The mismatched pair of bay geldings was eager to get into their stalls and at their feed, and since they were good horses, she was not going to disappoint them. It had been a long day.

"After last night?" her companion said wearily. "I've been scrying every place we stop."

Noreen snorted. Last night they were staying in a crofter's barn when the darklings came slithering out of the corners. Fortunately, they got the torches blazing and drove the creatures out, but not before they lost a couple of the guards. Now, the caravan master was not pleased because more than half the men had sworn this stop was where they were getting off. As it was, Master Fergus had just finished paying wages. He grumbled about the cost.

And this was not the first time, she knew. They had been plagued with misfortunes since before they left Caer Elenthorn.

"Did you ever stop and think that scrying may be the reason we're having all our problems? Master Braidwine *did,* after all, tell us that using any magic other than the ones he specified would put us in danger."

The little man sighed and smiled up at her when she turned to look at him again. "Since when did you become my conscience, Noreen?" he asked.

"If you're going to ask, then you know that I'm going to tell you," she said.

He nodded. "Fair enough. I better get into the carriage and make sure everything is secure there."

"And I better get these hay burners in their stalls before they start dragging me halfway across the world," she said.

She took hold of the headstalls and started forward. Neither Brawny nor Bellow showed any inclination to lag.

The room was small, and there was only one pallet, so Rhoyd slept on a makeshift bed of camping gear that Conor had thrown together in one corner. *Well, I'm supposed to be asleep.* After dinner, Conor had told Rhoyd some hoary tale of bones coming back to life, and though Rhoyd had closed his eyes when the candle was extinguished, he could not make himself go to sleep.

He wasn't about to tell Conor that. One other time, Conor told Rhoyd a scary tale, and Eithne threatened to sew Conor's mouth shut as he slept if he dared tell the lad anything so frightening again. Rhoyd figured it was because Eithne had been unable to sleep as well, but he vowed then never to let Eithne know when a story frightened him...if he could help it.

So Rhoyd lay on his bedding, stretching senses the way his Aunt Genna had taught him. He had always been good at sensing others, but Genna taught him to hone that skill so that he could find other mageborn. He took every opportunity he could to practice, and since they arrived in Torlea, he had been using them to test other folk who were staying in the inn. Conor and Eithne, he knew their essence by heart now. Conor's was all bronze and steel, warm and strong and always a welcome sensation. Eithne's was quicksilver and bright to Rhoyd's perception. The power she possessed as a True Healer burned white in her when she used her "gift" to heal those with a need. Rhoyd could feel it just like he could feel magic.

He reached beyond their familiar auras and slowly worked his way through the inn. It was sort of like stretching fingers to touch people in Rhoyd's opinion. And depending on whether or not they were mageborn, they didn't usually notice him doing so.

Tonight, however, something was different, and he noticed it the moment he slid his awareness into the upper halls on the other end of the corridor from where he shared the room with his adopted parents. Just beyond that wall, he knew there were stables and a courtyard, and in that yard he sensed something totally different. He could not say that it was malignant, but it was...different. So he probed it, trying to ascertain its true nature. He had certainly not felt this essence last night. Indeed, he had started to feel several odd currents of magic in the air when the sun was setting, as though a miasma were crawling around the perimeters of the village. At first, he had figured it was just the story playing havoc with his nerves, but now as he lay touching the new currents of essence, he realized that in some way it was connected to what he sensed now. It hinted power under a cloak, but as he tried to examine it more clearly, it sank deeper and evaded him.

Rhoyd frowned and sat up. He took a deep breath to deepen his concentration and tried to push past the fog the other was throwing up to stop him from scrying. But just as Rhoyd tried again, he bumped into a solid wall of resistance that actually slapped at him. The ethereal blow knocked his awareness back as though someone had clouted him with a quarterstaff. He yelped, lurched back and bumped his head for real against the corner wall behind him. And that made him yelp again.

"Whuhhhh...?" Conor sat up swiftly, one hand stretching towards the long dagger he always kept at his side or under his pillow when he slept. Rhoyd winced and bit his tongue rather than give another shout. He cringed in the corner as though expecting a blow. "Rhoyd?" Conor said softly.

"Sorry," Rhoyd said. "I was dreaming."

"About what, lad?"

"About the bones," Rhoyd said and felt relieved that the shadows would hide the lie, for he knew his face started to burn. "I thought the bones were coming after me and..."

"Shhhhh." Conor crawled off the pallet and knelt in the corner at Rhoyd's side with a quick glance over at Eithne. She had yet to stir. "It's all right, lad," Conor said and held out his arms, and Rhoyd quickly claimed their warm protection. "If I'd known that story would frighten ye, I would not have told it."

Rhoyd said nothing. He was still feeling guilty about the lie. When Conor first took Rhoyd in and called him son, Rhoyd had promised then that he would never hide truths again. Now he felt bad because he had broken that promise, and Conor was being so kind. So he just leaned into Conor's shoulder, enjoying the warmth until he yawned.

And fell asleep.

TWO

Morning brought Eithne up first. She looked startled to see that Conor had Rhoyd tucked under one arm. The lad was coiled against her husband as though he were the only safe haven in the world. Eithne sighed and shook her head. No doubt that story Conor told was to blame. She would have words with him for that. Rhoyd was too young for such frightful tales...

Carefully, she stepped over the pair of them and pulled on her baggy trews and over tunic. She looked at her stockings and frowned. She should probably wash them and her other pair, but now was not the time. So she pulled on her boots, tucked in her trews. By the time she had finished dressing Conor opened his eyes. He looked at her and smiled.

"Morning, woman," he said.

Eithne looked down at Rhoyd, then met Conor's gaze.

"Aye, well, he was not sleeping so well."

"You really need to stop telling him those wicked stories," she said. "He's young, and he's impressionable."

"He's not that young, woman, and you ne'er said such things when I told those tales to Taran," Conor said.

"Taran wasn't mageborn," she said.

"We ne'er knew that fae certain," Conor said softly. But she knew what he meant. Taran had not lived long enough for them to learn if his bad dreams had been mage sign or just another vivid imagination running wild.

Rhoyd stirred then, and Eithne pursed her lips into a tight line, hoping the lad had not heard her speaking of him. He opened his eyes and fluttered a smile at her and she sighed. *Too many handsome men in my life,* she thought and smiled back.

"Hey, lamb," she said and knelt beside the bed. "Sorry to hear you couldn't sleep."

Rhoyd frowned as though not sure what she meant, then a bit of realization dawned in those cerulean eyes. His face flushed as well.

Conor was getting up, pulling on his own clothes. Eithne took a moment to help Rhoyd get his clothes together. He seemed a little uneasy to have her dressing him this way, but to her, it seemed perfectly natural to assist a young lad to tuck in his long shirt tail. She had done it for their son Taran before he deemed himself too old. *Before the bandits took him from us,* she thought with a sigh.

"And she says I spoil ye," Conor said with a grin.

Eithne merely finished the chore by brushing Rhoyd's hair out of his eyes and making certain his face was clean. "There," she said. "None the worse for the night, I imagine. You know it is rather dangerous to sleep next to Conor."

"Why?" Rhoyd asked, almost hesitant.

"Because the big barbarian might roll over and crush you in the night."

Rhoyd giggled a little.

"Woman, ye have no respect for yer man," Conor said.

Rhoyd laughed harder then.

They descended the stairs with Conor in the lead. He glanced over the faces of those who occupied the inn and noticed a dozen or so that he had not seen last night. Two of them sat apart at one of the smaller tables. Guards by the look of them, though they wore nothing to indicate whom they paid fealty to. Mercenaries like him, then? Conor nodded. Could this mean there was a caravan moving through after all?

He left Eithne and Rhoyd at one of the tables. "Be back in a moment," he said and sauntered away.

The men looked up at him when he approached.

"Good morrow, lads," he said. "Conor Manahan's the name."

"I'm Bowen Haldane," the closest said in a congenial manner. Conor took in the sight of a handsome face with icy blue eyes and a head of straw-colored curls barely hidden in the shadows of a cloak hood. "And this is Warden Blackstone." He gestured to his companion, a scruffy, middle-sized man whose dull brown eyes squinted up at Conor in suspicion. "You here to sign up for the caravan?" Bowen continued.

"Depends on the caravan," Conor said. "I was given to understand Caperton was not shipping for another fortnight."

"Naught to do with this Caperton, whoever he is" Bowen said and grinned. "This one arrived late last night. The men on it are looking to be relieved as they have worked it all the way from Caer Elenthorn."

"That far," Conor said and kept his thoughts private. Why would a caravan be coming out of Caer Elenthorn so early in the year? "How many wagons?" he asked instead.

"Eight, I hear," Bowen said. "Mostly furs and dry goods. Anyway, if you're interested, talk to that man over there in the corner." He gestured to a private booth in a shadowy corner where a man who looked like two dumplings squeezed into a leather doublet sat looking at a ledger. "That's Master Fergus, and he is in charge of the recruiting."

"Thanks," Conor said. He crossed the room to the table, casting a swift glance back at his small family to reassure himself. Eithne had already harangued breakfast out of the innkeeper, and was encouraging Rhoyd to eat. Rhoyd was wrinkling his nose over something. Conor shook his head and approached the corner.

"Master Fergus?" Conor said.

The eyes that rounded up at Conor were not the friendliest color. They reminded him of black river stones gone dry, and they narrowed at the sight of Conor. The reek of old boiled cabbage hit Conor's nose. He managed not to grimace in disgust as he wondered whether the man had partaken of the "neep" stew last night.

"Aye, I'm Master Fergus," Fergus said. "What do you want?"

Conor cleared his throat, fighting the urge to take too deep a breath. "My name is Conor Manahan, and I hear ye be hiring for a caravan."

Master Fergus sighed, his eyes appraising Conor. "Well, I could use another man, especially a muckle one like you," he agreed. His gaze went across the room to Eithne and Rhoyd. "Your family?"

"Aye," Conor said and nodded. "My woman is a trained healer, too."

"Really, from what temple?"

"She was trained at Caer Loughan, and on the battlefields of the Last War she was especially valuable. In truth, she is a True Healer."

"You're a militiaman turned mercenary, then?" Master Fergus asked. "What rank did you hold, if you don't mind me asking?"

"I was Sergeant of the Watch in the High King's Frontline Militia," Conor said. "I served under Baron MacDonnell of

Dun Ferlie. And I've been working caravans all over Ard-Taebh since the war ended."

Fergus grunted. "What about the lad?"

"He's a good lad, if that's what ye mean," Conor said. "No trouble at all, and he don't eat much."

Fergus sighed. "We're not running a nursery," he said.

"He needs none, and anyway, the woman does her part to keep an eye on him. And he assists her with her herbs and such."

"Very well," Fergus said. "The pay is two silver sgillinns a day plus meals. We'll pay the woman three brasses a day and her meals as well, but the lad will cost you two brass sgillinns to feed as long as you're working for us."

"You can take his meals out of my pay," Conor said.

"Good," Fergus said. "We leave at noon today."

"We'll be ready," Conor said.

Fergus turned his ledger around. "Make your mark then, Sergeant Manahan."

He watched closely as Conor wrote his name clearly in the ledger. Fergus nodded again.

"Yer educated," he said. "Not many I get can write their names."

"I hope ye won't hold that against me," Conor said.

"No, I will not." Master Fergus said. "But we shall see what Captain Camhin says." Fergus smiled. "He's the money behind this caravan, and he's not so fond of men more educated than himself."

"Then I shall endeavor not to embarrass the Captain," Conor said.

Fergus merely stretched his hand, and Conor took it to indicate the bargain was set. The skin was surprisingly cold and dry for such a fleshy man. With a nod, Conor turned on his heel and stepped back to his table with as much dignity as he could manage. Both Rhoyd and Eithne looked at him expectantly as he sat down with them.

"We've work at quite a nice pay," he said, then reached over and touched Rhoyd on the nose. "And you...keep the glamorie out of yer chores. I suspect these men will not take kindly to having one of the mageborn among them. Promise?"

Rhoyd rubbed his nose and continued to devour his food, but there was a smile there all the same. He nodded to show his agreement.

"So who are we working for?" Eithne asked. "I thought Caperton's son was not sending out a caravan yet."

Conor pointed towards the shadowy corner. Eithne glanced over that way.

Rhoyd paused from taking a bite of bread. "The one who smells like rotten turnips?" the lad asked and wrinkled his nose again.

Conor winced. "Ye can smell him from here, can ye?"

Rhoyd nodded, still grimacing in disgust.

"Well, let's not be letting him know that then, aye?" Conor said. "Could be bad for my reputation as a mercenary if ye go telling the caravan master that he stinks like auld neeps."

"I won't," Rhoyd said. "So long as I don't have to ride downwind of him."

Conor chuckled until he saw the stern look of disapproval Eithne directed at him.

"What?" Conor said.

"Don't encourage him," Eithne said.

"Who?" Conor and Rhoyd asked simultaneously.

Eithne opened her mouth, looked from one to the other and then shook her head.

"Blessed Brother, why do I bother," she said, concentrating on her own breakfast.

"Because you love us?" Rhoyd asked.

Conor bit his tongue and looked elsewhere because Eithne's face turned livid with astonishment. But then she smiled, reached over, caught Rhoyd's chin and gave the lad a gentle shake of admonishment.

"I can think of no better reason other than I may have just totally lost my wits," she agreed. Then she looked at Conor and added, "He's getting more like you every day, Brother help us all."

Conor did smile then.

"Is it just me, or do I sense *a hole next to that big fellow?"* his internal companion asked.

"What do you mean?" the Demon-Bound asked.

"Well, I see three people at that table, the man, his woman and the lad, but I only feel two of them. It's as if the lad isn't there at all."

The Demon-Bound managed not to frown since doing so might upset his mortal companion, but it was true. He fleetingly concentrated on the boy, and there was nothing there. No essence at all. At least none that he could sense. But as he did so, the lad looked up; brilliant cerulean eyes going wide as he quickly glanced around the room.

Horns, he felt me, too! He ducked back under his hood, grateful for the runes of misdirection woven into the inside of the cloak. The lad glanced his way, then at others, then sighed and went back to his meal.

How could an ordinary child do that?

"*Clearly, he is not an ordinary child,*" his internal companion said.

"*Then we had best be careful. First his father has mage blood, and now a child that cannot be felt.*"

"*Are you thinking what I am thinking?*"

That was possible, the Demon-Bound would admit to himself. Perhaps he should not have told the father about the caravan, but to not tell him might have been an even bigger mistake. His new mortal companion, while under his thrall, might have blurted something. The mortal seemed to be good at that. Last night, when he got drunk, he began to regale another man about his adventures on the road. *And when I tried to make him be quiet, he became restless and moody.*

The Demon-Bound would have considered finding another to shield him, but it was too late. He sensed that the caravan had arrived, and that they were staying in the stable yard of this very inn.

So he would just have to be careful and hope that the lad's invisible essence meant nothing. Then again, considering that their enemy had been so good at hiding—that the Other had lost its last flesh, could this lad have been the new vessel?

But how would he have gotten ahead of me? I left him bleeding out of the old body he had claimed as his host just before dawn two days ago. I had hoped that he would sink into the ground and be forced to stay there because I knew the sun was rising.

In some ways, I should be grateful to the cowardly one. Had that man not been such a sniveling child in the dark— had he not ran away from his post, screaming into the night that a demon was after him—I would never have learned where the Other hid.

Alas, it cost the coward his life, and forced me to kill the Other's host and then flee to keep from revealing myself to the rest of the caravan and the agents.

All the more reason to stick around and find out what was going on.

If that child is the new host, I shall have to keep a close eye on him.

THREE

Conor and his family arrived at the main gate just before the noon hour. The caravan was there, and it had apparently grown to nine wagons in a row since he'd spoken to Fergus. Eight of them were standard supply wagons, covered with canvases and at least one of those was dangling barrels of water and salted beef... *Cook's wagon,* Conor thought. It had been placed last in line.

Odd. A cook's wagon is usually kept in the middle.

The remaining wagon, however, struck Conor as odd the moment he rode up to the line. It actually looked like a noble's long box carriage of the sort that would have a small palace inside. The exterior was carved of dark wood and its small windows were draped with black curtains. Two heavy-set black drays pulled it, and their driver was actually riding on another large horse and holding lead reins instead of sitting on the box seat, almost as though the man had no desire to be closer than he had to.

Conor glanced at the faces of the men on horses who were gathered towards the front. He recognized Master Fergus. The dumpling had thrown a garish green cloak with a hood over his doublet. Out here in the open, his stench was less noticeable. As soon as he saw Conor, he shouted, "Hoi, Manahan, over here."

Conor rode over, leaving Eithne and Rhoyd near the end of the wagons. Bowen and Warden were among the men gathered in a semi-circle. All of the men were hooded and cloaked against the chill of the early spring weather. A few of the faces peering out from under hoods looked vaguely familiar, like they might have served on other caravans with Conor before. He saw recognition in at least one pair of eyes.

"This is the last man, Captain Camhin," Master Fergus said. "One Sergeant Manahan."

"The title is no longer valid," Conor said and traded looks with the captain. *Camhin? Doesn't that have something to do with dawn in the old tongue?* Conor pushed those thoughts aside and continued, "I haven't been in the militia since the Last War. I have the papers to prove it."

Camhin was rather nondescript in appearance. Like the others, he wore his hood pulled forward to shadow his face, and with the chill of the morning, Conor could hardly blame any of them. Being Keltoran, he had no problem with the chilly weather. Captain Camhin had a common face, and the sort of common color of hair and eyes that would be readily forgotten. But he looked at Conor with a critical eye, and Conor wasn't sure if he was being measured or misjudged. Then Camhin shrugged.

"Sergeant Manahan," he said. "I hear you have a family."

There was something almost odd in the way Camhin said it. In fact, there was a slight smile dressing his lips.

"Aye, and they'll do their share," Conor quickly said.

Camhin merely nodded and turned his attention back to the whole pack of men now gathered. "Fergus will give you all place assignments. No man is to break his place unless we are attacked. And for your own sakes, stay away from the middle wagon. Any man caught nosing about there will find himself alone in the woods. Am I understood?"

Every man nodded. A few, Conor noted, cast furtive glances at the wagon in question, then threw their gazes forward as though hoping the looks were not noticed.

Captain Camhin merely clucked to his horse and rode back to speak to the driver of the dark carriage. Conor glanced at his wife and son. Rhoyd was smiling at something Eithne was saying. Good. She was keeping the lad too distracted to notice the carriage.

And I'll have a talk with him later, Conor thought.

With Rhoyd, it was best to nip curiosity in the bud before it could lead to disaster.

The sight of the dark carriage had not set well with Eithne when she laid eyes on it. For one thing, it drew Rhoyd's attention like lodestone to the North Star. But she had managed to distract the lad by pointing to the wagon master's shape. "Conor would say he looks like two dumplings stuffed into a doublet," she said.

"More like four dumplings," Rhoyd said and smiled. "Five if you count his head."

"Or eight," Eithne countered and smiled.

"Ate too many dumplings is about right," Rhoyd said and laughed. "And too many old turnips as well."

"Who ate too many dumplings?"

Eithne turned at the sound of that voice. It had a familiar ring. But she only found was a nondescript man on a horse that she realized had been speaking to the guards just moments before. He looked at her in an overly familiar way that made her want to blush.

"I beg your pardon?" Eithne said.

"Captain Camhin at your service, ma'am," he said. "Your husband says you are a healer."

"Yes, I am," Eithne replied.

"Good. We can always use a wise head," Captain Camhin said. "Oh, and it's not terribly wise to make fun of the man who is responsible for keeping the wage books, though I will agree that Master Fergus probably has devoured more than his share of dumplings and turnips. And frankly, I would advise never riding downwind of him."

"Sorry," Eithne said. "I meant no ill."

"None would have been taken, I am certain," Captain Camhin said and winked. "Master Fergus has a sense of humor about his shape. Though I am not certain about his smell." He glanced at Rhoyd who was frowning at the captain. Camhin narrowed his eyes.

"Something the matter, boy?" Captain Camhin asked in a gruff voice.

Rhoyd shook his head and looked at his hands.

"I would ask that you and your lad ride with the cook's wagon towards the end of the caravan, if you don't mind," Captain Camhin said. He looked at Rhoyd again. "And if you are wise, lad, you will obey the orders I have given everyone else and stay away from the box carriage in the middle."

"Why?" Rhoyd asked before Eithne could.

Captain Camhin leaned closer. "Because while curiosity is the reason cats possess nine lives," he said, "young lads should remember that they are not so well blessed."

Rhoyd hitched back as though startled by the threat. Eithne started to scold the man, but he looked at her and nodded.

"I expect you will keep your son under control, ma'am," he said. "For his own good. I can't be held responsible if anything happens to him because he was given more than a healthy share of freedom. We'll be traveling through some dangerous areas, and I would not want him to be hurt."

Captain Camhin pressed heels to the flank of his horse and rode back towards the wagons.

"Well, I never," Eithne said and frowned. "What a rude little man."

Rhoyd stared after the Captain as though some thought he preferred not to share was flitting through his head. His eyes narrowed. He took a deep breath, and Eithne wondered if he was using his magic now.

"Rhoyd?" she said. "Remember your promise to Conor."

Rhoyd let out the breath in a huff and rolled his eyes as he nodded and looked aside.

"Never mind him, Rhoyd," she said and smiled encouragingly. "We don't really care what he has hidden in his ugly old carriage, do we?"

But even as she spoke those words, Eithne felt in her heart that Rhoyd *did* want to know, and she was going to have to keep one eye on the lad at all times.

She turned Maudie's head towards the cook's wagon, encouraging Rhoyd to follow her as she made her way there.

FOUR

The cook's name was Noreen, and she was a large, thickset woman, almost as tall as Conor. She wore her long brown hair braided back from what was a plain but honest face, and she dressed in trews, a linen shirt, and thick leather boots that matched her jerkin. Rhoyd noticed that her arms were thickly muscled more like a man's, and when she caught him staring at her, she flexed one and smiled indulgently.

"How did your arms get so big?" Rhoyd asked.

"I was in the Last War," she said and laughed.

"As a cook?" Rhoyd asked.

"Nay, lad." She leaned down from her wagon seat, still managing to guide the team of drays with a single hand. "I was a soldier."

Rhoyd reared back, fixing her with the look he reserved for some of Conor's less believable tales. "You? But you're a woman."

She laughed heartily and sat upright. "So pleased that ye noticed, lad," she said. "But I really was a soldier. You see, when I was a lass hardly older than you, I decided I didn't want to be a farmwife, so I stole my brother's clothes and ran away to war. And because I was such a big lass, the recruiters mistook me for a man, gave me a sword and a shield and taught me to use them. I killed me a lot of Haxons in them days. But then one night I got drunk and forgot meself when someone bet me that I couldn't throw one of the other soldiers. So, I stripped off my armor and my shirt to wrestle another man. And I won. The poor sod didn't quite know what to grab without getting his eyes blacked." She started to laugh at the memory.

Rhoyd smiled, though he didn't have a clue as to what she found so funny. He pointed towards the front where Conor was riding. "He was in the Last War too," Rhoyd said.

"Aye, militia, I'll warrant." Noreen nodded and flicked the reins and shouted, "Gie on, Bellow!" when one of the horses tried to hesitate.

"How do you know?" Rhoyd asked.

"I can tell by the way he wears his gear," she said. "I would like to have been in the militia, but I wasn't that good a fighter."

"And now you're a caravan cook?" Eithne said from the other side of Rhoyd.

"Aye, well," Noreen said with a sigh, glancing from Eithne to Rhoyd. "They won't hire me as a guard, so I come as a cook. Of course, when there's fighting to be done, you can bet your sweet mare, some of them guards will hide behind me."

"Moonface is a gelding," Rhoyd corrected then asked, "Why won't they hire you as a guard if you can fight?"

"Like you said, lad. I'm a woman." Noreen frowned a little. "But then, I don't really mind. It's work. And I ain't got no little 'uns to tie me down. No man to push me around. Not that many could." She grinned at him.

"Have you been with this caravan since it started?" Eithne suddenly asked.

Noreen hesitated just a whit. Rhoyd saw her look forward as though making sure no one was listening. "Well, I suppose. I mean, I came on in Caer Elenthorn with some of the first 'uns like Master Fergus." Noreen shrugged her great shoulders.

"And Captain Camhin?" Eithne asked.

"What about the captain?" Noreen asked suspiciously.

"Well, I assume since he is the man running the caravan that he was there as well."

"Oh...well, he come to Caer Elenthorn with the dark carriage." Noreen frowned as though not pleased by what she had said.

"But I thought the caravan originated in Caer Elenthorn," Eithne said.

"Oh, yes, ma'am, the caravan did indeed come from Caer Elenthorn. But that carriage came down from Kellerscroft, and Captain Camhin was a-leading it during the daylight as he is now."

"I see," Eithne said. "Doesn't that strike you as odd that he would lie to the men?"

"Not really," Noreen said and she actually smiled. "He's been all hush-hush and tight-lipped since the beginning. King's business and all. "

"Really? What sort of King's business, may I ask?"

"I ain't quite sure," Noreen said with a furtive glance towards the wagon up ahead of them. "I ain't exactly privy to the Captain's matters."

She's not telling everything, Rhoyd thought. He watched the way Noreen kept looking elsewhere as she spoke. The temptation to scry her was strong, but not with Eithne this close. Perhaps later he would try it.

"I would think having been with the caravan all that time, you would have learned something," Rhoyd said. He caught the look of admonishment Eithne fixed on him.

"Well, I don't think I should be telling such tales, as I needs these wages," Noreen said with a wink. "But I will tell ye that any man who sleeps near the dark carriage starts having nasty dreams after a few nights. So if you're smart, you'll set your beds as far from it as possible. And stay away from it. I hear the Captain has a nasty temper when someone breaks his rules. Been more than one man lost his job for messing about that wagon."

"We shall endeavor to take your advice, Mistress Noreen," Eithne said. "The last thing Rhoyd needs is bad dreams." And she turned an arched eye on him as she spoke.

Rhoyd looked aside, biting his lip.

Staying away was not exactly what he had in mind he was willing to admit only to himself.

The road wound out of the hills and took to following the meander of a river. At least it was more open here, which Conor thought was to their advantage. Bandits were everywhere these days, and at least open country was not to the advantage of thieves and rogues.

As the day wore on, the caravan stopped twice: once so they could rest the horses and the men and once because there was a huge rut in the road that seemed to concern Captain Camhin. He did not want to roll the dark wagon over it straight away and insisted on getting down and looking at the ground very carefully. Conor was not quite certain what all the fuss was, as the four leading wagons had rolled over the rut without a problem.

"Ye'd think it was full of precious glass, the way he's carrying on," Conor said. He was watching all from afar. Captain Camhin insisted Conor stay near the front. He didn't like that position since it put him so far from Eithne and Rhoyd.

"Aye," Bowen said and shifted in his saddle as he tugged the hood of his cloak forward to shade his face. He was riding closest to Conor, and had edged his horse closer in spite of the order to stand post and never break formation. "Creed says the captain makes them stop and examines the ground at every rut and every ford."

"If that be true," Conor said, "it's no wonder they've taken so long to get this far south."

Bowen nodded then stiffened for Master Fergus had cast a warning glance in his direction. He guided his horse back to his own post, and Conor sighed. Captain Camhin suddenly nodded and gestured for the driver of the dark carriage to go on. Conor shook his head. *All that, and for what?* The dark wagon rolled easily over the rut, and once it had reached the other side, Camhin took his usual place just ahead of it. Master Fergus then called the caravan to move on, and Conor clucked to Battlebrute.

Aye strange, that was. Because Conor realized there was something in Camhin's gesture that looked vaguely familiar.

He just couldn't quite put a finger on what.

"So, what do you think?" the captain asked as they stopped to water the horses. Noreen was hauling buckets for Brawny and Bellow when he appeared at her side.

"About what?" she asked, surveying the area to make sure no one was close enough to hear them.

"About the Keltoran?" he asked, and she saw him smile.

"You know him, don't you?" she asked. She set the buckets down in front of Brawny and Bellow and loosened the reins so they could drink. Brawny took to drinking right away, but Bellow wanted to play with the bucket a bit, forcing her to pick it up again and hold it so he didn't spill it all over her boots.

"Yes," Camhin said. "I do know him very well, and I never thought for a minute I would ever see him again."

"Why?"

The captain sighed. "It's a long story. I wonder if he really forgave me."

"For what?"

"Nothing," the captain said. "It was long ago. I expect he has forgotten, and he certainly does not know who I am."

Noreen arched one eyebrow at a comical angle. "Don't sell

the man short," she said. "Keltorans are not stupid as folks would believe."

"No one could ever sell Sergeant Conor MacManahan short," the captain said with a grin. "Still, keep an eye on his lad."

"Why?"

"Because boys that age are eaten up with curiosity."

"And curiosity is the reason cats have nine lives," Noreen responded. "The lad's as curious as they come, but you've nothing to fear. I put a bee in his mother's head about King's business and bad dreams."

"You told them about the bad dreams?" Camhin glowered at her, his face shifting just slightly and looking rather unstable. "Sometimes I wonder whose side you're really on, Noreen."

"Your side, of course," she said with a frown. "I'm here to back you up, remember? So far, all I've done is make meals and pretend to be something I'm not. And you better relax. You know what happens when you get agitated."

He started to open his mouth to spew some tirade, but obviously thought better of it and pulled his hood forward, taking several deep breaths to ease the tension. His face stopped and relaxed to its ordinary countenance once more.

"We all have our jobs," Camhin said softly. "And anyway, you volunteered, remember?" He mounted his horse again and rode off.

"Aye, I remember," she muttered under her breath. But she didn't remember volunteering to put up with being treated like a lackey.

Ah, well, she thought and shook her head. *I've better things to fret about.* Besides, Bellow had now decided that her sleeve was a good place to drool and slop water. She resisted the urge to pop him between the eyes to teach him better manners.

Last horse she did that to collapsed in a heap and didn't get up for days.

FIVE

Eventually, the caravan reached a broad lea, and there, Captain Camhin ordered camp be set.

Bit windy for a decent fire, Conor thought. *He* would have been inclined to select the flat below the hill, down out of the wind, but Captain Camhin insisted this was the better spot.

Also, instead of having the wagons drawn in a circle, he had them strung out in a line, which meant the men guarding the first wagon had to walk a long way to get their meals. *Has this man actually ever worked a caravan before?* Conor was starting to have his doubts. Such a formation would also leave them open to attack, though he would admit that having the caravan on such a high hill in such an open area might stop that from happening.

Still...

Conor drew first watch. Not his favorite since it meant standing at attention while others moved around and set up camp and had their meals. His would be cold supper since cooks rarely kept hot meals for the men coming off the first watch. Too bad. Big woman they called Noreen probably fixed a good board. She had a military way about her.

"She was a soldier," Rhoyd's voice piped from behind Conor. He turned with a start to find the lad holding out a steaming mug of broth and some fresh bread.

"How did you know what I was thinking?" Conor said carefully.

"You kept looking at her, and when we stopped to water the horses at midday, I heard you tell that man Bowen that she acted more like a soldier than a cook," Rhoyd said. "But I wasn't in your head. I can't go into your head unless I touch you. Mostly."

Conor bit back the desire to ask just how the lad *could* get into another man's head. There were some things about mageborn he would rather not know.

"You stand there and hold the mug," he said as he took the bread. Dipping the latter in the former, Conor filled his belly, wryly noting that the broth was thick and meaty and the bread was soft and sweet. *Quite good.* He would have washed them down with a bit of ale, but being on duty was not a time to indulge in drink. So he satisfied his thirst with the rest of the broth and the flask of water. Rhoyd hung around dutifully—or was there more to that impatient look in his eyes? He did glance furtively towards the line of wagons, and most particularly at the dark carriage.

"You're to stay away from that," Conor said.

"Captain Camhin already told Eithne that," Rhoyd said, sounding a little put out. "He said lads didn't have lots of lives like cats..."

"Oh?" Conor said and frowned. "Why would he say that?"

"I don't know. I don't trust him," Rhoyd said.

"Why?"

"He doesn't feel right," Rhoyd said. "Not in a bad way, mind you, but he just feels wrong. But then so do several of the men around here."

Conor raised an eyebrow as the words trailed off. That was as cryptic a statement as any that had ever crossed the lad's lips. He glanced down at Rhoyd. The lad's gaze wandered once more to the dark carriage.

"You best get on back to Eithne and help her finish setting our camp," Conor said. "It'll be dark soon, and I don't want ye wandering away from the fire. Aye?"

Rhoyd took a deep breath and nodded, fluttering the black locks that flew around his face.

"Your word is your bond," Conor said. "Do you swear?"

Rhoyd nodded again. Briefly, he slipped arms around Conor's waist and hid his face in the thickness of the mercenary's plaid. Then he pulled back and hurried away.

Conor watched him disappear the length of the wagon line, then turned his eyes back out on the world.

Why was he having trouble believing this was going to be a peaceful night?

Come sunset, Captain Camhin became an invisible presence, and that bothered Rhoyd. The man's horse, a dull looking chestnut that was as nondescript as its rider, was tethered with the rest in the line. But of the captain himself, there was no sign. Rhoyd had cautiously scried for him as he wandered back to help Eithne with camp. Oddly, when Rhoyd tried to scry the dark carriage, misdirection sent his senses wandering to the other wagons either up or down the line, as if the carriage was not where he saw it. And when he tried harder, the same essence that had slapped him away in the inn now struck at him like an angry hornet. He gave up, rather than keep trying, lest he give away what he was doing.

Eithne already had the camp set. It was a dry night, so she did not bother with the tent. Besides, the wind that whipped across this hill and played tag with Rhoyd's long black hair would have pulled the tent over. As it was, the flames of their campfire had to be kept low behind a wall of stones so that it would continue to burn. Rhoyd could have kept it burning with magic, but he had promised Conor not to.

Besides, he would rather figure out where Camhin had gone.

"Where's the mug?" Eithne suddenly asked as Rhoyd sat on a log and stared off across the camp at the wagon row.

"Conor still has it," Rhoyd said.

"But you were supposed to bring it back," she said, cocking her head and staring accusingly at him.

Rhoyd fought the urge to roll his eyes and bound back to his feet. "I'm sorry. Shall I go fetch it now?"

Eithne shook her head. "No, it's getting dark and Conor wanted us to stay by the fire."

Rhoyd narrowed his eyes. He suspected a conspiracy was afoot now. To keep him out of trouble, like as not. *I don't make trouble,* he thought.

Not intentionally.

Eithne must have caught his look. She opened her arms and said, "Come here, you little rogue."

He went to her willingly, letting her take him into an embrace.

"I think you need a chore," she said and pulled him back to the log to sit down. "And I have herbs to sort."

"Out here in the wind?" Rhoyd said.

Eithne smiled. "Yes, you're right. The herbs *would* be rather difficult to keep track of. In that case, you can help me gather some fruit, because I saw a small patch of wild blackberries just down the hill there."

"You use blackberries for herbs?" Rhoyd said.

"They are wonderful in tea," she said. "Come on. Grab the

small water pail from the kit. Let's go see if we can fill it up."

"It will be dark," Rhoyd said. "And you said that Conor said we're not supposed to leave the fire."

"Yes, well, I think we can manage under this moon. But just in case, we'll take a lantern as well."

Rhoyd tried hard not to laugh. She was determined, he decided, and he was not going to argue with her any more. He fetched the pail as she fetched the lantern and lit it from the fire. Together, they made their way down the hillside to where the patch of thorny blackberries grew. Eithne set the lantern off to one side so the light fell on them, then they crouched with the pail between them and began to gather the thick black fruit.

It was messy work. Rhoyd's hands were stained purplish from the task, as was his mouth because it was hard to resist eating a few of the berries. Strange to find them so this early in the year, but there were still places all over the north of Ard-Taebh where the weather defied convention. These berries were lush and ripe, and the tiny bits popped on his tongue when he squashed them against the roof of his mouth. All else was forgotten in the joy of the task, of being helpful at something that reminded him of when he was smaller and he and his mother would go gather berries from the forest outside Claggen. Those were the happier times of his childhood. His mother taught him to make daisy chains and to weave grass into a tiny basket and fill it with berries. Never more than one or two would fit in them, and she would insist on leaving them for the birds. "They will take the fruit for food and the grass for their nests."

Rhoyd paused as his throat thickened with the memory. He did miss his mother, even after all this time. He pulled his lower lip between his teeth and took a deep breath.

And froze.

Something had moved in his peripheral vision, a shadow gliding across the ground. Rhoyd turned towards the motion and it vanished, or grew still. There were so many shadows beyond their light, and even the moon was not yet high enough to cast its waning glow. But mage eyes had the power to see into those shadows, and as Rhoyd stared at them, one of the shadows stared back.

Rhoyd opened his mouth to shout a warning when the shadow sprang. *A darkling!* His sudden reaction to its presence brought Eithne turning around. At the sight of a blanket of darkness with a maw full of teeth and red eyes she screamed, and that cry was enough to get the creature's attention. It honed in on Eithne, twisting in midair, preparing to drop on her. Rhoyd seized up the lantern and aimed its feeble light on the darkling. *"Solus!"* he hissed and the pale candlelight suddenly flared as bright as the sun. The brilliant ray of light nearly cut the darkling in half. It screamed and fell to the ground, scrambling to retreat, looking like a torn blanket oozing some sort of brackish blood. Shouting, Rhoyd threw the lantern at the darkling, and it landed on the creature's back. It shrieked as the light ate away at its amorphous body, leaving only an oily residue.

At that moment, shouts sounded from above.

"Rhoyd, the light!" Eithne said, and he understood what she meant.

He quickly whispered *"Solus dubh!"* and the brilliance faded back to candlelight.

Barely in time, too. Men were suddenly thundering down the hill, swords in hand. Conor was among them, swiftly gaining the lead with his longer legs. He managed to get to them first, brandishing his blade in readiness.

"Eithne? Was that you that screamed?" Conor asked.

Rhoyd helped Eithne crawl to her feet. She nodded. "It was me," she admitted with a shiver.

"What happened, woman?"

Before she could answer, a horse raced down the rise. How Captain Camhin had gotten the beast saddled so swiftly was a mystery. But he was there, on his plain-looking beast, glowering down at the gathering.

"What happened here?" he demanded. "What was all the screaming?"

"Beg pardon, sir, it was me," Eithne said.

"And just what were you doing so far from camp in the gloaming?"

"We were gathering blackberries," Eithne said and pointed to the bucket someone had kicked over in all the excitement. Rhoyd glanced at the berry stains on his hands then quickly hid them behind his back.

"Why were you screaming?" Camhin demanded.

Eithne gestured towards the oily patch that had once been the darkling. "That thing attacked me."

Men muttered and shifted back and forth. Rhoyd sidled over to Conor, uncertain.

"And just what was that thing?" Camhin said as he dismounted and walked over to crouch beside the patch. And Rhoyd felt just a hint of mage senses scouring the ground.

He's mageborn... Rhoyd managed to hide his surprise and looked out at the dark.

"I think it was a darkling," Eithne replied.

"Indeed?" Camhin stood up and stared at her. "And just how did you defeat it?"

There was a moment of hesitation. Rhoyd felt Conor's hand on his shoulder when he tensed. *Conor knows it was me...he knows I used magic...* Conor always knew, for as a Keltoran descended from a mage line, he possessed the skill to "feel" magic when it was used. Rhoyd took a deep breath, ready to defend his reason for casting a spell.

"I threw the lantern at it, of course," Eithne said, quickly recovering her wits. "I always heard that darklings were afraid of light because it could kill them."

"Yes, so it's been said," Captain Camhin said and glanced at the lantern. He seemed to be contemplating something. "Well, then, the danger is obviously over. I suggest we all get back to camp and set watch fires, just in case there are more of them lurking out there."

He glanced over where Master Fergus stood at the edge of the knot of men. "You heard the captain," Fergus said. "Back to camp, and get the watch fires burning bright."

Rhoyd watched the expressions on the faces of some of the men. Bowen was there, looking thoughtful. The one they called Warden was glowering at Eithne. Behind them, Rhoyd spotted Noreen. The cook's face was set in a solemn scowl.

Slipping out from under Conor's hand, Rhoyd snatched up the fallen bucket of blackberries. Less than half had spilled on the ground. Eithne took it from him, pushing his hair out of his eyes and offering a reassuring smile. She glanced up at Conor, a hint of a plea visible in her eyes. He nodded.

They held back a little, following at the tag end of the small party of mercenaries as they headed back up to the camp. Conor knelt long enough to allow Rhoyd to clamber up on his back and rose again. Rhoyd slung his legs around Conor's waist and arms around his neck to hang on. *I'm getting too old to be carried this way,* he thought, but there was a comfort in the action that he could not explain, like he needed Conor's strength and protection all the more at that moment.

"Ye used the glamorie, didn't ye?" Conor whispered.

"He didn't have a choice," Eithne whispered back, coming close beside him. "He saved my life."

"Oh, I'm not faulting him, woman," Conor said softly as he glanced over his shoulder, and in the dark Rhoyd saw a smile tug the corner of his mouth. "No more than I fault ye for taking the blame."

Eithne rolled her eyes and poked Conor in the ribs. He chuckled and glanced back at Rhoyd again.

"Ye look like ye've been kissing a blackberry miss," Conor said. "Hope ye saved some of her kisses for me."

"You can have what we didn't spill or eat," Eithne was swift to assure him.

"Yer such a generous woman," Conor replied.

Rhoyd leaned his head against the back of Conor's neck and turned so he could glance back down the hillside.

It only occurred to him then to wonder what a darkling would be doing out in the open. They preferred the shadows and the mist.

There was no mist here, and no trees. Only the shadow of the long grass and the blackberry patch. Not enough to hide such a creature.

So why was a darkling out roaming the open moors under the waning moon?

A mystery, to be sure. Like Captain Camhin, the man who looked unnoticeable and felt wrong.

And was mageborn as well.

"It was him," **the captain** said to Noreen as she was locking down her wagon for the night. "I know it was him."

"Who?" Noreen asked. She was getting a little tired of the way the captain always started talking without letting her know what was on his mind.

"The lad," he said and frowned at her. "*He* used magic to stop that darkling—I just know it."

Noreen nodded. She had felt spells being cast, strong spells too, but she had assumed it was Camhin and not the lad. "So what was the screaming?" she asked.

"His mother," Camhin said. "The darkling attacked them and she claims she killed it with the lantern, but there was magic, I tell you. That lantern might have frightened it off, but it was not powerful enough to kill it."

Noreen shrugged. "You never know with darklings. Some of them turn to smoke if you light a candle."

"That was an older one," the captain insisted. "It would have taken more than lanterns and candles to kill it. A torch, maybe, applied directly to it, but not a lantern."

"So what do we do?" Noreen asked. "Leave them behind the next village? I don't think the Keltoran will take kindly to being fired. I heard a couple of the men talking. They know him, too. He's got a good reputation among the caravans."

The captain sighed. "Yes, I know. And no, we cannot let him go without a good reason. But we should keep an eye on him and the lad. Especially the lad."

Noreen shook her head and continued her work. "Don't you think you better get into your wagon, sir? You know what happens when you get agitated and tired."

The captain nodded. *Yes, he knows,* she mused. He wandered away, heading towards the middle of the line where the dark carriage sat.

Noreen glanced out at the small camp set not too far away. The Keltoran was returning with his son and his wife. He set the lad down and ordered him to behave, and the lad saluted. The Keltoran growled and mussed the lad's hair. Then the lad retaliated by trying futilely to tackle the big man, who merely lifted the lad so he was upside down and began to burnish his thin ribs with strong finger. They both laughed and the lad yielded. Then the Keltoran wandered off, leaving his son and wife to guard their camp.

A happy little family, she mused, and oh so briefly, she felt her vision cloud. She hoped this trip was not going to be their undoing.

While she had never married, she had been a mother once, long ago. Her own son had grown up and gotten old, and passed away quietly in his sleep, and there were times that Noreen still missed him. She had left her homeland then and gone on to other adventures, including the Last War.

But she had never forgotten her son.

With a sigh, she tied off the last of the boards and crawled back into her wagon. There was cold supper waiting for the men who needed it, but she had no reason to stand over it while they fed. She needed her own sleep instead.

SIX

Conor returned to his watch post to finish his stint, and he was grateful when the next man came to relieve him. Camhin ordered them all to carry torches, which was not to Conor's liking. He was not a man who wanted to be a target in the dark.

Relieved of his duty for the rest of the night, Conor made his way along the wagons. The dark one looked ominous at night, and even though he kept his distance, he felt the whisper of a breeze on the small hairs of his hands. There was magic here, and it was not the glamorie of his son.

But it was familiar in some strange way that Conor could not quite understand. Some faint memory stirred in him, forcing him to draw away from the vicinity of the dark wagon, to widen the berth he gave it as he made his way back to his pallet.

Eithne was still awake. She busied herself washing her stockings in a small bucket of water and laying them close to the fire to dry. Conor could not keep from smiling at the sight of her with her bare feet planted on either side of the pail sitting between her thighs. She looked up when he approached and raised a quizzical eyebrow to see his expression. "I see you are in a much better mood," she said.

"I was ne'er in a bad one," he assured her, then glanced at Rhoyd. The lad was asleep, wrapped in two double ells of Conor's plaidie. In fact, all that was visible above the tartan wool was a mop of black hair.

"Exactly what did he do out there to make you willing to cover for him?" Conor asked.

"That bright light spell of his," she said. "It was harmless...well, I suppose not to the darkling."

Conor nodded and pulled off his sword belt and seated himself beside her. He had thought as much. "Did anyone else see?"

"I don't think so," she said, wringing out the last of her stockings. "I took him down there to get him away from the temptation to scry that dark carriage. So in some ways it is my fault he was forced to resort to his spells. Do you forgive me?"

With a sigh, Conor pulled off his boots. "I'll have to think about it, woman," he said. "Are ye going to wash my stockings too?"

She grimaced. "Your stockings should be burned," she said.

"Aye, well, I guess I'll have to wash them meself," he said, and yanking them off, he started dunking them vigorously into the pail, splashing water here and there.

"Oh, Conor, stop that, you're getting me all wet."

"Am I now?" he said with a leer and leaned down to kiss her.

She seized up the bucket, tipped it in his direction and sent water washing down his trews.

Rhoyd told himself he was just having a dream. That the world was not all purple and blue. That the grass was not really red. The trees did not have faces slipping in and out of view like spirits. Their branches were not made of tatters of grey hide and bleached bones.

But it seemed awfully real at the moment and try as he did, he could not pull himself out of it. He was in an ancient forest, and bare-branched trees kept trying to snag him. And somewhere out in the shadows beyond, the essence of whatever stalked him left a bitterness that tasted like cinnamon on his tongue.

And he was lost. The trees thickened and formed walls, and Rhoyd was forced to follow what now looked like the stones of a cave. No, a tunnel, and it grew narrow so that his shoulders touched the sides as he fled. The ceiling lowered and forced him to duck, then to crouch, then crawl. The world was closing in on him.

Then he was in a box, a chest of stone like a sarcophagus. He beat useless fists against the stone lid that held him inside. At least until the lid moved and the dark flooded into the depths where he lay. He flailed at the blanket of shadow that slipped over and under him, drew him upright, held him suspended in the air. No, it was the claw of a dragon so black she seemed more like a hole into a void. Her obsidian eyes caught glitters of light as they fixed on him.

He flailed as she brought him up into the air. White fire filled his hands, and he cast it at her. She shrieked and let him fall, and he landed in a heap on cold ground, flailing at the darkness moving around him.

And then he saw the chest, a thing of wood so white, it burned his eyes. He shaded them and rose cautiously to his feet, stepping closer, putting out a hand.

When he touched the wood, the lid rose slowly. Rhoyd stood and blinked at the space within.

And then Rhoyd screamed. For the bones of some creature that stood so much taller than he and reeked of the essence of bitter cinnamon sprang from the box and lunged at him.

Blessed Brother! **It took a lot** to get Eithne to rise from a good sleep. Conor, of course moved like lightning, leaving her to flounder. She took a moment to orient herself. Someone was screaming.

Then she realized that someone was a small lad tangled in blankets and bedding on the other side of the fire. Conor scrambled around to Rhoyd's side, and the moment he touched the lad, Rhoyd started to flail and kick. But Conor was bigger and wrapped strong arms around the struggling form and dragged him close. Eithne crawled out of the pallet to join him in subduing Rhoyd.

"Easy, lad, it's me," Conor said. "It's me, Rhoyd."

Men were approaching from all sides. Conor turned a hard look at them.

"It's all right. He's all right. He's just having a bad dream."

There were mutters as though they did not believe him, but they backed away. Eithne saw Master Fergus shake his head. Captain Camhin was nowhere to be seen.

Eithne decided it didn't matter. She took Rhoyd's face in her hands. "Rhoyd, open your eyes," she said. "Please open your eyes."

Cerulean blue suddenly did open. The struggles ceased. Rhoyd took deep gulps of air, staring at her for moments as though he did not know who she was. Then slowly, he shifted and looked up at Conor.

"Bad dream?" Conor said.

Rhoyd merely struggled to shift around, seizing handholds of Conor's shirt and plaidie, pressing himself against the man as though that were his only anchor in the world. Conor looked at Eithne and sighed.

"I'll brew him some blackberry sage tea," she said and ruffled Rhoyd's hair.

Conor nodded. Eithne hurried over to her packs. Fortunately, there were still a few blackberries left over from the ones they gathered earlier in the evening. She crushed their juice into water then set it to boil. Meanwhile, she dug out the sage leaves and crushed and sprinkled some of them into a cup. When the water boiled, she poured the hot liquid over the leaves and let it simmer and brew.

Rhoyd seemed to have calmed down by the time she was done. In the distance, she noticed some of the men were watching warily. She handed the mug to Rhoyd, letting him hold it, and stood up to glare at them.

"There is nothing more here for you to see," she said firmly. "Our son merely had bad dreams, no doubt caused by the dreadful creature that attacked us down by the blackberries, so you can all go about your business and leave us to ours."

Glances were traded all around, then like whipped curs, the men drifted away, returning to their pallets and their posts. Eithne shook her head and turned back to find Conor wearing a wry smile.

"Remind me never to get on your bad side," he said.

"As if you would never do so?" she said and crouched once more. Rhoyd managed a little smile, in spite of looking wan. "Go on, my lamb. Drink your tea," she said. "Then you can tell us all about it."

Rhoyd nodded and sipped the brew carefully because it was still rather hot. At length, he handed the mug back to her, half empty and looked at his own hands in thought. "I saw those bones again," he said.

Eithne set a stern look on Conor who inclined his eyebrows in denial. "Well, those bones are only a figment of your imagination and Conor's bogie tales," she said. "So why don't you bring your pallet around and lie with us? Conor and I will keep those nasty dreams away."

Rhoyd turned a worried look in her direction. "I...I don't think it was an ordinary dream," he said and glanced up at Conor as well. "I think it was a...a..." Rhoyd crossed his own eyebrows as though searching hard for the word. "I think it was what Aunt Genna calls a portent."

Eithne saw Conor frown. She sighed.

"Well, portent or not, you bring your pallet around the fire," she said. "Conor will keep you safe, I'm sure."

"Better do as she says, lad," Conor said. "Or she'll make me share your wee pallet with you instead."

Rhoyd nodded and gently disengaged himself from Conor's grasp. With a sigh, he gathered his blankets and bedding. Conor stood and lent a hand, and they all returned to the far side of the fire to retire once more.

He dreams, his internal companion said. *He dreams of bones.*

Yes, so I heard, the Demon-Bound thought.

This is not good. He knows.

Then we must watch him and wait and see.

Why not just get rid of him now?

Because I don't think he is carrying the Other inside him. But I do think there is something about him that warrants watching.

Such as?

Can you not feel it?

His companion barely sifted the air around the camp. *Oh, my...*

Yes, he thought back. *He is...*

Then we must watch over him as well.

Yes, we must.

SEVEN

Rhoyd felt better the next morning as he saddled Moonface and helped Eithne to break their small camp and pack the horses. The dream did not return, for which he was grateful. But in spite of that, he had felt some strange miasma hanging around beyond the caravan. It hovered in the dark like a wicked presence waiting to spring. Strange, for he also felt something else was there, something that hid just like the dark when he tried to scry it. Something unlike anyone or anything he had ever felt before. Demon essence laced it, but not like the demons he had met and destroyed before. In fact, there was something almost human about it.

Rhoyd would have mentioned this, but since Eithne had taken his dream as nothing more than the remnants of one of Conor's tales still haunting the boy, he felt certain she would scold Conor if Rhoyd even hinted there was some magical danger afoot. Granted, he knew that men like these were probably superstitious and would think him as much a bogie because he was mageborn. The Last War had left "too many fools," as his Aunt Genna would say. Conor was more inclined to say it was a matter of "old wounds." The Last War had been a time of terrible tidings for all of Ard-Taebh when the Hound of the Blackthorn swept across the land and brought his army of Haxons and evil creatures to prey on mortalkind. Here in Elenthorn, the worst damage was done. Whole cities destroyed by magical, murderous monsters that before then people thought were just the stuff of stories.

And now they thought mageborn were all kith and kin to the same creatures that plagued them during the Last War. Even Conor had said that men saw what destruction magic could bring, and how they were helpless to stop it.

"No man likes to think he has no power over his own fate," Conor would have said.

Rhoyd was inclined to agree; especially since there were times he thought he had no control of his own. He still was not sure that he understood it all. His Uncle Fenelon's spirit was always insisting Rhoyd had a destiny that would one day mean life or death for all humans.

But how could he, one small lad, be so important? Aunt Genna refused to say anything on the matter when she was teaching Rhoyd spells. She was disinclined to let anyone tell Rhoyd he was special. So much so that she actually refused to take him to meet the Council of Mageborn, even though Fenelon insisted that they needed to know the *Ard Magister* was real. *As if anyone would think I was special...*

Rhoyd sighed and finished tightening the girth, only to realize there was a shadow hanging over him. He turned with a gasp, half expecting another darkling.

But no. It was only Conor.

"Are ye all right, lad?" he asked and reached out to check the girth.

"I'm all right," Rhoyd said.

"Why don't ye ride with me today," Conor said and smiled.

"But you're working," Rhoyd said.

"I think we can manage," Conor insisted with a wink.

Rhoyd nodded. He *did* want to ride with Conor.

At least then, he would not be so inclined to think of his dreams and his future.

Conor had so hoped it would turn out to be an uneventful day. The caravan was sticking to the open areas, so it would be more difficult for bandits to attack unseen. The sun was warm, but it was still early enough in the year to feel good on a man's head, for the air held a slight chill to remind them that winter was not entirely gone. Rhoyd stayed preoccupied with one of his books. He rode behind Conor, braced by the bedroll, and now and again, Conor would feel the book gently pressing against his back.

Well, at least it meant the lad was behaving himself.

"So what are ye reading?" Conor asked.

"One of Uncle Fenelon's journals," Rhoyd muttered and turned a page.

Conor frowned. "Does yer auntie know?"

He felt the rock of the lad shaking his head. "No," Rhoyd said. "Uncle Fenelon said not to tell her."

Conor arched an eyebrow. He still had difficulty coming to terms with knowing that the lad conversed freely with the spirit of an ancestor as though the man were still alive and in the same room. In Keltora, spirits were considered naught but bad omens, and mageborn were often asked to exorcise them. Living up to one's ancestors didn't mean living with them.

"So, what's he writing about?" Conor asked.

"Putting fire in a bottle," Rhoyd said.

"Sounds rather dangerous, that."

"It was," Rhoyd said. "He blew out a door at Dun Gealach the one time he tried it."

"You're not thinking about trying that, are ye?" Conor ventured.

Rhoyd hesitated then said, "No," in a way that Conor felt certain the answer meant just the opposite.

"I should hope not, because I dinna want to hear tell of you trying that at the White Hart. Meg would make short work of you for it."

"What she could find left of me, it would be short work indeed," Rhoyd said in such a droll manner, Conor laughed.

Rhoyd suddenly snapped the book shut and sat upright. "We're not alone," he said.

"What?" Conor loosened his sword and his shield, drawing the targe from its hook.

And just in time. An arrow thunked into the wood, coming from somewhere downhill, along with several of its kin. One of the guards screamed in pain, caught unawares. Then the bodies of many men in mismatched armor and clothes sprang up out of the grass like fetid weeds.

"Bandits!" several voices heralded at once.

"Hold on, lad!" Conor pulled Battlebrute around so that the warhorse could do his part. The big dun squealed and struck out with fore hooves and teeth while Conor lay about with his blade. He was keeping the shield back to help cover Rhoyd, determined to protect the lad from bandit axes and swords, but there were so many men rushing out of the patches of tall grass like rats converging on a midden heap.

One of the bandits lunged up and seized hold of Rhoyd's leg, trying to yank the lad off Battlebrute. Rhoyd shouted and whacked the man on the head with his book. The wood, copper and leather bindings about the vellum had just enough weight to do the trick, and the bandit crumpled with a groan.

I've got to get out of the thick of this before the lad gets hurt, Conor thought.

But just as he was wheeling Battlebrute around to retreat, another arrow flashed close to Conor's face. He flinched, rolling back, and Battlebrute responded to the shift in weigh and reared to strike out with fore hooves. Rhoyd yelped as he was caught off balance. He dropped his book, and before Conor could think, the lad was scrambling to get off the horse and pursue his precious tome.

"Rhoyd, no!" Conor shouted.

Too late, the lad was on the ground snatching up the journal when another bandit rushed at him. Rhoyd looked up and stretched his hand out, and shouted, *"Gath saighead buail!"* without thinking. The flash of blue left his hand and struck the bandit high in the chest with enough force to knock him off his feet.

Conor yanked Battlebrute back down, scooped up the lad, and flung him across his lap. Then pressing heels to the dun's sides, they surged over the top of a couple of men who were on the attack. Shouting, Conor rode back to the nearest wagon. To his good fortune, it turned out to be the one driven by the cook. Noreen stood ready with a sword, looking just like one of the battle maidens of old. Conor practically tossed Rhoyd onto the wagon seat beside her.

"Stay here!" Conor snapped at the lad and turned Battlebrute back into the fray.

The bandits were still fighting, but now many of them were starting to flee. Conor rode through their numbers, sword lashing like a whip. He cut down half a dozen men before the rest of the bandits finally figured out that they didn't have a chance and fled. Guards rode over them, slaying as many as they could who were on the retreat.

And then it was over. A field of carnage lie about them. The guards had fared well, though there were injuries aplenty that would need Eithne's healing skill.

It was then that Captain Camhin rode up, looking angry and brandishing a sword stained with blood. *Well at least he was in the thick of it,* Conor thought. *And not off hiding like some coward.*

"Damn," Captain Camhin said, sneering at the field. "These vermin will stop at nothing."

"We routed them well enough," Conor said. "We're all still alive."

"Yes, and fortunately, none of them were able to get near

the dark carriage."

It was on the tip of Conor's tongue to blurt that he did not think any man would want near that wagon, but he kept the thought to himself.

"Aye, well, that's why ye hired us, I imagine," Conor said.

Camhin glanced at Conor with narrowed eyes, and once more, Conor was struck by the humor hiding behind them, and the sense that he should know the owner better than he did. *Breeze on the small hairs.* The sensation assailed his skin as though magic were being cast. Before Conor could comment on that, Camhin clucked to his horse and rode over to check on Master Fergus.

Conor sighed and glanced over at the cook's wagon. Rhoyd was sitting there, clutching his book, watching while Mistress Noreen showed off some moves with her sword.

With a shake of his head, Conor clucked to Battlebrute and set out to find Eithne.

EIGHT

There were no dead among the guards, for which Eithne was grateful. The first man to take an arrow had been lucky for it had merely pierced his shoulder. She removed it, cleaned the wound, called one of her healing prayers, and the Blessed Brother answered her. The guard whose name was Warden, expressed his gratitude as he marveled at having use of the arm again so soon.

Other injuries were not as severe. These guards were apparently as good as her Conor when it came to wielding their blades and shields. Some wounds were minor enough to require no more than comfrey paste and bandages. One needed stitching. The rest were little more than scrapes, and the men who had them insisted on cleaning their own wounds. So she let them, taking a moment to make sure the injuries were no more serious than that.

She had finished the last man's bandage when she saw Conor riding over, looking dour.

And no sign of Rhoyd.

"Oh Blessed Brother," she muttered and rushed over to greet him. "Where...?"

"The lad's with the cook," Conor said. "He's fine."

He looked uneasy all the same.

"What?" she asked as he dismounted.

"He used his magic to stop one of the bandits."

Eithne frowned. "Do you think anyone saw?"

"In the thick of battle, it's hard to say, but we should stay on our toes all the same," Conor said.

"You're not angry with him, are you?"

"Nay, woman," Conor said, glancing around. "He only did what came natural when he found himself in danger. But I'm not so keen on being left behind by this lot, should one of them have seen him. We could survive, but if there are darklings roaming about in the open, I'd be hesitant to be left behind."

"Eyes and ears open then," Eithne said and glanced towards

the cook's wagon when she heard familiar laughter. Rhoyd nearly fell off the bench.

"Eyes and ears open," Conor agreed.

Master Fergus motioned the men who were not standing watch at the moment to gather on towards the front, so Conor seized Battlebrute's reins, mounted up and started on. Eithne watched him ride over to the huddle of men then set her sights on Rhoyd and Mistress Noreen.

Better get word to Rhoyd that he should be on his guard and his best behavior.

Master Fergus had little more to say than to congratulate the men on a job well done.

"And without a life lost," he said. "Now we must detail men to pile up the corpses of the bandits we killed and set them afire, and then we must move on without further delay. As it is, we shall not reach the village of Stonelay, so we will have to camp in the open again. This time, there will be a full ring of watch fires on the outer perimeter and double watch."

Conor said nothing, though he saw the expressions of some of the men and knew they agreed. Double watch would be harder on the men riding detail the next day. Few would get a full sleep.

Still, he did not blame them if bandits were attacking in broad daylight in open fields—*just as darklings are attacking in open fields at night.*

Not a thought he cared to have in his way.

They set to work, hauling the corpses into a pyre and setting it ablaze. Then they set off across the moors. Conor made certain Rhoyd was in Eithne's company and that they both stayed close to the cook's wagon before he took his post.

The rest of the day went uneventfully. Captain Camhin was adamant about staying out of the forests, which meant they often left the road and wound their way across rough tracks of open ground. In Conor's opinion, that slowed them more than anything, that and the fact that the Captain seemed particular about the terrain itself. He never allowed that black wagon to roll over ruts or streams without first getting off his horse and looking at them. And every time they came near any menhirs or even just a scattering of broken stones, the Captain would examine them as though studying a war map and he was plotting a charge. What he could see was beyond

Conor's reckoning. If Camhin behaved this way all the time, then it was no wonder that the guards kept changing.

Except for Mistress Noreen, Conor thought.

What had Eithne said? The woman had come on in Caer Elenthorn, and that the black carriage actually came from a town near the Ranges. Strange place, the Ranges. Mountains so tall one could not scale them in even a week. A place of ancient power, some said, and ancient magic. A few tribes of Haxons still roamed there, though they seemed more civil than their northern kin. Stone folk lived in those mountains as well. And he had heard tales of bogie beasts, demons and the like. And giants and trow.

And they call my stories strange.

He wondered just what this mysterious cargo was. The main wagons contained provisions and trade goods, but not that dark carriage.

Don't start acting like the lad, Manahan, Conor scolded himself. Rhoyd's curiosity for the unnatural was bad enough.

And ye knew that raising a mageborn would not be easy...

Conor shook his head. Besides, he was noticing that one of the guards was whispering to one of the wagon drivers, and that now and again, their glances would whisk in Conor's direction then flit away.

Horns! he thought. What were they blathering about?

The guard—Warden, Conor realized—pulled his mount around and rode back to where Conor was. Battlebrute snapped at Warden's mount when it got too close. The dappled gelding laid its ears back and jerked its head away, but did not retaliate.

"Something on yer mind?" Conor asked, looking at the man.

Warden nodded his head, bouncing the curls of brown shot through with wisps of silver. His dark eyes narrowed up at Conor.

"One of the men said your lad was mageborn," Warden said. "Said he hit one of the bandits with a bolt of light. Is that true?"

"What does it matter is he is or isn't?" Conor said and scowled at the man. This was precisely what he had hoped would not happen.

Warden rubbed his chin. "Don't matter none to me 'cos he's just a lad. But there's some that might think otherwise."

"Then some had best keep their tongues behind their teeth," Conor said sharply.

Warden smiled. "That's what I told them. My friend Bowen, he thinks they're all nervous and looking for a scapegoat."

Conor looked straight at Warden. "Any man touches my lad will answer to me," he said.

"Don't get your tripes in a knot, Keltoran," Warden said. "No man here has that kind of courage as long as you're alive. Besides, they's more interested in what he can do to them shadow things."

With a sigh, Conor shook his head. "He'll do naught unless I tell him," Conor said. "I won't have men speaking against him because of what he is."

Warden nodded. "Do you think he can see what is in that black wagon?" he asked with a cock of one eyebrow.

"What do you think is in it?" Conor asked.

"A king's ransom in gold," Warden replied. "I think the captain's just an act, and the shadow things is his doing just to keep us from taking a peek."

"Whatever is in that wagon is none of our affairs," Conor said. "Ye'd do well to remember that. And my lad knows that he'll answer to me if he so much as tries to find out what's in it."

Warden frowned and dragged his horse back so that Conor pulled ahead.

Conor decided to himself that Warden was a man worth watching as well.

"Warden?" Bowen said, pulling his hood forward to shade his eyes. "He's got a head full of turnips."

"Fancy words for a friend," Conor said.

Bowen shrugged. "He's not actually a friend. I mean I know him, and I've worked a few caravans with him, but he's not a man I'd call friend. More of an acquaintance instead. He does his job, but by the horns, he's as dense as a post at times."

Conor sought Bowen out when they stopped to water the horses and rest a bit later that afternoon. The scouts had ridden ahead to seek a safe camp. As Master Fergus said, they had not reached the village that was their next stop, so he had men out looking for a place that would suit Captain Camhin.

It was getting harder to avoid the forested areas now, for they were started to extend in all directions. The Captain did not want to go through them at night, though.

"Aye, I rather thought that meself," Conor said. "Still, he thinks that wagon contains gold and that all the bad things a-happening are the Captain's doing. And that my lad can tell him what is in there."

Bowen sighed. "That's my fault, actually," he said. "When your wife did her healing on Warden's wound, he thought it was magic. I told him it was naught but Diancecht's will and her prayers, but he wouldn't believe it. Apparently, he saw when your lad clipped that bandit with a mage bolt, though I tried to convince him it was nothing more than pain flash from being wounded by an arrow. Warden then said when your lad and woman were attacked by the darkling he didn't believe that she had killed it with the lantern. He was certain your lad had done that as well."

"How do you know about healers and mage bolts?" Conor asked suspiciously.

Bowen smirked. "My granddad died in the Last War, and he told stories in his letters about mageborn and their battle magic."

"Yer granddad was a man of letters?"

"Nay. My dad was a healer, trained in the temples. But he went to war with my granddad, and he wrote the letters for him."

Conor nodded. "So ye are the man who told the others about my lad?"

Bowen nodded. "I just told Warden. If others know, it's his doing. But I'll do what I can to make sure none of the others get the wrong idea about your lad."

"Ye'll have my gratitude," Conor said.

"Good," Bowen said and smiled.

Someone called for mount up. Conor pulled Battlebrute away from the water and checked his girth, then climbed into the saddle.

They would be making camp soon. He just hoped Bowen was a man of his word.

Well?

Well what?
You saw what he did.

Yes.

Is he?

The Other—no, he is not the Other.

But is he.

Yes, he is. By the White One's tail, I never thought I would live to see him, but it is most certainly the one.

But I thought she said he would be an orphan.

She said his parents would die when he was young. Could be that has not happened yet?

Sad.

Why?

I was rather starting to like the big man.

He smiled under his hood. *Like him? In what way?*

He just seems like a good man.

Yes, I suppose you're right on that account. And young is irrelevant to one of the mageborn. He could be much younger than anyone knows.

Or much older. Age or not, he has the ancient blood.

Yes, I feel it too.

So—if something happens to the father and the mother on this trip, do we let it and do nothing?

He sighed. That was not something he wanted to think about.

We do what the Balance of All Things requires—no more and no less.

His internal companion echoed his sigh. *I suppose you're right. But if it's not yet their time?*

We do what we must to maintain the Balance of All Things.

Even if it means letting them die?

I don't want to think about that right now.

But he knew well enough that when the time came, the White One would send him to seek out this lad again.

He just hoped it was not during this caravan's run. He had more important things to do for now.

NINE

The distant cry of a predator jerked Rhoyd out of sleep. He sat up, groggy and uncertain, lashing about with mage senses. Then the realization of where he was outweighed his confusion. He pushed his hair out of his eyes and looked around.

On the other side of the campfire, Conor's soft burr matched the even rise and fall of his chest. Beside him, Eithne did not even stir. Rhoyd smiled, reassured that all was well if both of his parents were sound asleep. Drawing a deep breath, he lay back down and looked up at the stars. The Warrior constellation was high overhead. Beside it, the Great Dragon coiled over the Boar who was racing to join the Unicorn on the horizon. Between them, pinpoints of light flared and careened across the dark, only to vanish. Conor once said that meant the gods were shooting arrows of fire at the shadows to keep them at bay.

He was thinking of that explanation when light flashed bright in the corner of his vision. Rhoyd sat up, wondering if one of those godly arrows had fallen to earth, and looked to his left. The dark cloaked wagon was there, and a bit of unnaturally white light peeped between the black leather curtains.

Mage light! Rhoyd pushed mage senses at the source and felt the hum of power. A mageborn was in there working spells.

Rhoyd threw back his blankets and pulled on his boots. Neither Conor nor Eithne moved. Quietly, Rhoyd rose to his feet. All around him, he heard the murmurs of the caravan guards at their posts, the whicker of horses and the low of oxen. Night birds sang a chorus amid the snores of sleeping men. These were more than enough sounds to disguise the soft tread of his boots to ordinary ears as he carefully picked his way across the caravan camp and crept up to the wagon.

He sensed the probing fingers of the wards before they could give *his* presence away. Rhoyd froze in place and concentrated on them, closing his eyes and drawing tiny whispers of essence from the earth beneath his boots to extend his power. The caster had laid them out like a web and anchored them to the ground. Another step, and Rhoyd would have been on that web, and the caster would have been aware.

Hmmmm, Rhoyd thought as he opened his eyes. He crouched and held out his hand. The spell did not appear to rise above the ground at all. Standing up again, Rhoyd walked around the wagon, testing the ward's edges. And when he reached the front, his mage senses perceived that the tongue of the wagon touched the ground just outside the grid of the wards. Rhoyd smiled and stretched mage senses to test the wooden tongue. It was not hooked to the wards. Odd. Why had the caster failed to realize that not all who approached his wagon would be limited to the ground...unless those "things" Noreen mentioned could not fly. Rhoyd shook his head. Careless, he thought. Why, anyone light and agile could walk right up the wooden tongue.

Rhoyd carefully put one foot on the tongue, mindful of the iron harness rings and chains. For good measure, he whispered *"Tosd"* in the mage tongue to make certain they did not rattle. Then lightly, he planted his other foot on the wide wood of the wagon. Like the wire walkers he had seen at one of the village fairs Conor took him to, Rhoyd walked up the tongue and reached the wagon unnoticed, or so he hoped.

He glanced out at the camp then carefully crawled into the wagon seat. It creaked just a little, and he stopped, heart pounding with excitement. And it occurred to Rhoyd that Conor would be angry if he were caught sneaking about like a common thief, but determination and curiosity overshadowed the brief fear. Rhoyd could now hear a voice speaking words of a spell. *"Solus ceangail du so linnseach,"* they muttered.

A binding spell. Rhoyd leaned and pushed fingers against the curtain flap covering the window behind the wagon seat. White light flashed, filling Rhoyd's eyes and temporarily blinding him. Then he managed to blink and adjust his sight.

A man cloaked in dark blue stood with his back to Rhoyd. The raised hood kept Rhoyd from seeing much more than the hands that gestured and the fringes of straw-blond hair. Unable to tell who it was, Rhoyd leaned a bit so he could look around the figure.

A white cloth laid over something shaped like a long coffin was the source of the glow. Rhoyd could see runes and glyphs carefully embroidered around it edges.

The sound of a footfall alerted Rhoyd to the fact that he was about to have company. He let go of the flap and bolted, heedless of the alarm it was likely to raise. With a mighty leap, he hit the ground outside the web of wards and rolled.

"Who's there?" a gruff voice shouted.

Rhoyd bolted for the nearest wagon and went under it, whispering , *"Bi ann sgath!"* Just in time too. He spotted the heavy boots of a guardsman racing up on the scene. Lying flat on the ground and as still as stone, Rhoyd saw several others join the man. He also saw the flap at the front window of the wagon open enough to reveal a hooded head.

Oh, Horns, Rhoyd thought. *Don't let him see me!*

He could feel the mage senses of the other flickering about inquisitively. Rhoyd remained as still as the ground beneath him. Then more men gathered, the hooded figure pulled back, and the scrying ceased. Rhoyd let out a deep sigh of relief.

"What's wrong?" one of the guards asked.

"I thought I heard someone running away from the dark wagon," the other replied.

"Spread out and search the camp."

Horns, Rhoyd thought. *If they wake Conor, I'm done for!*

Indeed, as he looked over, he could see that Conor was stirring and sitting up.

What to do?

He didn't *know* what to do! But if Conor discovered Rhoyd was missing—and he would, Rhoyd felt certain—there would be questions asked that Rhoyd could not answer.

So he stayed where he was, fuming in his mind, wondering how long it would be before he was discovered.

Conor was rousted first by the noise in the camp. Men were shouting, and he sat up, reaching for his long dirk and looking around. Eithne stirred a bit then grew still. He saw no reason to awaken her as he glanced over at the second pallet...

...And saw that it was empty.

Horns, where is the lad gone now?

It occurred to Conor that Rhoyd might be off relieving his nature...or not. It also occurred to him that whatever had stirred the men in the night could be connected to his missing son. So he rose to his great height, dragging his man's plaidie about him for warmth and scoured the area.

No sign of Rhoyd.

With a grunt, Conor crossed the ground to join the men. "Hoi, what's the noise about?" he asked the closest man.

A guard named Galdon turned around. "Someone was near the dark wagon, they say."

Conor nodded. "Bandits?" he asked.

"Dunno," Galdon said. "Creed there heard someone running, but he's seen no one."

It was then that Captain Camhin seemed to materialize behind them. "What is the meaning of this?" he asked.

"Someone says they heard someone near the dark wagon..."

Camhin scanned the area. "I see no one save you men," he said.

"Aye, well no one was seen," Galdon admitted. "But Creed is certain he heard someone running away."

"Check the perimeter of the camp," Camhin said. "See if any of the posts have been compromised. You, Manahan, where's that lad of yours?"

Conor frowned at the captain. "If you're suggesting my lad had anything to do with this..."

"I just want to make certain he is safe, that is all," Camhin said with a wry smile. A smile that looked strangely familiar to Conor, but it disappeared before he could recall just who had smiled at him like that in his life.

But then Master Fergus made an appearance, filling the air with the odor of old turnips again. He and the Captain put their heads together. And Conor decided it would be a good time to see if he could find Rhoyd.

TEN

The gathering of guards thickened, and then Conor was in on it, and Rhoyd decided it was no longer safe for him to stay where he was. He had to get around the last wagon. Then he could claim he was off relieving himself and hope Conor did not notice the lie.

So he pulled essence and whispered a spell of misdirection, and cautiously crawled out of the far side of the wagon from where Conor stood.

The plan, he told himself, was to head for the last wagon, to slip into the trees there and really relieve his bladder in case someone wanted proof. At the moment, he felt like he could have pissed a river with very little effort. Funny how lying on the cold ground, trembling in fear, could encourage such a need in him.

"Faic mi cha!" he whispered in the mage tongue as he passed the supply wagon. Then the cook's wagon where Noreen was rousting herself and coming into view with a skillet in hand. She wielded it like a battle axe, and Rhoyd felt certain she could have split a man's head with one blow. He whispered *"Faic mi cha!"* once more as he passed her, and watched her turn the other way.

One more wagon and there would be but a short sprint to the woods. He rushed past the end, perhaps a little more carelessly than was wise.

The arm snagged him before he could think. He opened his mouth to scream, but a large hand clamped over the cry.

"Wheesht, lad," Conor said. "If yer gonna use the glamorie, ye best remember that I can feel it."

Warm bronze essence flooded the air around Rhoyd. He relaxed and leaned into the wall of chest that he was pinned against.

"You've some explaining to do, lad," Conor said softly.

Rhoyd nodded. He gave in as he was released then led from the end wagon past Noreen.

"Evening, Mistress," Conor said as they walked by.

"Evening," she said, fixing Rhoyd with a puzzled stare. She was probably trying to figure out where Rhoyd had come from.

Horns! The Demon-Bound thought.

Horns, indeed, the one inside him agreed. *Quite a remarkable little fellow, he is to figure a way past the wards.*

Too remarkable. That was dangerous. What if he had broken the spells?

I think I would be thankful that the Other did not see him.

We can only hope the Other did not see him.

Horns! I didn't think of that! We must watch him more closely.

But how can we without giving ourselves away?

True, the one the Demon-Bound had claimed to hide his essence behind was starting to grow restless under the bondage. The fact that he had dared to ask the Keltoran to have the lad scry the wagon. *And by the Balance, if that lad should break the spells scrying the wagon...*

He had no doubt that the lad could do just that.

We watch, he thought.

That was all they could do for now. Because until he knew where the Other hid—assuming the Other was there—he did not dare reveal himself.

Not yet.

Eithne was aroused by the chill of the night as much as Conor's return. She had felt cold air on her back, and was about to turn over and see what happened to the blankets when she spied Conor and Rhoyd coming back to their small camp. Conor wore that grim look he reserved for moments of silent anger, and Rhoyd...he had his head ducked.

"Blessed Brother, what is the matter?" she asked as she sat up and drew the blanket around her.

Conor motioned for silence, though. And just then, Captain Camhin walked over.

"Found him, I see," Camhin said.

"He was off taking a piss," Conor said. "Got scared by all the noise and hid under the last wagon, actually. It's a wonder Mistress Noreen didn't mistake him for a bandit and clout him with her skillet."

Camhin raised an eyebrow as though not sure he believed

the tale. "What frightened you, lad?" he asked. "What did you see?"

Rhoyd looked terribly reluctant to answer that question.

"Go on, lad," Conor said and crouched at Rhoyd's side. "Tell the man about that shadow ye saw."

Rhoyd's brows quirked a hint, but it was more than enough for Eithne to see. Still, the lad took a deep breath and pointed towards the woods not far from their camp. "It was a big shadowy thing," he said. "I thought it might be another darkling..."

"A darkling, you say?" Captain Camhin said. "Then I believe we should set out more watch fires for the rest of the night. Best way to keep darklings away is to light lots of fires." Camhin looked at Conor. "Darklings," the Captain repeated and shook his head. "Well, then, lad. I would suggest you don't wander out of camp the next time you need to relieve your nature."

"Yes, sir," Rhoyd said and lowered his head.

Captain Camhin shook his head again and turned away. "Darkling," he muttered, and he seemed to be chuckling as he said it. Eithne watched him saunter back towards the dark wagon and disappear behind it. She waited until then to turn and look at Conor and Rhoyd.

Conor was still crouching, and he had Rhoyd's shoulders in a firm grim.

"Well, now," Conor said in a low voice. "We're both going to be in a bit of a fix if he learns we both lied. But I think yer in more of a fix since ye owe me an explanation. What were ye doing out there in the dark?"

Eithne watched the exchange quietly. Rhoyd took a deep breath. "I saw a light," he said. "Not a shadow and it was coming out of the dark carriage."

"And what else did you see?"

"There's a mageborn in there," Rhoyd replied. "He was casting a binding spell on a white blanket."

"A mageborn?" Conor said. "So there *is* a mageborn among us? I thought I felt magic in the air that was not your glamorie. Did ye get a look at him?"

Rhoyd shook his head. "He was hooded. And the other guards were coming and I had to run."

Conor nodded and looked over at Eithne, then back at Rhoyd.

"I owe ye a stint across my knee for that prank," he said. "But we'll save it for another time. Now you stay away from that cursed wagon."

"It's not cursed," Rhoyd said. "The spell was a good spell."

"Good or bad, I don't like the feel of this," Conor said. "Ye'll keep yer distance from that carriage, or I'll see to it you ride standing in the stirrups. Understand?"

Rhoyd nodded.

Conor released Rhoyd's shoulders and pushed a hand through the black thatch of the lad's hair. "Get to bed now," he said firmly.

Again, Rhoyd nodded. He slipped over to his pallet and crawled in, curling up in a knot and closing his eyes.

Conor sat down on the pallet with Eithne and caught her look. "What?"

She smiled a little. "You're too soft on him," she said.

He frowned at her then shook his head. "Aye, I suppose I am," he muttered and looked across the fire.

"There's nothing wrong with tempering mercy with justice, or justice with mercy," she said. "It's one of the things I have always admired about you."

Conor looked back as though not sure whether or not she was teasing him. She smiled, rose to one knee to kiss him, and then sat back down. Conor followed her, forcing her to lie down on the pallet as he slid his arms around her.

"You're soft on me, woman," he said. "But then, I'm soft on you, too."

Eithne smiled and snuggled close, relishing his warmth and his musky smell as she closed her eyes.

ELEVEN

"It had to be him," the captain snarled as Noreen was slicing bread for the board.

She shrugged. "All I know is that I didn't see him run past, but I did sense magic, and then there was the Keltoran coming back with the lad in tow."

"I'm starting to wish I had told Fergus we didn't need another man," the captain said. He picked up a slice of bread and started tearing it into smaller pieces. "But Conor Manahan is the best there is. He always was a fair, honest, trustworthy, decent man."

"People change," Noreen said. "War changes folks. I know that. You know that."

"But he left the war before it ended..." He paused and sighed, and took a bite of the chunks he had torn off.

Noreen got the impression he was not telling her everything.

Damn it all, how can I help you if you keep secrets from me!

He was entitled to them, but she wished he would be more open about the things that mattered. Like why it was he thought so well of the Keltoran.

"We're just going to have to keep both eyes on him from now on."

Noreen grinned. "You know, there is a way."

"What?"

"Let me go talk to his father. I'll tell him I heard some of the men nattering about the lad, and that I don't like what I'm hearing, and if it makes his job easier, there's room for more than one on my wagon."

"Brilliant!" the captain said. "That way, you can keep him out of trouble."

Noreen nodded. She glanced over towards the camps. The Keltoran was already up and approaching the boards to look over the cold breakfast she had laid out for the men.

"Take off. I'll handle this," she said.

The captain nodded and slipped away. Noreen walked over to the boards and smiled at the Keltoran.

"You look chipper for a man who was up in the dark chasing small hearth rats," she said. "What can I get for ye?"

The Keltoran smiled. "Do ye know how to make bannocks?" he asked.

"I do indeed," Noreen said. "Easy as falling off a stone. How many do ye want?"

He told her and she chatted with him as she mixed the batter and started heating the griddle on the fire, while remembering something her mam used to say about hearts and stomachs and men.

In no time, he was a fast friend.

"All up!" Master Fergus shouted.

Rhoyd sat up with a groan. The temperature had dropped in the night, and now it was chilly. He tightened the blanket and his tartan cloak around him and glanced around, knuckling sleep from his eyes.

"So he rises," Conor said. He was packing the horses. Eithne was nowhere in sight.

"I guess," Rhoyd said cautiously. It was hard to decipher Conor's mood at the moment. "I'm sorry," he added, in case that was what was needed.

Conor raised an eyebrow and glanced over at the lad. "For what, lad?"

Rhoyd took a deep breath. "Last night," he said. "I should have awakened you instead of going off on a lark."

Conor nodded and returned to his chores. The tightness of his jaw that said he was fighting laughter. "Aye, that you should have," he said. "And I would have told ye that it was nonsense. Now, there's a bannock for ye, and an apple. Eat up."

Rhoyd frowned. But it wasn't nonsense. He had seen the light, and the mage.

"Except I know there is not something right in all that has been a-happening here," Conor added. "So I want ye to give me yer word, and I want ye to keep it. No more larking about in the dark. You see or hear something, you wake me up, aye?"

"What if you're on watch?" Rhoyd asked.

"Then ye come fetch me," Conor said. "Cos if ye dinna do

so, I'll be fetching the flat of my hand across the seat of yer trews."

Conor glanced over, one eyebrow raised. Rhoyd bit his lip. The words were stern, but there was humor hidden in the expression Conor presented. Rhoyd took a deep breath and nodded as he crawled to his feet.

"I promise," he said.

"Yer hand on it?" Conor said and held out his own hand to seal the pact.

Rhoyd crossed the space between them and extended his hand. It was tiny compared to Conor's, and his fingers could not even reach half way around the mercenary's wrist, while Conor's overlapped about his arm. But they shook on their bargain like men at a market. Conor, however, didn't let go. He squatted so he was looking up at Rhoyd.

"Now give us a hug," Conor said.

Rhoyd smiled and threw arms around Conor's neck.

"Oh, and ye'll be riding on the wagon with Mistress Noreen today," Conor added.

"Why?" Rhoyd asked and pulled back.

"Just to make certain ye stay out of trouble," Conor said with a wry smile.

"I said I would," Rhoyd said indignantly.

"I know ye will try," Conor said and tapped Rhoyd's chin. "I'm making it easier for ye to keep yer word. Besides, Mistress Noreen seems to have taken a shine to ye. Best take advantage of that. I hear she's thinking of frying up some apple tarts tonight."

Rhoyd smiled. "All right," he said. "I'll ask her to tell me more war stories."

"Good lad," Conor said and rose from his crouch. "Now eat yer breakfast then get yer gear packed and ready. We'll be moving out here shortly."

Rhoyd nodded and snatched up the food as he looked about for his kit.

"And nary a man alive that day
Could stand against the wind
Of the Mighty Maudie Maggie May
The Maid of the Hulan Glen..."

Eithne tried not to roll her eyes as Rhoyd and Noreen belted that chorus for the tenth time. She was starting to have doubts about letting the lad ride with the cook. Granted, Conor had taught him songs of which Eithne did not approve, but this...

With a sigh, Eithne glanced at the pair. They were howling with laughter now, and Rhoyd nearly fell backwards off the wagon seat, but Noreen steadied him with a free hand.

"Your turn, lad," Noreen said.

Rhoyd's face split into a wide smile, and he started belting, "Gin ye'll be my lassie..." in his sweet alto voice.

Conor! Eithne thought. *We shall have words about these unsavory songs tonight.* At least three of "Rhoyd's turn" had been songs she knew Conor taught the lad. She wished she could see what Conor was doing just now but he was on the far side of the caravan and further up the line as well. No doubt, he was one of those she heard chuckling in amusement at this bawdy display. Then again, she supposed she should have been grateful because the men were not concentrating on the fact that Rhoyd was mageborn. She just wasn't sure that a reputation as a singer of lewd songs was a fair trade.

Of course, Conor had told her that it was for the better. That some of the men on this caravan had discovered Rhoyd's heritage, and that it would be better for the lad to stay with someone who could protect him should Conor not be available. Eithne had sniffed at the suggestion that she could not protect their son as well as this muscle-armed cook with the easy manners, but resigned herself to the idea with the reminder that she was not one who believed in violence to settle matters. If men had swords and she only had her staff, she could defend herself well enough, but she might not be up to defending Rhoyd, too. Though she would certainly try.

Lost in her thoughts, she failed to notice at first that a horse was pacing her own. She turned suddenly to find one of the guards at her side. Eithne just managed to keep from gasping aloud for his presence startled her. But then she recognized him as the man from whom she had removed the arrow yesterday. What was his name? Warren? No, Warden. He was peering at her with an amused expression. She frowned in return.

"Sorry, Mistress, didn't mean to startle you," Warden said carefully. "Just realized I never got a chance to say thank you for the fixing of my shoulder." He reached up as he spoke and rubbed the spot. "Quite a talent you got there."

Relief washed over Eithne. She smiled and nodded. "It is the Blessed Brother to whom you owe your thanks," she said. "I am merely His servant here among the living."

"Well, next time I am near one of your temples, I'll make a donation," he said and flexed the arm.

"Is it still troubling you?" Eithne asked. "I can fix you a tea when we stop..."

"Oh, no," Warden assured her and shook his head and smiled. It was an absurdly gentle look for the otherwise gruff man. "I was just...curious."

"About what?"

"Is it magic?"

Eithne raised her eyebrows. "It's no more than the Brother's Will," she said.

"But there was a healer in our village, and all he knew was potions and granny cures and herbs...though he was a fair hand at setting bones and stitching wounds. But he could not make fever go away, nor close a wound with his prayers and his touch."

"Ah," Eithne said. "Well, you see, the Blessed Brother does not always give his gift to everyone who follows his teaching. Indeed, his gift seems to blossom as randomly as mageborn skills..."

"Like your son?" Warden said.

Eithne looked at the man. He was still smiling. "What do you mean?" she asked.

"Oh, I know what he is," Warden said. "I know what he did yesterday when the bandits attacked."

Eithne opened her mouth, uncertain of what to say. Conor had worried that some of these men might grow hostile if they learned what Rhoyd was.

"Oh, you've nothing to fear from me, Mistress," Warden quickly assured her. "I owe you for my life. I'll gladly see to it that no harm comes to your lad."

"Well, that's very thoughtful of you, but..."

"Oh, not at all," he assured her. "You just remember. Old Warden owes you a favor. And maybe he will expect one in return."

With that, he clucked to his horse and rode away. Eithne watched him go up front of the caravan. She turned to look over her shoulder and spied Captain Camhin riding off a short ways, watching her with thoughtful eyes. Oh, Blessed Brother, had he heard that conversation?

Taking a deep breath, she glanced over at the jolly duet. Rhoyd was still singing, but his eyes held a worried look. She spurred Maudie and rode over to look for Conor.

"Warden," Conor said with a grimace as Eithne told him what had transpired. "He's the man what asked me if Rhoyd could look into the dark wagon for him. He's convinced there's gold in there."

Eithne sighed and glanced aside. "I am starting to wish we had waited for Caperton's caravan," she said.

"Well, we can always jump caravan in the next village," Conor said. "Take what pay we've earned and head south for Caer Tamnagh."

"Back through the mountains and across the river," she said softly. "And it still rough weathered there...I don't know, Conor."

Conor shrugged, his eyes never leaving the woods they had entered. Camhin had ordered all men to keep their eyes on the trees, and Eithne was starting to understand why. There were a lot of shadows here.

"We have to make a choice," he said. "If these men start thinking they can use our son to their own ends..."

"Is there none we can trust?" Eithne said. "Besides the venerable Mistress Noreen who apparently knows more bawdy songs than you."

Conor managed a smile. "She would have made a good companion in the Last War," he said with a chuckle. "A woman who can fight and cook and sing like a soldier."

Eithne could not help but reach over and slap his thigh since that was the closest part of him she could reach. "Men," she said.

Conor laughed. "It's all right, woman. You're more than enough for me," he assured her. "But as to whom we can trust? There's that fellow Bowen. His da was a healer, and he knows about mageborn and holds them no grudge, and he said he would help watch Warden. So I dinna think we've anything to get our knickers in a twist over yet."

"Not even Captain Camhin?"

"What about the captain?" Conor said.

"I think he heard what Warden said to me."

Conor was silent for a moment, as though mulling this.

"Well, there's something about the captain that keeps making me wonder if he's the problem or the cure, I will admit," Conor finally said. "But I suspect that if he thought there was something wrong with mageborn, he would have come out and said so."

"Why do you say that?"

"He's got a glamour about him," Conor said.

"What?"

"Rhoyd says so," Conor added.

Eithne raised eyebrows. This caravan was turning out to be stranger than she had first imagined.

"So are we leaving at the next village?" Conor asked.

She sighed. "We should at least wait until we reach one of the larger towns," she said.

"Thought so," Conor agreed. "Now you best get back to the cook's wagon. Oh, and ask Mistress Noreen if she knows *The Randy Bandy Cock,* as I would love to hear her sing it."

"You!" Eithne slapped his thigh again and jerked Maudie away. "I will do no such thing."

"You're a hard woman," Conor called after her so that more ears than her own could hear. "Must be why I love you so much."

Her face flushed red as a beet. Some of the men in hearing range chuckled.

TWELVE

Rhoyd saw Eithne ride away, and he was wondering why when he felt the odd sense he was being scried. He turned quickly towards the source of the sensation.

Captain Camhin had ridden up on the other side of the wagon. "Mistress Noreen," he said. "Are you now nursemaid as well as cook?" he asked cheerfully.

"Nah, this is me new apprentice," Noreen shot back with a twinkle in her eyes. "We're gonna teach him how to make men lust after yer tarts..."

Camhin actually laughed, and the sound was alien to his appearance. In fact, for a moment, Rhoyd thought he saw the glamour around the man fall just a whit, and what was revealed to mage eyes was a thinner man with long, fair hair and grey eyes. But the image quickly vanished.

"Well, he's rather small for a cook's apprentice, isn't he?" the captain said.

"We'll fatten him up," Noreen said and reached over to poke Rhoyd in the stomach.

Rhoyd wriggled and watched as the captain suddenly guided his horse around behind the wagon and came up on Rhoyd's side.

"You know, lad," Camhin said. "You are creating quite a stir."

"Me?" Rhoyd frowned.

"Aye." The captain leaned closer. "I know what you saw last night." He whispered so only mage ears could hear. "I know that you were the one the guards thought they saw near the dark carriage."

Rhoyd stiffened and slid closer to Mistress Noreen, uncertain.

"It's all right, lad," she said. "He's not the enemy, even if he acts like it at times."

"You're quite amazing," Captain Camhin said, and with alarming agility, he climbed from the back of his horse onto the wagon so that Rhoyd was sandwiched between them.

"I've never met a mageborn who could not be felt with a little scrying. It's your magic that gives you away, you know. You really must learn to cloak your spells. Have you not been trained to do so?"

"I want off this wagon now, please," Rhoyd said, looking at Mistress Noreen.

"You're safe with us lad," the big woman said, and her eyes locked his, and he felt power in her as well. Rhoyd's jaw dropped nearly to his knees.

"You're both mageborn," he said.

"Aye, that we are," Camhin said. "And now, you have the power to undo all we are fighting for by your knowledge alone."

"What do you mean?"

"Would you like to see what is in the dark carriage?"

Rhoyd stiffened. "No," he said.

"Too bad," Camhin said. "We could certainly use your help."

"No!" Rhoyd said and lurched out between them. Before either of them could stop him, he flung himself onto the back end of one of the wagon horses. The beast did not take too kindly to the sudden weight and bucked, flinging him off to one side...right in the path of the wheel.

There was a scream of, "Whoa Bellow, Whoa Bawdy!" and Mistress Noreen was clearly trying to halt her wagon. Rhoyd heard someone hiss *"Talamh utag!"* in the mage tongue, and like a hand, the earth heaved and rolled him out of the way...barely in time. The wheel stopped right on the spot he had been laying. But that put him into the path of Camhin's horse, and his sudden appearance frightened the animal. Rhoyd scrunched himself into a ball as he had been taught to do when he was small and some of the horses in his real father's smithy misbehaved. Hooves slammed the ground to either side of him. There was a general outcry from several sources then hands were on him, lifting him from the ground. He turned to find Eithne was pulling him up. Camhin was off to one side, hauling his skittish mount under control.

"Rhoyd, are you all right?" Eithne said.

He nodded and scrunched himself against her, burying his face in her tunic. She slipped reassuring arms around him and made cooing noises to comfort him and he clung to her, wishing the rest of the world would just go away.

"I'm so sorry, Mistress," he heard Noreen say. "He was standing up when the wagon hit a rut. I couldn't catch him...I'm sorry."

Rhoyd shifted so he could look at her. There was a power in her eyes, and in Rhoyd's head, he felt a voice filter through.

"Please, lad, for the sake of the world, don't give us away," Noreen begged. *If the dark ones realize who we are and what we carry, the world will be lost to a new Darkening before its ready to face that day...*

For the sake of the world? he thought.

"And what was Captain Camhin doing on the wagon as well?" Eithne asked.

"He was asking if we knew another song," Rhoyd said softly and looked up at Eithne. "I'm all right, really..."

"Oh," she said, though the suspicion in her eyes never faded. "Well, as long as you're not hurt. I suppose next time you'll know better than to stand up on a wagon crossing rough ground."

Rhoyd nodded and pulled back. Eithne took the edge of her sleeve and wiped the dirt off his nose. Then she stood up and helped him to rise.

"Are you certain you're all right?" she asked. Conor was riding back now, his expression dark with worry.

"I'm fine," Rhoyd said. "I won't stand up to sing anymore."

"I should think not," Eithne said.

"Do ye want to ride with me, then?" Conor asked.

Rhoyd shook his head. "I'll ride with Mistress Noreen," he said. "She hasn't finished teaching me that song."

He looked at Noreen as he spoke. Relief covered her face. And that of Camhin. He mounted his horse, bowed to them all and rode back to his place near the dark carriage. Rhoyd, with Eithne's assistance, crawled back onto the cook's wagon.

He took his seat at Noreen's side and looked at her expectantly. Then someone gave the wagons the order to roll on. Conor hurried back to his post. Eithne mounted up and stayed at Rhoyd's side.

"So what shall we sing now?" Noreen asked.

"Do you know *The Traitorous Giant?*" he said.

Noreen winced. "Can't say as I do," she said.

Rhoyd launched into a song about a giant that stole a magic stone from the realm of Cernunnos, and the trouble he had when the god discovered the theft.

Well, now they know, his companion thought.

Yes, though I don't know what good it will do them. He's just a boy.

He is the Ard Magister. Fenelon would have fits to hear you say that he's just a boy.

The Demon-Bound sighed. *Yes, I suppose you're right—were he here he would have words for me.*

Then we should consider ourselves fortunate that as a mage spirit, he is confined to the place where he died.

Small favors, the Demon-Bound thought as he nodded, pulling his hood forward. Though the sun was not filtering through the trees, there was something about this place that bothered him.

He wondered if the boy felt it. And the captain. And the cook.

Oh, they feel it, his internal companion said. *Even if they do not show it, they feel it.*

The Other.

Very near.

Not good news. *Stay alert then.*

Oh, we shall...

They had managed to get through the forest unchallenged, but Captain Camhin ordered torches in spite of the abundance of daylight filtering through the boughs of large ancient oaks. Conor thought this odd. There was hardly any undergrowth. In fact, he could not recall seeing a forest so bare of shrubs and short growth. Not even grass. Just the dirt and leaves and scatterings of upright stones, and the occasional patches of moss or ferns. Even with the roll of the landscape, one could see for a good distance.

On the other hand, Conor was all too aware of the way the forest felt. It reminded him of other bogie places he had encountered in his lifetime. So he stayed alert, and was not surprised when Rhoyd and Noreen stopped their contest of songs. Something about the woods required silence.

And then he realized it was because they heard no birds.

But they made it through without trouble and continued along the rolling pastures of braes that seemed to make up a lot of Elenthorn's landscape.

Stonelay came into view as the caravan rounded the curve in the road where it wound along the edge of a large hummock. The latter was clearly an old broch whose walls had been ransacked for the stones…no doubt to make the fences that penned in the sheep and kept cows out of small gardens. Like so many farming villages that started back up after the Last War, Stonelay was little more than a collection of stone and thatch cottages where most of the livestock roamed at will. The broch had probably been some seat of power before the Haxons razed this land. Conor remembered one of his commanders saying that nobility in the north was rare as whole families went to war and were slaughtered defending their land and their people. And that many a lady was forced to take some farmer to replace her husband in bed, thus making him little more than what Conor heard called a "dirt noble."

Clearly the folks of Stonelay had no lord to manage for them. And like many in the north who had lived through the Last War, their eyes filled with suspicion as the first of the caravan appeared among their homes. Master Fergus rode up and asked for a headman. At length, one came out of a central building larger than the rest. He was an old warrior with a patch over one eye, and was accompanied by several younger men armed with little more than pitchforks, staves and knives. Fergus spoke to them from the back of his horse. There were nods and grunts, and eventually, the headman accepted Fergus' offer of his hand.

What he had bargained for was little more than fresh meat for the cook's wagon, and in trade, he gave them goods.

Conor and the men stayed mounted. They watched as Fergus let the villagers remove some of the crates from one of the wagons. He noted too how the villagers stood far back from the black wagon. Some of them whispered among themselves and pointed at it. Captain Camhin rode around it in a circle, keeping a keen eye on the crowd. His nervousness could not be disguised.

With a sigh, Conor glanced at Rhoyd sitting on the cook's wagon. The lad was alert, like a fox scenting a predator larger than itself. His blue eyes scanned the crowd, and he frowned. Conor could not help but wonder what mage eyes could see that he only felt a hint of. Then suddenly Rhoyd stood up and stared over at the pens, and Conor directed his attention there as well.

At first, he saw nothing, but then, the sheep began to mill and shove against one another in a panic. What they fled from, Conor could not say. He stood in his stirrups for a better look. Nothing but sheep, as far as he could tell.

At least it looked like sheep. There was one ram that did not seem to be joining the bustle...in fact, the other sheep were fleeing from the vicinity of the ram whose eyes started to glow red with unnatural fire. Its white coat shimmered and darkened, and it began to change shape and size. The wool thickened and hardened into scales as it rose on its hind feet. Within moments, it lost almost all resemblance to a sheep...except for the head, where those curling ram horns remained.

"Demon!" someone screamed, and at that point, panic ensued. Villagers took one look at the monster and fled for whatever hovel they could find.

Conor dragged Battlebrute around, jerked his sword free of its scabbard, and charged the pen with a shout. Several of the guards did the same. The demon crouched as though to leap, leering at the men who rushed for the pen. It showed no fear as Conor and one other leapt their horses over the low stone wall and attacked it. Conor was first to reach it, and he slashed down on its head. The creature writhed out of the path of his blade and swiped at him with razor-sharp talons. They bit through the leather of the saddle, snagged the girth rings and jerked.

The saddle came lose with a snap, and Conor was airborne. He landed on top of the fleeing sheep that had not yet been able to get over the stone wall. They scattered and dropped him in a heap on the ground. A guttural scream of pain tore the air. Scrambling, Conor got his feet under him and turned.

The demon had grown larger and it had snagged both the man and his horse by the throats and was dangling them in the air. Opening its mouth, it bit off the man's head and heaved his corpse towards Conor, forcing him to dodge, and then it tore the horse's head off and began to devour it as well.

"Horns!" Conor shouted and looked around. Battlebrute had managed to get out of the pen with the sheep. So much for depending on his battle mount. Then again, considering that the demon was eating a whole horse, it just proved that the old hay burner was wise in his own way.

Some of the guards started shooting arrows at the beast, but they bounced off its scaled hide. The demon snarled, tore a haunch off the horse and threw it at them. Someone else came in with a blade and tried to slice the monster's leg, but they might as well have tried to fell a tree. The blade bounced off the demon's hide.

"They're impervious to steel!" Captain Camhin shouted. "Conor, get out of there! Now!"

Conor decided that was as good an order as any. He turned and ran for the wall...but he had hardly gone more than a few long strides when a long coil of a tail tripped him. He fell, only to feel the tail wrap about his leg like a rope and haul him up into the air. Somehow, he managed to hang onto his sword, and he tried hacking at the appendage as it drew him over to the demon. Those red eyes looked into his, and the beast seemed to smile. Shouting, Conor struck again, but his blade skittered. Clearly, the beast's scales were better than any armor he had known. Still smiling, it batted his blade aside.

"Put him down!" a small voice shouted.

Both Conor and the demon turned. Standing on the rim of the stone wall was Rhoyd, and in his hands was a ball of white flames. All the remaining villagers and the men in the caravan had gone silent. In fact, even the sheep seemed to have grown still, as though no one could quite believe their eyes.

"I said put him down now!" Rhoyd ordered. "Or I'll burn you!"

The fireball got bigger. Conor felt himself lurch as the demon contemptuously flung him. He landed among the sheep again. Scrambling to his feet, he watched in horror as the demon turned its attention on the lad. Rhoyd stood firm as the demon crouched and then lunged.

The white fire in Rhoyd's hands became as bright as the sun and shouting in the mage tongue, Rhoyd flung it at the demon. The creature screamed as it fell into the burning orb. Flames blossomed around it, but it continued to race at the lad as though determined to take his life even as it died.

"No!" Conor shouted, and he heard Eithne echo his sentiments. There was nothing to stop the momentum of the beast as it rushed at Rhoyd, like burning shot from a catapult. Neither of them would reach the lad in time.

But then, there was a wall of woman flinging herself in from the side. Mistress Noreen tackled Rhoyd and jerked him off the wall, throwing both her and the lad to the ground just as the flaming demon passed over the stone rim. It hit the ground and splattered into a multitude of smaller flames and sizzled with a stinking black smoke.

Then all at once, it was gone, leaving only the lingering scent of rot and a few tiny bits of flame dancing around in the dirt.

Conor charged to his feet, racing across the pen. Eithne, Captain Camhin and several others were charging in as well. As Conor reached the wall, he could only see Mistress Noreen on the ground, and she was struggling to get up quickly. Then he spotted Rhoyd, face down in the muck, sputtering like a small bantam as Eithne reached his side first and drew him upright. He turned and looked at the imprint in the ground where the demon landed, and broke into a grin. Mud plastered his face, making his blue eyes more brilliant than ever as they blinked at the tiny scattered embers of magic fire still smoldering on the ground.

"It worked," he said breathlessly, then sank to the ground when his knees failed him.

"Oh, look at you," Eithne said and started scrubbing the mud from his face.

Conor crawled over the stone wall, feeling like an old man as he sat down beside the lad and glanced at the faces of the villagers and the guards.

Not a one of them had yet to move. They stood around, their mouths open, and stared at Rhoyd.

Well at least they're not attacking us, Conor thought as he closed his eyes.

THIRTEEN

Conor had yet to say two words to Rhoyd, and that was starting to worry him more than a little. The headman of the village loaned them the use of his hut. Eithne fussed like an old hen as she got Rhoyd cleaned up, and he gave in to her rather than protest that he could do it himself. Now, he suspected would not be a good time.

As Eithne made Rhoyd change clothes, Conor collected his saddle and brought it inside, and now he was working a fresh strip of leather in to replace the one that held the girth rings and stitching it into place. Rhoyd watched the whole process, waiting.

He's angry, Rhoyd thought. Conor might not be showing it, but Rhoyd could feel it all the same. Yet he wasn't sure that the anger was directed at him.

Maybe he's angry because I killed the demon and he didn't. But what was I supposed to do? Let it kill him?

Rhoyd took a deep breath.

"You should consider yourself fortunate that Mistress Noreen was there to save you," Eithne said suddenly. "And that when she pushed you down and landed on top of you that you didn't break any bones."

Conor made a noise. It might have been a stifled laugh. Rhoyd glanced cautiously at his adopted father. Eithne finished brushing her fingers through Rhoyd's hair and sat back on the chair she was using.

"Now I must go see to the men who were injured," Eithne said. "You stay in here with Conor and behave yourself."

Rhoyd nodded and hugged her. He had been surprised that she stayed with him instead of going to the men who had been waylaid by the horse's haunch. But their injuries were not serious. A few small cuts and bruises. Still, Rhoyd had never known her to put *"need's call"* aside for him. So he knew that what he had done had frightened her.

She stood up, crossed the room and went through the door. There was a common room on the other side where the rest were gathered. Rhoyd glanced over his surroundings with a critical eye. It occurred to him that there was no other way out, save the small window. If this was meant to be a prison...

"Come here," Conor said.

Rhoyd sighed. This was it, he supposed. The lecture? Or would Conor keep his earlier promise to dust trews if Rhoyd broke his word.

But what was I supposed to do? Let him die?

He bit down the urge to say so aloud and crossed the chamber to stand before Conor.

But all Conor said was, "Get the knife, lad, and cut this near the knot. If I let go, the saddle might slip."

Rhoyd pulled out the small dagger he carried on one hip—a gift from Conor last year—and carefully slipped it between Conor's hands. Deftly, Rhoyd sliced through the bits of waxed linen thread and pulled his dagger away.

"Thank ye, lad," Conor said.

Rhoyd shrugged and blushed, unsure why he should be thanked for such a simple thing. Until he saw the look in Conor's eyes.

"I...I'm sorry I had to break my word," Rhoyd said.

Conor lifted the saddle and put it aside. He opened his arms, and Rhoyd did not hesitate to slip into the proffered comfort.

"As am I," Conor said. "But I'm not sorry that ye did. Otherwise, I would not be here to forgive ye."

The startling reality of those words hit Rhoyd in the gut like cold steel. He snuggled closer, closing his eyes, hiding his face in Conor's plaidie and relishing in the scents of the man. A large hand moved up and down his back in comforting strokes that loosened the knots there.

"When I was in the Last War, I fought a demon," Conor said. "A shadow beast, it was. Took over the body of some unfortunate and tried to kill me...nearly did. But for my friend Michan who was our battle mage, I don't think I would have lived to tell you the tale."

Rhoyd nodded. He remembered that tale.

"Of course, you killed a whole wheen of them in Harrowdown, remember, so I suppose my one battle is nothing to you."

"All your battles are good," Rhoyd said and drew upright

to look into Conor's weary expression.

"That thing...is that what's been hanging around outside the caravan? The thing I've felt?" Conor asked.

With a deep breath, Rhoyd stretched mage senses. A miasma squatted far out in the old forest beyond this place. Slowly, he shook his head.

"No, it's still there," he said carefully.

"What's going on here, lad?" Conor asked.

Before Rhoyd could open his mouth and reply, the door opened. Captain Camhin and Mistress Noreen strode in and shut the door. Rhoyd felt Conor tense. The Captain turned and set a glower on Conor.

"Why didn't you tell us that your son was mageborn?" Camhin demanded.

"Why?" Conor said. "So you could look at him the way you're looking at him now? As though he was an abomination of nature?"

"No," the captain said, "but it would have helped to know that sooner than later. I would not have allowed you to come along had I known."

Conor nodded. "I see," he said. "Then, if this is yer way of coming to tell us that we have to leave the caravan, we'll stay here and let you go on."

"You can't stay behind now, MacManahan, not after what your boy has done."

Conor reared upright. "How do you know my full name?" he asked.

"Because I...," Captain Camhin said, his usual assuredness faltering. He looked at Noreen and she shrugged.

"It's your call, m'lord Magister," she said with a smile.

Captain Camhin gestured to the door. Noreen turned and threw the bolt. She was surprisingly military in the action. Once it was thrown, she turned back and planted herself there like a soldier.

"What the..." Conor stood, pushing Rhoyd back as though ready to defend the lad.

"Please, do not be alarmed, Conor. Clearly, my mistake was not revealing myself to you sooner."

Camhin changed as well, his nondescript form shimmering and becoming thinner, and more acute. Rhoyd frowned, for this was quite like the man who had been in the dark carriage last night. *Well...maybe,* he thought since he had not actually seen the man's face. But the essence was there, the magic Rhoyd had felt then was on this man.

"Michan?" Conor said. "Michan O'Brannach? Is that really you?"

Michan? Rhoyd thought and looked up at Conor. The battle mage Conor had called his friend.

"Yes," Michan said and took a deep breath. "Look, I know I owe you an explanation, but..." He hesitated, glancing towards the door. "I must have your word that what is said in this room remains in this room, and that you will not reveal me to any of them." He gestured towards the world outside.

"Yes, I think you *do* owe me an explanation," Conor agreed. "But you have my word as your old friend. Your secret is safe so long as it brings harm to none."

"Fair enough," Michan said. "Though I can't really make that promise. I have an important mission to fulfill here. I have to get this caravan to Caer Keltora without any more incidents."

"Why?" Conor asked.

"It's best you don't know," Michan said. "Less apt to put you or your family in danger. But what I can tell you is this. That was not the first demon to attack this caravan, and I suspect before we reach the Highland Ranges, there will be others."

"Why the ruse?"

Michan pulled a chair over and sat down. "Because there are those who know who I am. Noreen and I are part of a special courier sent to the Ranges to collect something of great importance to all the world. But as soon as we were put in charge of our cargo, it became apparent that there were others seeking it as well, and though the Demon-Bound did his best..."

"The Demon-Bound?" Rhoyd suddenly said. "You mean Alaric Braidwine, the bard?"

Michan's eye narrowed on the lad. "How do you know the name of the Demon-Bound?"

"Uncle Fenelon told me about him."

"Uncle Fenelon?" Michan leaned forward in his chair, staring at Rhoyd. "Fenelon *Greenfyn*?"

Rhoyd nodded.

"He's your *uncle*?" Michan glanced at Conor. "I didn't know you were related in blood to Fenelon Greenfyn."

"Very distantly," Conor said. "Through my real mother, as I've been told...but the lad here, he's closer in blood than I."

"What? How?" Michan looked terribly confused now. "How can your son be...?"

Conor sighed and crouched and slipped an arm around Rhoyd. "My son is dead, Michan. Killed by bandits years ago. Rhoyd is my adopted son. His name is Smytheson, and his mother was Alycia Greenfyn who is sister to..."

"Genna Greenfyn, yes I know her."

"That's the lad's Auntie what teaches him spell craft in the winter."

"But if that's true..." Michan stopped and looked hard at Rhoyd. "By the breath of the Dragons," he whispered. "No, this cannot be." Michan got up and walked over to Noreen. She looked as startled as he did. "This can't be."

"What can't be?" Conor insisted firmly.

Michan took a deep breath and whispered the words of a spell, and the glamour fell over him, turning him back into Captain Camhin.

"Perhaps we should gate to Dun Gealach now," Noreen suggested.

Michan shook his head. "That is precisely what the Dark Ones are hoping we will do. As long as we keep it off the ground and under the cloak of spells, they cannot be certain where it is or which caravan it is on. But if we try to move it by magical means, then The Demon-Bound has said that our enemies shall know where it is, and they will follow and seize it at whatever cost."

"More than one caravan?" Conor said.

Michan nodded. "Six caravans, taking six different routes to Dun Gealach," he said. "All guided by a mageborn traveling under an illusion and pretending to be mortalborn. It was hoped that by doing so, we would keep the dark powers confused."

"Doesn't seem to be working," Conor said.

"As far as we know, it *is* working," Michan insisted. "All of the caravans came under similar attack when we were still able to communicate. We decided then to end communications and hope that by doing so, the enemy would be confused. But now we have a new problem. Those of us who were mageborn were under orders not to use magic unless an extreme matter arose. But now that Rhoyd here has used magic, no doubt we will see more trouble."

"So if we leave, the trouble will follow us and not you."

"Exactly," Michan said. "And knowing what I know now, I cannot risk that."

"So what do we do?" Conor asked.

"Rhoyd will have to stay with Noreen at all times. She can cloak him with the cloaking spell that is protecting her and her wagon. And he must not practice any magic for the rest of this trip...is that understood?"

Michan looked at Rhoyd as though challenging the lad to say otherwise. Rhoyd sighed and looked at Conor.

"That'll be easier said than done," Conor said with a half-smile. He pushed a fond hand through Rhoyd's hair. "But he'll try."

Rhoyd nodded. Yes, he would try. Promise? That might be a more difficult.

FOURTEEN

"He's going to what?" Eithne looked up at Conor, and if she had been taller, he suspected she would have gone nose to nose with him now.

"He's going to ride with Noreen for the rest of the trip," Conor said.

"But why are we going all the way to Caer Keltora?" she asked. "I thought we were working the caravan as far as the border of the Highland Ranges and then heading south on a caravan to Gwyrn..."

"I know...but this is important," Conor said.

"Important how?" she insisted.

Conor sighed. He had given his word not to reveal Michan or his mission. Still, his wife would not allow him any peace if he did not give her an answer that would satisfy her. "Very important. This cargo is bound for the High King's palace, and they want only the best to guard it...and ye know I am one of the best mercenaries in all of Ard-Taebh. Besides, they're doubling my purse...and yours. Which means ye'll have a nice fat donation for yer god's temple when we get back to Loughan."

Eithne took a deep breath and glanced at Rhoyd. The lad put all his attention to slowly rewinding the waxed thread for Conor so he did not have to look at her. He had been warned as well. But Eithne was not one to take any matter lightly, and she had learned to read the lies in Rhoyd's eyes much better than Conor ever had.

"Very well, I suppose we can put off visiting the temple in Gwyrn for another year," she said softly and looked back at Conor.

"We can go there after we leave Caer Keltora," Conor said. "There will be plenty of time."

"So there really *is* a king's ransom in gold in there," she said.

Conor said nothing. No reason to compound the lie.

"And at any rate, this will give me a chance to visit the

temple in Caer Keltora," she added.

"That it will," he said. "We could even rest there a few days before heading for Gwyrn.

"But I'm still not certain it will be wise to let Mistress Noreen look after Rhoyd," she added. "For one thing, he is not her responsibility, and for another, I'm not so sure she won't crush him the next time she falls on him."

"I'll be fine," Rhoyd said and raised a mischievous smile. "Next time, I'll get out of her way."

Eithne merely rolled her eyes. Conor said a silent thank you.

One obstacle out of the way, he thought. *Now if we can just get to Caer Keltora without any more trouble.*

But they still had Tamnagh's mountains and the Highland Ranges to pass through first.

The forest seemed a lot more cheerful now. Rhoyd wondered if killing the demon was responsible for the calm he now felt. He wasn't sorry in the least that he had killed it, for it was going to kill Conor, and Rhoyd just couldn't let that happen.

He was tempted to stretch mage senses and see if the outward malaise was gone as well, but Michan had said there must be no magic used. And to Rhoyd's surprise, Conor had agreed. "But what if another demon is out there?" Rhoyd had protested, for all the good it did.

Michan insisted that he would deal with it.

Rhoyd bit his tongue rather than ask how, considering Michan was not using any magic beyond the illusion that turned him into Captain Camhin and the wards on the dark wagon. This was the mageborn Conor had told so many stories about over the last three years, and though Rhoyd had detected a hint of old anger buried in Conor, the mercenary still counted Michan his friend.

A friend he's known much longer than he's been father to me, Rhoyd thought with a sigh.

"You're being awfully quiet," Noreen said.

Rhoyd glanced at her. Outwardly, she still looked like the "cook," but now that he knew there was a faint *glamorie* on her, he could still see the mageborn under the mortalborn illusion.

"Where are you from?" he asked abruptly. "I mean, where were you really born?"

Noreen arched one eyebrow. "Why do you ask?" she said.

"You're not from Ard-Taebh at all," he said. "You don't feel like you are."

"I thought you were not to *use the glamorie,* as your da says," she said in an accusing manner.

Rhoyd refused to be put off. "I can feel things even without *using the glamorie,"* he retorted, imitating her poor imitation of Conor. "And you don't feel Ard-Taebhean. Besides, you're too tall for a woman."

Noreen's mouth curved into a smile. "And you're too smart for your own good, lad. The Council is going to *love* you."

Rhoyd frowned, wondering what she meant by that. "What Council?" he asked.

"Council of the Mageborn, of course," Noreen said.

Rhoyd shook his head. "Aunt Genna says I can't see them...not yet."

"Why not?" Noreen asked.

"She said they thought Fenelon was mad before he died," Rhoyd said. "She said they would not accept me now, and that I should wait until I was ready."

Noreen smiled. "Wise woman."

"So where are you really from?" Rhoyd insisted.

"Does it matter?" she asked.

He nodded.

"Well, as you said, I am not from Ard-Taebh." She leaned a bit closer as thought about to reveal a terrible secret. "I'm a Haxon," she said.

Rhoyd narrowed his eyes. "A Haxon?" he said. "But you don't look like a barbarian."

Noreen laughed. "And what do you *think* a Haxon looks like, my lad?"

Rhoyd frowned. In truth, he had never seen a Haxon. At least not one of whom he was aware. "Well, they wear a lot of raggedy old animal skins...and they never bathe."

Again she laughed and shook her head. "Better the Council doesn't meet you yet, my lad," she said. "You've got a lot to learn about the world. When the Great Cataclysm tore the world apart, not all Haxons went to Carn Dubh, you know. The scholars and priest and even some of the warriors followed the Stone Folk through the Ranges and eventually settled in Ross-Mhor and called it *Rhunwud,* and they intermarried with the Tree Folk who lived there."

"*Tree Folk?*" Rhoyd had never heard the Ross-Mhorians called that before.

"Aye. We called them that because they lived up *in* the trees. Anyway, some Haxons married into the Tree Folk Clans. Other's kept to their own kin. *My* family was of the latter disposition. I was raised to believe my blood must remain pure because some say my kin are blood kin to the Hammer Maid herself."

"The Hammer Maid? Who was she?" Rhoyd was finding all this history fascinating now. So many things he had never heard before. He could not wait to impress Aunt Genna with this new knowledge when he saw her next winter.

"Chosen of Thunor," Noreen said. "She who bore the Eye of True Seeing, and who carried the Thunder Hammer that was Mjolnir's twin. She is said to have shattered the body of the Dark Mother before one of the Shadow Lords managed to kill her and escape with the Dragon's Tongue. And he took it to Shadow Vale so the Dark Mother could be reborn, but the White One's Avatar managed to stop him and hid the tongue for all time."

"Was this Hammer Maid tall like you?"

"Taller, some say. She had the strength of ten men, so the Shadow Lord who slew her had to be sneaky about it. They say the White One put her up in the Stars, and that when the next Darkening comes, she will be born again in one of my kin's blood to help the White One's Champion of Light."

Rhoyd glanced up, but all he was flickers of blue sky through the winter-worn branches and thin new spring growth of leaves on the trees.

He would have to remember to ask her to show him where the Hammer Maid was.

Or ask Conor.

Eithne watched the lad closely, for in spite of Conor's reassurances, she felt a little uneasy to have him riding with Noreen. It seemed strange to her too that Conor had been so accepting of letting Rhoyd ride there. Usually, when there was danger, Conor wanted the lad close, but he had handed Rhoyd over to the cook's care with no sign of a fuss, all because Captain Camhin thought it wise?

That did not sound like Conor at all.

And Rhoyd was not looking as cheerful as he had before.

He was solemn-faced even now as he spoke with Noreen. Was he frightened by something?

Frowning, Eithne guided Maudie closer to the wagon, though not so she was in sight line.

"...So who is this White One?" Rhoyd asked.

"That depends on who you ask," Noreen replied, and Eithne was struck by the fact that the woman's voice was more cultured and possessed a slightly foreign accent. "Some say she is Mother of the Universe. Others call her She Who Sits At The Center Of All Things. Still others whisper that she is a beautiful white dragon, and that those who have seen her are blinded by her brilliance."

"Have you ever seen her?" Rhoyd asked.

"Well, when I was a little girl living in Blue Oak, my old grandmother was blind, and according to my father, she had seen the White One when she was but a lass..."

Eithne sputtered. "Stuff and nonsense," she muttered. Noreen was filling the lad's head with fancies as wild as anything Conor had ever told the lad. Tapping heels to Maudie's sides, Eithne urged the mare to move forward. She was going to stop this right now.

But just as she rode up to the wagon seat, she found two sets of eyes staring at her with incredulous looks of uncertainty. The sight stilled her tongue, for it suddenly occurred to her that blurting her opinion aloud as she had, Rhoyd would hear her.

"Is summit the matter, Mistress Manahan?" Noreen asked, and her accent had returned to the broad course speech of the common folk.

"I...uh..." Eithne took a deep breath. Her face was flushing warm. "I just wanted you to know that I do not approve of telling Rhoyd these stories, that's all."

Noreen arched an eyebrow. Rhoyd actually frowned and said, "I told you she was eavesdropping on us."

Eithne's face now turned bright red. Without another word, she drew Maudie around and headed towards the last wagon.

She would have words with Conor about this later for certain.

FIFTEEN

The forests were more frequent, and Captain Camhin was obviously displeased to have to go through them. And as the day wore on, Rhoyd found Noreen's company wearing as well. Oh, he liked her and all, and her stories were funny. And she gave him an apple from the barrel in the wagon and promised him there would be apple tarts for dinner. But she spoke of the war mostly, and of her girlhood in Ross-Mhor.

"I had seven brothers—just like the Hammer Maid," she said.

Rhoyd tried not to frown. She seemed quite insistent on mentioning her relationship to this "Hammer Maid" as though it were of importance to him.

"Did you meet the Demon-Bound himself?" Rhoyd asked, hoping to steer the subject in a direction that interested him, namely, magic.

"Not a good place to speak of that one, lad," Noreen whispered. "The trees might have ears..."

Rhoyd did frown this time. He glanced at the thick-bodied oaks they were riding past. The bark did seem to have faces. One tree in particular looked as though it were a sleeping old man. Rhoyd cocked an eyebrow, and just for sport, he threw his apple core at it, hitting it square in what would have been the forehead.

And was startled when the tree actually opened an eye and winked at him.

Rhoyd hitched back hard with a gasp, bumping into Noreen.

"Hey, what was that for?" she asked.

Rhoyd shook his head. "Nothing," he said and watched the tree closely as they rolled on by it. The one eye closed again, and the tree looked like nothing more than a tree.

"You should be more careful," she said. "You don't want to make me spook Bawdy and Bellow."

"Sorry," Rhoyd muttered. "What is this place anyway?"

Noreen shrugged. "Haven't a clue, lad, though I will admit that it has a bit of a bogie feel to it. Why? Do you sense something?"

"No," Rhoyd said and shook his head again.

Noreen frowned as though she did not believe him, but she said nothing more on the subject. "As I was saying, when I was a little girl, I had seven brothers..."

Rhoyd sighed and leaned to rest his elbows on his knees and his chin on his hands. Would they ever stop? It seemed like they had been moving forever. He was starting to wish he had been able to save Conor from the demon without magic...

Like there was a way to do so, he thought as he ignored Noreen's monologue about Haxon folk and Hammer Maids and the ravens of some one-eyed god she called Wotan.

Horns, would they ever be out of these trees?

He was certainly afraid of never knowing that answer, when the wagons finally rolled out of the forest and into a clearing. Ahead, the road wound around several knolls. Some scouts had apparently been sent ahead, and now they were riding back. They were too far away for even mage ears to pick up what was said, though, but they gestured off at the rolling horizon. Rhoyd stood up to get a better look, but could see nothing.

Well, not entirely nothing. He could see Conor standing watchfully in his stirrups to stretch. He could see Eithne riding alongside the row of wagons rolling to a slow halt. Rhoyd could see the other guards on horseback scattering out to keep watch, including that fellow Warden that Conor had warned him about. He could see Michan too—*Captain Camhin,* he reminded himself—hovering nervously around the dark wagon, and Master Fergus when he rode over to meet the captain, and leaned to speak to him.

"...those old ruins are dead," Master Fergus said assuredly. "Nothing lives in them. The men need a rest, as do the horses, and there is water there..."

Captain Camhin cocked an eyebrow and then nodded. "Very well. But we will not take the wagons up into the ruins themselves. Tell your men to form the row of wagons on the sunniest side of the knoll."

Fergus frowned. "They'll not be happy for the lack of shade."

"It's cool enough," Captain Camhin said. "They'll manage."

Fergus turned his horse around and rode back to the head of the line.

Oh, good, Rhoyd thought. *We are going to stop.*

The wagons rolled on, following the path around the knolls, and soon enough, Rhoyd saw what the scouts had reported. Atop one of the knolls stood the remains of a stone wall, and just beyond it were a scattering of monoliths and past that, a small corrie so that the whole affair looked like the open mouth of some giant beast. He was thinking what a fascinating place that would be to explore when the first wagon stopped just past the opening in the broken wall. Others lined up behind it, though the dark wagon was taken a little more out into the field. Noreen drove her team skillfully into place.

Rhoyd hopped off the wagon almost as soon as it rolled to a stop and started swiftly for the stone walls of the old ruins.

"Hey, where do you think you're going?" Noreen called.

"I have to..." Rhoyd said emphatically, and he did a little dance to indicate just why.

Noreen rolled her eyes and shook her head. "All right, just don't go far," she said.

"I won't," Rhoyd said and bolted. He slipped behind the wall, pretending to reach for the lacings of his trews. Then carefully, he peered around the end.

Noreen had turned to deal with the horses. As soon as she was occupied, Rhoyd sprinted for the next section of wall on up the hill. He made it just before she turned back to glance in his direction. Rhoyd ducked down with a sigh.

Horns! He was starting to wish someone *else* had killed the demon. Then he would not be stuck on the wagon with the mage woman who would not answer his questions as well as he liked.

Rhoyd sat down, feeling the stone, the earth. This was an old place, but it was not ancient. Not a barrow mound, at any rate. He could not sense death under the ground when he briefly risked scrying it. In fact, this place was quiet, rather like a temple. He could see oak leaves and mistletoe carved into some of the stones at what might have once been a gate. Those markings were a sign of Diancecht's followers. Perhaps this had once been a shrine for healers?

Rhoyd glanced back to make sure no one was looking then carefully crept across the grass, down into a dry moat and up the gap. Wind picked up the wild strands of his black hair and whipped them into his eyes. He blinked and shook them away, and then placed one hand on the weather surface of the rubble, letting mage senses sink into it as he closed his eyes.

Visions sprang up in his mind. Men and women fleeing as Haxons forced their way through the wooden gates that had covered this opening. Faintly, he could hear the echoes of their screams as the barbarians rushed into the compound and began to slay the men and seize the women. Warm blood splattered Rhoyd as a Haxon lopped off one healer's head. Rhoyd gasped and let go, opening his eyes.

And then a hand clamped down on his shoulder. The weight of it startled Rhoyd. He lurched forward, bolting through the broken gate, tripping, falling, and rolling over on his back as he dredged his frantic mind for his mage bolt spell.

But it was only one of the guards who stood over Rhoyd and not a Haxon invader. The man held up his empty hands to reveal that he was not holding a weapon.

"Hey, sorry, lad," he said. "Didn't mean to startle you." He held out one hand and smiled. "My name's Warden. I works this caravan just like your old da. No one to be frightened of. Here, come on, let's get you up from there."

Warden continued to offer the hand, leaning a bit. The man smelled of old leather and unwashed skin. Rhoyd was reluctant to accept that offer of assistance. He rolled over onto his knees and got up, keeping back a few paces.

With a shrug, Warden lowered the hand. "Guess I scared you," he said. "Didn't mean to. Just wondered what you were doing?"

"I was just looking around," Rhoyd said and shot a furtive glance down the hill. It occurred to him that the caravan was almost completely out of sight.

"Ah," Warden said and nodded, scratching his head as he glanced around too. "I used to like to look around old ruins when I was a lad too. Find anything interesting?"

Rhoyd shook his head. He rather doubted it would be wise to tell the man about his vision.

"Aye well," the guard said and crossed his arms nervously. "Just old stones and grass...nothing interesting at all. Not like that black wagon. Now that's a fine mystery, ain't it?"

He inclined his head in the direction of the caravan.

"I don't know," Rhoyd said. "I'm not supposed to go near the wagon."

Warden nodded again. "Yeah, that little captain is being a

bit prickly about it. I mean, the way he acts, you'd think there was some sort of treasure in there, wouldn't ye?"

"I guess," Rhoyd said and shrugged. "I better go now. Noreen will be looking for me."

"Aren't you the least bit curious as to what they's hiding in that wagon?" Warden asked.

Rhoyd hesitated. Of course, he was curious. After seeing the spell being cast on the box under the cloth...after learning that Captain Camhin was none other than Michan O'Brannach. How could he not be when he knew there was magic in that wagon?

"So, you're one of the mageborn," Warden suddenly said and leaned against the gate stones so that he was blocking the way out.

"Yes," Rhoyd said, suddenly wishing he had not come up here at all. He closed his hand, ready to cast a spell if Warden should take another step.

"So...why can't you tell me what's in the black wagon?" he asked.

Rhoyd frowned. "Why do you keep asking me about the black wagon?" he asked. "I don't know what's in it..."

"But you could see into it, can't you? They say mageborn can do that." Warden stepped forward.

"I'm not supposed to use magic when I'm riding caravans," Rhoyd said as he took several steps back to keep his range intact.

"Like you didn't use it when them bandits attacked? Or when that demon almost killed your da?"

Rhoyd stiffened. "I didn't have a choice," he said.

"You have a choice now," Warden said. "Just come here and tell me what you see in the wagon."

"It doesn't work that way," Rhoyd said.

Warden's expression grew hard. "Look, boy, I want to know if there's gold in that wagon, and you're gonna tell me."

The guard lunged so suddenly Rhoyd almost didn't get his hand up in time. *"Beag gath siud buail!"* he said and the small mage bolt leapt from his hand, catching Warden in the cheek. It was meant to do little more than a sting, but it made the guard angry. With a curse, he came at Rhoyd hard and fast, slinging the back of a hand. Before Rhoyd could dodge, the blow caught him up the side of the head and sent him reeling into the grass.

As Rhoyd tried to scramble to his feet, Warden seized him and dragged him up. One hand closed over his throat and the other covered his mouth. He was shoved back towards the wall.

"You're gonna tell me what's in that wagon or I'm gonna beat...urk..."

Warden's face went white, and his grasp fell away, leaving Rhoyd struggling to stay balanced. He tumbled in a heap against the wall and looked up at Warden. The man was dancing on tiptoes, his turning a sickly shade of grey-green. Behind him was Noreen, her features hardened with a scowl. She was holding a hank of Warden's hair in one hand so that it was nearly torn out of his scalp, and her other hand clearly had hold of the man in a manner that made Rhoyd wince.

"I could break your neck, you stupid sod," she growled. "I could rip your manhood out at the roots. I should...and I will if I see you anywhere near this lad again. Do I make myself clear?"

It was impossible for Warden to nod. He swallowed and whimpered, "Yes."

"Then get back down to the caravan, and forget about that wagon, or I'll have a few words with Master Fergus and you'll be left alone in these woods. I'll make certain of it."

Noreen slung him towards the gate and through it as though he were little more than a straw man. Warden went to his knees, clutching his groin. He scrambled, getting back on his feet and half ran, half fell down the hill. He didn't even look back.

Rhoyd froze when her angry glower turned back on him.

"Didn't I tell you not to go far?" she asked.

"Yes, ma'am," Rhoyd whispered.

"What do you think your father would do if I told him what just happened?"

Rhoyd bit his lower lip then let it go. "He'd...kill Warden."

"That he would. And Warden has enough friends that might want revenge enough to put a small dirk in your father's back for it. I should tell your father that you disobeyed me, and I suspect you'd have to ride standing if I did."

Rhoyd winced.

"Now, let's go back down that hill, and don't you go pulling any such nonsense on me again. I may not be your da, but I won't hesitate to put you over my knee and give you a walloping you won't forget."

She thrust her hand toward Rhoyd. He took it, letting her pull him to his feet and herd him for the gate.

Escape for now was clearly not an option. He had a strong feeling that Mistress Noreen was a woman of her word.

Conor had just finished loosening Battlebrute's girth when he spied Warden fleeing the ruins like a frightened hare with a bogie on its tail.

"What the..." Conor muttered.

He quickly tethered the old dun warhorse and turned to see what was afoot. Warden looked like he'd seen Arawn himself. He kept looking back over his shoulder in fright as he stumbled and rolled his way down the hillside.

Drawing a few inches of steel, Conor started for the rise...and stopped when he saw Mistress Noreen come out of the remains of an opening in the wall. She was pushing Rhoyd ahead of her. The cook wore a scowl that Conor could see even from this distance, and there was no mistaking the hunch of the lad's shoulders.

Something had happened, and Conor decided he'd best find out what before word got around camp. He started towards his son with long strides that ate the ground. They were nearly at the bottom of the knoll when Conor confronted them. Rhoyd looked both uncertain and relieved. Mistress Noreen looked as though she might chew stones.

"What's wrong?" Conor asked.

Rhoyd rushed forward to clamp arms around Conor. Noreen's frown darkened as Conor looked at her.

"A close encounter of the sort we were hoping to avoid," Noreen said and flicked a glance about the caravan grouping.

Conor glanced down at Rhoyd, then pried the lad free and met his startled gaze. "What is she talking about?"

"It wasn't my fault," Rhoyd said. "And I didn't do anything. That man Warden was trying to throttle me and Noreen threw him down the hill."

"Hold on, back up," Conor insisted. "What do ye mean, Warden tried to throttle ye?" Conor glanced sharply at Noreen. "I thought ye were supposed to be keeping an eye on him."

"I was," she said defensively. "But he told me he had to take a piss, and the next thing I know, I see him sneaking up the rise into the ruins and that fellow Warden was hard on his heels. If I hadn't gone up there looking for him, no telling what would have happened."

Conor sighed and looked at Rhoyd. "Is it true?" Conor asked. "Did ye give her the slip just so you could go larking about the ruins?"

"I gave her the slip because she wouldn't stop telling me that story about the Hammer Maid," Rhoyd said. "I'm tired of riding with her. I want to ride with you."

"You were told to stay with her," Conor said. "For yer own good, I might add, and now ye nearly got yerself strangled by that brute Warden. What did ye do to make him come after ye like that?"

Rhoyd jerked back, and a mixture of hurt and anger took over his face. "I didn't do anything," Rhoyd said. "He followed me because he wanted me to tell him what was on the dark carriage. I told him I wouldn't and he became angry and attacked me." Rhoyd paused and looked down. "And then Noreen came and picked him up and threw him down the hill." His gaze rose, and there was a hint of mirth. "That was sort of funny to see."

Conor merely scowled.

Rhoyd sighed as though realizing his humor was not appreciated at the moment. "I'm sorry," he muttered.

"Not as sorry as I should make ye," Conor said and Rhoyd flinched. "But I've no time for that now. Ye'd best get back to the cook's wagon and stay with Mistress Noreen, and I better not hear tell of ye giving her the slip again or we'll have more than words about it. Understand me?" Rhoyd nodded and looked at his feet again. "And as for you." Conor looked up at the cook as he spoke. "Ye know he's no ordinary lad. Ye have to keep both eyes on him or ye'll answer to me if anything bad happens to him."

Noreen raised an eyebrow, but said nothing to argue. She put a hand on Rhoyd's shoulder and firmly guided him towards her wagon.

Conor turned and started away. There was anger in him that needed to be set free before it rose hot enough to make him *and* the lad both regret it. He marched down to where the men were milling. Warden was there, sitting on a stone as Conor walked up to him. The sight of the tall Keltoran striding purposefully across the ground obviously bore ill. Warden sprang up as though he was going to flee, but he held his ground instead, glancing warily at those around him.

Without missing a beat, Conor lashed out with a fist. He caught Warden full in the nose and sent the man sprawling hard to the ground. Several of the guards started to rush in and defend the fallen, but Conor raised a hand to show he was not going to do anything else. A couple of them ran to Warden and pulled him over on his back. He squealed in pain, holding his nose as blood gushed through his fingers and down his chin and onto his clothes and leather jerkin.

Conor pointed a finger at Warden. "Ye touch my lad again, and I'll make what Mistress Noreen did seem like a child's pat. I'll wrap yer tripes about yer ears and use them ta hang ye, I will. I'll cut out yer heart and feed it to ye!"

"What's this?" Master Fergus pushed his way into the fray, his cabbage stench filling the air. Several of the men stepped back and waved hands before their faces or pinched their noses. "Manahan, what are you doing to this man?"

"Letting him know what 'twill happen is he ever lays a hand on my son again," Conor said.

"What?"

"Let me through!" Eithne's voice broke through the muttering and took on an authoritative air. "Let me pass!"

Men stepped aside to let Conor's healer wife into the center of the crowd. She took one look at her husband standing there glowering at the man on the ground, and at Warden, and rolled her eyes.

"I might have known," she muttered and knelt beside Warden who continued to whimper like a child. "Oh, stop fussing and let me see," Eithne said, and Warden gave in as she pulled his bloodstained hands away from his face and began to examine his nose. "Broken," she said. "We'll fix that straight away, and then you can go clean up."

She blessed Conor with a look that said there would be words about this later then set to work. Conor took a deep breath and stepped out of the crowd. Broken. That was going to hurt.

He didn't want her to see him smile.

Damn him! The **Demon-Bound** thought. *Is he trying to get himself killed?*

Perhaps when we reach Cullstane, we should look for another to take his place? his internal companion suggested.

Assuming he lives so long. I should have found another. I was desperate...

Well, there is nothing we can do now but keep both eyes on him and hope he heeds the Keltoran and stays away from the lad.

If he doesn't I may have to kill him myself.

And let the Other know where you are?

Hang the Other. That lad is the last hope of the world. I cannot allow him to be harmed because The Balance of All Things would be harmed in the process.

Then we should find you another shield as soon as possible. But for now...

We watch. And pray he has learned his lesson.

Never mess with a Keltoran, his companion said with a chuckle.

Indeed, the Demon-Bound replied.

SIXTEEN

Blessed Brother, what gets *into him?* Eithne fixed Warden's nose quickly enough. Some of the men stood off to one side watching the process with morbid fascination as she set the man's nose then called her healing prayer. Once that task was completed, she felt tight as a new-strung bow.

She quickly headed over to where she could see the dun warhorse tethered. Conor was there, sitting on one of the multitude of stones that decorated this lea around the ruins. He was looking at his knuckles, flexing them as though to ease some pain.

Serves him right, she thought. She did not approve of fighting without a cause. *What possessed him to hit that man so hard?* Granted, she knew that Warden had been one of those Conor fretted about when Rhoyd used his mage bolt spell. And the man had approached her as well, asking questions she thought were really none of his affair. Had he taken that inquisition one step farther?

She walked over to where Conor was sitting, claiming a bit of the space at his side. He did not look at her. He merely muttered, "Have yer say, woman, and make it short."

Eithne narrowed eyes up at him. "Was there a reason?" she asked.

"He tried to throttle our son," Conor said. "Is that not reason enough?"

Eithne's little gasp caught in her throat. "Is Rhoyd...?"

"Fine, as near as I can tell. Noreen apparently got there afore Warden could do much more."

"I should go look to him, just in case," Eithne said and started to rise. And froze.

Captain Camhin was riding up on his horse. He had the look of a man not pleased with his task. "What in the name of Cernunnos was that all about?" he demanded as he dismounted and strode over to the pair.

"A matter between men," Conor said. "The cur made the mistake of laying hands on my lad."

"And just what did the lad do that brought this on him?" Captain Camhin demanded.

Conor rose so suddenly, Eithne nearly fell off the stone in surprise. "He refused to help the man ferret whatever yer hiding in that dark carriage, that's what," Conor said. "So the bastard tried to throttle Rhoyd and force him to use his magic."

"What?" Captain Camhin snarled. "Of all the...this is what comes of you not keeping that lad of yours under control."

"Me?" Conor took two steps forward and towered over Captain Camhin like a fury. "'Twas yer woman what let the lad out of her sight. Had he been with me, he'd have never gotten into trouble, Michan."

Captain Camhin's jaw dropped, and it was as though his face shimmered slightly.

"Michan?" Eithne said and stared in surprise.

The captain's eyes flashed a glance her way then turned back to Conor. "This is not the place to speak that name," he growled. "I'll meet you in the cook's wagon, and we will discuss this matter *there!*"

Captain Camhin turned and strode back to his horse, snagging the animal's bridle and turning for the rest of the caravan.

Eithne glanced at Conor. "You called him Michan," she said carefully.

"He's right, this is not the place to speak his name, woman," Conor said.

"I want to know what is happening, Conor, and I want to know now."

"Then we'd best get over to the cook's wagon," he said and started after the captain.

Eithne shoved her hair out of her eyes and followed in a huff.

Someone had certainly better explain all this to her.

Rhoyd watched as Noreen carefully etched glyphs into the corners of the wagon. *Glyphs of silence,* he thought. And glyphs of warding and distraction, meant to send any one who approached off in another direction. Aunt Genna had taught him those.

It seemed strange even now to watch Noreen perform the spells. She did so with her own essence, closing the world away from the wagon and those who were now gathered within.

Rhoyd glanced at the faces: Conor, Eithne and the captain were going out of their way not to look at one another. He frowned. When all the adults took on *those* looks, it was apt to spell trouble for him.

"It's set," Noreen said.

"Captain Camhin" took a deep breath and let his illusion fall away. Rhoyd heard Eithne gasp, "It really is you, Michan."

Michan nodded. "I am sorry to have to deceive you, dear Eithne," he said.

She took his hands in her own. "And how are you?"

"Doing rather well, I can assure you," he said with a half-smile.

"And Sorcha?"

Michan took a deep breath. "Sorcha died peacefully in her sleep two winters ago," he said. "I'm sorry to have to tell you that."

Eithne nodded.

"So why are we all here?" Conor said stiffly. Rhoyd sidled over next to the man and sat down. Without looking, Conor slipped a comforting arm around his shoulders. The weight and the warmth were reassuring.

"We are here because you came very close to revealing something I would rather these men did not know," Michan said. "I warned you before, Conor. Now matters are apt to get worse."

"And I told ye that if it was that important to keep yer secret intact, we could leave," Conor said.

"And I told you that now that Rhoyd has revealed what he is, it would not be safe for the three of you to go off alone."

Eithne glanced sharply at Conor. "Why didn't you tell me that was the real reason we were staying with them?"

"Because I made him promise not to," Michan said quickly. "So you can blame me for that."

"So what's the real reason for all this frippery and illusion?" Conor asked. "Ye might as well tell me, Michan. I'm tired of not knowing, and I swear that if you don't, I'll pack up my family and leave right now, danger or none."

Michan sighed. "I told you that my cargo needed to get to Dun Gealach as soon as possible. I told you that there are five other wagons out there. And I told you that it was important not to use magic."

"Why?" Conor asked. "What is going on here that make

men so edgy? What are ye protecting in that wagon that men would think was the king's gold?"

"I wish it was the king's gold," Michan said. "That would certainly be a lot easier to transport."

"Not when yer likely to attract every robber from here to the Highland Ranges and beyond," Conor said.

"Bandits would be a blessing," Michan said. "But what I carry in that wagon is not gold or gems...just bones."

"Bones?" Rhoyd piped up before anyone else could.

Michan glanced at the lad. "Not just any bones," he said carefully. "How much do you know about the mageborn they call the Demon-Bound?"

Rhoyd shrugged. In truth, he only knew what he had read thus far in Fenelon's old journals, and what little Genna would tell him when he asked her. "Alaric Braidwine is a mageborn bard who bonded his soul with that of a demon," Rhoyd said. "Uncle Fenelon says Alaric lives in the Ranges now, and that he is the Avatar, and that he holds some sort of key."

Michan looked thoughtful and nodded. "Do you know how he became the Demon-Bound?"

Rhoyd shook his head.

"Legend has it that he once carried the soul of a bard named Ronan Tey, but Ronan was not who—or what—he seemed. Alaric Braidwine was forced to choose to be master of a demon or slave to a demon. He chose to be master, but that meant he would never be free of the demon any more than it would be free of him. But it had an ill effect on him as well. Bonded to the demon as he was, he began to take on demon traits until he could no longer stay in Ard-Taebh without others discovering his secret."

"He became a demon?" Rhoyd asked.

"As close to a demon as a man can become without losing his humanity," Michan replied.

"And what has this to do with the contents of that wagon?" Conor asked.

"The bones, as I said, are no ordinary bones. They are the bones of the Betrayer."

"The Betrayer?" Eithne said.

"The demon who tricked Alaric Braidwine—the demon who would have been his master had he been foolish enough to allow it—was the Avatar of the White One, the one they believe is the mother of creation," Michan said. "But he betrayed her as he betrayed Alaric Braidwine, and his soul was apparently sundered from his body. His hide was removed and used to make a special map. And his bones were hidden in the Ranges in order to maintain the Balance of All Things. He tricked the real Ronan Tey and used his body to escape, but apparently, there was one who wanted the secret Ronan was now guardian of, and that one took Ronan's physical life. Not ready to be so easily defeated, the demon prepared Alaric to be his new vessel, and was going to steal Alaric's body. But the other demon that Alaric was forced to bond with in order to save his own life gave up its freedom to help Alaric defeat the Betrayer."

"Why are these bones so important?" Conor asked. "Why would men want the bones of a dead demon?"

"Not men," Alaric said. "A blood mage and a powerful one at that. One we all hoped was defeated in the Last War."

"The Hound?" Conor rubbed his chin. "But I heard that mageborn captured him and sundered him, and that King Conor MacMorroch had him beheaded."

"Among mageborn, Conor, death is not always what it seems. For mortalborn, it's an end. To mageborn—and even to those who possess mage blood in their family line—it's merely a transition from the corporeal to the incorporeal. Depending on how the mageborn dies, his or her spirit can survive."

"Blessed Brother, do you mean to say that the Hound is not dead?" Eithne touched her finger to her lips in dismay.

"There are very few who know the whole tale," Michan said. "Six mageborn went out to capture Cudraeighean. One of them sacrificed her life that the other five might succeed in capturing him. They sundered his power, but not his life. The High King wanted that privilege for himself...revenge for the death of his father at the Black Battle, some said. The problem is it was known even then that the Hound possessed a Soul Stone."

Rhoyd leaned forward with new interest. He had heard Aunt Genna *and* Uncle Fenelon mention those.

"And with that stone, it was believed that when the Hound was executed, he managed to send his life into that stone. But no such stone was found on his body by the mageborn after he was executed, so they suggested that his body be sent away, separated from his head, in the hopes that he would not be able to rise again. I have been told by others that a new rumor has begun to spread...that the Hound did indeed find a new home for his soul, and that he is waiting in the Ranges, biding his time before he begins a new campaign against Ard-Taebh and even the rest of the world. From the Ranges, he could conquer the entire continent."

"And what has all this to do with the bones?"

"To rule the world, Cudraeighean must set into motion certain events, and one of those is that he must bring back the Dark Mother, sister to the White One, and let her bring night back to the world as she did in the age of the Shadow Lords. But first, he will have to find where her physical remains are hidden. With the bones of the Avatar who hid her corpse in the first place, the Hound could do just that. The Demon-Bound knew this, so he went to the place where the White One had hidden the Betrayer's bones. He brought them to the end of the Ranges at great danger to himself.

"I and several other mageborn are members of a group that has been entrusted with the task of gathering and protecting the various artifacts that a monster like Cudraeighean could use to bring back the Darkening. The Demon-Bound contacted us and charged us to take the bones to a safe place."

"And why is this a danger to us?" Conor asked. "Why would we be at risk if we left now?"

"Because if Rhoyd is truly the nephew of Fenelon Greenfyn several times removed—if he is the one they call The Ard Magister, The Twice-Blooded Once-Born—then he is in danger, for the though Cudraeighean has not fully regained his power, he has already spread his minions across the land to search for the one mageborn who might have the power to defeat him when the Darkening comes. He knows about the prophecy that brought this lad to life, and he will do whatever is necessary to assure that there will not be such a mage powerful enough to stand against him the next time he seeks to conquer the world. By allowing Rhoyd to use magic near the bones...I fear we have probably alerted his minions to this lad. So I cannot, in good conscious, allow you and yours to leave before the bones are safe in Dun Gealach."

"And once we get to Dun Gealach?" Eithne asked.

"The Council of Mageborn will be forced to acknowledge that many of the things Fenelon Greenfyn said all those years ago were true."

"They'll want to keep Rhoyd there, will they not?" Conor said.

"Quite possibly," Michan said.

"Then we cannot go to Caer Keltora with you," Conor said, "for I will not let any man take this lad from me until he is ready to go away on his own. I gave him my word on that, and I'll not back down."

Conor stood up and the wagon rocked.

"You may not have a choice, Conor," Michan said. "If this lad is truly the last hope of the world, we cannot risk his life."

Conor shook his head and reached down to offer Rhoyd his hand. "I'm through with this, Michan," he said. "We're leaving."

"Conor, let's not be so hasty," Eithne said. "If the danger is as real as Michan believes..."

Conor looked at her, and she at him. Rhoyd took Conor's hand and rose to stand beside his adopted father. For a moment, no one said a word.

"We do not have to take him to Dun Gealach," she said softly. "With that, I will support you. But I do not want to be out in the world alone if there is a chance someone will come after Rhoyd...so we should stay with Michan and help him deliver the bones to Caer Keltora."

"And what about the men...the ones like Warden who think Rhoyd can magic king's gold out of the dark carriage for them?"

"We are two days from the township of Cullstane," Michan said. "Warden will be seeking new employment when we get there...I can guarantee that much. For that matter, we are likely to take on a whole new crew of mercenaries."

"Why?"

"Most of them don't want to stay with us after a sen'night of riding with the dark wagon. Even though I have spells set to keep the bones from touching earth and being detected through earth or water or air, they still reek a bit of the demon essence they once carried. The men start having bad dreams..."

"All right," Conor said. "But the lad rides with me from now on."

"Only if you agree to ride with the dark carriage," Michan said. "I could certainly use your skills to protect it from the rest of these men."

Slowly, Conor nodded. "So be it," he said. "And if that

bastard Warden comes anywhere near me or my lad..."

"You have my permission to *ding his neb* to the bottom of his toes," Michan said and smiled.

"'Twas not his nose I was thinking about dinging," Conor said. "I'm more inclined to ask Mistress Noreen if she knows any good recipes for a man's sausage..."

"Conor!" Eithne said. "Don't be rude."

"Oh, I do, indeed," Noreen said and laughed.

Rhoyd sighed. So he would not have to stay with the cook's wagon after all.

That was a relief.

SEVENTEEN

Riding close to the dark carriage made Conor itch. Had he not been in the saddle, he would have sworn he was sitting on an anthill instead. It was hard not to squirm and scratch like a dog. How could Rhoyd just sit there on Moonface, reading that journal as though nothing were amiss? The lad's expression was intent when Conor glanced his way.

Michan now wore his Captain Camhin face and rode on the far side of the dark carriage. Noreen had moved the cook's wagon up behind them. So the men who had been driving the fourth wagon now fell back into the fifth place in line, and they looked rather relieved for it.

Conor wondered if they had sensed what he was feeling now. A faint bitterness like cloves sat on his tongue, familiar in a way. He could not remember why he knew.

He wanted to ask Rhoyd what he felt just now.

Ahead, he could see Warden slouching in the saddle. His nose was not so red or swollen, but he rubbed it as though it still irritated him. Now and again, he would toss a glance back at Rhoyd, but as soon as he saw Conor watching, he would turn his eyes forward again. There was definitely something going on in that man's mind, and Conor was not sure he liked it.

Warden was plotting something. Conor just wished he knew what.

Rhoyd made a sound that was a cross between a soft laugh and a snort, and Conor drew his attention back to the lad. Anything to keep from thinking about the discomfort.

"So what has you so amused, lad?" he asked.

Rhoyd looked up. "Uncle Fenelon is telling about his meeting with Alaric Braidwine."

"Read it to me," Conor said.

Rhoyd raised an eyebrow. "Here?"

"Read it to me," Conor said.

Rhoyd took a deep breath. *"Wendon was leading the new fellow off, telling him it would be in his best interest not to communicate with me in any fashion. I could not resist, I will admit. Wendon is always such a prig and a pig. The nickname I tattooed magically to his wide backside in glowing letters suited him...Warthog... And Wendon, being as thick as a pile of stones, didn't even notice, but the new chap did..."*

"Why is that funny?" Conor asked.

"I never thought of using magic to put a bad name on someone that glows," Rhoyd said.

"If you ever try that on me, lad, I'll tattoo your backside with the flat of my hand," Conor warned.

Rhoyd cocked an eyebrow and peered out from under his hair. Amusement stretched the corners of his mouth into a grin. "I wasn't going to do it to you," he said and looked forward. "I was thinking about that fellow Warden. I could write *clout me here* on the back of his head and see if anyone took up the suggestion."

"That one's got a thick skull, lad," Conor said and smiled slightly. "Doubt he would notice."

"You're probably right," Rhoyd said and closed his book. He slipped it into his pack and guided Moonface a little closer. "I'm getting tired...can I ride with you a while?"

Conor looked at the hopeful expression being angled at him. "Yer getting a wee bit old for that, aren't ye?"

Rhoyd sighed. "Am I?" He looked disappointed as he glanced at the wagon.

Conor grinned and leaned so he could slip an arm around the lad's waist and pull him over onto Battlebrute. Rhoyd quickly settled down, still clutching the reins. Conor took them, slipping them over Moonface's head to allow the grey gelding some room and not crowd Battlebrute who never took kindly to other horses being too close.

"Will you tell me a story?" Rhoyd asked.

"Now?" Conor said.

Rhoyd nodded. Conor sighed and rested his chin on the lad's head where Rhoyd was leaning back into his chest.

"Aye, well... How about I teach ye a song instead?"

"Will Eithne approve?" Rhoyd asked.

"Probably not," Conor said.

Rhoyd chuckled. "All right," he said.

Conor launched into *The Randy Bandy Cock*. He saw Captain Camhin leaning around to look across the front of the dark carriage at them. The "captain" shook his head and grinned. Several of the guards chuckled, and a few joined the chorus. Even Mistress Noreen added her voice to the affair. Soon, the entire caravan's mood rose above the gloom.

Only Warden continued to sulk.

Well before night fell, the caravan stopped and set up camp in a clearing. They were well away from the nearest brook, which Eithne thought was absurd. She wanted water to make tea and was going to have to walk a good ways just to fetch it. Nor would Michan—*Captain Camhin,* she reminded herself—allow her to take Rhoyd along to help. "We have plenty of water in the barrels," he said.

"Stale water," she retorted. "I want fresh running water. The tea will taste much better that way."

"Since when did you become so particular?" he asked.

"Since when did you become such a boor?" she replied with a glower.

The "captain" rolled his eyes and muttered about the minds of women being set in stone, and Eithne decided then and there she would not wait another moment for the permission of any man. Let him be stubborn. She would go on her own and if anything did happen to her, she hoped he would feel guilty about it.

She took what looked like a path through the tall grass towards the copse where the stream ran, carrying her pail in one hand. In the other, she was holding her staff of oak wood, carved with mistletoe and leaves. Not that she feared going there alone, but lately, with all that had happened, it was probably a good idea to have some means of deterring trouble.

Besides, she could scream loud enough if she needed to.

She stepped into the line of trees that bordered the brook, threading her way through a tangle of laurel trees that grew thick upon the banks of the small stream. There was still more than enough light outside the forest, but now that she was under the trees, the path was less visible. So she wasn't too surprised when she tripped over a root and sprawled across the ground.

Oh, Horns, she thought. Her staff landed on the ground before her, but the pail rolled away and disappeared beyond some roots. Still swearing under her breath, Eithne crawled to her knees and peered into the dark where the pail had gone. *I should have brought a lantern,* she thought. The hole into which it had rolled looked like a badger den, and she was reluctant to push her hand in for fear some small creature with teeth might still occupy it. She could not afford to lose her small pail, as it was the one she liked to keep for making the various teas she both drank and used for her patients. Only the Brother knew when they would reach a large enough city for her to purchase a new one.

Still on her knees, she drew her staff around and carefully poked it into the shadows. Nothing came bursting out at her, but she did hear the thunk of her staff clattering dully against the metal of the small pail. She poked around a bit more to be certain, then got down on her stomach and reached, trying not to think of spiders and beetles and snakes and other small vermin that might be living inside instead of a badger.

Her fingers barely brushed the rim of the pail. Eithne strained, pushing her arm deeper even though it meant nearly shoving her face into a root. But she managed to catch the edge and pull the pail towards her. Relieved, she sat back on her haunches, looking perturbed at the condition of the pail. It would have to be scrubbed out now.

She sighed and started to get up again, when a shadow slithered out of the corner of her eye. Eithne gasped, clutching the pail close and turned towards the movement. Some of the limbs of the laurel were moving up and down as though someone—something—had recently passed by and brushed against them.

The wind. That was it. Just the wind...

But wouldn't wind make all the limbs around her move?

Oh, I am being foolish. She grasped the handle of the pail tightly in one hand, picked up her staff with the other, and scanning the trees to either side, she crawled back to her feet. There was nothing there, though she had to admit she could not see so well into those shadows as she would have liked. *I should have insisted on bringing Rhoyd, and let Michan be damned,* she thought. Rhoyd could see into shadows. He could make light.

And that is the exact reason we are in this mess.

Fetch the water and go back, she told herself. She would have herself screaming if she didn't stop this nonsense. *There is nothing there but the wind and...*

Weight crashed through the limbs to her left. With a startled squeak, she turned towards the source. The tree there was moving quite violently, and there was no way it could be the wind and she knew it. She turned and started running, heedless of the trail, eager to get out of this copse and back to the safety of the camp.

But it occurred to her then that she was not quite sure where the path was, or which direction to go. So she stumbled on, flailing at her surroundings with her staff, and it was then that she hit something large and soft that stank of death. She tumbled again, falling into water, floundering to get up again.

Here, the trees above parted enough to let her see that what she had fallen over was a dead mule. Something had been eating on its flesh, for there were ragged tears in the skin of its haunch. A badger might do that...or a bear. *Oh, Blessed Brother, please, let it only be a bear.* Conor had told her how to frighten bears though he had also told her one should never stand between a bear and its meal.

Get away from the mule!

She rose again, struggling in her now damp clothes, backing away from the carcass only to trip over something smaller and more human... It was a man whose face had been torn off. Then the trees near the bank where the mule lie started to tremble and Eithne heard a snarling sound. Something thrust its head through the tangle of trees, and it was certainly not a bear. Eithne wasn't sure what it was, except that it bore some resemblance to a minor demon, for it only had three claws and a head that resembled an oversized rat. It fixed beady eyes on her and hissed like a cat.

She decided that now was as good a time as any to scream.

Rhoyd had wanted to go with Eithne—he had heard her asking the captain who said no—but Noreen would not let him out of her sight. He thought of asking Conor, but he was off with the other guards getting his watch assignment.

Rhoyd looked up at Noreen. She bustled around her wagon to prepare the meal, calling to the two guards who had been assigned to assist her.

"Here," she said to Rhoyd and thrust a stack of trenchers into his hands. "Come make yourself useful."

Rhoyd hesitated. There was something wrong here. He could feel it. He just didn't understand why neither Michan nor Noreen noticed. His tongue was taking on the familiar burn that he felt around the bones. But instead of the bitter-sweetness of cinnamon or cloves, this was like something pungent and rotten. *Like bile.* He glanced off towards the copse where Eithne had gone. The sense of malaise was stronger down there. He stretched mage senses.

"Here! Don't do that!" Noreen said and punched his shoulder hard enough to stagger him so he dropped the trenchers on the ground.

Rhoyd turned with a shout and slapped at her hand. Noreen looked startled.

"What's got into you?" she asked.

Rhoyd backed off a step. "Eithne's in danger," he said.

"Oh, right, you just want another excuse to run off and…"

A scream pierced the air.

"Eithne!" Rhoyd turned and did not wait for anyone else. He dashed down the hill towards the copse that hit the stream.

"Rhoyd, wait!" Noreen called.

He refused to listen. And he had enough of a head start that he was almost at the copse before the thunder of other feet came close enough that someone could seize him by the arm. Rhoyd flailed at the grasp. He could hear snarling and snapping, and the sounds of Eithne alternately shouting and screaming.

"Rhoyd!" Conor snapped and jerked him back. "Let me lead!"

Rhoyd held back just long enough for Conor to push ahead. He glanced back in time to see Noreen and Captain Camhin and a couple of other guards arriving. Like a small army, they pushed into the thickness of the copse.

"Horns, ye canna see a bugger thing in here…" Conor snarled.

Rhoyd hissed, *"Solus,"* yanking essence from the last light of the sun. He willed the ball of white light that flared to life to fly ahead of Conor and light the way. Behind him, he heard the captain curse. Rhoyd didn't care.

The light illuminated the ragged trail and allowed Conor to quickly pick his way among rambling roots of laurel. He rushed into a clearing quite suddenly where a commotion and a din were taking place. Rhoyd arrived in time to see that Eithne was not on the ground. She was up in the branches of one of the trees, and she was flailing desperately at something that looked like a rat's head on a skinny imp's body. It was trying to scramble up the tree after her, and she was making good account of herself with that oak staff, beating the creature about the head and screaming and shouting.

Conor moved in swiftly. Minor demons he had encountered enough of in the Last War, and Rhoyd cheered as the mercenary lurched at the beast. It turned with a hiss and sprang at Conor. Unlike its greater kin, it was not impervious to good Keltoran steel. Conor shouted and lopped off its head with one clean blow. It bounced off the carcass of a dead mule and turned to mush. Its body collapsed and began to deteriorate as well.

"Keep your eyes open," Captain Camhin ordered, though Rhoyd had a feeling none of these men would see anything else. The miasma was still there, keeping its distance, but the essence of a demon was gone.

Eithne scrambled down from the tree, rushing towards Conor. "Are ye hurt, woman?" he asked as he pulled her close.

"I think I'm all right," she said. "It didn't bite me, though it did scratch me."

"We better get back to camp and attend that," Captain Camhin said. "Demon scratches from a minor beast may not be as dangerous as those of a greater demon, but they can still fester and become infected."

"Yes, I well remember that from the Last War," Eithne said, looking hard at him. She pulled back from Conor and searched around for her pail, picking it up. Rhoyd could see that her staff was a bit clawed and chewed as she passed him. "I shall have to beg my tea water from Mistress Noreen's barrels after all, I imagine," she said as she gave the mule a disgusted look. "And I will say a small prayer for this poor wretch and his beast."

She walked past them all as though more than eager to leave the copse.

Rhoyd decided to follow her quickly.

The odor of the dead mule was nauseating him more than the bile taste the demon's essence inspired.

EIGHTEEN

Conor could not help but notice that Eithne pressed herself tight against him as she slept that night. It was unusual for her to do so, for her nature was as fierce as a battle-seasoned warrior about many things. Yet tonight, the experience must have been playing on her nerves because she lay close to him, and even in sleep, her fingers would not be dislodged where they twined into his plaidie. Like she believed that creature would return.

Michan didn't seem to think that demon was there for a particular reason. Like as not, he insisted, it was one of many pestilences still remaining behind after the Hound's invasion of the northern lands. "That creature was as mindless as a rock," he had whispered to Conor on their way back. "It feeds and that is all it knows how to do."

Conor wanted to remind Michan that darklings were just as mindless, yet they had seen a fair wheen o' them doing things against their very nature, he kept the thoughts to himself and said nothing. As long as it wasn't something that had been purposely placed there to attack the caravan, Michan was not concerned. And its death by steel was not as apt to alert whoever pursued the box of bones as much as the mage light Rhoyd had conjured.

"Really," Michan had said, his nondescript face set in a worried frown as he watched to make certain no one else was listening. "He has got to stop using his magic."

"Magic is as natural to him as breathing is to the rest of us...Mi...Captain," Conor said, almost slipping again. "We're still just beginning to learn the extent of his power. If you ask that Auntie of his, the lad was born to shite gold."

"You say that as though it bothered you," Michan said.

Conor shook his head. "Nay, for it bothers me more that none will let him just be what he is, a lad who has some growing to do before he can take the responsibility of the world onto his shoulders."

There had been little else to discuss, but they had reached

the wagons by then. Conor had his duties. The "captain" had his as well. Though to Conor's surprise, Master Fergus did not give him a watch, but rather told him that he should stay with his family. That was unusual. Conor had never worked a caravan, no matter how many guards there were, that he did not stand at least one watch through the night.

It made him wonder what Michan—*Captain Camhin,* he reminded himself—had told the Master of the Caravan.

Aye, well. To sleep a full night would be a blessing. He closed his eyes against the night, quite ready to sink into slumber.

Only to sit up abruptly when he heard men shouting. Somewhere towards the front of the wagon line, excited shouts filled the air. Eithne muttered and sat up as well. "What?"

Conor was already crawling to his feet. Rhoyd sat up, brushing hair and sleep from his face as Conor reached for his plaidie and his sword.

And then he heard a voice shout, "Wild boar!"

Horns. The angry squeals of the pig were a frightening sound. Conor turned to Eithne and Rhoyd. "Get up on the cook's wagon...now!"

She needed little encouragement, though Rhoyd was only half awake as she dragged him along. Conor waited just long enough to make certain they were safe before he snatched up his targe and flung it over his back. Then he ran to saddle Battlebrute as quick as he could. A scream of agony broke the night. A man had just been gored. Conor checked the girth to make sure it was secure, then flung himself into the saddle and rammed heels into Battlebrute's ribs. With a squeal, the dun warhorse reared before surging up the slope towards the head of the wagons.

There was chaos. Not one boar, but two were savaging their way through the ranks of men. Useless blows rained on their backs. Horns, did these men not know that the shoulder blades of a boar were thicker than any man's armor? That their tusks were as sharp as steel? *Fools!* He rode hard up behind one of the beasts as it was swinging around to attack one of the guards, and leaning down, Conor slashed at the boar's hind leg, severing the hamstring. It screamed and went down, rolling over and exposing its throat, and one of the guards saw this and went in for the kill.

Conor turned his attention to the other boar. Several

archers had managed to pin arrows in its flank, but none had stopped it from charging. Captain Camhin was there on his horse, waving his sword at the beast. Conor would have laughed at the sight, for clearly Michan had never hunted wild boar. But then it charged at "the captain's" horse, and before he could bring his blade around, it rammed the gelding hard, ripping its belly. The horse squealed, rearing and falling over, taking Captain Camhin to the ground with it. He could not roll free, and the weight of the wounded mount pinned him down by one leg. The boar slashed at the horse again then set its sights on the man.

It seemed like no one knew what to do for several moments. Conor pummeled Battlebrute with heels to get the warhorse going hard and fast. There was one place—if he could hit it with his sword. Boar's heads were as heavily plated as their backs, but just behind the ear.

Conor charged down on the boar. It half turned as though realizing it was about to be attacked and slashed across with those wicked tusks, but Conor pulled Battlebrute aside in time to keep it from goring the war horse or ripping open his leg. At least its attention was off Captain Camhin who was still trying to get free of his fallen horse. But now it looked at Conor with eyes of madness. And then it charged.

Conor flung himself out of the saddle and pushed the horse away. He waited until the last possible moment, knowing that the creature was agile as it was deadly. Then he shifted aside, turning like a dancer and crouched, and with both hands clutching the grip of his long sword, he rammed his steel up in under the jaw of the charging beast. The creature ran itself all the way up his sword, and Conor had to let go as it flung on past him and crashed into one of the wagons. The wagon shook and even lifted off two wheels in spite of the cargo it held, but then the boar fell under it and the wagon rocked but did not overturn.

Conor took his time approaching. The beast did not move. He walked around the wagon so he could see its face. The eyes were glazed in death, and his sword was buried up to the hilt.

Horns, it will take a bit of work to get that free.

With a sigh, Conor hurried over to where Master Fergus and some of the men were extracting Captain Camhin from under his dying horse. The animal's screams of pain quickly ended when one of the men cut its throat. Conor took one look at the captain and knew from his expression that he was having a hard time holding his spell of illusion because of the pain he was in. But then Eithne came rushing onto the scene pushing the men aside. She took one look and said, "I think your leg might be broken. Conor, get him into Noreen's wagon now."

Conor took over the chore of holding the captain upright. He could see the grey eyes flickering and heard the faint whisper of, "Please, don't let them see my face..."

Noreen arrived then, as did Rhoyd, and the four of them were barely able to whisk the captain out of sight of the rest of the before he fainted and lost hold of his illusion spell.

"How is the Captain?" Master Fergus called from outside the wagon. Noreen went out to keep the caravan master from coming in. That left Conor to assist Eithne as she set the bone in Michan's leg. It was a clean break, at least, she was pleased to note, and having Michan unconscious was a blessing as well. She did hate to listen to men scream when she was rearranging broken bones.

Rhoyd sat off to one side now. She would have sent him out, but she knew neither Conor nor Michan would have approved. And after her encounter earlier with that creature, she knew it would not be wise.

"There's talk that those beasts were not here by mistake," Fergus said. "I must speak to the Captain."

"The healer has him sedated so she can fix his leg," Noreen said. "He'll be right as rain once she heals him, and then you can ask him your questions."

"Look, I have never worked a caravan where so many odd and dangerous things keep happened in so short a space of time," Fergus retorted. "It's as though we are under a curse. I must have a way to reassure these men before they mutiny and desert us."

What Noreen said after that was muffled. Eithne briefly wished she had Rhoyd's sharp ears. It would have been nice to know what was going on out there, but she had more than enough to concentrate on here. Conor held the splints in a powerful grasp as she tied them off. Once the leg and splints were finished, she closed her eyes and laid her hands on the leg to say her magical prayers.

"Blessed Brother, hear my plea." The words whispered across her lips. The healer god answered quickly, allowing his power to flood through Eithne and into Michan's leg. She smiled as the warmth spread, and when she stopped, she took a deep breath and opened her eyes.

Michan moaned. The wagon shifted as Noreen clambered back inside. Michan groaned again and muttered, "Am I on a boat?"

"Nay," Noreen said cheerfully.

Michan opened his eyes and looked up at Eithne...and smiled. "Ah, a vision," he said.

Conor leaned over.

"Another vision—not quite as appealing but..." Michan tried to sit up, but Eithne would not let him.

"Too soon," she said.

He nodded. "Did anyone see me?"

"We got you in here quick enough," Noreen said, "but old Fergus is about to have a cow. Can you pull your illusion back in place?"

Michan shook his head. "I need to rest. What is he having a cow about?"

"The men think those boars were not natural."

Conor was nodding. "They may not be so wrong there, Mistress Noreen," he said. "Boars rarely roam at night."

Michan frowned. "But that would mean someone woke them up and drove them here."

"Aye, though I canna say I felt any glamorie. Rhoyd?" He glanced at the lad who was ensconced in a corner, half dozing.

Rhoyd stirred and shook his head as he yawned. "I didn't feel anything then," he said. "But I was asleep."

"As were we all," Michan said and frowned. "Can I sit up now, Eithne?"

She sighed, knowing she could tell him no, but he was not likely to listen. So she helped him up, and Conor did so as well.

"You thinking what I'm thinking, then?" Noreen asked.

Michan looked over at Rhoyd. "Your magic is causing us a lot of grief, lad. I do wish you would refrain from casting it. No doubt the light you called when we rescued Eithne gave away our location again."

Rhoyd looked unhappy to be blamed. Conor stepped around so he was between Michan and the lad.

"Leave my son alone, Michan," Conor said.

"Or what?" Michan retorted. "You promised to keep him under control."

"Captain! Is that you?"

Fergus again. Eithne rolled her eyes. Michan looked startled because the wagon was shaking, and before Noreen could block the way, the back flap was thrown aside. Eithne pulled her cloak around and covered Michan's head. He nearly threw it off then stopped himself.

"Captain?" Fergus said.

"I'm...fine, Master Fergus. Just...tired." Michan was struggling to imitate the voice that they knew as the captain.

"The men..."

"Mistress Noreen has already told me," Michan said. "You can tell the men that there was nothing unnatural about the boars. Probably got awakened by that thing we killed down in the woods earlier."

"Oh...aye," Fergus said. Then frowned. "Why are you hiding under the healer's cloak, sir?"

"He was cold," Eithne said. "Shock. Once he warms up, he will be fine. But he needs to rest and stay warm and still for a while, so if you don't mind."

Master Fergus looked from Eithne to Conor to Noreen and shrugged. "Ye might want to go fetch yer horse, Manahan. He's bitten three 'o my men so far." He turned and let go of the flap, and they all heard him mutter, "Don't know how he can rest with all them in there."

Eithne sighed. Conor was smiling at her.

"I'll take the lad and fetch Battlebrute and go back to our camp," he said, and gestured for Rhoyd to follow him. "He's going to fall asleep here and now."

Eithne nodded as Conor hopped off the wagon then helped Rhoyd down. "I'll be there in a moment."

"Well, Captain, if you cannot hold an illusion, maybe you'd better stay in the wagon for tonight." Noreen smiled almost lasciviously as she said that.

Michan rolled his eyes.

"And I'll sleep in yours," she added.

"Thank you," Michan said. "But that means you'll be with the box."

"It'll be fine," Noreen said. "I'm not afraid of some moldy old demon bones."

"It's not the bones I was thinking about," Michan said.

Eithne rather wished he hadn't put it that way.

A sense of urgency had started washing over Rhoyd as he sat in the wagon, so he was glad when Conor whistled for Battlebrute and started back towards their small camp. Admittedly, he was tired, and would be glad to get back to his pallet, but almost as soon as the chaos broke, Rhoyd kept sensing something was not right. Something more than the fact that boars did not usually roam in pairs unless the other was a sow, and certainly not at night.

He truly had felt nothing when the excitement started, but while they were in the cook's wagon, that was another matter, and even now as they approached the camp, the urgency had not gone away. He stretched mage senses as soon as he arrived.

"What's wrong, lad?" Conor asked as he came close.

Rhoyd wrinkled his nose. Conor stank of blood and death. He had washed the crimson stains from his hands once they had Michan inside the wagon, but there was still a swatch of boar's blood up his arm and down the side of his tunic.

Still, he ignored the stench and waved a hand around him, gesturing at the camp.

"Someone has been here," he said.

"Who?" Conor asked as he removed his warhorse's tack and laid it aside.

Rhoyd deepened his concentration, but either he was too tired or this was little more than the fragment of some older essence that was teasing him. With a sigh, he let go and shook his head. "I don't know," he said. "It's like I can sense someone was here. I don't know. It's confusing."

He wanted to say that everyone in the world left some hint of essence that he could sense. It was like having someone walk by in old clothes that were musty, or someone who needed a bath. One smelled them whether one saw them or not, and the odor might be little more than a faint scent being carried away by the wind.

Sometimes, magic was too hard to explain.

A big hand rested on his shoulder and gave him a reassuring shake. "Maybe ye should sleep on it," Conor said. "A good sleep will do us both some good. And maybe in the morning, 'twill be clearer?"

Rhoyd nodded. Maybe, if he remembered at all. He yawned and crawled into his pallet, hardly able to keep his eyes open. Conor knelt to draw the blankets up to Rhoyd's chin, and then ruffled his hair in a gesture of fondness.

"Good night, lad," he said.

Rhoyd hardly muttered his own response before sleep took him.

Conor continued to squat beside the pallet, even though it was clear that Rhoyd had sunk into a deep sleep. He smiled and shook his head, allowing his hand to once more brush at those ebon locks before he stood up and looked around.

Their camp was in a bit of a shambles, but it had been left that way when Conor tossed off his bedding, scrambled for weapons and practically herded his small family over to the cook's wagon for their own safety. He could not help but wonder what had made the lad think anyone had been here. The quick departure to deal with the boars had caused Conor to toss things about a bit. He glanced at the packs, the only thing still neat in the midst of the scene. Shaking his head, Conor finished brushing down the marks the saddle had left on Battlebrute. Once the warhorse was settled, he poked up the fire and went looking to his own bedding. He had thrown the blankets about in his rush, and one of them had landed across his saddle pack. He picked it up...and paused.

His saddlebags lay as he had left them, but as he stared at the way the top one was knotted, he frowned. He had a habit of tying the ends back through behind the flap since they were long and sometimes reached down far enough to tickle Battlebrute's flanks. But the loose ends of the top one now dangled free. Conor frowned and decided that he was getting sloppy. He tucked them back into place, wondering if he should look inside. But he shook his head. There was naught in that pack but old matters from his militia days. The standard he had knifed off his tunic when he left the militia was tucked in there, along with a leather sword belt, a pair of bracers, his extra gauntlets and the dagger he was awarded for winning a footrace. He smiled to himself. He had taken the dagger when Eithne refused him a kiss.

A footfall on the grass alerted him. He turned to find Eithne approaching.

"How's yer patient?" he asked.

"He'll live," she said with a smile. "He is staying in Mistress Noreen's wagon for the night. She is going to sleep in his."

Conor glanced off towards the line of wagons. The cook was going to sleep with the bones. Somehow, he had a feeling if anyone could protect them, she could.

"Is something wrong?" Eithne asked.

Conor shook his head, and said, "Just tired, woman. Killing boars is hard work on a man of my age."

"Oh, poor man," she said. She stepped closer as he turned and finished sorting the bedding. He looked up in time to see her grimace.

"What?" he asked.

"You stink of blood," she said.

"Shall I go down to the water and wash me self?" he asked.

Eithne glanced towards the woods and shook her head. "There's still water in my pail from the barrel. Use that."

Conor looked at the pail. "Bit small far a man o my size to bathe in," he said and winked.

"Just get the tunic off," she said. "And sit down."

Conor stood to remove the tunic and sat down again to oblige her. Eithne fetched the pail with its remains of water, and even dug a bit of linen out of her pack. She came over beside him, dipping the linen in the pail, and began to wash the drying blood off his arm. Her probing fingers quickly found a nasty looking bruise.

"I thought you said you weren't hurt," she said when she prodded it and he flinched.

"I wasn't until you started scrubbing my skin off, woman," he retorted with a grin.

"Men...such whiners." She finished washing him off then frowned at his tunic, tossed carelessly aside. He knew what she was thinking. The blood would never come completely out of it. She had washed enough of it from his tunic before. He could count every stain and knew almost all of them, including one he had never quite removed. Conor shook the thoughts away and looked at her and smiled.

"Will you make it better?" he asked.

"I shall certainly try," she said and smiled back.

She didn't refuse to kiss him then.

Noreen set up the wards and worked the spells of protection and misdirection before she locked the door of the dark carriage. Inside, the black wood burned white with the sheen of pure light from the cloak over the chest. She was tempted to lift it—peer under at its contents, but she knew better than to mess with Michan's spells. He'd just have one of his royal fits. And besides, to do so meant that she risked exposing this precious cargo to those who sought it.

She settled down on the bench that served as a bed. It was padded with a thin mattress. Rather spare for a man of the Captain's airs. She took him for a young noble the first day she met him, and was not surprised to learn he was a man of breeding. But like a lot of short men, he behaved like a mad cock, always ready to strike.

It was a wonder she agreed to come along. But she had known the Demon-Bound for nearly fifty years now, and knew his mission was important. His request that she go along had pleased her. He knew she had little else to do.

The bedding was a little shorter than would cover her. Noreen shook her head and spread the two blankets to cover her length.

She should have brought her own blankets. With a sigh, she closed her eyes.

The hum of magic around her was like a soothing lullaby, and soon put her to sleep.

Damn, the **Demon-Bound** thought. Death had been everywhere, spurring baser lusts. His internal companion was struggling to take charge, and were it not for his knowledge of the greater spells passed on to him by the Elderkin that once possessed him, he would have given in, charged into the fray, devoured those boars in a couple of gulps.

And given ourselves away, his internal companion intoned with just a hint of disappointment.

But now that the battle was over, though the lingering coppery scent of blood still tempted him, he felt that the world was all wrong.

His world. His shield was missing, vanished on the wind, and though the Demon-Bound cautiously searched for the essence he used as a disguise, it could not be found.

So the Demon-Bound stalked the campground, vainly seeking the one he needed to hide himself. But it was as though the very earth had swallowed the man, essence and all.

This is not good, his internal companion muttered. *Without him, we might be discovered.*

True. He would need to find another—quickly.

It was then that he saw the guard called Creed standing watch, looking wary as a deer. Strong essence filled the man, made stronger by his unease. But he was steady as well, and not a hint of mage essence could be felt in him.

He will have to be the one, the Demon-Bound thought.

So he wandered over casually, offered Creed his hand, and gently wove his essence into that of the man.

And wondered the whole time if the Other was to blame.

NINETEEN

Eithne rose at first light, gathering Conor's tunic and a small pouch of cleaning powder as well as a large pail, and headed for the stream in the woods. This time, she chose to go in uphill of where the dead mule lay. Conor's tunic stank enough without adding the taint of the dead beast. Besides, the trees were thinner on the higher ground, and though she had to walk farther, she decided it would be worth the trip.

Too bad I didn't think of that last night, she thought.

She found a spot where the water formed a pool close to the shore, and where the shadows were pale. There, she knelt, dunked the tunic, and let it lay in the cold water as she filled the pail and mixed in a bit of the cleaning powder, stirring it to make a milky, sudsy solution. Pulling the tunic out of the stream, she wadded it down into the pail and tried to scour the boar's blood from it.

As she worked, she could not help but glance around at the woods. Granted, she did not think any of those dark creatures would be here in the early morning light, but it would not hurt to stay alert. There was a different feel to the place. Birds sang in the trees. On downhill where the mule's carcass rotted—and sent an occasional whiff of odor to scourge her nose—she heard jackdaws and ravens quarreling. She tried to ignore them and concentrate on the task at hand.

The stains were proving more stubborn than she liked. *I should have dunked it in cold water last night,* she thought. She scrubbed it hard with the little brush she carried for such tasks, and while most of it came out, it was clearly time to talk to Conor about getting him a new tunic. Of course, she knew what he would say. *"Tis naught wrong with this one, woman."* To him, every stain was a bit of history. She had often had to wrangle it off of him to wash it at all. Conor seemed to think that clothes only needed replacing if they were rags. This one was getting threadbare as it was. He would not part with it because he had been wearing it since the day their real son died. As far as Eithne was concerned,

Conor needed to let go of that part of his past. Why, he still had his militia one tucked away in a saddle pack, and it was even worse looking than this one. If ever she got a chance, she would toss that one on a midden heap as well.

She shook her head. "When we get to the next large town," she muttered aloud as she stood up and wrung out the wet wool cloth, "if I have to purchase the cloth with my own sgillinns—or borrow them from Rhoyd—I am going to buy an ell or two of wool and make him a new tunic. This nasty old thing must go. Why, he looks no better than a bandit in it."

A chuckle sounded from close by. Eithne gasped and turned towards the source of the sound. In her anger, she had stopped being alert.

Someone stood in the deeper shadows on the opposite bank. She could not see who it was. Her heart thundered heavily against her ribs as she realized that this time she had come to the water without her staff and had no means of defending herself.

"Who's there?" she called. "Show yourself!"

The figure flitted away so abruptly, she wondered if he had been there at all. Frowning, she tried to peer at the place where he had stood.

"Mistress Manahan?" Master Fergus was suddenly at her side. Eithne gasped and turned again, ready to fling the wet tunic and kick over the pail as distractions, but the caravan master put up his hands. "Is something the matter?" he asked.

Eithne pointed to the place across the water.

"There was a man there," she said and pointed. "Did you not see him?"

Master Fergus peered across the stream and shook his head. "I see no one," he said. "Except a foolish woman jumping at shadows."

"I beg your pardon?" she said and turned back to glare at him.

"Forgive me, Mistress Manahan, but after what happened here last night, I would not have thought you would have returned here."

Eithne sighed to calm herself. "Sorry, but it's a bright morning, and Conor's tunic got a bit bloody last night."

Master Fergus looked at the wad of cloth and smiled. "You're a good wife, then," he said. "Mine makes me burn my clothes from time to time."

The light-heartedness of his words made her laugh. Rhoyd was right. Master Fergus did resemble five dumplings in a doublet if one counted his head. But seemed a nice man too in spite of the odor clinging to him. She could see that now in the crinkle around his eyes and the soft smile that spread his lips even in the shadow of his hood.

"Are you done?" he asked, gesturing to the bucket.

"Oh, yes," Eithne said. "I'm afraid it won't all come out."

"Then I would suggest you follow my wife's way and burn it—though since it's wet, that may not be possible at the moment," he said. "Come, I'll escort you back."

"Surely, you did not come down here just to do that?"

"Oh, no, I was taking another look at the mule and its master to see if I could figure out who they were," he said. "Then I heard you call out and thought I'd better see what was amiss."

"As I said, there was a man over there," she said. "I thought he was going to attack me."

Master Fergus eyed the shadows then shrugged. "Well, then all the more reason to get you back to camp," he said.

He gestured that she should take the lead, and she did when he picked up her pail and carried it for her. She glanced over her shoulder at the far bank one more time, but she still could not see anyone. *But there was someone there. I saw him.* She let a little frown dress her eyebrows.

"By the way, Mistress Manahan," Fergus said as though he thought mundane conversation would ease her distress. "How is the captain?"

"Oh, I am certain he is doing well," she said. "I shall look in on him as soon as I return to camp."

"I'll come with you, then," Fergus said. "I have matters to discuss with him."

"What matters?" she asked.

Fergus cocked an eyebrow in amusement. "Well, I do not think I should rightly tell you, Mistress."

That was most certainly a rebuke, Eithne thought. Of a sort that only made her curiosity stronger. "Really, if it is something that could affect the captain's health, I should know," she said.

"Well, was nothing more than the fact that we lost two men last night," Fergus said. "One of them was trampled and gored by the boar."

Eithne nodded, she remembered that unfortunate all too well. There had been nothing she could do for him. "And the other?" she said. "I only saw one man seriously harmed by those beasts."

"The other has simply disappeared," the caravan master said with a shake of his head. "He went on dark watch, and come the dawn, he was not at his post."

"Which man?"

"Warden," Master Fergus said.

"Do you suppose he deserted?" she asked.

"Possible, but not likely," Fergus said. "There was blood, you see. A large dollop of it on the ground."

Eithne stopped and looked at the caravan master. "Do you believe he met an ill end by the hand of another?"

Fergus shrugged. "It was one of the reasons I wanted another look at the mule. I thought that whatever had killed the beast might have taken Warden as well. But I found no clue, and no fresh signs of feeding. So I fear it may be that Warden was indeed killed and someone has concealed his body. The only question is where?"

Eithne nodded. "Poor Warden," she said.

"Poor?" Fergus repeated. "The man who threatened your son? The man your husband swore he would kill if he came near the lad again?"

Eithne frowned at the caravan master. "Are you implying that my husband had anything to do with Warden's disappearance?" she asked in a hard voice. "For if you are, let me tell you that Conor Manahan is not a man to go butchering another in the dark. He is no coward, and he would never kill a man unless forced to do so."

Fergus waved a hand. "I am not saying anything of the sort, Mistress," he said. "I am merely stating a fact. I have no evidence other than the blood. Without a body, there can be no crime declared."

She heaved a sigh and shook her head. "Conor has never ever killed a man that he did not meet in a fair fight," she said.

"And I believe you," Fergus said. "Now, let us return to camp so you can look in on the captain and I can report this matter to him."

Slowly, she nodded. But in her head she was feeling a bit peevish. How could he accuse Conor of having anything to do with the disappearance of one like Warden? She was willing to bet the blood was left over from the boar and that the man had simply gone off because he was tired of working this cursed caravan.

Or maybe another demon had taken him.

Conor opened his eyes to the bright light of dawn just as he heard the thump of something wet tossed on the ground. He squinted at the sight of his small, dark-haired wife glaring at the fire, arms crossed over her chest. She looked like she had a bee in her breeches, and Conor wondered if he had done something to enable that mood. He sat up carefully in case he had and smiled for her.

"Morning, woman," he said.

She glanced at him, half startled. Then slowly, she sighed.

"Good morning," she returned.

"What have you been up to, love of my life?" he asked.

The words softened her expression just a little. She kicked at the bundle of wet cloth, and he realized that it was his tunic. "Trying to make this clean and sweet," she said wearily. "But it refuses to let go of its stains, just as you refuse to let go of it."

Conor arched an eyebrow and tried not to frown. When Eithne started speaking in riddles that involved him, he never knew quite what to expect. "I'm sorry if I vex ye by being a practical man," he said.

She sighed again, this time a short huffing breath and shook her head. "I would not have you any other way," she said. "But that tunic has got to go, Conor. When we reach the next township, I am going to get you another."

He glanced at the wet wad of blue cloth that was fading a dull shade and patterned with a smattering of stains. "If it makes ye happy," he said.

She hesitated. Then she came over and knelt beside him and kissed him. He wanted the kiss to linger, but she drew back and brushed his grizzled cheek with one hand. "Of course, it makes me happy," she said. "I won't have to scrub my knuckles off trying to get the stains out of a new one. Now, I have to go check in on *Captain Camhin,* as Master Fergus wants to speak to him as soon as possible."

"What's the stinky auld dumpling in a stir about now?" Conor asked.

"He lost two men last night," she said.

"Two?" Conor said and frowned. "But only one man fell under that boar I hamstrung."

"The other merely disappeared in the night," she said. "Leaving nothing more than a patch of blood where he stood watch."

"Which man?"

She hesitated. "Warden."

Conor frowned. "We're better off without that one," he said.

"Master Fergus seems to think he was murdered in the night."

"Without making a sound?" Conor said. "It would take a man of great skill to kill another so quietly."

She said nothing for a moment. That deepened his frown.

"And it wasn't me, if that be what ye were thinking," he said a little more stiffly than he intended.

Eithne shook her head. "I know in my heart that it was not you," she said and leaned to kiss him again. "But if I were you, I would be more cautious when I threaten men in the future. Master Fergus remembers that you said you would kill Warden."

"If he lays a hand on my son, aye," Conor said. "But sneaking about in the dark to slay men is not my way, woman."

"I know," she said and smiled. "Just be careful, please."

She leaned and kissed him one more time. He held her, not willing to let her go just yet, but she pulled back and shook her head. "I have to go."

With that, she drew herself to her feet and hurried towards the cook's wagon.

"Aye, just like you, woman," he called in a teasing way. "Get a man all ready and then dump him for another."

"Oh, you wish," she called back before she climbed into the cook's wagon.

He looked over and saw a pair of blue eyes crinkled over a smile.

"What are you grinning like a jackanapes about," Conor said, and tossed his blanket across at the lad who tried too late to scramble out of range.

Rhoyd giggled like an imp as the blanket buried him.

TWENTY

Once the main portion of the camp was aroused and fed for the day, they prepared to continue on their journey. More than one comment was made about the disappearance of the man called Warden. Eithne was fully aware that when Master Fergus reported the matter to the captain—who had regained his ability to hold the illusion—that Captain Camhin looked in her direction. Though Master Fergus did not voice his suspicions, she knew that several men heard Conor's threat.

Well, she thought. *The captain can use magic to determine who might be guilty of the crime...* But she was painfully aware that he could not share this knowledge without revealing himself. And this made her fret all the more that eyes would turn on Conor and try to blame him for the man's disappearance.

She dearly hoped Warden had deserted. She truly hoped that the blood was that of a boar and not his own. There was a moment in which she thought she might take Rhoyd to the place and have him scry, but it occurred to her that she had no idea where Warren was standing watch at the time. And there were other bloodstains on the ground.

Mistress Noreen was taking the deaths of the boars in stride. She had spent the earliest hours of the morning skinning and cleaning the carcasses for travel. "We'll have a fine roast tonight," she said. "No use in letting this meat go to waste." She hung both carcasses up in her wagon once the captain was out of it. Eithne was rolling up the bandages from the splint she had removed from the captain that morning.

"But won't most of it go to waste?" Eithne asked.

"When we reach the town tomorrow night, I'll get salt barrels to pack the rest in."

Eithne had looked at the wagons. There were already several barrels tied to its sides, all marked with symbols to denote their contents.

"Doesn't look like you'll have room for more barrels," she said and smiled.

"There's room inside. And that way I can keep the water barrels for water alone and the flour barrel for flour and the vegetable barrel for vegetables...oh, and I mustn't forget the ale and the wine barrels. These men would have hinny fits if I let their ale get salty."

Eithne nodded. That struck her as a wise plan. She was beginning to see that Mistress Noreen was wiser than she first thought. Wise enough to confide in, perhaps.

"So, what do you think happened to Warden?" Eithne asked.

"That lazy, good-for-nothing son of a whore?" Mistress Noreen said with a snort. "Good riddance, I say. I hope a demon ate him."

"But do you think he met with a foul end?" Eithne ventured.

"He had a foul end, if you ask me." Noreen chuckled. "But I ne'er much liked him when he signed on. Something about him gave me the willies. Ne'er could understand how he and a nice lad like Bowen became friends."

Eithne narrowed her eyes. "Friends?"

"Aye, they signed on together. In fact, I got the impression Bowen was the one that talked Warden into coming along."

"Why do you say that?"

"Something Warden said when he was drinking," Mistress Noreen said. "That Bowen said it would be good for them both. Of course, he was complaining about the dangers and the fact that your son was mageborn. And I remember Bowen reaching over and punching his shoulder and telling him to mind his tongue or lay off the drink, so I took it as more ale than thought."

"When was this?"

"That first night from the place where you and your husband signed on," Noreen said. "Well, that takes care of those beauties. Best get Bawdy and Bellow hitched up now."

Eithne frowned.

First night?

How had Warden known so soon that Rhoyd was mageborn?

The adults were being rather closed that morning. Rhoyd sensed the mood as he checked the girth on Moonface's saddle. It wasn't just Conor and Eithne. It was everyone in camp. He had seen a number of them conferring in small groups, and their eyes would always stray to Conor if he was in the vicinity. And Conor seemed more wary as he moved about saddling Battlebrute and Maudie.

Something was definitely wrong, and Rhoyd hated it when the problem was not a magical one. Magic was easy to deal with, easier than adults being secretive and moody.

He wondered what had them all a' stir? Was it the boar attack last night? The demon in the woods? Maybe they were blaming Rhoyd for all the trouble. Maybe Conor's wariness was his way of making sure none of them tried to harm Rhoyd.

He wished he knew. He felt a little uneasy about asking.

Perhaps he should ask Noreen. But he reminded himself that Conor had decided to keep him close, and he would not have a chance to ride with her at all.

He was contemplating this when the captain approached on foot, looking none the worse for his injury. Indeed, Eithne's healing had done so well, he only walked with a slight limp.

"Master Manahan," Captain Camhin called.

"Sir?" Conor said, though there was a hint of cheek in the way he said it. He stopped adjusting the stirrups to turn and look at the captain.

"I find myself without a horse, and wondered if your wife would loan me hers for the day, at least until we get someplace where I can purchase another."

"That would be up to my wife," Conor said and cocked and eyebrow. "Ye'll have to ask her."

Captain Camhin nodded. "And so I shall."

"You can ride Moonface," Rhoyd said quickly. "I can ride with Noreen."

Both the captain and Conor looked at Rhoyd. "Thought you were tired of the cook's company, lad?" Conor said.

Rhoyd shrugged. "It was just a thought. Moonface is more surefooted, and younger than Maudie, and he would be a better mount if there was a bandit attack."

Conor cocked an eyebrow. Captain Camhin raised both of his.

"Can't argue with that," Conor said. "Maudie is a bit of a lazy auld besom at times."

"Then I suppose I shall accept the offer with the good grace and common sense with which it was presented," Camhin said.

Rhoyd smiled and loosened his pack full of books from the

saddle to take with him. He held out the reins to the captain who took them and gave Moonface an appreciative look. "Thank you, lad," the captain said, though he had yet to lose the puzzlement in his look.

"He won't shy at much," Rhoyd said.

Captain Camhin nodded, readjusting the stirrups. He climbed cleanly into the saddle and gathered the reins. Moonface was quiet as still water.

"A very nice mount indeed," the captain agreed. He applied a little heel, and Moonface stepped forward at a walk. "Very responsive. My thanks."

Rhoyd nodded and watched as the captain rode off. He turned and saw the look in Conor's eyes. Conor motioned Rhoyd close. With a sigh, he obeyed.

"You stay out of mischief, and you stay with Mistress Noreen no matter what," Conor said.

"I will," Rhoyd promised.

"Off you go, then," Conor said.

Rhoyd hurried towards the cook's wagon. Noreen was tying down the flaps in the back, and Rhoyd stopped a few feet away as the stench of fresh blood assailed him.

"Whew...what's that?" he said.

"The boars," Noreen replied. "What are you doing mucking about? Shouldn't you be getting ready to ride?"

"I'm riding with you today," Rhoyd said.

"Are ye now?" Noreen asked.

"Captain Camhin needed my horse," Rhoyd added. "He wanted Maudie, but she's old and not good in a fight."

"Aye, well that was generous of you," Noreen agreed. "I suppose that means you're not going to try and give me the slip today?"

"Do you promise not to tell me all about the Hammer Maid again?" Rhoyd returned.

Noreen smiled. "All right. Get on board, then."

Rhoyd ran around to the front end of the wagon. He tossed his pack up then clambered up into the seat. Noreen finished her inspection, and then crawled into her place, taking up the reins and the whip.

Quiet pervaded the entire day. The weather was good and the path was clear. Conor had to admit to himself that he was pleased with the peace. The caravan made good time on that day without sighting a bandit or a bogie. Just hawks and stoats and a brace of deer that managed to escape into the forest before any man could draw on them.

At length, as the shadows began to grow, they reached a clear glen that the captain declared was a good place to stop for the night. Even Conor noticed that there was nothing bogie about the place. It was wide enough to afford a good view, and the water was in the open. Watch fires were placed around the camp, and Noreen boiled a flank of one of the boars in a great cauldron, seasoning it with spices from her stores. She pulled out rounds of cheese and flat bread and apples as well.

Having a meal of fresh-cooked meat seemed to set well with everyone present. The men's moods were not as dark as they had been, and Conor started to wonder if Warden's departure was even being noticed. He saw Bowen laughing with several of the men, and he hoisted his tankard in Conor's direction in a salute.

"He certainly doesn't seem upset with the loss of his friend," Eithne muttered as she followed Conor to the boards to collect their meals.

"Who says they were friends?" Conor asked.

"Mistress Noreen," Eithne replied. "She said it was Bowen who convinced Warden to sign on to the caravan. She also said she couldn't figure out how a nice lad like Bowen could call a lout like Warden his friend."

Conor arched an eyebrow in thought. That was news to him. While he knew that Bowen and Warden had signed on at the same time—they had been sharing a meal in the inn the day Conor met them and learned of the caravan—he remembered Bowen saying that they were not actually friends. *Why would Bowen tell me this if they were friends after all?*

He opened his mouth to voice that thought when they reached the boards. Mistress Noreen was slicing thick chunks of the boiled haunch to serve the men. Beside her, Rhoyd was passing out pieces of flat bread and chunks of cheese and whole apples.

"Will ye look at that, woman," Conor said with a grin. "Our lad's gone to be a scullery. I knew all that reading was never going to amount to much…"

Rhoyd looked up and stuck out his tongue.

"And such manners he's learning," Conor went on with a

grin.

"Ah, he does a fine job when he's not dropping apples," Noreen declared.

As if on cue, one of the apples did slip from Rhoyd's grasp and arc through the air. He tried to catch it, but it bounced off the edges of his hands and went rolling down the table. Rhoyd had to abandon it in order to keep from dropping the bread and cheese as well.

"Horns," the lad hissed.

The apple was just about to fall off the end of the table when Bowen arrived and caught it. Conor frowned at his sudden presence, for he had not seen the man approach.

"Waste of good apples," Bowen said. He set it on the table and walked on as though naught were amiss. But his eyes flitted briefly to Conor as though taking his measure.

Rhoyd collected the apple and offered it to Conor, startling him out of his thoughts. He took it, weighing it in his hand, and wondered how Bowen had gotten there so quick. But there was a bustling behind him as more men joined the line. Someone groused, "What's holding you up, Manahan?"

"So, are ye eating that or debating it?" Noreen asked. "I got more mouths than yours to feed, you know."

"Eating," Conor said and held out his wooden bowl for a portion of the boar meat. "And you and I need to have a bit of a talk afterwards," he added in a low voice.

"So long as your wife isn't the jealous sort," Noreen said with a wink at Eithne.

"You're welcome to him," Eithne tossed back with a wry smile. "But I'll warn you, he snores..."

"Now, woman, don't be maligning me manhood," Conor said defensively. "And anyway, I only had in mind to share a few war stories. I suspect the mistress is more woman than even I could handle."

"We'll see about that, long-shanks," Noreen said and leered as she slapped a large slice into his bowl.

TWENTY-ONE

Eithne was stitching stockings when Conor collected Rhoyd and brought the lad back to their camp. They arrived, singing some verse the lad must have learned from Mistress Noreen. Eithne said nothing and they stopped before her and finished the performance. She merely shook her head. At least Conor was in a good mood, which was more than she could say for herself. Since the evening, she had been pushing down a sense that all was not well in her little world.

Rhoyd was tired from working with the cook, and it wasn't long before he was in his pallet slumbering.

Without his old tunic, Conor had wrapped the ells of his plaidie about him for warmth. He seated himself at the side of their fire and glanced out over the glen.

"Is something bothering you?" Eithne asked, hoping to alleviate her own unease by ferreting out his thoughts.

"I've been thinking about what ye said," Conor said. "About Warden and Bowen being friends. You see, Bowen told me he was no friend of Warden, even though he knew him and had worked several caravans with him."

"Well, it does seem odd," Eithne agreed. "But then why would Mistress Noreen think they were friends?"

Conor shrugged. "I ne'er got the chance to ask. She was busy, and there was too many hanging about, and she wanted to have a cold board set fae the men what come off watch in the Dark Hour."

Eithne nodded, putting her stitching aside. She wished she could sort it all out. "Do you think we should tell the captain?"

Conor shifted and glanced towards the dark carriage. "He'll be holed up making magic, like as not, and not want to be disturbed tonight. But maybe tomorrow on the ride in, I can speak to him."

Eithne sighed. "I wish we had not come."

"If wishes were horses, woman." Conor grinned at her. The look took away the last of her resolve. She bit her lip and looked elsewhere.

"I know," she said, unable to stop herself. "But I have this odd feeling that something terrible is going to happen."

Conor leaned so he could look at her. "Ye haven't gone and gotten the sight, have ye?" he asked. "Or has Rhoyd said something?"

Eithne rolled her eyes. "Our son is not the only one who can have feelings." She drew her knees to her chest and shivered a little, not sure if it was the cold or the unease.

Smiling, Conor shifted and slipped an arm around her shoulder. "And I would never doubt those feelings for a moment," he said softly.

She sighed and leaned into him, relishing his warmth, eager to slip under that plaidie with him hard against her.

But there was Rhoyd to consider, and they were not using the tent, and she could not—no matter how much she ached for Conor's touch—bring herself to make love here in the open with so many about. She had seen it before. Camp whores and their men rutting under blankets where all could see.

"I love you," she whispered.

Conor glanced down at her. "What makes ye say that now?" he asked.

She sighed. "I don't know. I just..."

Conor lifted her chin and drew lips to hers. The kiss lingered long enough to make her forget her sense of discretion. She drew the long end of the plaidie over herself and let nature take its course.

Eithne fell asleep after they made love. Conor tucked blankets around her and stood to stretch, his plaidie drawn tight. Normally, it was he who snored like an oaf after, but there was something about the act—something in her very urgency—that set ill in him. As though the unease she had hinted at before had been passed to him.

So he decided to take a walk around the camp to loosen the thoughts and the muscles. Once more, he had not drawn watch, and he was starting to think that Michan was using glamorie to change the draw. The other men looked at him almost suspiciously when the lots were cast. For this was the third day in a row that Conor had drawn the white stone—the sign of day watch.

By now it was dark and men not on duty were under their

blankets or the wagons. He could see the ring of watch fires and hear the calls of the mercenaries set about the camp. Mistress Noreen had a lantern set up and a board set out. Cold table consisted of dried meat and fruits and cheese and bread and a keg of ale to wash it all down.

As he wandered on past the boards and out beyond the dark wagon, Conor took a deep breath. The scent of the glen carried on the night breeze. It reminded Conor a little of home, though it lacked the salty tang. Seanbrae where he was born was close to the sea, sitting on an inlet that rolled wild out of the braes. A wide river that men could not tame, even with a bridge, so one had to travel inland just to cross.

He thought of the glens of his youth as he now wandered the camp. If he narrowed his eyes, he could almost pretend that these braes were one and the same...

A shadow moved at the corner of his vision. Instincts honed by years of training pushed into focus. The shadow was that of a man in a cloak, and he was hunkering and flitting from stone to stone, moving away from the camp.

Away?

Conor frowned. He tightened his plaidie about his shoulders and shifted his long dirk so that it was within easy grasp. Cautiously, he started after the figure that was now coming close to one of the guards. Surely the man would see.

But no, the guard turned and stretched and yawned, and the cloaked one glided by ghost-like. Conor advanced at a steady pace. This was not good, men at their posts and a thief or worse slipping out of camp right under their noses. Conor kept sight of the figure creeping past the outer rank of guards, and as before, the man turned away and scratched himself absently. The shadow came but a few feet of him, and yet he did not see it.

Not good at all. Conor picked up his pace. The cloaked one was making tracks towards one of the few copses dotting this wide glen.

Why?

Conor had reached the inner rank of guards. He walked past the man who had stretched and yawned, and to his surprise, the man stood with eyes closed. *Asleep on his feet,* Conor thought, and he was tempted to awaken the man. But he wanted to keep up with his quarry and could not risk such a delay. So he walked on, leaving the sentry asleep and made for the next rank of guards.

He half expected the next man to stop him as he walked right by, but this one was still more concerned with whatever made him itch. The guard never looked up. Conor cast his glance left and right, and noticed that other guards were just as distracted. Horns, there could have been a horde riding full tilt across the glen, and not a man would have seen before it was too late.

Conor walked on, picking up his pace to a long-legged lope through the tall sedge. The thump of his boots on the ground was quiet enough, but he slowed his pace when he reached the edge of the copse.

No wind stirred here. Conor stood in the edge of the shadows and let his eyes adjust to the gloom. He could barely hear the whisper of cloth slipping through the trees ahead. Focusing on that sound, he stepped into the first rank of trees.

Ancient oaks, snarled old men of the forest, surrounded him now. He picked his way across soft moss among a garden of roots. These trees must have been here since the Great Cataclysm, for they were giants. Very few saplings were nestled into their roots. Among their gnarled limbs, faint glimmer of moonlight flecked the ground with diamonds of light. The mottled pattern they laid on the ground and the trunks of the old oaks was the perfect place for a Keltoran and his plaidie to blend in.

Conor was but a few trees in when he heard a moan. His hand went to his long dirk. He jerked steel free, keeping it hidden under his plaidie lest a flicker of moonlight on steel should give him away. Was it the wind in the branches? *There is no wind.* He hastened towards the sound as quiet as an assassin at work.

The moan sounded again from a different direction. Conor hissed an oath under his breath and turned towards the sound. It occurred to him now that he was inside the copse, he could not tell much about the direction from whence he came. Another moan interrupted his thoughts, this time from farther away.

Horns, is this one of the haunted woods? As a youth he had wandered such bogie places, and now as he stood trying to get a sense of direction, the small hairs began to rise. There was something—or someone—in this wood who reeked of magic. He felt it as sure as he felt any of Rhoyd's glamorie.

And with it, he caught the scent of blood.

What in the name of Cernunnos? This was something that needed Michan's attention and not his. *I've no skill against glamorie!* Best he return to camp and tell Michan that something foul was afoot this night.

He took a deep breath and tried to orient himself to the direction of the moonlight. Cautiously, he moved towards what he hoped was the direction he had come. If only he could glimpse one of the watch fires. He was no coward in the dark, but to come so far into dark wood without a glim of light was foolish. *Gormless, that's what you are Manahan,* he thought.

He pushed around the trunk of a rather large tree when a shadow moved. Conor froze. There was a thinning ahead of him. He hoped it meant he was close to the edge of the trees, but that shadow was moving across his path, and to move now would give him away. Indeed, the shadow paced back and forth like a feline debating which way to go. Conor crouched and moved forward, still clutching his long dirk tight in one hand. He waited until the figure stepped off to one side and appeared to be looking away then charged.

There was a startled shout as Conor broke out of the trees. The figure turned clumsily—stiffly—not at all like a man used to moving fast. That gave Conor the advantage, and he charged at the unknown foe, seizing him by the throat and raising his blade.

"Name yourself or die!" Conor snapped.

And then he froze as the wide-eyed terror was revealed in the gleam of moonlight to be Master Fergus. The old wagon master had thrown up one hand to defend himself. The other was reaching for his short dagger.

Conor quickly let go and stepped back.

"Forgive me, Master Fergus," he said. "I mistook you for a stranger."

"It's you who is growing stranger by the day, Manahan," Fergus retorted, rubbing his throat. "I damned near pissed my breeks when you came charging out of there like some monster wild beast. You should be more careful!"

"Sir?" Conor frowned.

"What in the name of Cernunnos are you doing skulking down here in the trees anyway?"

Conor took a deep breath and pushed his long dirk back

into its sheath. "Trailing shadows in the shape of men," he said. "I spied someone from up in the camp a-heading towards these woods, and decide to follow when I saw them walk right past the watch unseen."

"And how did you get past the watch?"

Conor frowned now. "Same way the shadow did," he said. "I walked and found one man asleep, another in need of a bath to rid him of fleas. What are you doing down here?"

"I was walking the watch and came up missing a man," Fergus said. He pointed towards an open space. Conor frowned. There had been a man there. He had passed him as the guard dug around his groin.

"That man was scratching at himself," Conor said. "He ne'er saw me pass."

"Well, he's not there now. Just his quarterstaff a lying off to one side."

"Then perhaps that was the moaning I heard," Conor said.

"Moaning?" Master Fergus looked as though he did not believe Conor.

"Aye," Conor said. "When I stepped into the woods, I heard moans, and I could not tell if it was man or beast or the groaning of wood. But I felt magic in there, and I smelled blood."

Fergus looked at the trees. Uncertainty masked his expression.

"Then we shall wait for first light to see what lies in those woods," he said. "And I pray to the gods that we do not find a corpse."

Conor nodded. "May haps we'd best return to camp," he said carefully.

"Indeed," Fergus said. "You lead the way."

Conor arched an eyebrow. Was that the caravan master's way of saying he did not trust Conor?

He sighed and started on. When they came back in the morning, he would insist on bringing Rhoyd. Michan would object, he knew, but the lad might be able to sense what had happened here.

For now that Conor was outside the trees, the dark taint of magic was gone.

TWENTY-TWO

Captain Camhin was not happy with the delay, but Fergus insisted on taking a small party of men to scour the woods for the missing man as soon as it was light enough to see. Conor offered to assist, and to bring Rhoyd, but Fergus decided that would not be wise. He insisted that Conor and his son stay at camp, whispered something to the captain, and then left with his small band.

So Conor was not surprised when Camhin turned a puzzled look in his direction.

"Did you really threaten his life?" the captain asked.

"I followed a shadow into those woods last night," Conor said. "I felt magic and smelled blood, and I couldn't find my way out, and when I did, there was this shadow waiting for me. How was I to know it was him?"

They stood side by side at the crest of the hill, watching as the men moved into the trees. Conor had sent Rhoyd back with Eithne to help her break camp.

"A shadow," Camhin said thoughtfully. "And now we are missing another man. You do realize now that Master Fergus thinks you are to blame, don't you?"

"I had naught to do with either man going missing and you know that," Conor said.

The captain sighed and nodded. He grew still as though he were concentrating on something. But then he took another deep breath and shook his head. "I sense nothing down there, Conor. That's the strange part."

"Nothing? No magic?"

"Not even life," the captain said.

"Then how could I have felt it?" Conor asked. "How could I have known there was death and magic in those trees?"

"How indeed," Camhin said. "Perhaps life with your son has made you more sensitive to magic?"

Conor shook his head. "I was always sensitive to magic, and you know that."

"Yes, alas I cannot let them know that I know that," Camhin

said wryly. "Did you know the man who disappeared? I think Fergus said his name was Ganlon."

"Canna say that I did," Conor said. "I work a lot of caravans, ye ken. See some men often enough and ye learn their faces and their names. But some I see so far apart, I cannot say."

The captain nodded knowingly. Then stiffened as men started out of the trees dragging something behind them. Conor frowned. That didn't look like the body of a man. They came closer, then let go and stepped back. He and Captain Camhin started down the hill together.

The stench of death filled the air as soon as they got close. Conor steeled himself, expecting to see the scratching man Ganlon.

But no, it looked to be a small bear freshly killed. Just a mound of thick fur with paws. But then one of the men kicked it over to reveal the huge gap where its belly should have been. Conor peered closer and withheld a gasp. The bear looked as though something had eaten its insides out...

"Well?" Captain Camhin called.

"This would explain the stench of death," Master Fergus said. "There's no sign of the man."

"What in the name of Cernunnos could do that to a bear?" one of the men said.

"A darkling, perhaps," Captain Camhin said. "We should be on our guard."

"Darklings don't leave corpses," Master Fergus said. "I may not be a man who knows much about magic and bogies..." He looked at Conor as he said that. "...But I know that darklings eat all there is and leave nothing behind, save a patch of blood."

"A badger, then," the captain said wearily. "They are known to kill bears while defending their lairs."

Several of the men nodded that this sounded reasonable enough.

"Might be that a darkling ate Ganlon and Warden," one of the men said. Conor saw several men cast looks at him all the same.

Fergus frowned. "May haps," he said and cast a frustrated look in Conor's direction. "It would explain why there was naught to be found save the blood on the ground."

And if it is so, you owe me an apology, Conor mused. He kept his expression stoic.

"In that case," the captain said. "Our men will double the ring of watch fires and watch from inside them. Now we have delayed long enough. We want to reach Cullstane before dark."

Fergus nodded. He cast one more look at Conor before departing.

"Best keep a close watch on that lad of yours today," Camhin said in a low voice as the men were moving away. "I have a feeling that Master Fergus no longer trusts you, in spite of what the men think."

Conor nodded. That was advice he figured he could do well to heed.

Noreen was fussing about the barrels when Eithne approached, leading Rhoyd. The cook looked irritably at the ones hanging off the sides. "I know good and well I had that ale barrel higher," she snarled at Master Fergus.

"And just how can you know that?" Master Fergus retorted. He looked tired and irritable, and there was a bit of oak leaf stuck in his hair. "All them barrels look alike to me. They're probably shifting from the uneven road."

"Shifting my mother's foot," Noreen barked back. "You tell this lot that I better not catch any of them helping themselves to the stores at night."

Fergus waved her away with both hands and stalked off muttering about crazy women.

Noreen turned and spotted Eithne and Rhoyd.

"Morning Mistress," she said a little more cheerfully. "What can I do for you?"

"What's all the fuss about?" Eithne asked.

"Oh, this lot thinks I'm too dense to notice that they been messing with the barrels," Noreen said and shook her head. "I never tie one so low."

"So there's no chance it slipped?" Eithne asked, noticing that the barrel had a thin coating of flour on the lid. "Flour barrels can be heavy..."

Mistress Noreen arched an eyebrow and looked hard at the barrel. "Well, Horns, that is the flour," she said and shook her head. "Do me a favor and don't tell Fergus. I swore it was the ale."

"Mum's the word," Eithne said. "Conor says that Rhoyd will be riding with you again today. He and the Captain seem to think Rhoyd will be in some sort of danger because of that dead bear they found down in the woods."

Noreen looked toward the woods and sighed. "That were a strange thing, that man disappearing like that."

"Someone said darklings ate him," Rhoyd said matter-of-factly.

Eithne pushed a hand through the lad's hair and offered him an annoyed look.

"More likely he deserted, lamb," she said, but she could see that Rhoyd did not believe her. "At any rate, Conor said I was to charge you with keeping Rhoyd in one place." She looked at Rhoyd, "And you, my lamb, had better stay on that wagon."

"I will," Rhoyd said, looking annoyed.

Eithne pushed his hair out of his eyes and kissed his forehead. Then walked away, wondering why she still felt so much unease.

Rhoyd was tired of reading the diary, and Noreen was busy fussing at the horses, calling them lazy louts. And they took their time on the rise. So he put Fenelon's personal account away and dug out another book. This one was poorly bound, and its pages were loose. Someone had long ago tied a piece of twine around the spine to keep the signature in. Rhoyd had found it in Uncle Fenelon's library. The moment he touched its black leather cover carved with old runes that Fenelon had said were Haxon in origin, Rhoyd had known that this book was forbidden. Indeed, his Aunt Genna had found him lounging in one of the windows, peering at the script within, comparing the runes to notes Fenelon had left about Haxon languages. She had practically ripped it from his hands and with magic she had put it on a shelf far above his reach, one at the very ceiling of the room.

"There," she had said. "When you learn to levitate, you can have it back."

Rhoyd was not pleased to be scolded in that manner. Besides, he had learned the levitation spell ages ago. He just hadn't told her. As soon as she left the room, he had whispered to the air to move the book off the shelf and back into his hands.

Fenelon had applauded and laughed, and then told Rhoyd, "You better hide that somewhere else or Genna will burn it."

So he had hidden it in the bag, under the clothes along

with the journals. And when he had left Eldon Keep that first winter of lessons, he had taken all, including the notes.

On his own, it had not taken him long to decipher the runes. They were an alphabet, and once he had the key, translating the words was easy. Now he could read them as though he had been born a Haxon.

He now knew that what he possessed was a treatise on demons and their darkling kin. In fact, he recalled that there was a whole section of it devoted to the darklings. He had not really read it thoroughly before. Now seemed like a good time.

> *Darklings are thought to be the breath of the Dragon and the spawn of the Elderkin. None of their species were reported to have existed before the Corruption.*

Rhoyd looked over at Noreen. "What was the Corruption?" he asked.

Noreen arched an eyebrow. "Something it would not be safe to discuss just now," she said. "But suffice to say that in the age of the Shadow Lords, the Dark Mother corrupted demons and their kin."

"How did she corrupt them?" Rhoyd asked.

"Wouldn't know. I wasn't around then," Noreen said. "Hoi! Bawdy, walk on, you mangy..."

Rhoyd sighed. Clearly Noreen was no help just now. He flipped the book back open.

> *Darklings have no physical form unless it is imposed on them. However, at the moment they feed, they are known to assume a solid form. But once the prey is devoured—usually whole— they revert to their mist-like form.*
>
> *Some mageborn have been known to bind them as demons and familiars can be bound. Like demons, darklings are possessed of a secret name, and to know that name gives one the power to control them. Unlike demons, they are possessed of no serious intelligence. Their names are more common and easily discovered, for most of them are shadow beings and tend to have names that reflect that origin. And while*

they can be controlled, they often are useless for more than guardians. They can be bound to a place with boundaries of light or proper runes.

It is written that strong sunlight will disintegrate them, and that fire will keep them at bay, but that one must be careful of the shadows between fires, for in their mist form, they can crawl along the tiniest of paths.

It is rare, however, for them to wander out of places where the shadows are heavy, and though moonlight will not harm them, they seem to fear it.

Rhoyd arched an eyebrow. That made no sense. But then, he thought of the darkling that had attacked him and Eithne when they were plucking blackberries. Someone had to have been controlling it.

He was about to flip back into the book when Noreen gave a shout. "Hang on!" she called.

The wheel under Rhoyd hit a deep rut and jolted the wagon seat hard enough to bounce him. He managed to grab hold of the rail on one side. And it was then that his book chose to leap from his lap. He grabbed it, snagging it by the fragile pages and holding his breath.

Noreen cursed at the horses. Rhoyd gingerly kept his precarious hold on the book. When he felt safe enough to let go of the rail, he reached down with his other hand and pulled the book up. The pages flittered and flipped, leaving him trying to find his place in vain.

They stopped, however, with a page where someone had written, *Elderkin of the Shadows.*

Rhoyd peered at the page, the darkling lore forgotten, and he sifted through the runes.

Yet another type of the Shadow Beast is a creature of the Elderkin, a Greater Shadow Demon. Unlike its lesser kin, the Greater Shadow Demon possessed power of speech and the ability to wield magic. These beasts are rare, and this is a blessing, for it was said that during the age of the Shadow Lords, these Greater Shadow Demons were the agents of darkness.

Like all shadow kin, they had an aversion to strong light. Sunlight will destroy them, as will bright mage light and mage fire. They can call clouds of shadow to protect themselves, and this is often what gives them away.

But these clever creations of the Dark Mother, which are believed to have been around since the World was new, had the skill to cloak themselves in the human flesh of a living man, and with this cloak of flesh, they could walk around in the light of day and appear as men...

"That must be a terribly interesting book."

"Gah!" Rhoyd shouted and nearly lost the book again. He pulled it to his chest and looked over at the owner of the voice.

Bowen was riding up beside the wagon, his hood drawn to shade his eyes against the sun. He smirked.

"Sorry, lad," Bowen said. "Didn't mean to frighten you. Mistress Noreen, Master Fergus asks if you can spare a bit of fruit. One of the men on the front wagons has fainted, and he thinks it was the lack of food."

"Fools," Mistress Noreen said. "Rhoyd, be a good lad and crawl back into the wagon and get an apple and a sliver of cheese and bread."

Rhoyd hesitated then slowly crawled over the back of the bench, still clutching his book close. Only when he was in the wagon did he lay the book down and fetch the things the cook had asked for. He brought them back out and offered them to Bowen. The mercenary took them and saluted.

"My thanks to you, lad," he said and spurred his horse to ride on up front.

Rhoyd stayed back of the bench waiting for his heart to stop thundering before he collected his book and crawled back into the seat. Then he packed it away and took up the journal once more.

Perhaps he didn't need to be reading that particular book just now.

TWENTY-THREE

They reached Cullstane after another uneventful day, and Rhoyd was starting to believe that Warden had taken all the bad luck with him. *Good riddance, then,* he thought as they reached the town. It had walls of stone, much like Wenthorn, and small farms gathered around its base. A large keep centered the whole affair. Not some country village, but a real town like the one Rhoyd stayed in during the winter. He hoped this meant they would get to sleep in an inn. It would be nice to have a room, a roof and a soft bed. And warm food.

Assuming the Captain didn't want Rhoyd to stay with the dark wagon. He hoped not.

The caravan stopped outside the town and waited for the guards to come and look them over. Rhoyd stood up and peered at the rows of men along the walls and the banners displaying a large stone circled by smaller ones on a field of green. He was leaning a little too far when he nearly fell. Fortunately, Noreen snagged his arm and kept him from tumbling out of the wagon seat.

"Are you just naturally clumsy?" she asked with a good-natured grin, and Rhoyd smiled back, taking hold of something so he could lean out and see what was happening.

Master Fergus strolled down the line of wagons with one of the sergeants of the town watch. The man looked over the rosters that Master Fergus held out and nodded. "All in order," the sergeant said. He motioned to the gate guards to indicate that it was all right for the caravan to pass. One by one, the wagons started up and rolled through the stone gates.

Inside, they were directed to follow a road that would take them to the warehouses. Rhoyd noticed that the "captain" was keen on staying close to his wagon. He watched every person on the street, and Rhoyd wondered just who he was expecting to see. This was a town. Darklings rarely came into walled cities. Too many torches and too many people. Even the miasma that had hovered about the edges of Rhoyd's perception was drowned by the overwhelming multitude of essences. He sensed more people than he could ferret through without deep concentration.

Rhoyd sighed and sat back down.

The sergeant of the watch had assigned some of his men to escort the wagons on through the streets. Rhoyd thought this a bit odd, but then, thought Conor once told him that in some towns the watch worried that a new caravan coming in would mean that every thief would crawl out of their hiding hole. He said that it paid to make sure the cargo got safely to its destination to keep the caravans coming through.

They reached the warehouses without incident, though. Soon, they would be inside, and Rhoyd could join Conor and Eithne and have a meal. Rhoyd looked around for his pack as Noreen was negotiating her wagon through the opening. And just as he was lifting his bag into the wagon seat, cold brushed his nerves, and a bitter taste swelled on his tongue. *Demon! A demon spell!* Rhoyd jerked back around, looking for the source. He stood up quickly when one of the horses shied.

"Whoa, hey!" Noreen called, but the left lead gelding swung into the right hand beast, and in turn that one shifted directions. As a result, her wagon cut close to the opening, clipping one of the barrels. Rhoyd lost his balance and tumbled, and this time Noreen could do nothing to stop him. Fortunately, he landed against the footboard and managed to grab it to keep from falling.

"Horns!" she shouted and reached for him. The horses felt the shift and responded. There was a grate and a snap and the barrel dislodged from its mooring, hitting the cobbles hard. Wood exploded and boards splintered, and a shower of white meal fogged the air. "Whoa, damn rot ye!" Noreen said and let go of Rhoyd to jerk at the reins. "My flour!"

She managed to get the horses to stop and leaped off the far side of the wagon. Rhoyd scrambled to his feet and leapt off the wagon on the side where a cloud of white was billowing. Several of the guards, Conor among them, were dismounting and making their way closer to see what could be done.

Rhoyd started towards the mess as well. It was on the tip of his tongue to call air and make the cloud of flour settle. But the flurry of bodies rushing into the area created enough of a stir, and he decided that Conor might not be pleased if he cast any magic here in front of all the townsfolk.

He was looking to see where Conor had gone when someone

gasped.

At once, there was a crowd of men rushing over to peer at the mess.

But it was not the waste of flour or Noreen's curses that caused everyone one of them to stop.

It was the body of a man with a dagger in his back.

When the barrel broke, Conor's first thought had been that Rhoyd might be in danger. He had seen how the wagon lurched off to one side, and that his ever-curious son had been standing just moments before. The fear that Rhoyd might have fallen under a wheel came over him.

But then there was all the flour to try and peer through. And people were shouting about something in the flour as well. So when Conor managed to push through the shorter men and reach the mess, he stopped at the sight of a body. *Odd, why is there no blood?* Flour obscured the features and with the cloud of it hovering like an ominous fog, it was hard to see who lay there. Then someone came rushing in with water, tossing it on the man and washing the flour away. The face that was revealed was warped into a visage of terror. The man looked as though he had died of fright.

Howt awa! Conor thought. *'Tis Warden.*

Conor frowned. For between Warden's shoulder blades was a familiar sight. A dagger with a jeweled hilt—he knew it all too well, for it was the same dagger he had claimed as his prize all those years ago when he was courting Eithne and she refused to kiss him for winning a race. The dagger he normally kept in his saddle packs. *The saddle packs that were tied wrong...*

Conor stared at it in uncertainty. But then Fergus pushed forward and with him the Sergeant of the Watch.

"Does anyone know who this man is?" the sergeant asked.

Fergus cleared his throat. "It's a guard named Warden who disappeared three nights ago." He cast a look up at Conor. "It would appear the darklings that might have taken Gandon last night didn't get Warden after all.

Captain Camhin was moving around the edges of the crowd. He cast a worried glance in Conor's direction.

Horns, of course Michan would know that bloody blade.

"Does anyone know whose dagger that is?" the sergeant asked.

Conor cleared his throat. "It's mine," he said.

"Yours?" Master Fergus said. "I knew it!"

"Knew what?" the sergeant asked.

"He vowed to kill Warden," Fergus said.

For a moment, shock filled Conor's face. "Why you old goat," he snarled. "I said I would kill him if he touched my son again, but he ne'er did, and neither did I!"

"Take him," the sergeant of the watch ordered, drawing his sword and thrusting the point just inches from Conor's chest.

Several men surged forward to grab Conor. His instincts said fight, but he held his ground as they laid hands on him and pulled his arms out before him. Someone produced a set of manacles and began clamping them about his wrists. Others unbuckled his sword belt and drew his long dirk from his sheath. He swore under his breath, trying to stand strong against the jostling, and wryly noted that they did not notice the small dirk in the depths of his boot.

"No!" Eithne said. "This is all a mistake. My husband would never..."

The sergeant of the watch ignored her. Some of his men moved in to stop her advance as he held out the dagger, waving it before Conor. "You do not deny that this weapon is yours?" the captain asked.

"No, I will not deny that it is mine," Conor said. "But I did not use it on him. It was stolen from me the night the boars attacked our camp."

"Stolen?" the Sergeant of the Watch said. "By whom?"

"Well, if I knew that..." Conor said darkly, glaring at the man.

"Were there others who knew about the theft?"

Conor frowned. Rhoyd had said someone had been in the camp, and Conor had noticed his pack tied wrong, but he had not looked to see if anything was missing. And his hesitation did not go unnoticed. Still, he knew that if the dagger was in Warren's back, someone must have stolen it, and suddenly the boars appearing in the middle of the night looked suspiciously like some sort of distraction. *But why would anyone want to accuse me of murder?* He took a deep breath and shook his head.

"In truth, I did not tell anyone because I did not look," Conor said. "But I am telling ye that if I had killed the dog, ye'd have found his corpse in pieces. I've ne'er be so dishonorable as to stab that dog in the back, because I am not a coward."

"There are witnesses here who say that you threatened to kill him," the sergeant of the watch continued.

"Aye and I would have had he laid hands on my lad again, but I did not kill him, and I give you my word as a Keltoran..."

"The word of a Keltoran hardly matters in these parts," the sergeant of the watch said with a glower. "Take him away."

"NO!"

Conor glanced towards the sound of that cry. Rhoyd was pushing his way through the throng of men, wriggling like a ferret between impossible gaps. One of the guards turned and shoved the lad back, and Conor yelled in rage and shook off his handlers to throw himself at the man's back. Several men shouted warnings. Conor was never certain whether they were telling him to look out or the man he dove after. All he wanted to do was protect the lad. But someone slammed a cudgel against the back on his knee. His leg buckled. Eithne screamed and tried to get through as well, but there were others pulling her to safety. The man who had gone after Rhoyd now turned and with a snarl, he struck across with his own staff. The blow caught Conor in the shoulder, grating with pain, and sent him floundering off to one side. Hampered by the manacles, he could not get up as the man started to kick him in the ribs.

The blow never arrived. Rhoyd shouted and hit the man in the back with all the force his small body could muster. The blow sent the guard reeling off balance, and he stumbled across Conor.

"Hold!" That was Captain Camhin's voice. He pushed into the fray, Eithne and Noreen, and Master Fergus on his heels. "What is the meaning of this?"

"This man is accused of murder, and I will not have these people interfering!" the sergeant of the watch barked.

"This has to be a mistake. Conor Manahan would never kill a man without good cause."

"His knife was found in the man's back, and he does not deny that he would have killed him."

"That man has been nothing but trouble since he came onto the caravan," Camhin said, gesturing towards Warden's corpse. "What death he suffered, he likely brought on himself.

And I know this Conor for an honest man. If he says he didn't do it, then he is innocent. Besides, why would he have hidden the body where it was likely to be found?"

"What about his tunic," Master Fergus said. "I saw it covered with blood the night Warden disappeared. I witnessed his wife trying to wash out the stains..."

"Oh, that is absurd!" Eithne chimed in. "It was boar's blood, and it would not come out."

"Be silent!" the sergeant of the watch said. "I will hear no more nonsense. This man stands accused of murder, and it is for the magistrate of this township and the Lord Baron to decide if he is guilty or innocent. "All who wish to speak for him will be heard at the proper time. But until then, I will not have any of you interfering with this matter, or I will lock the whole lot of you in the dungeons. Now take him away."

A couple of guards pulled Conor upright to lead him off. He froze when he felt the whisper of magic coursing the air. Conor turned towards Rhoyd. The lad's eyes betrayed his intention as strongly as the raising of his hand. Captain Camhin turned a startled look towards Rhoyd, and Conor knew there was no way the captain could stop the lad in time.

"Rhoyd, NO!" Conor snapped and glared at the lad. "You gave me your word!"

Rhoyd hesitated, his eyes widening.

"Don't ye dare break yer promise to me, lad," Conor said. "Don't ye dare do it, or I'll never forgive ye if I live to do so."

The pain that flooded the lad's expression slammed guilt into Conor's gut. He kept his expression fierce, though it cost him. Then Captain Camhin crossed into Rhoyd's path, put a hand on his shoulder and guided him over to where Eithne stood twisting a bit of her cloak. Rhoyd went without a fight, and Eithne quickly clutched him to her, putting arms around his shoulders. Captain Camhin sighed.

"I'll do whatever I can for him, Rhoyd. I promise," Camhin said. He glanced up at Eithne, then over at Conor. "I swear."

Conor nodded, letting the tension fall away from his limbs as he was herded away by men nowhere near his stature. They pushed him along the streets at a hurried pace in spite of his painful limp, making for the gates of the guardhouse, hauling him through into a building that stank of things he did not want to even guess at. He was dragged down to a cell under the walls, forced to bend low under the beam, and pushed into the dark, dank corner where his manacles were hitched to a ring in the wall. He had little more than a small window to offer a bit of light. The air was nasty in his nose, bitter, rotten odors that raised the bile in his throat.

But he fought it down, punching it under with the outrage he felt in his heart.

I have been falsely accused of a crime I did not commit by my own dagger and my own words, he thought darkly.

He just hoped Michan made good his promise.

TWENTY-FOUR

"Why will you not let me see him?" Eithne said as she glared at the sergeant of the watch.

The sergeant was seated at a table in the foyer of the guardhouse, picking apart a leg of duck. Grease stained his tunic and dribbled down his fingers as he paused to look up at her.

"He is a murderer and a dangerous man," the sergeant replied.

"He is my husband, and your men beat him and injured him, and I can feel his _need,_" she complained.

The sergeant quirked one eyebrow and grinned lasciviously. "Oh, I can imagine his _need,_ my lady," he said wickedly.

It was all Eithne could do not to slap him. He seemed to know this, for he sat back, still gripping his duck.

"And besides, it is the rule," he said. "Until the Baron is notified, we cannot allow the prisoner to see anyone."

"Then I will speak to this Baron personally," Eithne said. "Where do I find him?"

"In the north forest, I imagine," the sergeant said. "He is accompanying the Duke of Highthorne on a boar hunt, and is not expected back for three days."

"Three days!" That was Captain Camhin. Eithne turned and looked at him. He had accompanied her because she refused to stay with the wagons and allow him to come and speak to these men. Conor's _need_ had assailed her as he was being dragged away. He might not let her see his pain, but she knew when it was there all the same.

"I cannot wait three days," Eithne said. "Infection could set into the wounds your men left on him. Now I want to see my husband now. I have a right to see him."

She started towards the entrance to the cells as she spoke. At once, there were guards in her way. Large bullies who blocked her path and glowered at her. And while she might have had the courage to take on any one of them alone, four of them now made a wall that she knew well enough she could not penetrate. She stopped, crossed her arms and tapped her foot impatiently.

"Madam, your husband is a murderer. It is likely he will lose his head."

She wheeled towards the sergeant, unable to hide her fury. "My Conor did not kill that man!" she snapped.

"His dagger was in the unfortunate's back, and his tunic was covered with blood."

"That was boar's blood, you insidious oaf!" Eithne said. "And his dagger was stolen!"

"You can prove this?" the sergeant asked. "Show me the evidence of his innocence, and I will set him free as soon as the magistrate and the baron have heard the matter."

Eithne hesitated. Of course, she had no physical proof and she knew it. But she also knew the accusations were false. She glanced over at Captain Camhin, pleading with her eyes. *Say something, Michan!* she thought.

Camhin cleared his throat and took a deep breath. "Could she not at least be allowed to heal him?" he asked. "She is a True Healer with connections to many temples."

"Why heal him if he is going to the axe man's block anyway?" the sergeant said.

Her temper took over. Eithne shrieked and rushed at the sergeant, willing to do harm for his words, but Captain Camhin was swift. He stopped her flight across the room, drew arms around her even as she struggled and screamed, "You dog, you monstrous cur! I am the daughter of the Duke of Gwyrn, and my father will have your manhood wrapped about your throat for that."

"Eithne, please," Camhin said softly. "Let us leave and discuss this in a civil manner—before you say something to damn both Conor and yourself—and the rest of us as well."

The sergeant merely smiled. Eithne shoved against the captain to break his grasp, and he allowed her to, holding his hands up in a gesture of surrender. With a dark glare at the sergeant, she stormed out of the chamber.

Captain Camhin caught up with her on the street outside.

"Eithne, please," he said. "You must be reasonable."

She stopped and wheeled on him. "How can I be reasonable, Michan?" she demanded, and the captain winced. "Conor is languishing in that cell, injured, accused of a crime he did not commit, and you want me to be reasonable? They are condemning him without even trying to see if he is innocent! I will not stand aside and allow him to die!"

"Nor will I," he insisted, seizing her shoulders and forcing her to face him. "I have not counted him my best friend during all those years of the Last War for nothing, Eithne. But I have an obligation, as do you, to stay calm and keep my head about this. Flying like a fury will not save him."

Eithne blinked. The words were as stinging as a slap. Yes, she had lost her head. The man she loved was hurt, and they would not listen to reason. Yet here was reason facing her now. She took a deep breath, fighting the sudden flood of tears that were pushing to escape.

"Oh, Michan, what are we to do?" she asked.

He winced again. "Eithne, please don't say my name, not here."

She nodded, giving in as he guided her back towards the entrance to warehouse where the caravan was stowing the wagons for the night. Rhoyd was sitting on Noreen's wagon, his face long with grief. He had wanted to come, but Eithne had refused to allow him to do so. She had feared the sight of Conor in a cell would have been more than a lad of his tender years should have seen.

At the sight of her, the lad hopped down and ran to her. She pulled him close, wanting to sob but afraid that doing so now would just upset him more. So she held him tight and ruffled his hair with one hand.

"Did you see him?" Rhoyd asked.

"They would not let me," Eithne said with a sigh. "But I am sure that he is well."

He looked up at her then, and a frown furrowed his brows. "Don't lie to me," he said. "I know he is not well. I can feel it as sure as I felt the magic that made that stupid horse shift the wagon so that the barrel broke."

Captain Camhin was suddenly at their side, looking at Rhoyd with a stunned expression.

"You felt magic turn Noreen's wagon?" he asked.

"Demon magic," Rhoyd said in a faint voice that only mageborn could hear.

"This is not good at all," Camhin said. "We cannot stay here if there are demons about."

"What do you mean?" Eithne glared at the captain.

"Let's get inside the wagon and discuss this," he said. "Noreen." He glanced at the cook and she nodded. Noreen opened up the wagon so they could all climb in. Once there, she carefully set her wards. Camhin waited until she was done to let his illusion fall away so that Michan stood before them once more. Eithne thought he looked a little pale. *The strain of the spell?*

"Now, what did you mean when you said you felt demon magic?" Michan asked, looking at Rhoyd. "You felt essence? Or did you actually feel a demon casting a spell."

"It was casting a spell," Rhoyd said.

"Could you tell the direction from whence it came?"

Rhoyd shook his head. "I was busy at the time, but I felt it, and then the horses hitched over and drove that barrel into the door."

"I see," Michan said, furrowing his brows in thought. "This is not good at all."

"What do you mean?" Eithne asked.

Michan took a deep breath. "It is as I feared. I had hoped it was not true, but before you joined the caravan, I was beginning to wonder if the servant of darkness we were dealing with was blood mage or demon kin. Darklings, while lower in intelligence than demons, are difficult to control, even for a mageborn of considerable experience. But one thing I witnessed when I was in the Last War was a shadow demon controlling darklings. Which might explain why there are so many of them following us around."

"But what has any of this to do with Conor?" Eithne asked.

"If it is true and we are dealing with some form of demon, in all likelihood, it does not want Conor around," Michan said. "His fierce protection of Rhoyd may be interfering with the creature's intentions. If it could claim the bones and destroy the Ard Magister before he is old enough to stand against its master, it would achieve the goals of the Dark Mother and bring back the Darkening to shadow the lands. This is why it is imperative that we leave as soon as..."

"Leave?" Eithne said. "Without Conor?"

"Eithne, if there is a demon about, we cannot afford to linger here. Rhoyd and the bones will be in danger."

"I will not leave here without Conor," Eithne said.

"Fine...you can stay here and I will take Rhoyd on to..."

"You will do no such thing," she said. "Rhoyd stays with

me. Conor would never allow him to leave."

"Don't you understand?" Michan said, advancing on her. "Rhoyd is in danger if he stays here."

"I'm not afraid of the demon," Rhoyd said suddenly. "I'll burn it like I did the other one."

"The one you burned was not a Greater Demon," Michan said. "If we are dealing with what I think we are dealing with, your courage will be useless..."

"We are not leaving without Conor, and that is all I will say on the matter." Eithne crossed her arms.

Michan took a deep breath. Eithne watched his expression shifting with his thoughts. Finally, he threw up his hands and muttered. "All right, but we must find out where this demon kin is hiding." He glanced at Noreen who looked just a little puzzled, and Eithne got the impression that something was passing between them because the cook's expression slipped into worry for a brief moment. But then Michan smiled as though reassuring her. "Noreen, take Rhoyd and scout around the camp," he said. "See if you can find any hint of the thing. Now that we know what we are looking for, it might be easier to ferret out the fiend. But whatever you do be cautious and don't let anyone else know. All right?"

"You can count on me to be the soul of discretion, sir," Noreen said and nodded. "Come on, lad," she said. "You and me is gonna go hunt us a demon for supper."

Rhoyd's face displayed uncertainty. Still, the prospect of hunting something with magic must have appealed to him because he nodded and followed Noreen towards the back of the wagon.

"Leave the wards up," Michan said softly.

Noreen nodded. She clambered out of the wagon and helped Rhoyd down.

Michan looked at Eithne in a solemn manner. "Now we can talk," he said.

"About what?" she asked.

"Look, I am not lying when I say that there is great danger remaining here. We must go on, and I really hate to do this because I love you and Conor both."

"Do what?" Eithne asked.

Michan rose, moving closer, sitting beside her.

"You must trust me, Eithne," he said. "I only do this because it is my duty to the Demon-Bound's cause that impels me to make such decisions. You do trust me, don't you?"

"Well, of course," she said. "But..."

"Take my hand," he said and offered his to her.

"Excuse me?" Eithne said, frowning.

"Please," he said.

Eithne looked at his hand. With a sigh, she laid her palm upon his.

Michan suddenly tightened his grasp around her hand. His other hand flew up and touched her forehead.

"Forgive me, but I have no choice," he said.

It was on the tip of her tongue to shout in alarm, but his touch sent a strange cooling sensation throughout her head, and he whispered words in his mage tongue. Cotton wool wrapped about her thoughts like a fog.

"Forgive me," he repeated. His voice was in her head, entwining itself like silver threads of a spider's web, softly, gently gathering all her will and her resistance until she had no thought other than those he placed there. "We must leave this place tomorrow morning, and you must come, and Rhoyd must come as well. Conor will be all right. I promise."

After that, she felt drowsy. Michan gently lowered her to the floor of the wagon and drew her cloak over her.

"All will be well, I swear," he whispered in her ear before sleep took her.

TWENTY-FIVE

Noreen led Rhoyd around the warehouse, and though Rhoyd stretched his senses carefully, he could find no sign of the demon kin or its magic. Had he been wrong? Had it been a blood mage spell after all? No, he was quite sure he had felt demon magic being invoked. He's encountered demons often enough that he knew their ilk. Their taint was as the burn of cinnamon or cloves or bile on his tongue. When he asked his Aunt Genna why, she had told him that demons—like mageborn and human—came in all shapes, sizes and varieties.

"Duff is a demon," she had told him then. "A small but highly intelligent one and I have him bound to me by his true name, just as any demon can be bound."

And Rhoyd knew that he had sensed this from the first time he met his aunt's raven familiar. For when he got around the bird, it put off the essence of cinnamon.

He wondered if it was possible to find the true name of the demon that had cast the spell. Perhaps he should go back and dig out his book on demons and see if there was anything in there to tell him how to find that true name.

"Do you sense anything, lad?" Noreen whispered in a low voice.

Rhoyd shook his head then paused. Actually, he was sensing something coming from the direction of the wagons. Magic? It was so faint that he wondered if he was just feeling the cloaking spell on Noreen's wagon.

"It's probably fled," Noreen said. "We best go back and tell the captain we cannot find it."

"Find what?"

The voice took both Noreen and Rhoyd by surprise. They turned to find Bowen standing off a short ways, his hood shadowing his face.

Noreen recovered quickly and smiled. "The captain has lost a key to his chest," she said. "We were just looking around to see if we could find it, that's all."

Bowen cocked his head. His eyes betrayed his thoughts.

He was not certain he believed her. "Well, if I see a key, I'll let you know," he said and walked away. Rhoyd flicked mage senses after the man, and to his surprise, Bowen turned and frowned over one shoulder as if to scold the lad, and then hurried on.

He felt that! Rhoyd thought.

Noreen put a hand on his shoulder, and Rhoyd gasped.

"You're jumpy as a toad," she said. "Let's go back to the wagon."

She herded him past the men who were milling around with Master Fergus. The Caravan Master's glance harbored no pity as he met Rhoyd's gaze. Rhoyd turned from those black eyes, feeling as though he were being shunned. He wished Conor were here to take the dumpling apart for his lies.

Back at the cook's wagon, Michan had resumed his Captain Camhin illusion. He was sitting on the wagon seat, staring morosely at his feet, and as the pair approached, he glanced up and frowned.

"Well?"

Noreen shook her head. "If it was a demon, it's gone now."

"Or just hiding," the captain said.

"Where's Eithne?" Rhoyd asked.

"She was exhausted from all the anger and frustration, and I can't say as I blame her. She's sleeping in the wagon now. Hope you don't mind, Noreen."

The cook shrugged.

"Is she going to be all right?" Rhoyd asked.

Camhin nodded, though he refused to look at Rhoyd at all, but locked eyes with Noreen.

"So what are we going to do about Conor?" Rhoyd asked.

The captain frowned just a little then tightened his mouth. "Leave that to me, lad," he said. "Why don't you get in the wagon and stay with Eithne? You look like you could use a good night's sleep yourself."

Rhoyd hesitated.

"Well, go on," the captain said a little more sharply. "Just because your father isn't here doesn't mean you can ignore my orders. Now get in the wagon and stay with your mother."

Rhoyd glared. He didn't like the way Camhin said that at all. But rather than argue, he crawled up into the wagon, going over the seat to enter the wagon itself.

Eithne was there, wrapped in her cloak, eyes closed.

"Eithne?" Rhoyd whispered.

She did not stir. He frowned and sank down at her side. Perhaps the captain was right. They should sleep and start anew in the morning. But it hurt him to think that poor Conor was trying to sleep in some stinky cell, all because Master Fergus had told those lies.

And why would he tell lies about Conor? I thought he liked Conor...

Puzzling indeed. Rhoyd wondered if he should tell the captain that, and tell him about Bowen knowing he was being scried. Bowen who always kept his hood over his head no matter how dull the day.

The book...

Rhoyd looked around. It had been in his satchel, and he had laid it under the wagon seat. He leaned over the board just behind the canvas curtain to look and froze.

"...I hated to do it to her that way, but it was necessary," Camhin was saying.

"Well, as long as the lad doesn't figure it out," Noreen said. "He's a clever little pup. If he learns that you are impelling Eithne to leave without Conor tomorrow morning, he might not be easy to control. There is a lot more power in him than meets the eye."

"Aye," the captain said. "He was well bred for what he is. But he is still just a child and power or not, if I have to subdue him, I will."

"So what are you going to do?"

"Well, you and I both know that to stop a mageborn, you must gag and blindfold him," Camhin said.

"That sounds like a mean thing to do, even to a lad of his years," Noreen said.

"But if it must be done, can I trust you to do it?"

Noreen sighed.

"If I must," she said. "But I'm not going to like it one bit. I've grown rather fond of the cheeky little hearth rat."

"It will be for his own good," Camhin said.

Rhoyd drew back, his heart thundering in his chest. He glanced at Eithne. *Impel?* Cautiously, he stretched mage senses and felt the whisper of a spell on her. Closing his eyes, he looked for the sigil. It was there, invisible to mortal means, but bright and shining to his inner eyes. A sigil of control. Michan had put a spell on Eithne that would allow him to control her mind.

I have to break it! I have to tell her what they are planning.
Eithne would never leave without Conor.

Rhoyd reached out with his finger when he felt a hum. The sigil was warded, and the ward had just been awakened.

There was a sudden thunder of feet on the front of the wagon. Two heads popped through the canvas.

"Don't," Camhin said, scrambling to get into the wagon.

Rhoyd rose and backed up a few steps, nearly tripping over one of the casks.

"You lied!" he said. "You don't care what happens to Conor. All you care about is that stupid box of bones."

"That box of bones could be the doom of mankind it they fall into the wrong hands," Camhin said. "Noreen, remember your promise."

Noreen sighed. "Come here, lad," she said and held out her hand.

"No!" Rhoyd snapped. "I won't let you gag me and bind me like some dog!"

With that, he turned and fled for the back of the wagon. He felt the captain pulling essence to cast a spell, but before it could be used, Rhoyd turned and hissed, *"Adhar buail!"* The air hardened into a fist, striking both Noreen and the captain, knocking them back through the front of the wagon. Outside, men shouted in surprise.

Rhoyd leapt out the back and dashed for the opening. Night was falling, and shadows were everywhere as he sprinted out of the warehouse and into the street. Behind him, he heard Captain Camhin shouting for men to go after Rhoyd and for Rhoyd to come back now. He ignored their shouts and the orders, ducking into one of the alleyways and running down the length of it. Somewhere around here, he knew the watchtower stood.

If he could just reach Conor before they caught him, then Conor would know what to do.

But to find that tower, he was going to have to use mage senses, and that would probably give him away. Still, he had to try. How else was he going to find Conor?

He ducked around the end of a shed that leaned precariously against the back wall of the stable next to the warehouse. Crouching, he took deep breaths to calm his own excitement. He knew Conor's aura well, and even here in a city full of men, that bronze warmth shone to Rhoyd like a beacon. The watchtower was apparently somewhere close by, because Conor's essence was strong.

Quietly, Rhoyd slipped out of his hiding place. There were torches here and there, and pools of shadow in between. He skirted the stables, heading away from the warehouse and towards the inn. Following the wall brought him to a small courtyard behind the inn. He would have to cross that, and he could see a gate sitting open on the other side. Quickly, Rhoyd sprinted across the cobble, trying not to make any sound. He reached the far side unchallenged, stopping near the open gate. Peering out, he could see an alley and at the end of that, a street. Stretching mage senses once more, he determined that the watchtower was on that street just down a short ways. Good. He took a deep breath and stepped through the gate.

"Rhoyd, where are you going?"

Rhoyd gasped and spun towards the sound. In his eagerness to head for the street, he had failed to check the other end of the alley. Someone in a cloak stood there, face hidden in shadows. But the eyes glowed like twin embers.

Rhoyd blinked. *He's a demon!*

"Who are you?" Rhoyd asked.

"That does not matter," the demon replied. "You really are all that Fenelon said you would be."

Rhoyd frowned. "How do you know my Uncle?"

"Oh, he and I go back a long ways," the demon said. "You could say we're very old friends."

Rhoyd took a few steps back. "You're a demon," he said. "My uncle would never have anything to do with a demon."

The demon chuckled. "I've been called worse things, I can assure you," he said. "Now, what shall we do? Go back peacefully, or must I take you by force?"

Rhoyd took another step. *Flee!* he thought. *Head for the street and shout for help.*

"Come on, Rhoyd, I have your best interests in heart, as does Michan," the demon said. "So let's not dally any longer. Come back to the wagons. You'll be safer there."

Rhoyd froze. "Michan? You know who he is?"

"With these eyes," the demon said, "there are no illusions that I cannot see through. Now come along."

"No!" Rhoyd said. "I have to save Conor, and I know what you did."

"What I did?" The demon sighed. "And just what did I do?"

"You killed Warden," Rhoyd said. "You put him in that barrel and made it look like Conor had done it."

"And why would I kill Warden? I needed him. His death has been rather costly to me. Now enough of this nonsense, lad. Come back with me and we will discuss this in a safer place."

The demon reached for Rhoyd, and the taste of cloves and cinnamon filled Rhoyd's mouth. He glanced up into the hood and spied familiar features. *Bowen?* It looked like Bowen, but with all the shadows it was hard to really tell. Demon essence burned in the man. There was no way Rhoyd was going to go back now. Not without Conor.

"Solus!" he shouted suddenly, jerking essence from the torches around the street. Brilliant light swelled in his hands, and just as the demon reached for him, Rhoyd shoved it into the demon's eyes and shouted, *"Solus feith!"*

The bright light stuck to the demon like phosphor. He shouted, "Damn, you, do you realize what you have done?" while staggering back, blinded by the light. As he fell away, Rhoyd dashed for the street, eager to get into a more populated area. He glanced back over his shoulder in time to see the demon crouching and shaking his head and snarling like a beast. His form had shifted into some amalgamation of a man and a large bat. He suddenly leapt into the air, his cloak furling around him and spreading like wings, he headed off into the sky.

At the sight of that, Rhoyd doubled his own speed. *Horns, he can fly!* As much as Rhoyd wanted to admire that skill, he wanted to escape even more, so he ran into the street and barreled across into a tavern. His abrupt entrance brought a number of heads snapping around to see what the intrusion was. But he did not stop for them. Instead, he continued to rush across the tavern, ducking among the customers, racing for the kitchen.

"No children!" the barkeep shouted. "Get out of here! Hey!"

Rhoyd ignored the man and sprinted out into an alley in the back of the tavern. There, he ducked down under the eaves of a shed in the shadows. *"See me not,"* he whispered and drew the shadows about him like a cloak. There he huddled, staring at the sky, wondering where the demon had gone. If his heart would just stop pounding in his ribs, he might be able to think.

Shadows are his realm, Rhoyd thought. He would have been safer in the light, but he didn't dare crawl out of the shadows just yet. Not until he could stop himself from shaking.

But at length, the trembling stopped. He saw no sign that the demon had tracked him into and out of the tavern. *But how could he if I blinded his demon sight?*

He wished he had that demon book with him now. If that demon had a true name, Rhoyd needed to find it. Because if he was what that book said he was, Rhoyd was going to need more than light spells to assist him.

Carefully, Rhoyd rose, following the wall. No more mage senses, he told himself. That was probably how the demon had found him. Demons could probably sense his magic as surely as mageborn like Michan. So Rhoyd needed to find his way to the tower without magic.

He slipped out of the alley, looking all directions and made for the watchtower

Clever little lad, his internal companion said.

Too clever for his own good, if you ask me. Horns, I didn't expect him to do that. I wonder if he guessed who I was?

Can't say, and anyway, you just underestimated him, that's all.

Tell me about it. The Demon-Bound sighed. Senses stretched to test the wind and the night, he could not figure out where the boy was, but he had a feeling he knew where the lad was going.

To rescue his father, of course, his companion said unbidden.

Aye and I fear he may be in for a disappointment. There are many guards on duty tonight. The lad is apt to get hurt.

Since when would that have stopped you?

The Demon-Bound sighed again. It would not, he knew.

I can't let him do this alone.

Now there's the spirit, his internal companion said and chuckled, a deep thrum that raced through his nerve endings, for he no longer had his own countenance. *What shall we do?*

To the watchtower, he said and shifted the wings that had

sprung into being so that he could sail towards the place. *You do remember that sleep spell of yours, I hope.*

Why of course, his companion replied.

Good. I have a feeling it will come in handy this night.

TWENTY-SIX

Conor's knee was killing him, and he wondered if his shoulder was cracked or just out of socket. He had watched the light creeping away as the sun slid down over the horizon. At least they had given him a cell with a small window so he could tell the time of day and get air. This place smelled rotten, and that was making him ill.

Since sundown, he had started to feel things, oddly magical in some respect. And his tongue kept giving him the impression he had been sucking on a clove. In some ways, it reminded him vaguely of something he had felt back during the Last War. As to what...his head was too fuzzy with pain to care, let alone remember.

Horns, Conor wished they would let Eithne come see him. He could have stood all the smells and the strange hints of magic better had she been allowed to heal him. But he had heard her shouting from the guardroom, and knew when the noise fell away that they had ordered her out.

Just don't do anything foolish, woman, he thought.

He tried to make himself as comfortable as possible on the stone shelf that served as a cot. At least they had let him keep his plaidie. He waded one part of it for a pillow and closed his eyes...

...And opened them again when he heard Rhoyd whisper, "Conor? Conor? Are you alive?"

"Alive," Conor replied, "But I must be dreaming because I think I hear my lad calling me."

He opened his eyes and turned his head. A small figure stood clutching the bars of the cell, peering through the tiny opening high on the wooden door. How he had managed to get that high was beyond reasoning. Conor sat up and groaned when pain reminded him that he was not a well man.

"Rhoyd?" he wheezed through gritted teeth. "What are ye doing here, lad?"

"I've come to rescue you," Rhoyd said as matter-of-factly as a lad his age could.

His face disappeared from the opening as he dropped to the ground and landed with a thump. Conor felt the tingle of more familiar magic as the lad whispered spell words. Within moments, the lock on the door clattered, the bolt was thrown back and the door opened. Rhoyd rushed in, stumbling over the uneven ground, practically throwing himself into Conor's arms.

"Easy, lad, I'm not all that whole at the moment,"

"Sorry," Rhoyd said, hiding his face in Conor's plaidie. "I...I..."

"Does Eithne know you're here?" Conor asked.

"She's a sleep, Conor," Rhoyd whispered, pulling back. "Michan put her under a spell so she would not fight him. He's planning to leave in the morning, and he said I had to go with him. But I don't want to go with him; I want to stay with you."

"Well, lad, I won't say that I am not entirely grateful for that, but I cannot just leave this place."

"Yes you can," Rhoyd said, pulling back and tugging Conor's arm. "The guards are all asleep. We can leave and no one will be the wiser. We'll go back to the warehouse and get Eithne and the horses, and we'll just leave."

"And I will be a wanted man the rest of my life," Conor said. "Is that how you want me?"

"I want you alive," Rhoyd said fiercely. "Eithne wants you alive. And the only way we are going to live is if we escape now. Otherwise, Michan will make us leave and that demon Bowen will kill me and take the bones, and all will be lost..."

"Whoa...Bowen is a demon? What are ye saying, lad?"

"Not here," Rhoyd said. "Come on, please."

Rhoyd would not stop tugging. *Persistent as a terrier,* Conor mused and eased himself to his feet. Horns, he felt ancient, and walking was a chore, but Rhoyd planted himself at Conor's side and tried to support him. Together, they half-staggered, half walked up the hall to the outer door. Rhoyd left Conor at the foot of the steps long enough to check and make sure all was still clear, then rushed back down and helped Conor to make the climb.

In the main room, men were slumped in their chairs. A group that had been playing High Ladies snoozed in the middle of their winnings. A strong hint of magic filled the place. Oddly, it felt nothing like Rhoyd's magic.

"Did ye do all this?" Conor whispered so as not to awaken them.

Rhoyd shook his head. "They were this way when I got here. The demon must have done it. It reeks of his magic."

The demon? Why would the demon do this? Conor thought.

Rhoyd left Conor to lean on the Sergeant of the Watch's desk. The Sergeant was lounging back in his chair, snoring like a drunken lord. When Rhoyd came back, he had Conor's weapons, including the dagger that had condemned him. Conor took it and looked at it, frowning. *I shall find a deep river for this piece,* he thought. Then again, why waste good steel? He shoved it into his belt and let Rhoyd assist him to the door.

Once they were outside, Rhoyd started them towards the inn that was near the warehouse. Horns, but it was good to be outside, but Conor caught himself looking over his shoulders, expecting men to come for him at any moment.

At the inn, they stopped in the shadows, and Conor could not help but notice how Rhoyd kept glancing at the sky.

"We need a plan," Rhoyd said.

"Do we now?" Conor said and rubbed the bridge of his nose. "Why?"

"We need a distraction. So I can run in and fetch Eithne and the horses and..."

Conor sat down on the nearest bench, his stomach clenching as pain assailed him. He took a deep breath to steel himself and looked sternly at the lad.

"Ye will do no such thing," Conor said.

Rhoyd frowned. "But..."

"Ye will go back and apologize to Michan for running away. And ye need to tell him about Bowen being a demon. Now here's the plan. When ye leave tomorrow, I will be waiting outside the gates. Ye ride Battlebrute, and I'll whistle for him, and he'll come to where I am."

"But..."

"Look, lad. It won't do ye any good to be running away now. I need Eithne's healing if I am to survive, but I'll not put you at risk just to have it. Now do as I say. Go back to the warehouse. I will get out of this city somehow."

"No you won't," Rhoyd said almost tearfully. "You're too weak to get out on your own. They'll catch you before you get to the gate."

Conor shook his head. "Cloak me in yer shadow spell, lad. I'll get out of the city and wait in the farm lanes."

"But what if you die out there?"

"I won't die," Conor said. "I've had worse in the war. But it will do neither of us any good to be here when those watch men awaken and find me gone. So you must go back and pretend to know nothing, and I will get over the wall somehow. Like as not, there's a postern on the outer gate that leads into the moat. Besides, if Eithne is bespelled, she's going to need you to break the spell, isn't she? Better we're all outside Cullstane if we're going to leave the caravan."

Rhoyd took a deep breath, looking at the ground. Then slowly, his eyes rose.

"You better be out there," he said firmly.

"You have my word on it, lad," Conor said and smiled. He pulled the lad close and kissed his forehead, then stood him back. "Now, cloak me and go."

Rhoyd nodded. Conor felt the whisper of magic chilling his skin as the lad said, *Bi ann sgaith,"* then stepped back.

"Be careful," Rhoyd whispered.

Then he turned and sprinted away.

Conor leaned against the wall. He waited until his head stopped spinning, then pulling the long end of his plaidie over his head like a cloak, he slowly crawled to his feet and limped across the street, making for the outer gates and hoping the lad's spell worked.

There were still folk out on the streets, and none of them seemed to see him as he stumbled past them. He made it all the way to the gates unchallenged, and even passed a small walking party of watchmen who did not even look his way. So the lad's spell was working. Good.

Alas, the gates themselves were barred. The portcullis had been dropped and the postern door was well guarded. So there would be no escaping that route.

Maybe he should have let the lad have his way.

No, 'tis bad enough I am free. When the watch find me gone, they will check every wagon of the caravan before they will let it out.

He was willing to bet Michan would birth badgers when they demanded to look into the dark carriage.

Conor sat down on a bench in front of a gate tavern full of laughter. His stomach growled in protest. He had not been given a proper supper. Tempting as it was to use coin to buy a bit of bread and ale, he knew that the spell would be broken by such actions. So he levered himself off the bench and sought another way.

There were stairs climbing the inner walls. Not all sections had guards, he noted. In fact, they were stretched thinner than he thought proper for such a long wall.

'Twill be to my advantage, though. With fewer men guarding the wall, it meant more places to climb over and out.

He selected a particularly shadowy section near one of the middle turrets. Carefully, he climbed the stairs, always aware that if he were spotted—even cloaked in shadows as he was—there would be a hue and cry. But he reached the top without a challenge and crossed the broad expanse of stone to peer between crenels.

The drop was perhaps three times Conor's height, but from the foot of the wall, there was another deeper drop into the dry moat. If he landed wrong, he would end up breaking his neck. He leaned and studied the stones. This wall was old, and showed signs of damage from when the Hound swept his army of barbarians and monsters through these northern kingdoms. This one had managed to stand, though he knew the city had been ransacked and overrun for a time with Haxons.

He would have to try and climb down, rather than risk an uncertain jump. He carefully inched into the space between the merlons, looked left and right to make certain no guards were visible, then turned around and sought holds for his toes. The crenellations were slanted part way to make it easier for a defending soldier to roll rocks on an invader's head. He hoped he did not slip.

As he lowered himself and sought footholds in the cracks of the stone, he quickly discovered that having a leg in pain was detrimental to any manner of gracefully scaling the wall.

I've no choice, he thought. Gritting his teeth, he started to wish he had brought a rope. He could have rappelled down more easily.

He was no more than a hand's reach from the end of the slanted crenellations, when his bad leg gave out. Conor grunted, grappling for a hold, trying to haul himself back up in vain. He was tired, and he was hurt, and he was hungry, and all those worked to weaken even a strong man like himself.

His scrabbling loosened bits of the wall underfoot, and his handholds crumbled as well. He could not stop himself from sliding backwards down the sluice.

He went airborne, dropping like a stone...until something snagged him from behind.

"Hang on," a voice said.

Conor turned his head and nearly screamed.

It was not a human face that smiled at him, but one that had taken some features of a handsome young man and mixed them with the features of a bat. The thing had wings and claws, and it was bearing him upward. The burn of cinnamon and cloves filled Conor's mouth.

Demon!

He did what any strong man would do.

He fought.

"Stop that! You'll make me drop you." The creature was flying away from the wall, rising higher than the tallest towers. Conor continued to fight, kicking with his good leg, twisting wildly.

"Let go of me, monster!" he shouted.

"Well, I like that," the creature said. "I'm only trying to help you. Otherwise you would have broken your neck."

But Conor was angry and frightened, and beyond hearing what those words actually meant. He reached into his belt and drew forth the dagger resting there. And turning, he tried to slash at the monster's head.

"Hey! Stop that!" the creature shouted, swinging around and flying rapidly towards the ground.

Conor would not stop. He was determined to break free.

"Very well, if you're going to be that way about it..."

The creature let go, and Conor started to fall. A howl of terror broke from his lungs, only to be cut short when he landed in a large pile of hay. He struggled and flipped, in spite of his pain, and spilled himself to the ground, blade still in hand, seeking his attacker.

All he heard was laughter, and in the moonlight, he could barely make out the silhouette of a form winging back towards Cullstane.

Horns. He sat down where he stood, nursing every pain and glanced about.

He was in a field just on the road.

Good, then he could wait here for the caravan. He just

hoped that Rhoyd would live up to his promise and tell Michan about the demon.

With a sigh, Conor burrowed back into the hay to settle in. He might as well make the best of it and sleep. This bed was certainly softer and sweeter smelling than the one in the cell.

Conor sighed. He would never be able to work a caravan on this route again. Accused of murder, he would be hunted in Elenthorn. He could always take his family into the highlands of Keltora and stay, but he rankled to think he was accused of a crime he had not committed. He almost wished he had killed Warden. Then at least he could have taken his punishment like a man.

No use fretting about it now, Manahan. Sleep. Get your strength back for tomorrow.

And just as he wrapped himself in his plaidie and lay down, the thoughts slipped into his head.

Why had the demon been trying to help him?

Why did it not let him fall to his death?

TWENTY-SEVEN

Going back was the hardest thing Rhoyd had ever had to do. In spite of knowing that Conor was right and that there was Eithne to think about, Rhoyd was reluctant to return at all. The captain's orders that he be gagged and bound were still floating in his head. And now that he suspected Bowen was really a demon...

...Or that a demon was pretending to be someone named Bowen. It occurred to him to wonder why he had never sensed demon taint on the man before.

But he had sensed a demon this day, both at the warehouse and in the alley. Something foul and fetid had accompanied the spell that shied the horses and broke the barrel.

How could Bowen have hidden such a strong essence?

Had it been Bowen at all?

Rhoyd frowned. He hated it when his head started running in circles. He wanted to go back and find Conor. He wanted to help Eithne. He wanted to leave the caravan.

The warehouse was lit up with a multitude of lanterns. Rhoyd crept up to the entrance and cautiously peered through one of the gaps in the wall. Captain Camhin was holding court.

"One small boy and you could not find him?" he said. "He can't have gone far."

"We looked all around the warehouse and the inn," Creed said.

Master Fergus glowered. "Did any of you think to check the watch tower?" he asked. "I'll wager the lad has gone there to try and free his murderous father."

Captain Camhin rounded on Fergus. "Conor Manahan is an honest and an innocent man, and if you open your mouth one more time, you will be looking for other employment. Do I make myself clear?"

There were grumbles from the ranks. Some of the men were clearly loyal to Master Fergus, old hands who had worked with him for many years, and they shifted and glowered at the captain with the looks of curs backing reluctantly down from a wolf with a bone they coveted.

"The boy is in danger," Captain Camhin said. "I have no doubt of that. Now I want him found as quickly as possible. Search in shifts if you must, but find him."

"I don't think you'll have to look far," Rhoyd said and stepped into the opening. He clasped his hands behind him to hide the fact that he was afraid.

Heads whipped around. Master Fergus frowned. Captain Camhin started to speak, but it was Noreen who came over and knelt before Rhoyd, showing concern.

"Here, lad, you gave us quite a fright," she said.

"Are you going to bind me and gag me?" he asked, fighting the tremble of his lower lip, not wanting her to think he was a coward.

Noreen leaned closer, "On my heart's blood, lad, I would never had done so," she said softly. "I'm not fond of that order, no matter who it came from."

Rhoyd swallowed. "I'm sorry," he said. "But I had to."

"Where have you been hiding?" the captain interrupted, coming over to join them.

"Behind the tavern," Rhoyd said. "I had to. The demon was after me and..."

"Demon?" Camhin drew closer, glancing over one shoulder. "You saw a demon?"

Rhoyd nodded. "And I think I know who the demon is," he said.

The captain glanced over the milling crowd of men, then back at Rhoyd. "Who, lad?" he asked softly. "Who is the demon?"

"I think it's that fellow Bowen," Rhoyd said and shot a look over the men who were reluctantly returning to their chores.

"That's absurd," Camhin said. "You might as well accuse me or Master Fergus."

Rhoyd frowned back. "But it looked like Bowen when it came after me in the alley near the inn," he said. "He attacked me, and I drove him off with a light spell, and he grew wings and he flew."

The captain was silent. "He grew wings?" he asked.

Rhoyd nodded again.

"And you're certain it was Bowen?"

At that, Rhoyd frowned. Now that he considered it, the face in the hood was nearly invisible even to mage eyes, as though the demon wore shadows on its face. "I think it was Bowen," Rhoyd said. "But...I didn't see his face fully. But I know it was him...it had to be him."

Camhin took a deep breath. "Look, Rhoyd, I cannot just accuse Bowen of being a demon any more than I can allow Master Fergus to keep saying that Conor is a murderer."

"Conor didn't kill that man."

"I know," the captain said softly. "I scried the body when I was able to, and there was no essence left in his flesh. His life had been torn from him, but not in the manner of blood magic. And there was no blood in the flour. Had Warden been stabbed in the back, even if he was not killed in the barrel, there should have been some blood mixed into the flour, but there was none. In fact, I doubt the blood that was on the ground when he disappeared was even his."

Rhoyd squinted. "Demons feed on blood, flesh and life essence," he said, remembering something he had read in the book.

"Exactly. Though sometimes they will feed on the blood and essence and leave the body whole. There was a black corruption around the wound in Warden's back. I saw it myself. That sort of corruption is seen when demons kill with their poisonous barbs. My guess is that the demon killed Warden and put him in the barrel to condemn Conor."

"Then why didn't you tell the watch men that?" Rhoyd flinched back, but before he could do anything else, Noreen caught his arm. He started to jerk away, but she merely cooed to him like a mother would, so he stopped struggling and glared at the captain once more.

"Because who is going to believe me, Rhoyd? Unless I reveal myself for who I really am, no one is going to accept that I know it was a demon that killed Warden."

"You would leave Conor to rot in that cell," Rhoyd said.

The captain shook his head. "I have already sent a missive to the Mageborn Councilor of the King of Elenthorn," he said. "A man will be here tomorrow to plea for Conor's release and pardon on the King's command."

Rhoyd bit his lip. *Oh, no!* he thought.

"What's the matter, lad?" the captain asked.

"Conor is not in the watch tower," Rhoyd said hesitantly.

"What?"

"I...got him out?"

"You what? How?"

"It was easy, actually," Rhoyd said. "All the men were asleep under a demon spell and I just walked in and got him out." *Might as well tell him all,* Rhoyd thought. "He's going to be waiting for us outside the wall when we leave."

"What?" The captain's face nearly shifted as his illusion faltered. He covered his face with his hands. "Well, that's a fine mess. My plan was to get him out tomorrow after we left and have him brought to us on the road by a spell gate. That way, no one could accuse us of having a part in his release."

"Conor hates spell gates," Rhoyd said. "He says they make him itch."

"Yes, I know," Camhin said. "The point is, now that he has escaped, we will not be able to convince them that he is innocent."

"We can if you tell them a demon killed Warden," Rhoyd said.

"They will need proof that I cannot give them," Camhin said.

Rhoyd opened his mouth to say that there was proof, when he spotted a shadowy figure not far away.

"Proof of what?"

It was Master Fergus who stood among the shadows. The captain rose suddenly and turned, reaching for his sword. Noreen rose as well, pulling Rhoyd behind her to protect him. He had to twist around her to see what was happening.

"Rhoyd seems to believe that a demon may have killed Warden," Camhin said, recovering his composure.

"Demons don't use knives," Master Fergus said and cocked his head to look sternly at Rhoyd.

"The demon stole the knife," Rhoyd said. "That was what I felt in camp the night the boars attacked. I knew that someone had invaded our camp, but at the time, I was thinking human. But now I realize that what I felt was the essence of a demon."

"And just where is this demon supposed to be hiding?" Fergus said.

"That is what we need to find out," Camhin said.

"We already know," Rhoyd said, and Fergus glared at him.

"No, we only have our suspicions," Captain Camhin insisted, giving Rhoyd a hard look that said, *"Shut your mouth!"*

"Really?" Fergus said. "Just who do you suspect?"

"I think it was Bowen," Rhoyd said before either Noreen or the captain could stop him.

"Aye, well," Fergus agreed. "There is something strange about that one, I'll wager. So why not ask him if he is a demon?"

Camhin closed his eyes. "Very well," he said. "And if he denies it, what then?"

Master Fergus shrugged. "We leave in the morning as planned, and the murderer will meet the axe man when the Baron of Cullstane returns from his hunt."

Rhoyd frowned. "Conor is innocent," he said.

"I've heard you singing that tune all night," Fergus said. "Find another. Let's go find this chap Bowen."

They did find Bowen. He was asleep under one of the wagons, and being awakened, he grumbled about not being allowed a decent sleep before he took dark watch. He looked up at those who surrounded him and smiled. Rhoyd squinted hard at Bowen's face, trying to imagine it with glowing eyes, but something about the features were different.

"A welcome committee?" Bowen said and yawned. "Is it dark watch already?"

"We would ask you a question," Fergus said in a tired voice.

Bowen shrugged.

"Are you a demon?" Master Fergus asked.

Laughter bubbled from Bowen's chest. "What?" he said.

"Are you a demon?" Master Fergus repeated. "The boy here seems to think that you are."

Bowen sighed and looked sharply at Rhoyd. "I suppose a lad who has lost his father will tell all manner of tales in hope of freeing the man," Bowen said. "Very well, is there some test for demons? Give it to me and then let me go back to sleep. I have the dark watch."

Rhoyd took a deep breath and stepped forward. He stared into Bowen's icy blue eyes. They had a depth to them, but no hint of magic or fire. Unconvinced, Rhoyd called a ball of white light into his hands. He thrust it towards Bowen who shaded his eyes.

"What am I supposed to do with that?" he asked.

"Take it," Rhoyd said.

Bowen looked puzzled, but he sighed and stretched his hands. As soon as the white ball of light came to rest on his palms, it faded.

Rhoyd could not believe his eyes.

"That's not possible," he whispered. "You stopped me in the alley. Your eyes glowed. I stuck white light in your face, and you howled and turned into a demon and flew away and..."

Bowen started laughing again, and the noise echoed with exhaustion.

"I'm sorry, lad," he said. "I think you'll have to look elsewhere for your demon."

"But..." Rhoyd's words died on his lips. He stretched mage senses, determined to scry Bowen to the depth of his soul, but there was nothing, not even a hint of demon essence. Only the bronze essence of a man. Rhoyd's throat tightened. How could he have been mistaken? *I saw him! He looked just like Bowen!*

Bowen must have seen the distress displayed on Rhoyd's face. His own expression softened into a smile of sympathy. "Look lad, I understand you being upset about losing your da. Personally, I don't think he killed Warden, but who am I to say anything?"

"I've seen enough," Fergus said and stalked away.

Noreen put a reassuring hand on Rhoyd's shoulder. "Come on, lad," she said. "Let's go back to the wagon. You need to rest."

Rhoyd pulled out from under her grasp and rushed back to the wagon on his own.

How could it be? He had seen the demon. He had seen it wearing Bowen's cloak.

But Bowen didn't have a hint of demon to him. At least none that Rhoyd could feel now.

Rhoyd crawled into the wagon. Eithne was still there, peacefully slumbering. He wanted to awaken her, to make her hold him so he could vent all his sorrow.

I've made a mess of everything!

He laid down next to her, tugging a blanket over him, fighting tears.

How could I be wrong about this? How could Bowen not be the demon? Now Conor will be a hunted man, and it will be my fault because I took him out of the watchtower.

He just wished Michan had said something sooner.

But how could he when I ran away?

Rhoyd pressed closer to Eithne, listening to the rhythm of

her heart and closed his eyes.

That was close.

Too close.

Do you think he will give up on you now?

No, I think he will try all the harder to prove who I am beneath this guise.

Perhaps you should tell him in private.

And risk having the Other know I am here? Not likely. Besides, considering how he reacted back there in the alleyway, I don't think he would take kindly to my "human" form trying to lure him away from the others now. I will just have to be careful. Fortunately, because I knew he would scry me as he did, I took precautions and used the essence of his own father that I borrowed when I rescued him to shield me.

That will fade.

I won't need it after tonight, I suspect.

What are you planning to do?

What I have planned to do all along. Get those bones to Caer Keltora before the Other can steal them and give them to his master.

Just wondering.

TWENTY-EIGHT

Eithne awoke from a dream where she stood on the edge of a field near the caravan and watched as Conor valiantly fought two boars. He managed to kill one, but the other...it struck him like a thief, tusks tearing into his back. Conor fell, and the maddened boar trampled and pummeled and ripped at him until there was nothing left but tatters of flesh and bone.

She opened her eyes and felt tears pushing behind them. Confusion grasped her mind. There was warmth at her side, pressing against her like a frightened child. She turned her head and saw the black tangle of unruly hair that always seemed to have a mind of its own.

Rhoyd?

Eithne sighed. "Poor lamb," she whispered. "You miss him as much as I do."

Carefully she sat up so as not to disturb him. He shifted and muttered in his sleep and grew still. She resisted the urge to bush his hair out of his eyes.

He needs his sleep, she thought and glanced around. They were inside the cook's wagon, though there was no sign of the large woman. *Mistress Noreen has done us a kindness, allowing us to sleep in her wagon in this time of mourning. I shall have to remember to thank her for her hospitality.*

Crawling away from the pallet, Eithne pushed aside the canvas covering the rear of the wagon. The hour was still quite early, and she realized that she had slept like the dead. Lanterns and the grey light of predawn softened the sharper edges of wood and revealed the shapes of men slumbering in pallets under and around the wagons.

She vaguely remembered that Michan had said something about leaving early, so she looked around for a source of water and a small fire to heat it with. And settled on setting one of the lanterns into a cleared spot and dangling the small kettle over it. She watched as the tiny pills of bubbles formed in the bottom and slowly released, and when the water boiled hard enough, she sprinkled it with tea and herbs, steeping them and pouring them into her mug, then squatting on her heels and warming her hands around the glazed clay.

Life is going to be so different now. She took a sip of the tea, holding it in her mouth to savor the flavor before swallowing. *But Michan is right. We must leave the past behind. It serves no purpose to carry the dead with you, for they only make the burden of grief heavier to bear. Rhoyd and I shall go with Michan to Dun Gealach. Conor would have wished it so. I shall offer my services as a True Healer to one of the temples in Caer Keltora, and Rhoyd shall have the opportunity to live among and be with mageborn who will protect him and teach him the ways of magic.*

A twinge assailed her, as though she had sat in one place too long. How could she think such a thing, to desert Conor to death and Rhoyd to strangers? Why Conor would never have given his consent. *We swore to never allow Rhoyd to be taken from us, and we will not...*

But then silvery warmth fogged her thoughts. Her hands were shaking. She nearly spilled her tea, and had to tighten her grasp on the mug just to keep it from falling.

How can Conor approve or disapprove? she thought with a frown. *He is dead, killed by boars three nights ago.*

Tears formed in the corner of her eyes. She would always miss him. How could she not miss the man she had given her heart to all those years ago when the gods had been so cruel as to take him from her?

She shook herself out of the misery. There was much to do before they left this morning. Besides, she had to be strong for Rhoyd's sake. She could not let him see her weep, as it would make him weep as well.

Eithne took a deep breath and sipped her tea and stared at the flame inside the lantern, trying to burn her thoughts away with the flame.

The shift of the wagon stirred Rhoyd from deep sleep. He opened his eyes and stared about him in confusion. He was inside a wagon, coiled into blankets that smelled of herbs and of Eithne. *There is something I have forgotten,* he thought as he slowly rose to a keener awareness. *But what?*

He sat up, shoving his hair out of his eyes and stared at the space beside him where Eithne had been lying. She was in the habit of rising early, he knew, but having her gone sent panic surging through him. What was it he was going to tell her?

Oh, yes. That he had helped Conor escape, and that they would find Conor outside the gates, and once she healed him, they were leaving.

Rhoyd threw off the blankets and scrambled towards the back end of the wagon. He pushed aside the canvas and looked out. Some of the men were rising to take care of feeding horses and getting them hitched. Others still slumbered. Rhoyd dropped to the ground and looked around, carefully stretching mage senses.

He found the warm silver of Eithne's essence close by and hurried towards the source. She was over by one of the windows, crouched close to a lantern, staring at the fire within it as she clutched her tea mug.

"Eithne," Rhoyd called and bolted across the warehouse.

She looked up when he stopped beside her, and such sorrow filled her eyes. But at the sight of him, she managed to smile. She patted the ground beside her, and he sat down. She slid her arm across his shoulders and pressed lips to his cheek.

"Morning, my lamb," she said.

"Are you all right?" Rhoyd asked worriedly. She didn't look all right.

"I'm fine," she said and pushed a hand fondly through his hair the way Conor always did. "We'll both be fine," she said. "We have each other, and that is all that matters."

Rhoyd frowned against his will. "And Conor," he said.

Eithne looked away. "We will always remember him," she said.

"But we can't forget him," Rhoyd said and lowered his voice as he leaned closer. "I mean, he's hurt. When I got him out of that watch tower, he was injured, so you're going to have to heal him when we get out of Cullstane..."

His words faltered as he watched her turn back, horror in her eyes.

"Eithne?" he said.

"Oh, Rhoyd, please don't do this. I want him back as much as you do, but we cannot change what has happened. Conor is dead, and we must accept that."

For a fleeting moment, he feared that something had happened in the night. That maybe she had found out that

Conor escaped. That he had fallen to his death or been killed by the watchmen while trying to get out of Cullstane.

"But he was alive last night when I left him," Rhoyd said. "He said he would wait for us outside the gate and…"

She put a hand to his lips to still his tirade.

"Oh, my poor lamb," she said. "You must have been having a dream. Conor died three nights ago. Remember the boars that attacked us? They killed him."

"No they didn't," Rhoyd said, and he jerked back when she tried to pull him close. "Conor is alive. He's waiting out in the fields beyond the walls. You'll see. I helped him to get out of the tower. He said he would be there. You have to heal him."

"Now, Rhoyd, you must not say such things, or you'll just find it harder to let go of him. Conor is dead, and you must accept that."

"Conor is not dead!" Rhoyd said and rose abruptly. "What is wrong with you? He's alive. These men tried to accuse him of murder. The watch took him to their tower, and I got him out and…"

He realized that her expression was one of great confusion. She touched her own forehead as though something pricked her there.

The glyph! Michan's spell!

Was that what Michan had done to her? Taken her memories of Conor's imprisonment away? Made her believe that he was dead?

Anger filled Rhoyd. How dare Michan do that to Eithne?

"Rhoyd," she said as she stood up and reached for him.

He pulled away before she could take hold of him and turned towards the dark carriage. Reason fled as he glared at the wagon. Snarling under his breath, he marched towards the dark carriage, stopping just a few meters away. Jerking essence from around him, he thrust a hand at the wagon and shouted, *"Adhar buail!"* He did not care who heard him now, so long as Michan did.

The dark carriage rocked as though hit by a trebuchet stone. From inside, Rhoyd hear a startled squawk.

There were shouts all around. Furiously, Rhoyd cast his spell again and again. With each blow the wagon rocked until it was lifted off two wheels, only to drop again.

"Rhoyd, stop!" Eithne rushed over to his side.

"Here now!" Noreen shouted and came at Rhoyd from another direction.

Suddenly there were men all around him. Rhoyd ignored them, casting the spell of air striking again and again, until Noreen was forced to grab him.

"Don't hurt him," Eithne cried.

Rhoyd howled and struggled in Noreen's grasp. Even with her holding him, he was screaming the spell words and making the wagon rock. He was determined to knock it over, or at least knock Michan out for what he had done to Eithne.

"Hit him!" Master Fergus ordered. "Knock the little beggar out!"

"Are you insane?" Eithne cried.

"Then do something to make him stop!"

"CEASE!" Captain Camhin's roar had an effect on everyone including Rhoyd. Like a chaotic frieze, they all stopped where they stood. The captain was hanging out of the dark carriage's door, looking disheveled and none too pleased.

"What in the name of Cernunnos are you doing?" the captain snapped as he glared at Rhoyd.

"You took him from her!" Rhoyd shouted and pointed to Eithne who was sobbing. "You made her forget him! She thinks he's dead! He's not dead!"

Briefly, the captain stopped, but his glare quickly returned. He pointed to Rhoyd. "Inside...now!"

"Sir?" Noreen said.

"Take care of her," Camhin ordered. "Fergus get these lazy bastards on their feet and this caravan had better be ready to move when I come out. Do I make myself clear?"

"As ice," Master Fergus muttered with a sneer.

"Then do it!" the captain shouted. "Rhoyd!"

Rhoyd almost fell as Noreen propelled him towards the dark wagon and occupied herself with leading Eithne away. As he stepped close to it, he felt the strange whispers of Michan's spells.

"Stop dragging your feet!" Camhin said.

Rhoyd picked up the pace, trotting over to the dark carriage. He had hardly reached for the door when the captain seized him by the scruff like an impudent pup and dragged him in, forcing him to sit down on the chest that centered the interior.

For a moment, Rhoyd looked around in awe. There were marks of power everywhere, and all of them tied to light. He could feel the magic, layer upon layer, and for a moment, he forgot his anger at Michan. The box beneath him thrummed with an alien power, and his tongue was sweet with the burn of cinnamon. Demon bones. They really were demon bones. He brushed the carved surface of the chest with one hand, marveling at the work.

The slamming and bolting of the door brought his dilemma back into sharp focus. He looked up as Michan's illusion fell away. The mageborn picked up a stool and set it so he could sit and face Rhoyd.

"Give me one good reason why I should not give you a sound thrashing," Michan said. "You have deliberately jeopardized this cargo with your antics just now, not to mention nearly given away who I am. Had you cracked these walls, you would have broken the protections I took so long to work into them and let the dark ones know where the bones were."

"Because Conor would turn you inside out," Rhoyd said plainly, though he twitched just a bit because he was not certain that Conor would not have thrashed him for what he had done.

"Oh, I have no doubt that Conor would do just that," Michan said and crossed his arms. "Friends we may be, but he clearly loves you above all else, which is why I cannot understand this behavior of yours. Do you want the Darkening to fall before its appointed time? Do you want the Na'Sgailean to rise from her prison and bury the world in shadow?"

Rhoyd winced. "I want Eithne to remember that Conor lives," he said.

"Well, that can't be helped, not for a few days, at least."

"Just undo the glyph," Rhoyd said.

"It's not that simple, my lad" Michan retorted. "Eithne is a woman of strong will, and I had to spend a lot of time weaving enough false memories to cover every aspect of the last few days. To simply remove the glyph would risk her sanity. It has to be removed in layers, and it has to be done over a period of days. I cannot risk staying here, not after all you have done."

Rhoyd flinched because Michan pointed to him, and for a moment, Rhoyd thought he was going to get clouted.

"But Conor will die if she does not heal him," he said quickly.

"What?"

"Conor was badly hurt. Those men beat him. His leg might be broken. He could barely walk, and he was bruised and his face was swollen. If you could have seen what they did to him..."

Rhoyd took an uneasy breath and looked down.

"Where is he?" Michan asked.

Rhoyd shrugged. "He said he would wait in the fields outside the walls."

"Is he there now?" Michan asked.

With a deep breath, Rhoyd closed his eyes. He stretched mage senses and felt the familiar bronze warmth of the man whom he loved as a father. Conor's essence was weak, but it was there. Opening his eyes, Rhoyd nodded.

"All right, here is what we will do," Michan said. "I got in touch with the man who is coming to claim Conor. He is mageborn, and he is going to tell the watch men that under the orders of the King of Elenthorn, Conor has been taken there to be healed. He will tell them that Conor has done no wrong—that he was acting under orders and that this is a matter for kings. They will not question him. This way, Conor can go on without being a wanted man."

"But he needs to be healed."

"I know, lad, but the shock of seeing him could be Eithne's undoing. I have seen folk bespelled this way die from shock when the truth is revealed before the false memories are removed. Now, you and Noreen will take Conor's horse and some supplies, and you are to tell Conor that he must go on and follow the west road, and that we will meet him at the Ford of Lea in two days. There is a croft there where he can be looked after until we arrive. By then, I will have removed the false memories, and Eithne will be able to heal him."

"But..."

"Noreen has some knowledge in the matters of healing. While she is not a True Healer, she knows how to set bones. She will give him a vial of poppy juice and willow bark to ease his pain. Then the two of you will come straight back here. We should be ready to leave by then."

Rhoyd opened his mouth.

"For once in your life, lad, do as I say," Michan said sharply. "The world depends on me getting these bones to Dun Gealach's deepest vaults, just as it will depend on you one day."

Lucky me, Rhoyd thought.

"Now go," Michan said. "And no more magic. Swear to me on the bones that you will behave."

"What if the demon comes back?" Rhoyd asked.

"If the demon comes back, you have my permission to turn it into a fireball," Michan said. "But nothing else. Now go and tell Noreen what I have told you."

He jerked his head towards the door. Rhoyd slid off the box, relieved to do so since it was tickling his backside. *Better tickled than thrashed, I suppose.*

"Oh, and Rhoyd," Michan said catching Rhoyd's arm and stopping him again. "Try to look like you've had a thrashing. It will make the men feel better about you if they think I can terrify and beat you into behaving."

"You wouldn't," Rhoyd said suspiciously.

Michan leaned closer, and suddenly popped Rhoyd on the seat of his trews. He jumped from the sting.

"Don't challenge me," Michan said. "Or I might. Now go."

Rhoyd pulled free without effort, but he knew it was because Michan's grip was light. He rubbed his face hard, especially his eyes and nose, hoping they would look red and puffy. Then he pulled the bolt and rushed out with a whimper, slamming the door.

Several pairs of eyes watched him with grins of satisfaction as and he pretended to snivel and wandered off in search of Noreen.

TWENTY-NINE

The rumble of hooves on grass woke Conor from his sleep. He lay still, feeling the stiffness of limbs assaulted and abused, then slowly he began to slip his long dirk out of the scabbard. Horses. Two of thcm, but the sound. Oddly, the tack on one had a familiar jungle. In fact, it sounded like Battlebrute.

Conor waited, not willing to give away his hiding place.

"Conor?" Rhoyd's voice was pitched into the air. "Conor, I know you're here."

Relief flooded Conor. Then the lad had done as he was told, and Eithne was waiting out there to heal Conor's injuries.

Only then did Conor move and the effort cost him. He gnashed his teeth and swore under his breath as he half crawled, half rolled out of his bed of hay hidden in the stacks.

"Horns!" he heard Noreen blurt.

Conor frowned as he crouched on the ground in pain. "You're not my wife," he said. "Where's Eithne?"

He looked from one to the other. Rhoyd took a deep breath and said, "She...thinks you're dead."

"What?" Conor tried to get up.

Rhoyd was already dropping from the great height of Battlebrute's saddle, a feat the lad had become adept at over the last three years. Battlebrute reached around as though about to nip the lad, but Rhoyd popped the dun's black muzzle with a practiced fist, and snapped, "Stop it, you stupid lug!" Battlebrute grunted and ceased his attack. Conor still marveled that his brute of a warhorse obeyed this tiny lad who had no fear of Conor's temperamental mount.

"It's a complex spell, actually," Noreen was quick to supply. "Michan put it on her so she would think you were dead and would not fight coming along with us when we left this morning. Of course, your lad here has seen to it that all our plans are folly."

"It's Michan's fault," Rhoyd said as Noreen dismounted. "He should have told me what he was planning. He should have told Eithne instead of scrambling her memories."

Noreen scratched her head. "That plan came a bit late

because I told him we had to do something or I was going to quit and leave him on his own," she said. "And anyway, it was my plan and not his."

"What plan? What are you two nattering about?" Conor asked.

Noreen was kneeling at Conor's side now, and he saw that she had a healer's kit.

"Michan got in touch with the King of Elenthorn's mageborn councilor. Magister Drennandale owes Michan a favor. He was going to have him go to the watchtower and say that you were the King's man and had acted on the King's behalf and name Warden as a spy and a thief. But since your lad got you out of that tower by putting the guards to sleep…"

"I didn't put them to sleep," Rhoyd retorted. "It was a demon spell!"

"At any rate, breaking you out created a whole new set of problems," Noreen said. "Can you get your boot off and let me look at that knee?"

Conor nodded struggling with the boots. Rhoyd came over to help.

"And these problems?" Conor urged, gritting his teeth and hissing when the lad tugged a little too fervently. "Easy lad."

"You were gone," Noreen said. "At any rate, we decided to stick to the tale of you acting on King's orders and have Magister Drennandale tell the watch men that he has already spirited you away because you needed a healer right away. As far as anyone in these parts if concerned, they have been told that you are to be forgotten."

Conor winced, for she had hold of his leg and was poking the ugly black bruise on the back of his knee in no gentle manner.

"Not broken," she said. "It would almost heal on its own in a week or so."

Conor frowned. "You should have brought Eithne and had her fix it," Conor said. "I cannot ride easy with that burning at the back of my leg. 'Twill make me feverish, and I will swoon and fall from the saddle."

"Keltoran pish and tattle," Noreen said. "And anyway, your wife cannot see you until we reach the Ford of Lea."

"Why not?"

"That's what I was trying to tell you," Rhoyd interrupted. "Remember last night when I told you that Michan had put some sort of mind glyph on her?"

"Aye," Conor said. "Something to make her forget me, you said."

"Well, it apparently made her believe you're dead," Rhoyd said. "And Michan says he can't remove it at once. It has to be removed in layers. Otherwise she could go insane."

"Why the little...I should have strangled him the day he told me he had bought out my commission," Conor groused.

"You'll have to tell me that tale some time," Noreen said. "In the meantime, here's what you must do. Ride west until you reach the stone bridge at the Ford of Lea. There's a croft there where you can shelter. Wait for us there. Should be about two days before we get there."

"And in the meantime, I have to suffer my beating like a man?" Conor said.

"I've seen to that," Noreen said. "You've food and water and a small cask of ale on your horse..." She opened the satchel and began to remove vials and small jars. "...And here's a couple of things to help. The poppy juice will ease your pain, but I don't advise more than a few drops at a time as I have seen men come to love this more than their wives. There's willow bark syrup in here. Take that when you go to bed. Mix it in water, not ale. It's bitter, but you'll get used to it. There are some other things in here, but I'll let you sort through those. Oh, and I brought you some cloud roots to chew on between doses of poppy juice. They're mild enough to keep you alert, but they will dull the pain, too."

She put the stuff back as Conor took a few drops of the poppy juice on his tongue. Noreen took it from him and handed him a chunk of bread. "Better chew on this now," she added. "Poppy juice is hard on the stomach when it's empty."

Conor took the bread and chewed it. Rhoyd brought him one of the skins of water so he could wash the bread down.

"West to the bridge at the Ford of Lea," Conor said between bites. "Two days of pain. How in the name of Cernunnos am I supposed to mount and dismount this mountain of a nag?"

"Very carefully," she said with a smile.

"Yer all heart," Conor said. "Get me up there."

Between Noreen and Rhoyd, he managed to mount Battlebrute. Being in the saddle was not the most comfortable place for him at the moment, but the poppy was doing its part. Noreen climbed back into the saddle of her dray, hauling

Rhoyd up behind her. Conor looked at the lad leaning against the large woman's back. He seemed small and vulnerable and tired.

Carefully, Conor guided Battlebrute over. Rhoyd's face flushed as he reached over and ran a fond hand through the lad's hair. Suddenly, Rhoyd threw himself the short distance, clambering into Conor's lap to throw arms around his neck. It took effort not to scream in pain. Conor welcomed those small arms even if they were about to make him howl. He fiercely hugged the lad to his chest.

"You mind Michan and look after Eithne," Conor said.

"I hate Michan," Rhoyd said.

"Here now, Michan is still my friend," Conor said, pushing the lad back. "He's only got your best interest in heart."

"He didn't believe me about the demon," Rhoyd said.

"That's because the man you said it was didn't have a lick of demon essence on him, lad," Noreen scolded.

Conor frowned. It occurred to him that he might be sending the lad back into a greater danger than the one he faced out in the wilds alone in such pain. Still, he knew Michan would not let anything happen to his son. *He knows I would hunt him down if he did,* Conor mused.

"You behave yourself," Conor said and tousled Rhoyd's hair again. "Now off with you. I'll see you at the Ford of Lea."

"You promise?" Rhoyd asked.

"Ye have my word as a Keltoran," Conor said.

Rhoyd hugged him again then allowed himself to be dragged back over onto the back of the dray behind Noreen.

"We'll take good care of him," she said. "You just take care of yourself."

Conor nodded. Noreen clucked to the dray and it started off at its lumbering pace. He watched as she and the lad headed back for the road. Rhoyd's forlorn face peered back over one shoulder. The sight twisted in Conor's gut. He was tempted to spur Battlebrute, ride after them, and snatch the lad back, but he knew the pain alone would make a mockery of his gallant gesture.

So he turned Battlebrute's head towards the lanes and the woods and the west.

I won't be far away, lad. You can count on that.

He squeezed gently so that Battlebrute started off at a leisurely walk.

THIRTY

"Where have you been?" Eithne found it hard to keep the panic and the anger out of her voice as Rhoyd and Noreen returned. She had been standing by the cook's wagon, holding the reins on Maudie and Moonface, when it occurred to her that she had no clue as to where Rhoyd was. The caravan was ready to roll, save the fact that the wagon was missing one horse, and she realized too that Battlebrute was gone.

But Conor is gone too...did we bury his horse with him? Oh, Blessed Brother, I wish I could remember.

Now seeing Rhoyd return perched on the dray behind the cook, Eithne's worry took forefront.

"You should have told me where you were going," she said. "I was worried sick."

"Oh, he's fine, Mistress Manahan," Noreen said and lowered Rhoyd from the great height of the horse to the back of Moonface. "We just went for a little visit, that's all."

"A visit?" Eithne repeated. "Where—to see whom? Conor would be very upset if he knew..."

She hesitated. *Conor would be upset? No, Conor cannot be upset if he is dead.*

She saw Rhoyd looking quizzically at Noreen, and felt her own face color. She must have looked like a fool just then.

"It's all right, Mistress Manahan," Noreen quickly said. "We was just taking that old warhorse out to find him a good home, that's all."

Rhoyd rolled his eyes. Eithne frowned.

"Then Battlebrute is not dead?" she asked.

"No," Noreen said.

"Didn't we lose a horse to the boars when Conor died?" Eithne asked. "I do remember a horse dying."

"That was the captain's horse, ma'am," Noreen said.

Eithne shook her head. "This is all very confusing. Why do I feel so confused? Rhoyd? You can't ride Moonface if the captain needs him?"

"Oh, it's all right, Mistress Manahan," Noreen said and

gestured off to where Captain Camhin sat on the back of a bay gelding. "He's got a new horse now, so your son can keep his palfrey."

Eithne stared hard at the captain. His nondescript profile was animated as he spoke to a man she had never seen before. The other fellow was tall and dignified, and dressed in rather courtly robes. He was seated on a lovely golden mare that pawed the ground impatiently.

"Who is that?"

Noreen shrugged. "Might be some official from the town," she said.

"From the Baron of Cullstane?" Eithne asked. "I should have a word with him about Conor's re..."

She stopped and swayed. *Conor is dead. He has already been released from his flesh.*

So why did she keep seeing an image of Conor being dragged away by the watch? It was faint, like a dream. They were outside this very warehouse when it happened, she was sure. *But how could that be?* she thought as the bloody image of Conor being trampled and gored by a boar rushed into her head and obliterated the other view. The trampling of her memories by that silvery fog staggered her. She dropped to her knees, releasing the reins.

"Eithne!" Rhoyd cried.

Eithne stayed on the ground and covered her face with her hands. Why couldn't she make the image of Conor's death go away? How could he be dead? But he was dead, and she had seen him die under the hooves and tusks of a wild boar.

Or had she?

Hands took her shoulders. She raised a tear-tracked face to find Captain Camhin kneeling before her. Rhoyd was beside her, and Noreen stood over them all, nearly as tall as Conor.

"Where is Conor?" she cried. "Where is he?"

"Shhhhh, it's all right," the captain said gently, and he put a hand to her forehead as though testing for fever. She felt a slight chill—a familiar chill—and the fog returned to blanket her thoughts. "Everything will be all right, Eithne," he said.

She blinked and brushed away the tears sliding down her cheeks, unable to comprehend why she suddenly felt calm.

Conor is dead, and I must accept that, and I must stay strong for Rhoyd, she thought. She looked down at the lad, kneeling beside her, his face masked with worry.

"We'll be all right, Rhoyd," she said. "The captain will take good care of us."

Rhoyd shot a look at the captain. "This is not good," the boy said in a low voice.

Captain Camhin nodded and smiled. "Eithne, you look tired. Why don't you lie down in Noreen's wagon? Noreen doesn't mind."

"But who will look after Rhoyd?" Eithne asked. "He is in danger and..."

"I will take care of him, I promise," the captain said. "You have nothing to fear. In a couple of days, all this will be forgotten, and you will be well again."

Eithne looked at him. "Am I ill?" she asked.

"You've not been yourself," he assured her. "But you will be in a couple of days."

She shrugged. "If you say so. The grief, I suppose. And I am rather tired."

They helped her to her feet and guided her towards Noreen's wagon. Rhoyd and Camhin saw to it that she settled down in the blankets. She closed her eyes as they slipped out of the wagon, leaving her to fall into a doze.

"She's getting worse," Rhoyd said, unable to hide his worry.

They had just ridden through the gates, a long lumbering caterpillar of wagons. Captain Camhin had decided that Rhoyd should ride with him, leaving Noreen to look after Eithne.

"She must be fighting the glyph in some fashion," the captain said as he surveyed the road leading from Cullstane and the farms that stretched fields and stone fencerows from the walls to the forest ahead. "There must be some memory I left unclouded that is conflicting with the memories I gave her."

"Then remove it," Rhoyd said.

"I am removing it," the captain retorted. "Each time I visit her, I slip a little more of the spell away. You can't hurry something as delicate as rearranging the memories and putting them back in the correct order."

"How do you do it?" Rhoyd suddenly asked. His aunt Genna had mentioned something about mind spells, but then she refused to let him know how they worked, or even how to use them. *"They are dangerous,"* she would say when he asked.

"And not something you will have any use for."

He was starting to wonder what he *would* have a use for. Genna seemed most determined to keep the greater spells out of his grasp.

Like that book of demons, he thought.

"I don't think it is something we should discuss out here in the open," Camhin said. "You never know who might be listening."

"Like demons," Rhoyd said and cast about for Bowen. He was still unwilling to believe that the guard was not a monster. *It had to be Bowen that I saw in the alley. I would swear it was Bowen, even when I saw him fly...*

"Like demons," the captain agreed. "But if you seriously want to learn the basics of the spell, you can watch when I work on Eithne. But you must be quiet and say nothing, or else her confusion will be greater."

Rhoyd nodded.

"And you must not tell your Aunt Genna either."

Rhoyd looked sidelong at the captain. "You know my Aunt Genna?"

"We're the same age," Michan said. "Or close. I was at Dun Gealach when your uncle Fenelon brought her to the Council of Mageborn and introduced her as his apprentice."

"Uncle Fenelon said she was a stubborn pupil," Rhoyd said.

"She's a stubborn lady as well," Camhin said. "The second time I met her was during the Last War. She was one of the Six, you know. As was I..."

Rhoyd frowned. He had seen that written somewhere. "You mean, my aunt Genna was there when they captured Cudraeighean Moran?" he asked.

The captain put a finger to his lips. "They believe it is never wise to say the name of the Hound," he whispered. "Otherwise, according to the Keltorans, he will seek you out in battle."

"The Hound is dead," Rhoyd said.

"So they say," the captain said. "But if the prophecy is to be believed, then his last death was not truly the end."

Prophecies again, Rhoyd thought. He got so tired of hearing about them. "His last death?"

The forest was looming dark and thick. Rhoyd suddenly realized they were about to enter the shadow of the woods that cloaked the road.

"Eyes and ears now, lad," Camhin said. "Ask questions another time. You stay here on the right, and I'll scour from the left. And remember—no more spells. If there is truly a demon about, I don't want to attract its attention. But if you *do* see anything, call out."

The captain dragged the gelding's head around and guided him behind the dark carriage to the other side.

So much for the chance to learn magic, Rhoyd thought and glowered after Michan.

Then he turned to study the forest and sighed.

THIRTY-ONE

The poppy juice wore off before the middle of the day. Conor was reminded of the time he'd tried to ride back from the battlefield after a Haxon danced a hammer off his ribs. No matter how he sat, there was no comfortable position for his injured leg or his shoulder. Every time Battlebrute stumbled over a gangly root, Conor would nearly bite his tongue in two. He tasted the blood and was beginning to fear that he would faint or fall. He dared not cry out, lest he attract unwanted attention. In spite of the reassurances that he was now considered a King's man doing the king's work of killing traitors, he did not trust that sergeant of the watch house not to try and hunt him down.

There's always the cloud root, he reminded himself. Not that he was fond of the stuff. He'd seen men chew it until they were too senseless and numb to know when someone thrust a sword in them. Still, if it would let him ride without pain, he supposed it was better than poppy juice.

He reached for the satchel Noreen had handed him and grunted as his shoulder gave a twinge of protest. For the most part, he was a mass of black bruises and aching joints. He kept telling himself that he had suffered worse in his life. Eithne had stitched enough of his wounds and fixed his broken bones, so he knew there were greater pains than these.

I've been spoiled by having a wife who can fix my wounds and ease my pain.

He certainly wished he had that wife with him now. And the lad. A morning gone and he was missing them terribly. He knew they were less than a quarter of a league behind him, and there was the temptation to turn around and ride back to where they would be.

But knowing that Michan used the "glamorie" on his wife so that she thought Conor dead. That galled him. Why did Michan have to put such a thought in Eithne's head? While Conor knew Eithne could be stubborn, he wondered why Michan thought it necessary to put such a glamorie on her.

He certainly hoped Rhoyd could find a way to break the spell.

He would certainly have words with Michan when he returned. Friend or not, the mageborn had better have a good explanation.

Because Conor was a man in pain, and that made him irritable.

I owe him a ding in the neb.

As a man of his word, Conor was tempted to keep that promise.

The thought cheered him somewhat. He bit off a piece of the cloud root and started to chew it. The overly sweet taste cloyed his tongue as the rough root turned to mush in his mouth. But it slowly spread its soothing numbness to his nerves and made the pain easier to bear.

He rode on in a better mood the rest of the day. And as the gloaming took the land, he found a deserted shepherd's hut in a clearing to bed down in.

Getting off Battlebrute was no easy chore. Fortunately, there was an old stump close by. He sidled the warhorse over to it and shortened the drop by a few feet. The problem was that his injured leg was the one he would be stepping down on as he dismounted, so he clung to the saddle as best he could and eased down. Battlebrute grunted and pawed restlessly, but stood his ground long enough for Conor to get the good leg out of the stirrup and under him.

He limped over to the hut and peered inside. There was space enough for him and the horse. Good, because he was certain he had heard distant rumbles of thunder. It was hard to say if there was a storm brewing, though the wind carried the smell of rain.

Tying Battlebrute inside and pulling off his saddle, Conor settled into the routine of making a small fire to heat water and brew the willow bark tea. There was bread and cheese aplenty in his pack now, and some strips of dried venison as well. All were welcome to a man with an empty belly.

Especially the ale.

Noreen had chosen well. It was heather ale.

Conor smiled. He knew better than to take much more than he needed to wet his throat and swallow his meal. A man chewing cloud root over the course of the afternoon could not risk drinking too much ale. It would not do to be numb and drunk at the same time.

Of course, he could recall a few times in the war when he had gotten so drunk he was numb. And one of them had been Eithne's fault, too.

He smiled briefly and sprinkled some of the willow bark mixture into the water when it started to boil. The small act was something Eithne usually did.

That thought froze him and tightened his chest. He looked out into the dark, fighting the urge to scream in rage. Screaming was not good when a man was in pain alone in the woods.

Besides, he could hear the march of rain moving closer through the trees. The wind was whipping up more. He finished his tea, doused his fire, and backed into the hut to finish his meal just as the storm began to brew.

He hoped the hut did not leak.

The storm came out of nowhere, though Rhoyd thought he had sensed it growing just before sunset. In the forest, it was difficult to determine direction, but he was almost willing to believe it had started right there where they were. It began with a sudden wind that whipped the trees into a frenzy, then lightning and thunder and rain.

The caravan halted right then and there, tied down canvases and sought shelter.

"Horns, we're leagues from a decent camp," Captain Camhin said.

They would have to stay on the road. There were no obvious clearings in among the trees. Rapidly, the guards and the drivers began to prepare for the worst. They tied the riding horses together between two large oaks. Some of the guards tried to shelter under the wagons, though it did little good. The way the wind whipped the rain, they were getting splattered and the downpour turned the road from dirt to mud.

Captain Camhin ordered Rhoyd into the cook's wagon with Eithne and Noreen before he settled into the dark carriage. Eithne was just arousing from her long nap. She looked at Rhoyd as though puzzled to see him, then sighed and said, "You're soaked!"

"It's raining," he said.

"Well, you must get out of those wet things at once," she said, and before Rhoyd could protest, Eithne was kneeling before him, working on the lacing of his clothes.

"I can do that," he said, pulling back and tossing a startled look at Noreen.

"Oh, I am certain our good cook has seen much in her time," Eithne said. "Now you get out of..."

She got up and started to approach him as she spoke when the wind whipped up fiercely and slammed against the side of the cook's wagon, rocking it. Eithne squeaked as she lost her balance and sat down. Even Rhoyd had to grab a barrel to keep from being knocked over. Noreen managed to stay upright, though she crouched and looked uncertain as she stared at the cover above.

"That was strange," the cook said.

She looked at Rhoyd. "It wasn't me," he said quickly.

"I didn't say that it was," Noreen retorted.

"What is that roaring sound?" Eithne suddenly asked.

There was a roaring sound, and with it, shrieks like a thousand beasts. Rhoyd felt his hairs standing on end. There was something unnatural and frightening to the sound. Rhoyd crawled over to the front of the wagon and peered through the canvas flap and strained on its tie-down ropes as it wrestled with the wind.

Darkness had claimed the world, the dark of storm clouds. Still, mage eyes could see in the faint gloaming that peeped between gaps in the raging firmament. At first, Rhoyd thought it was a giant serpent, twisting and undulating where it stretched between the trees on the road ahead and the distant sky. "Look!" he shouted.

Noreen and Eithne were suddenly around him, peering through the gap.

"Brother, preserve us," Eithne said. "Death wind."

"Death wind?" Rhoyd repeated, his heart thundering.

"I remember those from the Last War," Noreen said. "They say that the Hound would conjure them to tear through armies and scatter them like milkweed."

"Is it coming this way?" Eithne asked.

Rhoyd watched the wagging whirlwind. It was coming closer, inching through the forest. And he could see that trees were being torn up in its wake, for the air was filled with debris of wood and branches and leaves. Even around them, the world was growing so windy it whipped dirt and mud around to thicken the air.

"What should we do?"

"Take cover!" someone shouted, and it occurred to Rhoyd that others were seeing this as well. Men were scrambling out from under the wagons, heading for the trees. But in Rhoyd's eyes, that was a foolish place to go.

Their wagon lurched, and Eithne gasped. Rhoyd looked back over his shoulder in time to see Captain Camhin slipping in the back, drenched like an old rag. He threw off his illusion.

"Rhoyd, I will need your help," he said.

"What do you mean?" Rhoyd asked.

"The men must think it is you who is doing what I am about to do..." Michan said.

"But, sir..." Noreen said.

"This has to be done," Michan said. "Or we're all dead."

"Do you think you can manage, sir?" she asked.

Michan nodded.

"Now Rhoyd," he said. "Stand on the front of the wagon and raise your hands. Shout whatever nonsense you want, but shout it loud. I will do the rest. Noreen, I will have need of your strength."

"It's yours," she said.

"This is crazy!" Eithne cried. "You cannot send him out there to face a death wind. I've already lost my Conor! I will not lose my son."

"He'll be safe," Michan assured her and jerked his head towards Noreen who quickly made good use of her greater size to herd Eithne towards the back of the wagon. "Go on, Rhoyd," Michan said. "You'll be just fine."

Excitement overrode caution. Rhoyd pushed the flaps of canvas far enough apart to crawl out onto the wagon seat. The wind buffeted and assailed him, and nearly knocked him down. He struggled to stay on his feet, forced to brace himself against the back of the seat. Rain beat him and soaked him and plastered his black hair down like a thin layer of ink on his head. The sting of those icy cold droplets burned on his face and hands, but he did as Michan said and raised his arms and began to shout.

It was nonsense that spilled from his lips, a jumble of words and syllables with no real meaning. Behind him, he barely heard Michan chanting in the mage tongue, and he felt the mageborn's draw of power from Noreen and from the storm itself.

How can he stand to do that? Rhoyd marveled. *This storm reeks of demon essence.*

He nearly froze, shifting his gaze over towards the trees where many of the men watched him. Bowen was among them, smiling secretively. Not far behind him, Rhoyd could make out the dumpling figure of Master Fergus raising hands to keep the rain off his face and muttering to those around him. Around the knot of shivering men, Rhoyd felt the swirl of demon essence as well.

Somewhere in that knot of men, the demon was hiding.

But before Rhoyd could make sense of it or even decipher whom it might be, he heard the ripping of trees closer by. He turned and focused his attention on the death wind that was inching closer still.

He felt the power Michan summoned like a hard wind buffeting him from behind. The force of it flew forward, rushing past the rows of rocking wagons. *He's battling wind with wind,* Rhoyd marveled, and indeed, he could see that the wind Michan conjured rose and slammed into the death wind like a wave crashing into stones. There was a scream as force met force, and charged the air with static. Rhoyd saw little fingers of lighting dancing where the winds met. Some of them spread into a wall. Others scattered like fireflies in the dark. The roar went to a deafening height, pummeling Rhoyd with tremendous sound, and then silence fell hard on his already thundering ears.

For a moment, no one dared move. Rhoyd stayed where he was, hands still raised until he heard Michan whisper, "You can put your arms down now," in an exhausted voice.

Rhoyd did, nearly tumbling back into the wagon. He managed to sit on the wagon seat, and for a moment, he remained there, staring in awe. The rain had ceased to fall, and the black clouds had been dispersed. The faint rime of red-orange glowed along the bits of horizon barely visible through the trees. Amber fingers against the shadows of the forest.

Horns, he did that! Rhoyd took deep breaths, relishing the cleansing aftermath of Michan's spell. What power that had been to abate a fury like a death wind. Rhoyd could not stop shaking from excitement. *I never knew it was possible to use an air spell to do something like that!* His aunt Genna insisted air spells should be use in moderation for striking with air could have the same effect of striking with stone.

But Michan had done more than an ordinary air spell. There had been other things woven into the pattern, and Rhoyd wanted to know what they were. All at once, he forgot how much he had come to despise Michan. With a whoop, Rhoyd spun on the seat and almost fell off in his eagerness to get into the wagon.

Michan was sitting on the floor holding his head with his hands as Rhoyd popped through the canvas. Noreen sat wearily on a crate, looking drained as well. Rhoyd could sense that her life essence had been drawn into the spell, for a touch of it lingered, smelling like warm gold, lending a metallic taste to the air. Towards the back of the wagon, Eithne sat on a short keg looking stunned and confused.

Rhoyd dropped to his knees, holding his breath, anticipation burning on his tongue. He crouched in front of Michan and waited. Slowly, Michan looked up, and his expression was filled with suspicion.

"What?" Michan asked.

"Will you teach me that spell? Please?" Rhoyd asked.

"Why?" Michan said.

"Because Aunt Genna won't," Rhoyd said.

One of Michan's eyebrows flicked the merest of a gesture.

"Please?" Rhoyd said, trying to keep impatience at bay.

Michan glanced over at Noreen, then back at Rhoyd. "That spell is not a toy. Using it is not a game. It's a responsibility, and a mageborn has to understand that using such a destructive spell has its price."

Rhoyd sighed. "I know that. At times, I know deep inside that what faces me is never going to be a game. But Genna treats me like I don't need to know *anything*. Uncle Fenelon once said she was going to spoil it all and that I will not be ready because she would not teach me the greater spells now. He says I'm ready to learn them, but she thinks I'm too young."

A half-smile cocked one corner of Michan's mouth. "You're serious, then?" he asked.

"Yes," Rhoyd said.

"Well, I suppose it cannot hurt to know the fundamentals of that spell. But only so long as you promise that you *won't* use it on the road and..."

"Captain Camhin!" Fergus shouted from somewhere

outside. "Captain, where are you?"

"Horns!" Michan muttered. He took a deep breath and whispered the spell to restore the illusion, his face shimmering back into that of Captain Camhin.

"I'm in here, Fergus!" he called.

The wagon shook and creaked, and the canvas flaps behind the seat were wrestled open. Muddy and disheveled, Master Fergus pushed his head through the gap. The reek of him all drenched reminded Rhoyd of a midden heap.

"Ah, in here with the women and children, I see," Fergus said with a silly grin.

"Yes," the captain retorted. "I was worried about them. What do you want?"

Fergus rubbed his stubble and smeared a spot of mud into his chin. "Just thought you might actually want a report about the men," he said.

"Any losses?"

"No, but there are a few bumps and bruises. Mistress Manahan, if you would be so good. I've got one man needing his scalp stitched and another with a broken leg."

Eithne looked puzzled. "Oh, dear," she said. "Of course, I will come right away."

She fumbled around to collect her kit, and from the look on her face, Rhoyd got the impression she had not felt the *need* of these men.

Still, she started for the back of the wagon, kit in hand, then stopped and looked back at Rhoyd.

"Get out of those wet things right now," she said. "Else wise, I shall have to tell...to tell..." She hesitated, looking confused.

The captain frowned, and scrambled towards the back of the wagon. He took Eithne's hand ever so gently, and Rhoyd felt a faint trembling of magic on his own nerves. "Why don't I assist you, Mistress Manahan?" Camhin said. "That way, I can see the damage for myself. Noreen."

"Yes, sir?" the cook said.

"See to it that young Rhoyd gets out of those wet things."

"With pleasure, sir," Noreen said as the captain helped Eithne out of the wagon.

Rhoyd glanced sourly at Noreen, not quite liking the way she had said that. Beyond her, Master Fergus grinned like an ape, adding to Rhoyd's discomfort.

Noreen just winked at him, then turned to Master Fergus and snarled, "Get yer muddy feet off my wagon or it'll be cold tatties for breakfast."

Fergus disappeared from the gap with a chuckle. Noreen took up a large blanket and wrapped it about Rhoyd's shoulders.

"Now get out of them wet things," she said. "I have to check on the horses."

Rhoyd sighed with relief and began shucking out of his wet clothes as she left him to his privacy.

That was also close, his internal companion said. *Would you have let it come, knowing what it could do?*

The Demon-Bound frowned and helped Creed as he offered assistance to a guard who had been struck by a flying limb.

I would have had little choice, and the Other would have known me for who I am. Fortunately, Michan was quick enough with his spell.

Clever of him to make them think it was the boy.

Not really, he thought. *Not when there is so much at stake.*

Well, at least you didn't have to give yourself away.

Don't be so quick to cheer. I don't plan to celebrate until these bones are safe in a deep vault. Now we should go check on the Keltoran.

Why?

Just to make certain he survived this night.

Ah. May I ask why it matters?

Everything matters.

THIRTY-TWO

That was the strangest dream, Conor thought as he awoke early the next morning. Sun had not quite risen, though even in this small clearing, the abandoned shepherd's hut was shaded by the thick trees, but Conor had awakened because he had been certain that someone was standing there watching him. Someone with eyes like fire and a shadowy hooded face. The figure had whispered, *"Sleep, manling, for you will need your strength."* It had been on the tip of Conor's tongue to tell the monstrosity to go bugger itself as he didn't need any encouragement to sleep.

What he needed was to be healed.

Of course, as he rolled over in the morning, still wondering why he had assumed someone *was* standing over him in the night when the storm had kept the willow bark tea from doing its job, the stiffness of his body reminded him that he was not a well man. Some of the bruises were not feeling as troublesome, but the back of his knee felt stiff and unwieldy as old leather. When he moved, it sang a hearty protest from battered nerves.

He reminded himself then to roll over on his other side and get up with the strong leg under him. He had to wait a few minutes for the sickening dance in his stomach and head to abate, but he finally sat up and looked around.

Battlebrute was still tucked safely in one corner. All his gear was where he left it. Good, then it had to have been nothing more than a dream.

Pushing the thoughts aside, Conor scrounged in his pack for the poppy juice and a chunk of bread. A few drops and no more, he reminded himself. He was not looking forward to another day of riding the roads. *No choice, Manahan.*

Michan was going to owe him. That much he would make certain the mageborn knew.

I counted you as a friend all through the Last War, but ye disrupted my life then with all yer portend, and sent me away before the last battle could be met and won. Then ye come back into my life and disrupt it again, telling me my lad is in danger, sending me away once more, and making my woman forget that I live, all so that you can follow your portends.

Well, hang ye and yer portends. When I join ye at the Ford of Lea, I'm taking my family and leaving. Demons or no, yer not tearing my family apart.

The anger he felt towards Michan gave him the surge of energy he needed to get up and saddle Battlebrute. The poppy juice was working by the time he was ready to clamber onboard the warhorse's broad back and tightened his grasp on the reins. Battlebrute danced in one place, eager to take off.

Conor reined his old war mount back onto the road and gritted his teeth as they took off at as lively a pace as his pain would allow.

He wanted to reach the Ford in plenty of time. Because the anger he was nursing might turn against him once Michan and the others arrived.

He wanted time to get it out of his system to keep from dinging Michan's neb all the way to the bottom of his boots.

Eithne marveled at how brilliant blue the sky was the next day. She had slept well after the storm, for it had cleaned the air and left its fresh fragrance on everything.

Last night, the captain had stayed close to her as she moved among the men injured by the flying trees. There were a few bumps and bruises to wash down in witch hazel, a few cuts to treat with comfrey paste. A bit of stitching and one ankle to heal. She had felt so tired afterwards that Captain Camhin—*or was it Michan? How I hate the way my mind seems so distracted of late*—had brought her back to the cook's wagon. Rhoyd was asleep, coiled in the blankets. At least his wet clothes were hanging about to dry.

The captain became Michan then and there and insisted on holding her hand. "Really," she had told him. "I am all right. Truly, I know that fate has been unkind to me and Rhoyd by taking Conor from us, but I will be fine."

Those words, however, went as fuzzy as her head. She thought she was walking around in a fog for a time. Or a dream. Michan was there in her dream, and he was peeling back the layers from something that reminded her of a large cocoon. And she swore that there was a hint of a plaidie in the delicate threads. Inside it, something was alive, something familiar.

But when she had offered to assist him, he pushed her away and told her not yet. Not until he was done.

And then she had lost all sense of dreams and nightmares in a sound sleep.

Now it was morning, and she was up early as always, admiring the sky. Wondering if wherever Conor was, he was admiring it as well.

Oh, surely the sky in the Summerland is much more brilliant than this. She frowned. Why did she not think Conor would be in the Summerland when her mind still held trappings of his terrible beating at the hands of those...? *Hands? Since when do boars have hands?* She shook herself and prepared her kit for travel.

Master Fergus was also up early, and he sent two scouts to check out the road ahead as the wagons were preparing to depart the next morning.

Noreen was fixing the men a quick breakfast of meal mush and fruit, and Eithne had offered to assist when the men came riding back. They were new faces to Eithne, men that she was given to understand Master Fergus had hired in Cullstane where Conor...

Conor cannot be in Cullstane because Conor is...

She stopped herself, not liking the confusion that spun her thoughts like milkweed in a whirlwind. The fog was less prevalent in her mind, but the thoughts just would not stay focused for long.

But as she was drawing her thoughts back in order again, she heard one of the scouts say, "There are trees as far as the eye can see. The road is blocked by many an oak."

"What do you mean, blocked?" the captain asked as he joined the conversation. "One or two trees can readily be removed if we send men with axes ahead and..."

"Beg pardon, Captain Camhin," one of the scouts said, "but we be talking more than one or two trees here. It's as if every tree for nearly a quarter of a league got uprooted and tossed on the road by that death wind last night."

"How close to the south split are we?" Master Fergus asked.

"South split?" the captain asked.

"Aye, this here is not the only road to Keltora. There's a south road that follows this side of the Highland Ranges and cuts over a trail through the ranges south of Ben Uagh. It may add a day or two, but no more."

The captain did not look pleased.

"South split is clear," the scout said. "We rode a good tenth of a league past it before we found the road gone."

"Then we can take South Split," Fergus said.

"Is it a safe road?" the captain asked.

"Safe as they come," Master Fergus said.

Several of the men were gathering to claim their meals, drawing Eithne's attention away from the conversation. Among them stood Bowen, hooded as always. He narrowed his eyes, clearly following the conversation with interest.

Eithne frowned. She had thought Bowen was one of the men Michan said they would be leaving behind when they reached Cullstane. But there he was, standing among the men, his cloak drawn around him. He watched Master Fergus and Captain Camhin closely.

"Did you need something, Bowen?" Noreen asked.

Her voice startled him. He glanced at her as though not knowing her for a moment then slowly, a smile appeared.

"Nothing, Mistress Noreen," he said and slowly stepped away.

"Odd duck, that one," Noreen said quietly to Eithne. "He's starting to give me the willies, the way he comes and goes like a ghost. No wonder that lad of yours thought he might be carrying a demon. He don't move like a real man."

Eithne glanced cautiously after Bowen, but he had already vanished among the men. Then the captain and the caravan master called for the men to get ready to roll, distracting her.

"Where's Rhoyd?" she asked. "And where's Conor?"

Mistress Noreen looked puzzled. "Your lad's asleep. Conor..."

"Is dead," Eithne said before she could stop herself. She looked at Mistress Noreen. "Or is he?"

Noreen drew a short quick breath. "Perhaps you should talk to the Captain about that," she said.

"I will," Eithne said. "He should have been back by now."

"Back?" Noreen repeated.

Eithne frowned. The fog rolled in her head. She shook herself and walked away to finish preparations to leave.

THIRTY-THREE

"I don't like the look of this at all," Rhoyd whispered to no one in particular as he sat on Moonface and studied the forest. The caravan had reached the split, and it was clear that the way through to the Ford of Lea was blocked. Masses of trees had fallen to cover the road. Rhoyd longed to say something to the captain about how Conor would be waiting for them at the ford, but the captain had been too busy, and Master Fergus had been hovering close all day. So in spite of misgivings, they took the Split Road.

For a while, it had looked like the rest of the forest road they had been riding through, but then things started to change. Little things at first. Song birds were scarce. Instead, there seemed to be a lot of ravens about. The few early flowers grew less. Ferns thickened the forest floor, and the trees...they had a stunted shape. More than once, Rhoyd swore he saw shadows slinking through those trees. Darklings? Or just wolves? Something kept pace with the caravan while keeping its distance. Here, the trees leaned over the road and touched to form a canopy. Beneath their leafy boughs, the road was in shadows. Even with the strong sunlight of midday overhead, there was little light.

Captain Camhin ordered a halt while they were still in the sunlight.

"Are you certain this is a safe road?" the captain was asking Master Fergus.

"I've ridden way this many a time over the years," Fergus insisted "The next township along the route is Idleway about four days on, and a sen'night beyond that is the Duchy of Glenmarra that sits at the feet of Ben Uagh and guards the pass."

"This doesn't have the look of a caravan road," the captain said.

"Not every road looks like the King's Highways, Captain," Master Fergus said. "Relax. We'll be fine. It'll just take an extra day."

"Is there another way back up to the Ford of Lea?" Camhin asked.

"Why do you want to go there? Nothing but the road and the river and a few farmsteads. Next village after that is near a sen'night on."

"I know, but we were supposed to be meeting someone at a farmstead there. To pick up a delivery of goods bound for Caer Keltora."

"Don't remember any such order on the list, Captain."

"I got a letter about it in Cullstane," Camhin said.

"Did ye? When?"

Captain Camhin tossed a quick look towards Rhoyd.

"Well, there's no chance of going that way with the road blocked," Fergus said "Not unless you want to run the wagons through the woods, sir."

Rhoyd could see that the captain was struggling with this bit of information. He worried at the reins and looked at his dark wagon, and finally shook his head.

"No," he said. "But I think we should at least send a messenger through the woods to the Ford of Lea to deliver a message and tell them we will not be collecting..."

"Send a man into those woods?" Master Fergus said and frowned. "That's a daft idea. Unless he knows these woods like the back of his hand, he'll just get lost."

The captain took a deep breath.

What about Conor? Rhoyd thought.

"Then I guess we go on," the captain said wearily and looked at Rhoyd once more.

Fergus looked at Rhoyd as well and shook his head.

They ordered the wagons forward and started slowly into the darker wood. Rhoyd hesitated, looking toward the forest. He closed his eyes and took a deep breath, seeking essence in the air that he could draw to help him stretch mage senses. He wanted to see if he could sense Conor on the other road.

But something cold stood in his way. As his senses stretched, they met an icy wall that pushed back.

And then the captain was there, reaching over and grabbing his arm to give him a shake. "What are you doing?" Captain Camhin whispered.

"Trying to find Conor," Rhoyd said.

"Conor will be at the ford," the captain said, "and there is nothing we can do for now. Tonight—when we stop—I will scry for him. Make certain he is all right."

"But he has to be told we are not on the other road," Rhoyd said. "He wasn't well. He needs Eithne."

Camhin indicated for silence. Some of the men were looking at them now, the new hirelings that Master Fergus had gathered in Cullstane. Gruff looking men, they struck Rhoyd as more bandits than mercenaries.

He wished Conor were here.

"Later," Camhin whispered. "Now come on. We cannot delay any more."

He spurred his own mount and hurried back over to the far side of the dark wagon. Rhoyd wanted to yell at him, to call him a monster for letting Conor suffer. But he held his tongue because he looked over and saw Bowen riding back a ways. The man's gaze was troubled. He looked over into the woods when he saw Rhoyd looking back, pretending to be interested in something there.

Rhoyd looked down for a moment, then up again.

Bowen had vanished from the line. But before Rhoyd could say anything to the Captain, the caravan started to move. He was forced to turn forward and pay attention to the forest and the road.

The afternoon sun was beating down on Conor from between the trees. Another hour, he told himself, and he would reach the Ford of Lea. As he recalled from earlier caravans he had traveled with, as well as his years in the militia, there was a farmstead there with a mill. The locals grew wheat and made flour that had fed the bellies of militiamen such as himself in the Last War, once they had wrested it from the Hound's control.

The poppy juice was tempting him to take a few sips, but he told himself that it would not be wise, no matter how much his leg was hurting him now. Another hour's ride and he could find a bed for the night. And maybe someone would know a bit of granny skill, enough to ease his pain until Eithne could see to his needs.

He took a deep breath and closed his eyes. *How are they faring?* he wondered. More than once, he thought to ride back and meet them, but he resisted the urge. He had said he would meet them at the ford, and he was a man of his word.

He only wished he had not given it so readily.

He hoped Eithne and Rhoyd were well.

He hoped the snarling unease in his guts was the bread and venison and apples and not some portend of doom.

Portends...

He grumbled at himself for even thinking such a thing.

Michan was certainly going to pay for this.

Battlebrute snorted and shied. Conor had not really been watching the road, and now he opened his eyes and reached for his sword because the warhorse stopped dead still under him.

There was a figure on the road, wrapped in a cloak of dark hunter's green. The figure had the hood pulled forward so the face was hidden. *Brigand?* Conor thought. The cloak was awfully rich for a bandit.

"Conor MacManahan?" the man said, and Conor felt his stomach knot. This man knew his birthing name. He pulled his sword from the scabbard, though it weighed heavily in his hand and pulled at the muscles attached to his aching shoulder.

"Show yourself," Conor ordered, "Or by the Horns of Cernunnos, I'll run you through."

"That would serve no useful purpose, I can assure you," the cloaked one said, taking a step forward. "I am here because I need you to come with me."

Battlebrute hitched back and snorted nervously. Conor had never felt the old warhorse grow so tense. But then, he had never seen him shy from a stranger.

"Show yourself," Conor repeated.

"As you wish," the stranger said and pushed back the hood.

Blond hair, rich blue eyes, and a face that seemed both ancient and young. But it was not the indeterminable age as much as the strange eldritch shape of the man's features.

"You're not human," Conor said.

The man smiled. "I am human of flesh," he said. "I always have been."

"But not inside?" Conor asked.

The man sighed. "I was not aware that you could see into a man's soul," he said.

"Who are you?"

"Alaric Braidwine, at your service," the man said with a bow.

Conor frowned. "The one they call *the demon-bound?*" Conor asked.

"One and the same," Alaric replied. "Now that we have introductions out of the way, I must ask you to step down from your horse."

"Why?" Conor said. "Planning to steal this auld hay mucker would be a foolish idea. He doesn't take kindly to strangers."

"So I have seen," Alaric said with a faint smile. "But it is not your horse I need. It is easier to lead your horse through a gate than to ride him. In fact, you may want to cover his eyes."

"Why would I want to do that?" Conor asked.

"Because, the Other has led them off the road and they are not coming this way."

"What?"

"The one who carries the Shadow Demon within him has somehow diverted them from this road. He called a death wind last night and destroyed the road so they would have to go the way he wanted them to. They are riding into danger. They are going to need your strength and your sword."

Conor scrambled clumsily out of the saddle. "What do you mean, the Shadow Demon?" he insisted, reaching out and seizing Alaric by the shoulder. Alaric raised his hands to protest the gesture in vain. "Tell me what you mean."

Alaric cringed as though having a seizure, bowing his head. But when his face rose again, it was not the face of a man at all. It was something resembling a bat, and the eyes now glowed fiery red. With a snarl, Alaric broke Conor's grasp and shoved him so that he fell against his horse. Pain shot through him and he scrambled back, putting some distance between himself and the abomination he perceived.

"Wait!" Alaric cried. His voice was rasping and unearthly. "Do not flee. I should have warned you."

"Warned me?" Conor said, struggling to stay upright as dizziness swept over him.

"We will not harm you, but you must trust us," Alaric said.

"We?" Conor repeated.

"I...Vagner...I carry a demon inside me," Alaric said. "A Youngerkin. That is how I became the Demon-Bound."

Conor turned and tried to clamber back up into the saddle, though it was costing him.

"Wait," Alaric repeated. "I swear by the Silver Wheel—I

swear on She Who Sits at the Center of All Things—we will not harm you. Vagner just gets a little...testy when he thinks someone is attacking me."

Conor paused. The effort to mount his horse was taking its toll. He sank to the ground. "Do as you will then, monster," he said. "But let me die like a man."

Alaric sighed. Slowly, his features returned to their human state.

"You're not going to die," he said wearily. "Not as long as you don't try to kill me. And anyway, I am only trying to help you get back to where the others are. As I said, your son and your wife are in serious danger. For that matter so is the whole caravan. He has taken them to a place where his kin still dwell hidden from the light of day."

Conor frowned. "Why didn't you stop them?"

"I cannot. I am sworn to protect the Balance of All Things, and cannot interfere unless the Balance is threatened before its time." Alaric closed his eyes and opened them again. "As it was, I sent the bones of the betrayer on this journey because I thought they would be safer in the vaults of Dun Gealach. I came along in different guises so as not to arouse suspicion, but your son has betrayed me. And now he brings danger to all."

"My son is not to blame!" Conor snapped and lurched upright, pointing at Alaric with the sword.

Alaric shook his head. "I do not mean it that way. He saw through my glamour, forced me to hide deeper, and as a result, I have been careless. I should have remembered what the White One told me. Only those of the Elder Blood and the Twice-Blooded Once-Born would be able to see what I hid within me. But because he could see through Bowen, he betrayed me."

"Bowen? You were Bowen? Friend to that blackheart Warden?"

"Warren was a mistake. I tried to use him to hide myself, but he made matters difficult by thinking that your son could help him see into the wagon. I should not have overlooked his greed."

"Did you kill him?"

Alaric shook his head again. "No, but the one who carries the Shadow inside him did, just as he killed the other man that night when you were wandering around down in the woods. He used your dagger to throw the suspicion of that death on you. Now come, we are wasting time. Will you trust me?"

Conor studied the eldritch face. Instinct said that he should not trust this man who was no longer human inside. But knowing that his family was in danger, Conor knew he had no choice.

"I'll trust you," he said. "But you will have to go first."

"As I would have expected of you," Alaric said. "You're a good man. The White One knew what she was doing when she chose you to look after the last hope of the world."

Conor frowned.

"We must blindfold your horse now," Alaric said. "Then I will open the gate spell. I would rather we had a Walking Stone, but there are none close by."

"A Walking Stone?" Conor asked as he sheathed his sword and dragged a length of an old shirt out of his pack. Battlebrute threw his head around in protest, but Conor managed to get the cloth tucked in under the headstall of the bridle and tied it under the horse's jaw.

"Yes, in ancient times, the Old Ones traveled through Walking Stones to move around the world. One day, I will teach your son how to use them."

Conor narrowed his eyes. "*You* will teach him."

"When the time comes," Alaric said. "But not now, as I can see by the look in your eyes that it distresses you."

Conor sighed. "I was thinking more that it was all we needed, my lad knowing how to walk through stones. There are times he forgets to open doors, ye know."

Alaric looked puzzled.

"Auld joke. He gets to reading the books some times and forgets that there is a door in his way."

Alaric smiled. "I see."

"Shall we go?" Conor said.

Still smiling, Alaric closed his eyes and whispered, *"Geata foisgal..."* In the shadows of the trees, a small opening appeared, like a silver-rimmed eye opening. Through it, Conor could see a forest of great darkness. Alaric opened his eyes and stepped through the opening, gesturing for silence and beckoning Conor to follow.

With a sigh, Conor tugged Battlebrute's reins and led the warhorse through the gap.

It was like stepping into midnight. The world went as dark as the deepest part of night. Conor could barely make out the silhouettes of trees. He stumbled over roots at his feet.

"I cannot see my feet," he whispered.

Alaric glanced back, his eyes luminous like twin embers in the dark, and Conor hitched back at the sight, nearly blundering into his warhorse. "Sorry, I forget that mortalborn— even those descended from mageborn lines—are not able to see in the dark. Here…close your eyes. This won't last long, but it will help."

Conor was aware of a hand waving before his face. He closed his eyes as instructed when he felt fingertips on his eyelids, and heard Alaric whispering a spell. Conor's eyes went cold, then warm. He opened them with a gasp.

The world was there, visible in a strange, colorless sort of way. Like he was able to distinguish shapes, but they were all in hues of blue and grey.

"Come now," Alaric whispered. "We cannot tarry too long or the spell will wear off before we reach our destination."

"Our destination?" Conor asked. "We're not there?"

"I could not risk opening the gate close enough to be there right away," Alaric said. "As a man of war, you should understand that strategy."

Conor nodded. "All right then, if this is war show me the enemy."

"You may wish you had not seen him…" Alaric said. "Some say the sight of the Venomous Dark is so terrible, it freezes a man's blood."

"I'll worry about that later," Conor said. "Lead on."

Alaric nodded and carefully picked his way through the thickness of the trees. Conor pulled the cloth from Battlebrute's eyes and followed.

THIRTY-FOUR

"I don't like the look of this," Noreen muttered in a low voice that only Rhoyd and the Captain could hear. Rhoyd stretched and glanced back at the cook whose hands were white-knuckled about the reins. Her team danced nervously in the wake of the dark wagon, and Rhoyd was not so sure he blamed them for being unmanageable. This place was starting to play tricks on his senses.

For one thing, he swore the shadows were alive.

He so wished they had been able to take the other road. How were they going to let Conor know they would not be crossing the Ford of Lea?

Hoof beats got his attention. Master Fergus was riding back along the line. Was something the matter? The caravan master rode past Rhoyd, wearing a frown. The expression did not change as he guided his horse around behind the dark carriage and the cook's wagon, and up on the other side.

"Captain," he said. Rhoyd rode closer to the wagon to listen.

"Master Fergus?" Captain Camhin said.

"We're missing another man."

"Who?"

"That fellow Bowen," Fergus said darkly. "The one the lad said was a demon. You don't suppose the lad is the one..."

"Don't be ridiculous," the captain said.

"Begging your pardon, Captain," Fergus said and lowered his voice. "But we saw what he did to that demon in Stonelay and what he did to that storm last night, and the men are starting to grumble that ill luck has followed us since the lad's family joined our crew."

"I will hear no more such talk," Captain Camhin said in a steely voice. "Considering that Rhoyd and his family signed on well before some of the newer men, I find that rather unusual, don't you?"

"Sir, it cannot be helped," Fergus said. "The men saw the lad kill the demon—they saw him attacking you and your wagon. Maybe I was wrong about his da. Maybe the lad's been the problem all along. Maybe *he's* the one after that precious cargo of yours. I was in the Last War. I remember what mage folk could do. Even the young ones could kill..."

"That is enough!" the captain snapped.

Rhoyd swallowed hard. How could they think *he* was to blame for the deaths of those men?

"You tell your men that if they wish to make their wages and not get left behind the next village we come to, that they will put that nonsense out of their heads straight away. The lad may be mageborn, but he is no killer."

Fergus muttered something that even Rhoyd could not hear, and spurred his horse and charged forward. Rhoyd rode away from the dark wagon and just in time. The captain came riding around to his side of the wagon. Camhin's face was tight with anger.

"Get up on the wagon," he said.

Rhoyd blinked. "What?"

"I can't keep you safe if I can't see where you are," Camhin said. "And right now, the safest place for you is on that wagon. It's the one place they will be afraid to go near and try anything."

Rhoyd tried not to frown.

"Come on," the captain said and rode around so that he was forcing Moonface towards the wagon. "I'll tether your horse to the back of the cook's wagon after you get up there— now go!"

Rhoyd hesitated then sighed. He guided Moonface close to the front of the dark wagon. Camhin took the reins, and Rhoyd grabbed his satchel and pulled his feet out of the stirrups. Camhin kept the horses close as Rhoyd crawled from the saddle over into the driver's seat.

"Now stay there," Camhin said. "No matter what."

Rhoyd nodded, looking uncertainly at the pair of dark drays that pulled this box coach. They walked at a steady pace, led by a man on a third horse. The man leading them glanced tentatively at the boy then turned his eyes forward. Camhin must have tied Moonface back on the cook's wagon, because when he came back around to the other side, he was shy one small grey palfrey.

With a sigh, Rhoyd dug into his satchel. If he wasn't going to ride, he could read. He pulled out the book of demon lore, keeping its covers low so as not to let Camhin know what he was reading.

> *There is an old tale whose origin is claimed to have come from the first age of the world when the Great Dragons fought over the Balance of All Things and the first demons known as the Elderkin were born. When the Dark Mother slew the giant Ymir she plucked from him the essence of his rage and hid it within her shadows. And there it did fester and form into a shadow with substance, and that the Dark Mother did breathe upon it with her poisonous breath and gave it life, and it became known as the Venomous Dark, and that she gave it dominion over all her Shadow Demons.*
>
> *The Venomous Dark, for all its terrible power, could not bear the True Light of the White Ones, and so it skulked about among the shadows, seeking to serve the will of its mother, always looking for ways to destroy the light. And each time the world turned, the Venomous Dark would stand at the battle with the Lord of All Shadows, he who was the favorite son of the Dark Mother, and that the Venomous Dark would devour all followers of the Light who dared to step into the shade. But the Venomous Dark longed to devour the Champion of Light as well, and so to this end, it animated the dead and the dying, using their flesh to cloak its shadow essence and protect it from the Light.*
>
> *But the Champion of Light was able to see through the cloak of flesh and knew that the heart of the flesh was putrid and black as pitch. For the flesh of the living, when claimed by this evil is pale as dough and soft as butter, and gave off the odor of rot whenever it stood in the light too long...*

Rhoyd frowned and lowered the book. *The odor of rot?*

Why did that strike him as odd? The demon he encountered in the alley in Cullstane had carried the essence of cinnamon, not of rot.

Because there is more than one demon here...

That thought hit him as cold as ice. He scanned the wagons ahead and behind the dark carriage, standing up in the seat to peer over the top. Who? Who was it? He should have known. He should have realized.

"Rhoyd, what are you doing?" Captain Camhin called.

Rhoyd glanced over at the man. The illusion was flickering on his face.

"What's wrong?" Camhin asked.

"Your spell," Rhoyd whispered. "It's fading..."

The captain touched his face instinctively. He closed his eyes as though concentrating, trying to make the spell hold, but it was no good. His illusion was fading fast, and there was nothing he could do to make it stay. His face faded from the nondescript captain to that of Michan. Snarling, Michan jerked his hood up and over his head to shadow his features.

"Something is wrong here," Michan said. "We should not have come this way."

Rhoyd was about to say that this was a fine time to realize that, but his attention was drawn to his surroundings. All light of day had disappeared. The men were actually lighting torches and lanterns just so they could see. An unnatural night had fallen on the world, and under its shadow, Rhoyd felt magic that turned his blood cold. He looked around, trying to see in the dark and finding that even mage sight could not penetrate the depth of the trees. The forest was tangled and thick here, and it started to look as though there was no way out. Though Rhoyd tried to focus on the shadows under the thick canopy of twisted hawthorns, he failed. It was almost like being inside a void, except for the strange burn of the magic in the air.

Some instinct told him to look up. And that was when Rhoyd realized they were passing under not an archway of trees but a gate of black stone.

"Michan?" he barely whispered.

Michan raised one hand to indicate silence was the better idea. A warm wind was whipping up and sending a stench of rot to fill the air. Rhoyd put a hand over his nose, gagging at the nastiness that caught in his throat and embittered his tongue like rotten bile. The men of the caravan could be heard retching and moaning and cursing in the dark.

There was suddenly a shout from the front of the line. Horses screaming, the scream of wooden wagon brakes being applied, and the skittering of metal-shod hooves on something akin to stone. The caravan was coming to a halt and wagons were being forced into a circle around the sides of what vaguely looked like an old courtyard in the feeble light of their torches and lanterns. The dark carriage was forced to stop right in the middle.

"Fergus!" Michan barked. "What in the name of Cernunnos is this place?"

If Fergus heard, he said nothing, but his men were certainly raising a clamor.

"It's some sort of castle!" someone shouted. "Look at those carvings."

Rhoyd wanted more light, so he stood up and whispered, *"Solus mhor!"*

A ball of white light formed over the dark carriage and spread. He heard men gasp and shout as the shadows seemed to slither back and away.

It was a castle, a very ancient one with stones as black as pitch that oozed niter and slime and dark green moss. The walls of the courtyard rose high and disappeared under the canopy of hawthorns that appeared to be growing out of the very walkways above. The structure before them had seen better days. Its facade displayed the broken eyes of what had once been windows, and from every one of those, Rhoyd felt as though he was being watched. He glanced back towards the rear and realized that not all the wagons had come through, and that where the opening had stood, there was nothing but darkness of wood and stone and metal, as though gates had closed behind them.

"Where's Eithne?" Rhoyd asked. "Where's Noreen?"

But of the cook's wagon that had been just behind them, there was no sign.

"Damn it!" Noreen shouted. Eithne awoke when she felt the wagon lurch to a halt. Nearly thrown from the pallet she was using for a bed, she cursed and dragged herself out of the back where she had been taking yet another nap. *Blessed Brother, why am I sleeping so much?* She stopped, her eyes widening. The world had fallen into an unnatural dark.

"What's wrong?" Eithne asked. "Where are the other wagons?"

"In there somewhere," Noreen said. She reached under her seat and drew out her sword.

Eithne looked ahead of them and frowned. All that greeted her was a crumbling wall of stone that seemed to rise forever into the canopy of trees.

"But how? What?" Confusion not unlike what she had been feeling for the last couple of days began to fog her thoughts. Like she had lost something and come ever so close to finding it.

"Your guess is as good as mine," Noreen said, standing up and tying off the reins so the horses would stay. "One minute, we're on the road, the next we're blocked by those bloody gates. By the beard of the All Father, this is not a natural thing."

Eithne frowned. Who was this All Father? She shook the question out of her head. This was no time to ask.

"Where is Rhoyd?" she asked.

"In there with the rest of them, like as not," Noreen said. "You had best stay here, Mistress Manahan and keep quiet. These woods are not safe."

"And where are you going?" Eithne asked.

"I am going to see if I can climb that wall. It's old and it's not exactly even."

"Not without me," Eithne said.

"What?" Noreen glowered at Eithne. "This is a matter for warriors and mages, not healers, Mistress."

"And when warriors and mages are finished, who usually cleans up the wounds they leave behind?" Eithne retorted. "I spent most of my youth on the battlefields of the Last War, Mistress Noreen, and I have never shirked from doing the Brother's will. If my son is in there, I have a duty to get him out. I've lost his father, and I will not lose him... At least, I think I have lost his father. Or have I?"

She paused as the silvery fog frosted over her memories again. *Conor is dead? Is he really dead? Did I really see him die?* The thoughts raged about and she shook herself, for in her heart it was hard to believe that he was gone. *But he is not here,* she retorted in her thoughts. *And if he is not dead, then where is he?*

She glanced up again, noticing the puzzled look on Noreen's face. "Michan better have another go at you when this is all over," the cook said. She shook her head and leapt off the wagon seat, dropping to the ground with a lot more grace than Eithne would have thought possible for a woman so large.

But then, Blessed Brother, I do not think that Noreen is what she seems either.

What a strange thought. Eithne mentally pushed it aside and scrambled over the back of the wagon seat, following the cook. Noreen glanced back, and her expression said that she might be about to chide Eithne for not staying back, but her eyes reflected that she knew this was a waste of time. So Noreen wandered over to the wall and put a hand to it and closed her eyes.

She suddenly cursed in a foreign tongue, pulling back her hand as though she had laid it on a viper and staggered back.

"By the All Father, it cannot be!" she said.

"What cannot be?" Eithne insisted. "Please stop speaking in riddles and tell me what you feel."

Noreen's face was white as she turned back to Eithne.

"It's here."

"What is here?"

"They call it Nimheil-Dubh, the Venomous Dark," Noreen said in a whisper, and fear festooned her features. "It is the rage of Ymir, festered and nurtured in the shadows of the Dark Mother herself. Born to serve the Lord of Shadows and to have dominion over all shadow beings in his service, it was thought to have hidden itself after the fall of the Shadow Lords. It's in there, with all the rest of them."

Eithne frowned and looked at the wall. The stones seemed to ooze some malaise. She reached over and laid a hand on the surface, and found it cold and damp. And like a living thing, it held a *need*, but not the need of healing. The need of hunger and death.

But Rhoyd is in there and I will not abandon him. Oh, Blessed Brother, give me strength. Give me courage.

She took a deep breath and felt around the wall. There were chinks enough in the stones, and cautiously, though it spread its cold damp through her clothes and froze the very marrow of her bones, she started to climb.

"Eithne, wait!" Noreen shouted.

"I can't wait," Eithne said. "I must find Rhoyd."

"But you don't understand," Noreen said, and Eithne heard the large woman scrambling to climb the wall as well. "You have no idea what this place is—what waits above. You must let me lead the way, at least."

"Let you lead?" Eithne groused. "You nearly got my son killed more than once. I don't know why Conor trusted you."

"Because he had no choice," Noreen grumbled. "Michan

never gave him one, the cheeky little..." She paused in her tirade and started to climb. To Eithne's surprise, Noreen proved swift for her size, quickly catching up with Eithne halfway up the wall. "And you have to let me go first."

"I do not have to do any such thing," Eithne retorted and picked up her pace, only to slip. She squeaked and managed to find a foothold to keep from falling, and for a moment, she clung to the wall.

"Ah, yer man was right when he said you were a stubborn, fiery little besom. It's a wonder the big lummox puts up with you."

"How dare you speak ill of the dead!" Eithne stopped and turned her head to glare at Noreen.

"He's not dead, Eithne. He's alive and well. Well, at least alive. But he's waiting for us at the Ford of Lea, probably warming his heels at some crofter's hearth fire and wondering why in the name of Cernunnos we're not there already."

"The Ford of Lea?" Eithne frowned. "He's at the Ford of Lea?"

"Yes," Noreen said, "and the god's help him, but we've been diverted off that road and into this trap. I've a good mind to tell Michan that he has no commonsense for this work. How the Demon-Bounds could have trusted him with this matter is beyond my comprehension."

"I...I don't understand," Eithne said. "How can Conor be waiting for us at the Ford of Lea when he... When he..."

"Damn, Michan and his mind spell. I told you, Conor is alive, and if we don't reach the Ford of Lea, I am willing to bet he'll know we're in trouble and get back on the road looking for us, and that won't be a good thing since he is injured."

"Conor is injured?" Eithne glared at the cook.

"Aye, those watchmen were not so gentle when they took him prisoner. Don't you remember anything of the truth? Michan is supposed to be scrubbing the false images from your mind, damn the little..."

Eithne frowned for there was one image forming in her head, that of Conor going down on cobbles. The boar that attacked him stood upright like a man and wore the standard of the watch of Cullstane on his jerkin. She closed her eyes with a gasp. The scrambling noises drew closer, and she felt Noreen drawing close.

"Conor is...alive?" Eithne whispered.

"Aye, he's alive," Noreen said. "Now you best let me take the lead the rest of the way."

"Why?" Eithne asked, opening her eyes to glower at the cook once more.

"Because I'm bigger, and because I've got a sword, and I've got magic spells as well. And because those shadows up there are moving about just like living things."

"Oh?" Eithne looked up. The shadows overhead *were* moving a bit. From their darkness, the flicker of twin embers winked like fireflies. Or were those glowing eyes? *Blessed Brother, avert! Darklings!* Eithne swallowed and nodded. "Very well, you can lead," she said.

Noreen moved up the wall a short ways. She stopped long enough to stretch her hand and shout, *"Solus!"* Mage light flickered to life, a bare foxfire glow in the unnatural dark, but the light's presence cast far enough to make the shadows whimper and withdraw. Noreen started on up, and Eithne followed, praying to Diancecht that Conor was indeed well.

If only for the comfort the thought that he lived brought her.

THIRTY-FIVE

Alaric stopped so suddenly, Conor nearly ran over the top of the smaller man. *Man? He's part demon!* Alaric was looking up towards something higher, so Conor shifted his own gaze in that direction.

At first, all Conor perceived was that the world seemed a paler grey through the silhouette of trees atop what he thought must have been a high ridge. But then, as his eyes adjusted, he realized that he was looking at a massive, slanted wall built out of irregular-shaped black stone. There were trees growing in and among the crenellations and along what would have been the walk. There were also shadows creeping through the tangle of hawthorns. And the air was filled with a vaguely familiar mixture of essences. Conor could feel Rhoyd's magic—knew its call like the back of his own hand. But with that sweet essence, he felt a power unlike any he had encountered since the Last War. Those hawthorns were there for a reason, and he was willing to bet it had nothing to do with planting.

Bogie trees, Conor thought and frowned. "What is this place?" he whispered aloud.

"Not a place we want to be," Alaric replied. "But a place we will have to enter all the same."

"What do you mean?" Conor asked.

"That's mage light, if I am not mistaken," Alaric said and frowned

"Aye, and it's my son, if that's what you're about to say." Conor hid a smile when Alaric turned an astonished look in his direction. "I know his glamorie."

Alaric smiled. "Indeed. Now I understand why the White One said you would be a good man to raise the lad."

Conor felt his face warm with a blush. "White One? What's a White One?"

"She Who Sits at the Center of All Things and maintains The Balance of All Things," Alaric replied. "She who took the body of the giant Ymir and made the world on which we stand."

Conor cocked one eyebrow to indicate his uncertainty about all this blatherskite.

"We must make haste," Alaric said. "Tie your horse there. I will circle the beast with a ring of light to protect it from what resides in the dark."

Conor frowned, but he obeyed, hitching Battlebrute to the limb of a sturdy old oak that had managed to maintain its ancient presence in the midst of all these hawthorns, and even allowed glims of natural light to seep in and mottle the ground. Stepping close to it was like walking out of winter and into a warm spring.

Alaric, meanwhile, walked around the perimeter of the tree, whispering and touching the ground, and where he walked, light blossomed, raising a wall of brilliance.

Conor would have stayed and admired the beauty of it, but he heard someone scream.

"Come, I'll carry you," Alaric said, backing away from the circle of light, and as Conor followed the man turned back into a familiar form, that of a cross between a demon and his true self. Spreading wings, the creature stepped around behind Conor and seized him in surprisingly strong arms. Before he could protest, it rose into the air, bearing him along.

He just hoped they would not get tangled in any of the trees.

Eithne was grateful when Noreen stopped at the top of the wall long enough to give her a hand clambering up the last little bit. The path of foxfire light the mageborn woman had laid before them like a carpet seemed paler here. But then, considering what burned down in the courtyard, Eithne suspected no light would appear as bright. She shaded her eyes and tried to look into the brilliance.

But she could make out little more than a milling of men and restless horses.

"Your lad's got a way with making everyone else's magic look so feeble," Noreen said. Still, she whispered a spell of her own and laying fingers upon the forte of her blade, she said, "Solus feith." The steel took on an eerie glow.

"What's that for?" Eithne asked.

"Just in case," Noreen said. "I think I see old stairs over there."

She pointed to a place just beyond. Eithne saw what looked like the ruins of a gatehouse and next to it, crumbling stairs of stone that followed the inside wall to the ground.

"Yes, I think you're right," Eithne said and started towards them.

"Eithne, wait, I should lead in case..." Noreen's words were lost to a curse as the hawthorns snagged the larger woman's braided hair.

Eithne was about to say, *"In case what?"* but before those words could leave her thoughts, let along cross her lips something slithered between the trunks of the trees, staring at her with red glowing eyes. Eithne squealed before she could stop herself. The creature reared up, a blanket of darkness with a maw of sharp teeth, and swooped towards her.

"Get down!" Noreen shouted.

Eithne knew better than to disobey. She dropped to her knees on the rough stones just as that glowing blade cut the space where her head had been and slashed the black blanket of a beast in two. It screamed and fell, each half turning into rotten decay. The foul stench that rose clogged Eithne's throat. She gagged and coughed, waving her hands before her. Turning to back away, she looked up and saw that another creature was about to throw itself over Noreen from behind.

"Look out!" Eithne cried.

Noreen shouted and slashed the air behind her, cutting into the beast. It screamed and fluttered away, leaving more of the hideous stench.

Blessed Brother, we shall choke to death if we do not get off this wall.

"Go on!" Noreen shouted. "Save yourself now! Get into the light! *Loisg!*"

Fire blossomed even as Noreen shouted, and in its light Eithne saw that more of the dreadful creatures were surging out of the shadows of the trees to attack. There was nothing she could do but scramble for the stairs. She fell more than once, hearing Noreen shouting epithets and spells alike at the beasts as they tried to surround the mageborn woman. Eithne looked back at the conflagration that the hawthorns had become. She could see Noreen lashing away with her sword.

Blessed Brother, there is nothing I can do to help her. She had no skill with magic, and her staff was back down in the wagon.

Besides, one of the creatures was tearing itself away from

the attack and swarming through the hawthorns towards Eithne. She had no choice but to flee towards the stairs and the light below.

The creature pursuing her lashed out with a claw, shearing through her sleeve, ripping into her shoulder. Eithne shrieked from the hot, fiery pain and stumbled forward, determined to reach the light. She would not allow herself to be taken, not now. She practically threw herself towards the stairs, falling to her knees at the top, crawling down like a dog on all fours. The darkling had to stop at the edge of the wall just at the head of the stairs, for as soon as it lashed at her again, the brilliant light ate part of it away.

Eithne stopped long enough to right herself and turned to survey the scene below.

The edges of the white light were alive with shadowy creatures even more terrifying than the ones on the wall. These things had a variety of frightening shapes and moved upright like men, and yet she could see their features were nothing human at all. They looked like dragons and demons, like insects, like dogs and parodies of many other beasts. They were flailing at the men who were fleeing into the circle of light.

Among the men she made out one figure in a familiar cloak. Captain Camhin had lost his glamour and rushed about in his true shape. Michan had given up trying to hide himself. Like Noreen, he had attached a spell of light to his sword, and he was rushing at the edges of light, trying to fight off the monsters and help the men.

At the center of the maelstrom of white, she made out a small figure, arms upraised, standing on the seat of the dark carriage.

Rhoyd!

Eithne hurried down the stairs, determined to reach him, when she saw something up in the air. She raised her eyes and gasped.

Conor—at least, it looked like Conor—was descending out of the air, but from where she stood, he appeared to have four legs and wings and extra arms. His face was pallid and unnatural.

"Eithne!" he suddenly shouted and pointed. "There she is! Over there!"

Like something out of a nightmare, he flew at her. The fog

that had danced over her thoughts of late now smothered her with panic.

No, it cannot be him! He is dead! He is dead! I saw him die...I saw...I saw...

Confusion and fear surfaced. If Conor was truly dead, then what was that thing flying at her now, calling her name.

She decided not to wait around and find out. Prompted by the cloud of confusion and terror, she bolted for the inner gates, cutting through the edge of the light.

"Eithne, wait!" the strange apparition called. "Eithne, I need you!"

But she was beyond understanding. She only knew that she had to flee, and the only place to go was inside the keep itself.

THIRTY-SIX

It looked as though the whole world was burning. Conor saw Rhoyd standing in the middle of the light, and his heart sang with joy to know the lad was holding these foul creatures away with his magic. When he saw Eithne standing along the edge of that light, he felt certain all would be well.

At least, until she turned and fled for the darkness of the keep.

"Put me down!" he shouted at Alaric, and the creature flew across the path of light to the far side to set Conor on the ground. He staggered a few steps, then righted himself and started to rush into the dark.

"No wait, here," Alaric said.

Conor turned to bark at the creature that he had no time to wait, but he found instead the man had returned.

"Let me see your sword," Alaric said.

Conor raised the blade. Alaric seized it. "This is your only hope if there are more of these things in there. *Solus feith mhor.*"

Conor flinched as he felt his steel quiver with the surge of magic. His small hairs stood on end.

"Go, get her out of there. I will see what I can do to help Michan."

With a nod, Conor surged towards the gate, half limping, and he crossed out of the threshold of light. Horns, what would possess Eithne to enter such a dark and terrible place?

But when he got through the gate, he saw it was not dark, but grey from the feeble shards of daylight that managed to creep through the holes in what was once a grand hall's roof. He heard none of the sounds of creatures as he would have expected. No stoats, no ravens, not even a rat dwelled inside this place. A rank-smelling cold filled the place, something fetid as a midden heap and chilling as winter. Conor could see his own breath, and a glance at the damp stone walls showed him ice among the trickles of water.

Why was it so cold in here? Like winter had come to this

place. Long winter, such as he had heard about in the old tales.

He stopped in the middle of the grand hall and listened. No sound of footsteps echoed. Just the sigh of the wind whispering through the emptiness.

"Eithne?" he called, and his breath stirred the air and his words echoed around him. *Eithne, Eithne, Eithne...*

"Eithne, it's me," he called more quietly. "Woman where are ye?"

Had some fiend claimed her? Had she fallen into a hole? As his eyes adjusted to the barely visible light, he felt certain he saw several of them, cavernous maws in the floor from which foul odors emitted. There must have been a battle here long ago, and all that managed to grow were the hawthorns and the moss. There were trees perched here and there, making him wonder if someone planted them there on purpose? Some of them undulated with shadows that dared not step even into the feeble light that assailed their hall.

"Eithne, where are you?" Conor called.

He heard footsteps, someone running up behind him from the dark opening at his back. He turned swiftly, his grasp tight on the sword, determined to meet whatever challenge was there.

"Conor, it's me!" Michan threw up his hands.

"What are you doing in here? Shouldn't you be out there looking after Rhoyd?" Conor barked.

"Rhoyd is fine for now. Noreen managed to get over the wall and is going to help him hold the light. He's one tough little lad. Now where is Eithne?"

Conor frowned. "She came in here..."

Michan closed his eyes then gestured towards their left. "That way," he said.

Conor looked toward the left and saw an archway. Once it had been carved stone, and a fine tapestry would have covered it in winter. Now, little more than strands like a spider's web remained barely moving. Within the shadows, Conor could see a small figured hunched against the stones.

"Eithne?" he said.

She rose suddenly with a whimper and fled.

"Eithne, wait!" Conor bolted after her. *What was wrong with her? Why was she running away?* It was as though she did not know him.

He stopped in the opening. The patter of her soft boots had stopped again.

"Eithne, it's me," he said and stepped on through.

"Stay away from me, monster!" she suddenly cried.

Conor barely turned in time. A chunk of stone aimed for his head was all he saw. He barely dodged the blow that would have broken his skull, and felt thankful that the one who tried to bash his head with it was too short to reach the top. Lashing across with his free hand, he managed to knock the stone aside. Eithne screamed and kicked at him and turned and fled. Her path took her into a corner with no visible means of escape.

"Eithne!" he said firmly. "Woman, what is wrong with you?"

"No!" Eithne cried and backed away swiftly, stumbling over tree roots and broken cobbles as she fled the corner and sought another way to escape. "Stay away from me!" Tears streamed down her cheeks, mingling with the dirt ground into her complexion, but beneath the soil, her skin was pale with fear. She looked around as though seeking some weapon to defend herself.

"Eithne, wait!" Conor called, and he hurried after her as best he could with his leg screaming in pain. "It's me!"

"No!" she cried. "You're dead!"

"It's no good, Conor!" Michan shouted. "The spell is still in her head...I haven't been able to remove all the false memories. Her real memories just aren't strong enough yet."

Conor stopped and turned on Michan like a cornered bear. He reached out and seized the front of Michan's doublet, practically jerking the mageborn off his feet, in spite of the pain it fired in his battered ribs.

"Then you'd best remove them now!" Conor roared. "Because if you don't, I'll be removing most of your entrails with my bare hands."

"All right, all right," Michan said, holding up his hands. "But I have to touch her, and I can't get near her if you keep frightening her."

Conor swore and let go, shoving hard enough to push the mageborn off balance. Michan fell over on his arse, looking stunned. But then he scrambled to his feet and hurried past Conor.

Eithne was over at the other corner, stumbling around in the shadows, looking for an opening out of the ruined chamber.

At one point, she seemed to contemplate the height of a narrow window, no more than an arrow slit in Conor's opinion, but Eithne was small and wiry. If she managed to get up there, he had no doubt that she could worm herself through.

"Eithne," Michan said gently. "It's all right, I'm here."

Eithne turned and looked at him, her eyes glazed with wild fear. "No, you're dead. I saw you die."

"Eithne, it's me...Michan."

"No! You're a demon! You're in disguise. You're just pretending to be Michan."

"No, Eithne, it is me."

"No! Rhoyd was right, there is a demon here, and it's you...it's you...it's both of you..."

"Eithne!" Michan snapped.

But she would not listen to him. The madness narrowed her eyes as he came at her. She cringed against the wall, then shouting, she pushed away and shoved her hands into Michan's chest as hard as she was able.

Michan stumbled back, tripping over the broken cobbles and smacking his head. Conor saw Michan wince in pain, and the mageborn's face went white and he flopped back and moaned. Eithne flew past him, but in her haste, she seemed to forget the broken cobbles fringing yet another hole in the floor. She tripped over one of the loose stones and lost her balance as well, and before Conor could dive forward and seize her, she fell.

"No!" Conor shouted and threw himself at the hole. Gritting his teeth, he knelt at the edge and looked into the pit.

She was there, just a fraction more than his arm's length, clinging to part of the old braces. Her feet were scrambling for purchase on the wall.

"Eithne, give me your hand!" Conor called and lay himself down as best he could. His body protested every move, every touch, but he leaned over the edge and stretched a hand down towards her.

"No, stay away!" she wailed like a child. "Don't hurt me, please."

Conor swallowed. His shoulder was on fire, and every ounce of pain fought his need to stay focused, but he softened his features with worry and tried catch her eyes with his own. "Eithne, my wife, the woman I love. Please. Give me your hand before you fall."

"No, you're dead...I saw you trampled by the boar..."

"Lies," Conor said. "Just lies in your head, woman. Michan put them there to keep you safe, but they're just lies. I'm here, Eithne. I'll always be here for you. I told you that when I courted you, I told you that when you gave me your heart. You would not jump the fire, remember? You thought it was foolish."

She stopped struggling, looking at him.

"You gave me a son, and bandits took that son, but you stayed with me through the worst years as well as the best. And I'm not letting ye go now, woman. Just give me your hand, and all will be well."

Tears were flooding her cheeks now.

"I saw...I saw...men hurting you in the town, but then...you were gone and they said you were dead and...Conor? Is that really you?"

"Aye, woman, it's me, and I'm needing yer special skills because I'm hurt bad. Give me your hand."

She hung there, looking uncertain then slowly, she stretched one hand towards him. Conor leaned, though he felt himself nearly blacking out from the angle. He caught hold of her wrist and began to haul her up. She did not resist, but she did not assist either, and he thought his shoulder was going to come out of the socket.

"Michan!" he hissed through gritted teeth.

He heard Michan scrambling unsteadily to his side, and the mageborn looked as though someone had painted his face with flour, he was so white. But he reached down and seized Eithne's arm as well, and between them, they pulled her out of the hole.

For a moment, the three of them lay panting. *Like the old dogs we are,* Conor thought and grinned. Then slowly Eithne sat up. Her eyes were damp as he leaned over him.

"Conor?" she said, touching his face.

He smiled. "Aye, woman, it's me."

"What happened to you? Why did I think you were dead?"

"I nearly was," he said. "When they took me away from you and Rhoyd, I thought I was dead."

She traced his cheeks, then leaned over and kissed him. "Rest, my love," she said. "And I will make all your pains go away."

Her trembling hands touched Conor, feeling the lump on

his shoulder and the injuries of his legs. She closed her eyes and whispered, "Blessed Brother hear my plea..."

Michan rose slowly to his feet, his face awash with amazement as Eithne's prayers filled Conor with soothing warmth. His pains ebbed and flowed like tides throughout his body, and then slowly, they vanished, smoke on the wind, leaving him stiff and tired, but whole.

Her hands drew back slowly. The vague look returned to her eyes.

"Now tell me," she said, frowning at Conor as though he were a stranger to her. "How is it you look so much like my husband?"

Conor opened his mouth then shut it. He sat up and frowned at Michan. "You damn well better fix her mind, Michan. You damn well better have my Eithne back whole when I'm done."

Conor crawled to his feet.

"Where are you going?" Michan asked.

"To make certain Rhoyd is all right."

He started back out of the ruins, and the last thing he saw was Michan taking Eithne's hand, putting fingers to her forehead and whispering in the mage tongue.

THIRTY-SEVEN

The things that had come crawling out of the wall had frightened Rhoyd, and calling the light had kept most of them away, but now as he drained his own essence to conjure the light in this dark and dismal place, he saw two figures approaching. One was Noreen, her sword like a brand of fire. Her clothes were torn in several places, and a gash had been laid open on her cheek, and it trickled with blood.

The other. Rhoyd thought he should have known the other, for there was something familiar in his countenance. And as the other approached, it became clearer what he was seeing was a man with a demon inside him.

You? he thought, and his concentration almost died. *You were Bowen once.*

"Rhoyd, take what you need from me, lad," Noreen called, distracting him.

Rhoyd blinked as he felt her practically throwing her essence out to him. But he seized it and grafted it into his own, and felt relieved when the steady stream of her essence gave him more power.

But that's blood magic! Aunt Genna says I must never borrow essence from others.

He came close to severing the tie when he turned and found the other was crawling up onto the carriage with him. Noreen crawled up on the other side. Each of them touched him, offering him their power, and as it surged through him, he felt an odd mixture of magic both ancient and new. Demon's magic, man magic, and something that carried an essence he could not quite identify. Yet he thought that it might be the essence of a dragon, a white dragon.

He would have concentrated on it more, but suddenly, all the shadowy fiends just vanished. They sank back into the stones of the walls and down into the ground and up among the trees.

It's working, he thought. *I'm driving them away!*

Brief joy assailed him, lifting his spirits. This was wonderful, to have so much power that creatures of darkness feared him. Why would he ever be afraid of the dark again? He was all powerful, mageborn—*Ard Magister...*

The pride was short-lived.

"Something is not right here," Noreen said.

The other was looking about in uncertainty. "Why are they hiding?"

Cold suddenly seeped into the air, tendrils like ice chilling the air.

"No," the other said.

"What's wrong?" Rhoyd asked.

"You stay here," the other said, and he leapt off the carriage to wander around the ground. There was an eerie quiet in the air. The men of the caravan were huddling together, swords ready as they glanced thither and yon. Quick glances of unease. Furtive glances of fear.

Rhoyd leaned towards Noreen. "Who is he?" he asked, gesturing towards the stranger.

Noreen leaned even closer and whispered, "That, my lad, is Magister Alaric Braidwine—the Demon-Bound himself."

Rhoyd glanced back at the man. *The Demon-Bound? Here? Why?*

He would have voiced those questions, but the cold was growing sharper. Rhoyd took a deep breath and saw it whiten in the air. The light that he still held about them was glancing off the sheen of fog that rose and fell.

Where did that come from?

Alaric suddenly gave a shout. The ground of the courtyard was growing soft like old mud in a rain. Some of the men stumbled and slid as it went mushy beneath them. Things began to shoot out of it, tendrils like roots—or the arms of a sea creature Conor once showed to Rhoyd. They spread around the edges of the circle of light and began seizing what men did not clamber back up onto the wagons.

What the...

Before Rhoyd had time to think, the dark carriage heaved as though something had risen under it, and the sudden rocking threw him forward. Noreen caught him before he fell, but the whole motion wrecked his concentration. His white light flickered out like a candle in a strong wind.

And then the real screams began.

Conor hurried out of the keep. The cold he had felt inside now seemed to be spreading outward. *Why?* He quickened his pace, reaching the short ramp that led down to the main yard and slid to a halt.

Rhoyd's magical light was gone. Men shouted and screamed in confusion. Chaos had descended with the darkness.

Through it, he heard Alaric shouting the spell of light, and once more the feeble foxfire of a glow spread. The man had regained his demonic form and was flying up into the air to escape one of the long tendrils when it tried to snag him. The magic he invoked held something of a demon's essence and bitterness washed Conor's tongue. *Horns, the man is more demon than not!* he thought as he rushed down the ramp.

But as soon as he stepped upon the ground, his foot sank into unnatural ooze, and a tendril lashed at him. Cursing, he fell back, slashing at it with the glowing sword. The blade severed it, and the stump sprayed a cold black ichor as the amputated end splattered and turned into a stagnant-smelling liquid. Conor reared back from the stench and stayed on the stone ramp, glowering at the scene in the courtyard.

In the midst of it all, he saw the dark carriage rocking back and forth. The man who was on the lead horse was now throwing himself off the beast. A mistake to be sure, for he sank as though in shallow water, and he screamed in fright. And then there were the tendrils, like the arms of an octopus that flailed and snagged the man, dragging him into the mire.

The wagon was now clearly the target of the tendrils. They lashed at it, slipping in and out of the spokes of the wheels. In order to escape the grasping tendrils, Rhoyd clambered up onto the seat of the dark wagon. The tendrils seized the horses as they struggled to escape the mire in which they were sinking and wrapped about them like vines. The screams of the two black drays and the lead horse were horrible.

Conor started to charge forward again, but Michan lurched into his path. "No wait, it's not safe to stand on the ground," Michan said.

"Where's Eithne?"

"Asleep. The last of the spell drained her."

"Are you certain she's safe?"

"I surrounded her in light and warmth. Nothing will get at her, I promise you."

"You've made me many promises in your day, Michan, but

at the moment I'm having trouble..."

Both Rhoyd and Noreen gave startled shouts.

Conor looked up in time to see the horses dragged into the ground. The monster was wrapping tendrils around the wagon wheels as well, sliding them up into the axles without touching the wagon itself. Briefly, Conor thought that perhaps the spells on the dark carriage were going to keep the lad safe. But it was then he saw the billowing of smoke that rose into the air and arched over the top of the wagon.

Conor shouted Rhoyd's name, and heard the lad scream. Then at once, the whole mass of darkness began to descend into the ground. It sank through mud and dirt and stone.

Shouting again, Conor shoved Michan aside and ran for the sinking mound, but even as he reached it—as he flung himself at it—he landed on a solid surface of stone. Wet cobbles plastered with leaves and dirt stopped him.

"No!" He rose to his knees, scrabbling at the leaves and the dirt, trying desperately to find a way through.

But there was nothing there except stone and earth. He slammed the pommel of his sword against it for all the good it served.

The ground was solid again, and Conor had no way of reclaiming his son.

THIRTY-EIGHT

The faint light from the glow of Noreen's sword was the first thing to greet Rhoyd's gaze when he opened his eyes. In the heavy shadows, it was no more than a firefly's flicker, not even enough for mage eyes to work properly.

With a moan, Rhoyd tried to push up off the semi-soft uneven surface on which he lay. But one of his arms had fallen asleep from the awkward position in which it was cramped, and when he moved the arm, it sang a protest of needles and pins and pain.

Oh, horns, was it broken? No, he could wriggle the fingers, even if he could not see them move. But something was sticking deeply into him, almost to the bone, so he tried once more to get up, pushing off to one side. There was a tearing sound that he thought might be his sleeve, and a sting that could only have been the slice of cold steel. He yelped and rolled over only to discover the surface on which he had lain was higher than the rest of the ground. The short drop startled him so that he yelped again as he landed on his back.

Horns! He glanced over to find the mound in question was Noreen. It took him only a moment then to realize that she had broken his fall, and that the sharp pain had been caused by landing on her belt buckle. And that the buckle had just enough of an edge to tear cloth and gouge flesh.

He worked his other hand over and felt warmth and moisture on his own arm. The coppery scent reached his nose as he brought the hand back close to his face.

He was bleeding.

Awkwardly, he pushed himself upright and peered at the cook. She was not moving, not much. He put a hand on her ribs and felt a faint motion when she drew a shallow breath.

At least she was alive. Cautiously, he crawled up towards her head, hitting something with his own.

The wagon seat felt shorter than before.

The dark carriage?

Rhoyd felt around, letting his hands guide him. Yes, it

was the dark carriage on which he had been sitting before the monster attacked and he fell...

He had fallen, hadn't he? Sort of. He remembered his light failing when the carriage bucked beneath him and nearly threw him off. He remembered Noreen catching him before he landed on the ground. And then he remembered suffocating in a darkness that swallowed him. Long writhing tendrils that dragged them rapidly down through the earth as though it were water. He shuddered to recall how for a time, it had closed around him so he thought he was being sucked down in the gullet of some behemoth.

But then there had been a drop and a jarring stop...and then it all went blank.

He sat up carefully and grimaced.

"Noreen?" he whispered, not liking the odd echo of his own voice in this stygian dark.

She did not move, but his ears told him that something else did. Oh, it was faint, like the drawing of a breath. Like the leaves tumbled by a wind. Accompanying it was a slurping sound as though something fed.

And then there was the smell. Cold and harsh in his nose. Nauseating him as he drew each breath.

Whatever it was stank like pig droppings. No matter how hard he pinched his nose, the odor filled it like a noxious plague. Rhoyd's stomach churned. He was going to vomit if he did not wake Noreen up and find his way out of this hole. But it was pitch dark beyond the faint glow of the sword, and even mageborn could not see where there was no light. He would have called a globe of mage light, but he did not want to be a beacon.

Then again, he reminded himself that whatever dwelled in this dark and made it smell so bad was either already dead like the horses or not terribly fond of light. So he wrinkled his nose, drew essence from himself and whispered *"Solus..."*

And flinched when the dark gave a shriek and slithered away in a mass of tendrils and wet ooze. In its wake, he could see the half-eaten remains of the drays. Their bones jutted as though the flesh had been drained of nearly all fluid through the gashes in their hides. A trail of entrails lay scattered.

Rhoyd closed his eyes and moaned. That was the source of the smell. Once when Conor was slaughtering a deer, he had pulled the entrails out and commented on the fact that the beast had apparently not defecated yet that day. Rhoyd remembered that it had reeked much like what he smelled now. Well, maybe not quite as much.

We need to get out of here before I do vomit, he thought. Just at the edge of his light, he could sense that the dark putrid thing that had been feeding on the horses was waiting, hovering, eager to go back to its meal.

Rhoyd reached over and pushed Noreen's shoulder. "Noreen?" he said.

She did not stir. Her breathing was hoarse and labored. He shook her a little more, not certain what else to do, but she would not wake up. Leaning over her, he put his hand on her face. The flesh was clammy, and now he could see a trickle of blood descending from the other side of her head. He carefully moved so he could look closer.

Yes, it was blood. A bleeding gash.

And he had no idea how to stop it.

Or did he? Eithne once said something about pressure on a wound could staunch the blood, but what if he hurt Noreen worse? Horns, he wished Eithne was down here.

Well, no, he didn't because then there would be three of them trapped in whatever unknown realm this was.

Sitting up, he sought to draw essence from the air and willed his mage light larger. Its illumination spread, and he heard the slimy thing in the dark hiss and sputter and withdraw. The spread of light revealed that he was in some sort of chamber. Not a cavern as he would have expected, but a large room that stretched as far as a castle's great hall. He had seen such a hall in Wenthorn, one that appeared to go on for hundreds of meters. He made his light larger still, and the dark thing retreated behind arches of black stone.

Arches! Yes! If there were arches, this was a structure, and there had to be a way out.

But...I can't carry Noreen, and if I can't get her to wake up. He didn't really like the idea of leaving her here alone in this dark any more than he liked the thought of going forth on his own. But there really wasn't much of a choice.

I could draw a circle of light around her to protect her. It would take effort, he knew. He could find essence in the air, but there were other essences here that did not strike him as friendly. Shadow never made a good source for light spells.

There's magic in the carriage. Rhoyd touched the wood

with his free hand. He felt Michan's spells and the power that fed them tingle. The carriage was not sitting straight. It was leaning towards the front where he and Noreen had landed. So he pushed at the small wooden door behind the carriage seat.

At first, it refused to budge. Frowning, Rhoyd picked up Noreen's sword. A heavy blade in his small hand, but its steel was strong enough to use it to pry at the door. He heard a pop, and the door fell inward.

White light hit his face, more brilliant than his own. Everything in the carriage was glowing so bright he had to shade his eyes. Yes, more than enough power. More than enough light, for that matter. It rose and spread and the dark arches practically turned white, and the thing that was hidden behind them mewled and retreated even more.

She'll be safe enough, he thought. Still clutching her sword, he thrust it into the white light and whispered, *"Solus feith mhor."* The blade turned as white as the carriage then, and he quickly laid it back at her side, getting one of the hanging lanterns and setting the same spell on it. Now he would have the means of carrying a light that would not drain him.

Crawling down as low as the wagon would allow, he put a tentative foot on the ground. Nothing grabbed him. The ground felt solid underfoot. He sighed and lowered himself the rest of the way, standing and shining his lantern around.

The arches to either side still moaned with the sounds of the slimy creature that fled his light. The far end boasted what looked like a set of double doors, one of which hung off to the side. Rhoyd started towards it, ever aware as he moved away from the carriage that he was getting colder and his breath was fogging the air before his face. He wished he had his cloak. It was in the cook's wagon just now.

No matter now. If he moved faster, he might feel warmer.

He picked up his pace, opening all sides of the lantern to let more light play on his surroundings. Shadows seemed to leap away as he crossed the chamber and headed for the doors at the far end.

With luck, it would lead to stairs that would take him out of here.

Conor lurched to his feet as Michan and Alaric hurried towards the place where he stood.

"Damn it, where are they?" Conor snarled, turning toward them with a heart full of rage. He wanted to grab both of them, to run swords through them, but he held the desire in check. Now was not the perfect time to give in to the madness. His son was somewhere down in the earth at his feet, and Conor wanted only to find the lad.

Assuming he is still alive?

He hated himself for that thought.

Michan closed his eyes. Alaric knelt, and his form shifted to the slightly demonic shape as he passed a hand over the ground.

"I cannot sense them," Alaric said.

"Neither can I," Michan agreed. "The carriage has spells on it that should let me find it, but I cannot sense it either."

This is not good.

"We know it went down," Conor said. "There must be another way down there."

"Possibly," Alaric agreed. "But if this place is like so many of the ancient homes of the ones who served the Dark Mother in ancient times, then that path will not be so easy to find."

A muttering managed to steal Conor's attention. He glanced at their surroundings. The caravan guards were stirring now, like dogs shaking out of a dream. Their courage was returning, and Conor did not like what he saw in their eyes. The faces of the survivors of this strange battle were haggard and worn. The murmurs of discontent grew, and like a pack of wolves, they began to circle Conor, Michan and Alaric.

What is going on here?

One of the bolder ones—Conor recognized Creed—stepped forward and raised his sword, using it to point accusingly at Conor.

"How did you get here?" Creed asked.

Conor hesitated to say, *"I flew,"* since they might not have noticed his strange arrival.

"I saw him come out of the sky," a guard named Stoner said. "That one there is not a man."

Alaric looked at his accuser. "I can assure you that I am only one of the mageborn," he said.

"I ne'er saw a mageborn with wings," Stoner retorted, and others nodded in agreement.

"Listen," Michan said. "We've no time for this."

"And just who on the bloody horns are you?" Creed asked.

"I'm the man who hired you," Michan said. "I'm Captain Camhin."

"You don't look like the captain at all," Stoner snarled.

Michan took a deep breath. Conor could see the effort was costing the mageborn, and felt the faint draw of something pulling at his nerves. Michan whispered his spell, and the illusion flickered to life across his features. The men traded unhappy glances, and the murmuring returned. Michan let the illusion fall and swayed a bit from the effort.

"He's one of the mageborn, too," a guard named Hackett said. "No wonder we've had nothing but bad luck."

This is turning into a bloody nuisance, Conor thought.

"Aye, he's mageborn," Conor said, "and I've known him since my militia days. He was a good man then when he stood on the battlefields and fought against the Hound, and is still a good man now."

"And we're supposed to trust you?" Creed asked. "The last time we saw you, the watch in Cullstane was dragging you off to the tower for murdering Warden."

"I did not kill Warden," Conor said, "Nor Gandon."

"And what about Bowen? He's disappeared, too," Hackett snarled.

"*I* was Bowen," Alaric said.

"And you're the one the boy said was a demon," Creed retorted. "And now that we've seen you looking like a demon, we think the boy was right. So why should we take your word?"

"You can take words, or not, lads," Conor said. "But I've no quarrel with any of ye. I want to save my son, and I'll take down any man who stands in my way."

With those words, Conor raised his sword. Some of the men edged back as though not wanting to challenge this tall red-haired Keltoran. But Creed and Stoner held their ground, keeping their blades at the ready. Though nowhere near as tall as Conor, they were not small men by any means. And he had seen their prowess against bandits to know they would go down fighting hard if it came to that.

"You and yours are to blame for all this," Creed said. "You led us to this place all to hide that bloody black carriage of yours, and now you want us to stand down so you can do whatever nefarious work you have planned."

"We are not the men who led you here," Conor said.

"No, indeed," Michan said and looked up at Conor with a frown. "We're not the ones who chose this road at all."

"Who did then?" Creed challenged.

Michan scanned the crowd. "Surely you recall it was Master Fergus who insisted this was the right road to take…"

That set more murmurs going off. Conor looked around.

"Where in the name of Cernunnos is Fergus?" Conor asked.

The men quickly traded looks and searched their ranks. There was no sign of the caravan master anywhere.

"I saw him go inside," one of the men said. "He went inside when the battle started…ran away like a coward, he did."

"Are you sure it was Fergus?" Michan asked.

"You know anyone else who smells like rotten turnips?" the guard replied.

"Eithne is still in there," Conor said.

He started towards the keep. The men parted and let him pass. Alaric and Michan were on his heels as he rushed into the keep once more.

Light was going away. The daylight was heading towards the horizon, separated from this part of the world by the mountains and highlands of Keltora to the west.

"Where did you leave her?" Conor asked.

Michan took the lead, rushing towards the inner chamber where Conor had nearly lost his wife down a hole.

A circle of light glowed in the middle of the floor.

But Eithne was nowhere to be seen.

THIRTY-NINE

Eithne was having such a strange and sad dream. She was seeing Conor beaten and dragged away by several men dressed as town watch. When she tried to stop them, she fell into a deep pit, but just then, Conor had hold of her, and he was telling her that she was going to be all right. The reassuring sound of his voice was still echoing in her head when she opened her eyes.

Blessed Brother, where am I? All she could see was shadows and ice beyond a ring of lights. *Mage light?* Eithne slowly sat up, pushing her hair from her eyes. Yes, it was a ring of mage lights. Rhoyd sometimes set them around their camps, usually when Conor told the lad some horrid tale that was guaranteed to keep them all awake at night.

But Rhoyd didn't set these, she thought. Somewhere in the back of her mind, she had the vague impression that it had been Michan who did so. He had also told her to sleep and heal herself in her dreams.

How odd, she thought. *Why would he tell me that?*

And where were Conor and Rhoyd?

She stood up, gathering her cloak, which had been turned into a bed on the wretched-looking floor. Not the sort of place she would normally sleep. It was dank and smelly, for one thing. And how could there be ice on the walls when the place where she stood was warm?

And what were all those shouts about?

Well, she certainly would not find an answer here. Men were yelling in anger and in fear, and her sudden instinct was to find out why, for she knew whatever was going on, Rhoyd and Conor had to be in the thick of it. Perhaps they were being attacked by bandits?

She was about to head for the source of the sound when she saw a figure flitting past the opening to the chamber where she had slept. Frowning, Eithne stepped out of the light and hurried towards the opening of the arch. That was Master Fergus, and if she was not mistaken, he was limping and dragging one foot.

Poor man, he must have been injured in the fight.

Indeed, she sensed his need calling to her.

Blessed Brother, that cannot be allowed to stay. She hurried after him as he disappeared down the long length of the dark hall. For a moment, she hesitated, because she could not actually see where he had gone. And yet, his need called to her like a beacon.

It would be nice to see though, she thought.

She glanced back at the circle of lights. Michan had set them on loose cobbles and old floor stones. Hurrying back, she reached into the light. Rhoyd had taught her long ago that mage light was harmless to mortals. To her good fortune, one of the stones was loose enough that she could pick it up, and to her delight, the glow remained firmly attached to the stone.

This would serve as her lantern. She hurried back into the great hall. Master Fergus' need was still calling to her, though it was growing faint. She would have to run to catch him.

She bolted the length of the great hall, using the light of the stone to help her avoid the many holes in the floor. At the far end, there were archways that led to halls, and a doorway to one side. She stopped, letting her light play on the various openings in thought.

Blessed Brother, which way did he go?

Taking a deep breath, she closed her eyes. The *need* flourished through one of the arches. She opened her eyes and followed that trail of pain, noting to herself that it exuded a call of dying.

Master Fergus must have been seriously wounded. There was little time to lose.

The archway opened into a narrow corridor that did not exactly follow a straight path. Indeed as she followed swiftly along, she got the impression that it twisted and wound back on itself. But that was not possible, was it? Because even though she felt the floor turn at odd angles, she never thought she was going around any corner.

At least until she came to the stairs. They were there so abruptly she nearly missed her step, and just managed to catch herself. The stone, however, leapt from her hand and went bouncing down into the dark. Eager to reclaim her only source of light, she quickly followed it down. It stopped at the bottom, rolling up against what she thought was a stone.

But the stone moved and fled into the shadows with a startled squeak that could only have belonged to a rat.

Eithne thought of turning back then. Rats were not to her liking, for they were filthy creatures and carried fleas. But just as she picked up her stone, she once more felt *need* calling even more strongly than before. More than one person was in pain.

Blessed Brother, what is going on here?

She could not ignore that call. Though she could not help but wonder why Master Fergus would have fled into such a place. She knew that some animals ran away and hid when they were injured, but not men.

No matter, she told herself. The *need* continued to sing to her, and there was nothing she could do but follow.

Even into the dark.

Rhoyd felt like he had been wandering for a long time. And the halls in this place were not straight. They curved, much like the pathways of old garden mazes. In fact, this one reminded him of the sevenfold path Aunt Genna once left him in the center of. A stone maze out on a plain, and she had left him alone in the middle to find his own way out because she thought it was good for him to use his mage senses to find his way.

In this strange dark, beyond the light of his lantern, he wasn't so sure mage senses would work. He had tried to stretch them a little, but he kept meeting some dark barrier of cold and despair, and it frightened him into hoarding his mage senses and trying to use his wits instead. There were things in this cold dark that he did not like the feel of, old spells and old magic, and always that underlying stench of rot. It was not as bad here, away from the corpses of the horses and that mewling black thing with tentacles, but it was bad enough to make him wonder just how many creatures had died in this place and never been found again.

He suddenly thought of poor Noreen, unconscious back with the ruins of the carriage, with no company save that of the demon bones in the box. He hoped the light spells and the protections on the chest were keeping her safe. He would really hate to think that he had taken too long, and that the magic had died and left her vulnerable to whatever always slithered just at the edges of his light. The impression that something shadowed him in this dark would not go away, and it made him quicken his pace, mindful that to do so might be foolish.

So when the stench changed to the more familiar odor of rotten turnips, he stopped. What was making that smell? He wrinkled his nose in disgust and vowed that as soon as he got the chance to go back to Eldon Keep, he was going to search for a spell of protection against foul odors. Knowing Fenelon, there were probably dozens of them in his library.

Something moved at the edge of his light. Rhoyd stopped and raised the lantern to send the light farther along.

"Hoi! Stop that!" a familiar voice snarled. "You're blinding me, boy!"

Rhoyd lowered the light just a little and looked into the shadows with a frown. There was someone there, the rotund figure of five dumplings in a doublet.

"Master Fergus?" Rhoyd said.

"Aye, it's me," he said. "Would you put the light lower—I can't see with it in me eyes."

Reluctantly, Rhoyd did lower the light, but not so much as the caravan master liked. Fergus took a shuffling step forward, and then hesitated.

"How did you get down here?" Rhoyd asked.

"By the stairs," Fergus replied. "We're all looking for you, lad. Where's Noreen?"

Rhoyd relaxed, though not much. "Noreen's hurt," he said warily. "I left her back with the dark carriage."

"So the carriage is here as well?" Fergus said. "Take me there."

"We should fetch Eithne," Rhoyd said. "I think Noreen is dying."

"Nonsense, lad, she's a hale and hearty woman, our Noreen. It would take more than a short fall to kill her. Now take me to her."

"Why?"

"So I can help her, of course," Fergus retorted. "What's wrong with you, boy? Do you want her to die?"

Rhoyd shook his head. That was the last thing he wanted, to be sure. But a small part of his unease refused to relax. He wished Conor and Eithne were here.

"Well?" Fergus said. "What are you waiting for?"

"We really should fetch Eithne," Rhoyd repeated.

"Look, she'll be along shortly," Fergus said. "I told her I would scout in this direction." He turned back towards the dark. "Hoi! Mistress Manahan, I've found the boy!"

His voice echoed down the corridor.

"She'll hear that," Fergus said. "Now let's get back to Noreen before she does perish."

Rhoyd frowned, but he started back the way he had come, leading the caravan master who stayed just at the edge of the light. And as they hurried back down the twisted corridors, Rhoyd could not help noticing that Fergus' odor was even fouler than what he had left behind. The man smelled like more than rotten turnips. He smelled like an old corpse. And he shuffled as he walked, and his head had a peculiar angle to it.

"Are you all right?" Rhoyd suddenly asked.

Eyes that reflected the lamplight flicked their gaze upon Rhoyd. Fergus's smile was crooked.

"I'm fine," the caravan master said and glanced back over his shoulder into the dark. Rhoyd stopped where he stood.

"Is something the matter?" Rhoyd asked.

Fergus merely shook his head. "Must have been water dripping somewhere," he said. "Everything will be just fine once we get to the wagon. Let's go."

Rhoyd held his place, uncertain now. There was a growing miasma in the shadows that set ill with him, but Fergus gestured with his hands that they should continue, so Rhoyd turned and started back towards the chamber again. He took off at a slightly faster pace, eager to return to the safety of the light spells that protected Noreen, and to escape the sense that something lurked back there in the dark, something that Fergus could see. *But how could he see in the dark?* It occurred to Rhoyd then that the old caravan master had not been using a lantern to walk those corridors. And that whatever hid in the shadows in waiting had no desire to stop him. He noticed too that Fergus lumbered along like an unsteady bear awakened from its den, and that the caravan master stayed just at the edge of the light until they reached the chamber.

"Go on," Fergus said. "Get in there. Hurry. We mustn't delay."

Unsure why, Rhoyd practically ran the length of the great hall towards the circle of lights and Noreen. He stopped beside her and looked back. Fergus was staying well away from the light. His body quivered, and his hands seemed to shake.

"She's over here," Rhoyd said, never taking his eyes off the man. "On top of the carriage."

Fergus would come no closer. Rhoyd set his lantern down and waited, but the caravan master just hovered, shifting back and forth like some wary beast.

"What's wrong?" Rhoyd asked.

"The light is too bright for my old eyes," Fergus said. "Can't you make it go away?"

"Why?" Rhoyd asked and frowned.

"Because Noreen will die if I don't help her."

"But you're not a healer," Rhoyd said. "And this is just mage light, and men have nothing to fear from it."

"Take away the damned light, boy!" Fergus snapped.

"No," Rhoyd said. "Come into the light."

Fergus began to chuckle. "Oh, no, lad, you won't win that easily."

Rhoyd blinked. The voice that came out of the man was deeper and rasping.

"Who are you?" Rhoyd asked.

"You do not know? I would have thought those clever eyes of yours could see through my cloak of flesh as easily as they saw through the disguise of the Demon-Bound."

Rhoyd hesitated. "I do know you," he said. "You're the one they call the Venomous Dark. You're a shadow demon."

Fergus clapped his hands, walking the edge of the light. "Very good, my lad, though such knowledge will be useless to you now."

"What do you mean?" Rhoyd asked.

The Venomous Dark whispered and out beyond the arches, something stirred. Rhoyd dared a brief glance towards the movement. The tentacles were crawling around the edges of the archways, hesitant to come into the light.

"You do not understand do you?" the creature that stumbled around in human flesh said. "I know what you are. And I will not let you leave this place alive. Sooner or later, the captain's magic will fade without any natural light to feed it, and you will have nothing but your own essence to feed to the light. I can wait."

The hideous smile was growing loose and soft as though the man's face was slowly melting. Rhoyd felt his knees giving way under him, so he sat down on the edge of the carriage, meeting the glittering gaze when he heard a sound, and as he looked up, he saw a faint light. Footfalls padded through the dark behind the human flesh. The creature stiffened just as Rhoyd stretched mage senses and felt the quicksilver of Eithne's essence.

No!

"Master Fergus?" she said, her voice coming out of the dark.

The flesh of Master Fergus turned. Eithne was there, holding a glowing stone that exuded a glimmer of mage light. This close to the Venomous Dark, its power faded. Eithne looked at her stone, and then cast it aside.

No!

"Eithne, run!" Rhoyd shouted.

Eithne hesitated. Master Fergus' flesh suddenly doubled over, and he cried out in mock pain. "Oh, Mistress Manahan, you're just in time," he said.

"Master Fergus, are you hurt?" she asked and stepped closer.

"No, Eithne, he's not Master Fergus!" Rhoyd cried. He snatched up his lantern and raced towards the edge of the light; heedless of the danger he would put himself in.

But before he could get there, Eithne had reached for the caravan master to offer aid.

And he suddenly rose, grabbing her by the throat with one loose fleshy hand. She struggled, but the grasp was too strong. Rhoyd shouted again, preparing to cast the lantern at the man, but Fergus's flesh turned and stretched the other hand.

"Adhar buail!" he shouted, and Rhoyd was struck by a wall of air that flung him backwards and knocked the lantern from his hand. It skittered across the stones and fell into a crevice, and much to Rhoyd's dismay, vanished into those depths. He quickly rose, reaching for Noreen's glowing sword, but the monster shouted the spell again, and the sword skittered away before Rhoyd could lay a hand on it.

"Now, boy," the Venomous Dark hissed and cast a hideous smile at Rhoyd. "If you value her life, you will do as I say."

FORTY

Oh, dear, this does not bode well, Vagner whispered.

Alaric was inclined to agree. He had already seen how battle skilled this Keltoran was, and the sight of him glowering at the empty circle of lights was frightful. Were it not for carrying something within that could be counted even more fearsome, Alaric would have given in to the temptation to slip quietly away.

Conor took but a few moments to gather his wits. He turned quite suddenly and seized Michan by the front of his doublet, practically lifting him off the ground. Alaric felt Vagner tense within him, a demon ready to defend. *Careful,* Alaric thought. This would not be a good time to let the demon take over. Besides, Conor's anger was not directed at him, but at another target.

"Where in the name of Cernunnos is my wife, Michan?" Conor snarled.

"I left her here, I can assure you," Michan protested, squirming in Conor's grasp.

Alaric decided to let them sort it out. He turned and passed his hand over the broken ring of light. The essence of the healer was strong and silvery. He sensed no tragedy wrapped within it.

"She left of her own free will," he said calmly. "I sense no violence."

Conor growled like an old bear and let go of Michan, turning towards Alaric with the same fierce glower. "Then where is she?" he demanded.

Alaric shrugged. "She left. That is all I know."

"And I thought mageborn were supposed to know everything," Conor said. "What use is yer magic, demon man, if you cannot find my wife or my wee son?"

Alaric frowned and glanced at Michan. "Is he always this acerbic?"

Michan said nothing. He stopped straightening the skew of his doublet to stare at the ring of lights.

"What?" Conor asked, sounding calmer.

"One of the stones is missing," Michan said.

Both Conor and Alaric turned to look at the ring. There was indeed a small gap in the circle.

"Perhaps she took the stone with her," Alaric suggested. "She could be using it to light her way."

"Why would she do that?" Michan stopped and looked at Conor.

"I can think of only one reason," Conor said. "The *need* must have been a-calling her. And I can only think of one *need* that would draw Eithne to enter that darkness alone."

"Rhoyd," Michan said.

"Aye," Conor said. "So the question now is which way did she go?"

Michan closed his eyes. "That way," he said, gesturing back towards the main hall.

"I thought ye could not sense her," Conor said.

"Her...there is so much dark power here, her essence is a mere flicker of candlelight in a sea of shadows. But that light she took—*my* light—I can track that as easily as I can find my own face."

"That's a comforting thought," Conor said. "Considering that ye have not been wearing yer own face..."

Michan looked like he was about to refute that, then sighed and shook his head.

Ah, such wit, Vagner whispered, and the demon's quiet chuckle rumbled silently through Alaric. He hid his smile, for Michan's sake as much as any.

Michan headed back towards the main hall to follow the trail of his magical light's essence, and Conor was right beside him. Alaric had no intention of remaining behind.

Those bones were his responsibility.

He would see them rescued before they fell into the shadows.

Noreen wanted to open her eyes, but her head hurt so much, she just knew that the very act would send shards of pain racing through her. Apart from which, there was a great deal of shouting going on, and the echo of voices rattled through her head. She would have cast about with mage senses, but she knew that would hurt as well. So she fought the urge and concentrated on opening her eyes instead.

There was light, more of it than she cared to have. And even without using mage senses, she felt the magic in it. Some of it was Michan's to be sure. The rest. A dark miasma pushed at the edges of power that had been used to create a shield of light.

Horns, where in the name of Cernunnos was she? Vague recollections filtered through. The scream of the horses, the gathering of the dark, and the sensation of rushing into the bowels of the earth. The crash of wood and the pain of knowing that several parts of her had to have been broken by the fall before darkness claimed her senses.

And now...

"Why do you dawdle, boy?" a vaguely familiar voice growled. "Does her life mean nothing to you?"

"I...can't lift it," Rhoyd replied.

Noreen tried to shift her head. Pain wracked her, and she nearly passed out as it sent flashes of red and black across her vision. She managed not to scream.

"Then take away the light," the other said.

Noreen swallowed her pain and opened her eyes again, shifting them as far as her position would allow. She could see a shadow all around them. Smell the odor of rot and death. And see Rhoyd atop the broken carcass of the dark carriage. He had his hands on the white wood of the chest that housed the bones.

Oh, by the Hammer, no!

"I can't make the light go away," Rhoyd said wearily. "It's not my magic. It's Michan's, and he has it warded so only he can break the spell."

A curse echoed and a whimper of pain. Rhoyd lurched upright and stretched a hand. "No, don't hurt her!" he cried.

Her? Noreen wished she could move. She closed her eyes and tried to shift a little more. Pain. Her back. Her neck. Was her spine broken? Still, she shifted her head and let the swim of pain pass before opening her eyes.

Now she could see what had the lad so frightened. Beyond the corpses of the horses, Eithne was on her knees, her throat clutched in a hand that looked as though it were not much more than an uncooked pastry. It was swollen and blackening, too. And it belonged to a familiar face.

Master Fergus?

"Then bring me the bones," Master Fergus said in a

guttural voice that indicated he was having difficulty using it. "Or I will feed her to the dark."

As he spoke, Noreen became aware of the tendrils of some huge ungainly beast hovering off in the deepest shadows. By the Hammer, was that what she thought? One of the shadow beasts of ancient times? The Demon-Bound had told her of such creatures, but never had she seen one. Its fetid presence brought bile into her throat. *By the Hammer, don't let me vomit now.*

Rhoyd blinked then began to work almost frantically at the latch of the chest. He snatched up a bit of metal spring broken loose from the bottom of the carriage and tried to lever it in under the lock. Noreen took a deep breath and looked hard at him. She wanted to catch his gaze—to tell him what to do. She wished she could get up and help him, distract Fergus, get Eithne free, but her body was no longer a functioning entity. She could barely move her hands as it was.

But move one of them she did, scratching carefully at the dirt and broken stones. The motion got Rhoyd's attention. He hesitated, looking at her, eyes brimming.

"There is power in the bones, lad," she whispered. "Enough to stop him, but you must not let them touch the earth or the Mother of Darkness will know."

"Bring me a bone!" Fergus shouted. "I only need one!"

Rhoyd worked on the latch again, jerking the metal back and forth until the latch snapped. He tossed the metal aside, letting it clatter off into the shadows as he seized the edge of the box and shoved the lid back. Bright light flared in his face, washing him as pale as milk. He hesitated but a moment before he reached inside. With a deep breath, he drew out a large humerus that looked like a club in his small hands. Then he turned towards Fergus.

"I have it," he said.

"Bring it here!" Fergus shouted in his slurred speech. "Bring it here!"

As Noreen watched, an alien determination took over the boy's face. He clutched the bone in two hands like a bastard sword. Crawling off the wreckage, he carefully crossed the patch of light. But just as he reached the edge, he stopped and looked into the dark beyond Fergus.

"Captain Camhin?" he said almost too cheerfully.

Still, the name made Fergus swing his lopsided head

around towards the other end of the hall.

"Here's your bone!" Rhoyd snapped, and swung the humerus like a war hammer.

The moment the Venomous Dark looked towards the entrance, Rhoyd swung the bone around with all the might he could muster. It wasn't quite like using a sword or even the quarterstaff he had been training with, but it had the desired effect. The monster inside the man must have sensed something, for at the last minute, he turned back to see what was going on.

Rhoyd hit the monster square in the face, and to his surprise, there was a flash of white light before he heard the snap of bone and a squishy sound like he had hit a melon. Fergus' startled expression flew off into the dark, separated from the corpulent body.

The mushy hands released Eithne as the headless monstrosity staggered back. She sank to her knees, gasping for air. Rhoyd dashed forward and grabbed her hand, eager to get her into the light.

"Come on!" he said as he pulled her arm.

Eithne struggled to her feet and stumbled into the light, and just in time. Fergus' corpse tumbled to the ground in a pulpy heap where it lay and trembled and shook like some chicken that had its head wrung. But then, it began to ooze such an awful stench that made bile and feces seem fragrant by comparison. With the stench, an oily darkness began to spill from the neck hole and swell. Laughter filled the air.

"Stupid boy!" the rasping voice said. "What makes you think you can kill me that easily? All you have done is destroy the flesh that housed me."

Darkness billowed and surged into a large, nearly-shapeless form. Rhoyd saw eyes in the mass—hundreds of them staring at him, blinking. Awestruck at the sight, he stopped and stared back, releasing Eithne's hand, still clutching the bone that thrummed with demon essence.

Nimheil Dubh. Venomous Dark. The creature described in the tome on demons reshaped itself into a form somewhat like that of a man, but this "man" could not hold its shape at the edge of the circle of magic white light, so it fluttered and wavered and shifted and drifted like oil on water.

"You have only delayed your death," the Venomous Dark

said. "I have the patience of eons on my side. Eventually, the power that feeds the magic light will fade, or do you forget that he had to renew it almost nightly?"

Rhoyd had not forgotten. He swallowed and looked back at the wagon where the light did seem less than before. Michan was not here to renew those spells. And he knew his own essence would not last long if he used it to hold that light against this fetid dark.

I cannot let it fail. If it does, we are all dead.

He looked frantically over at Noreen.

"She cannot help you," Venomous Dark said, and its wavering mouth shifted into a black smile. "She is not long for this world. Of course, you could take her life and use it to feed the light."

"That would be wrong," Rhoyd said.

"But it would save her the pain of the death she now suffers," Venomous Dark said in a voice like honey. "Would you want her to suffer? Would you want your mother's screams to be the last sounds you heard in my dark?"

He looked at Eithne. Her face was white.

"So what is the price of our freedom?" Rhoyd asked.

"Give me that bone and I will allow the women to leave," Venomous Dark said.

"And me?" Rhoyd ventured.

"You are an enemy I cannot allow to survive to challenge the Mother of Darkness when she is reborn."

Rhoyd flinched.

"So what shall it be?" Venomous Dark asked. "Their freedom for your life and the bones?"

"Don't listen to him, Rhoyd," Eithne begged. "He is not to be trusted. Conor will find us...I know he will."

Rhoyd looked back at her. "Conor? But Conor is not here."

"Oh, yes, he is, Rhoyd," she said. "He came to save us, and he will save us."

Venomous Dark laughed. "What makes you think that your Keltoran father can defeat me?" the creature asked, and its form vibrated around the edges as its laughter continued. And again, where bits of it flitted into the edges of the light, it hissed like water on a hot griddle and faded.

Rhoyd looked at that. And felt the thrum of demon essence in his hand.

"I will give you a bone and you will go away and let them

leave?" he suddenly asked.

"Of course," Venomous Dark said.

Rhoyd tightened his grip on the humerus. Cautiously, he started towards the dark.

"No, Rhoyd, don't!" Eithne cried.

"Take care of Noreen," Rhoyd said.

She tried to seize him, but he sidestepped the grasp seeking to snag him. Eithne stumbled in his wake. Rhoyd reached the barest edges of the light and felt the eagerness of the shadows to claim what he held.

"Take it," Rhoyd said. "If you dare." And with that, he raised the bone and drew the essence of the demon that was still lying in the depths of the marrow. The power flooded him, flash fire in his blood, filled with light and edges of dark. *"Loisg!"* Rhoyd shouted and shoved the bone at the dark.

White fire so brilliant, it made that in the wagon seem dull by comparison, suddenly flared around the bone. But it was not ordinary fire, not mage fire, but demon fire. Rhoyd felt it smoldering some power in his soul as he willed it to reach for Venomous Dark.

The shadow demon screamed. The beast with tendrils retreated hastily as the wild demon fire spread fast and filled the chamber. Venomous Dark's shape flickered like smoke on a sudden breeze. Vainly, the monster fought to hold its shape, but the demon fire was too white. It burned brilliance into Rhoyd's eyes, blinding him as it clambered up and down his skin. Rhoyd battled the sting of it, fighting to maintain his grasp on the bone as he howled and charged at Venomous Dark, determined to smite the fiend into a thousand pieces.

The shadow demon twisted, seeking refuge and finding none. It screamed and fled, backing away as fire ate at it.

And then it found a bit of shadow just at the edge of the arch, and there it sang a spell of power, calling black lightning into its hands and throwing it at Rhoyd.

He tried to shift and get out of the way, and in his eagerness to escape the lightning's strike, he raised the bone before him like a shield. The black lightning lashed into the heart of the white fire. Rhoyd heard the snap and felt the burn of something digging into his hand and something striking him in the head as the bone was cleaved in two.

It must not touch the ground!

In a panic, Rhoyd juggled the halves, heedless of the

sudden gush of blood that trickled into his eyes. Like two brands, the bones continued to burn white, sucking the lightning into their marrow, and in turn shards of the lightning danced across Rhoyd's skin, burning him.

No, no, he could not let go! He reached for more of the demon essence, ripping it from the bones still in the box and screamed *"Loisg mhor!"*

The power hit him like a wall, slamming him backwards as white fire raced upward and outward. The beast behind the arches screamed and retreated. Rhoyd landed on his back, barely keeping the halves of the bone above the ground. For moments, all he could do was lie there and count the number of pains that assailed him. Then he forced himself to his elbows, determined to watch.

Venomous Shadow was caught in the fire, and this time the demon could not escape. It ate at his essence, reducing his undulating shape smaller and smaller.

"I will not die!" Venomous Dark screamed. "I will meet you again with the Dark Mother at my side."

The smallest bits of darkness slithered into the cracks and crevices of the floor and vanished. The white fire spread until the entire room was burning with pure white light. Demon essence was strong, and it sank into Rhoyd, whispering into his bones, making him too ill to think.

"Rhoyd!" Eithne screamed.

He felt her hands on him, and the moment she touched him, the fire abated from him. It fled, leaving bits of burning stone and old tapestries to make the room glow. Rhoyd slumped back, and Eithne caught him.

"Blessed Brother, Rhoyd, no..."

He blinked and looked up at her as she clutched him close.

"I'm all right," he whispered. "Really...help Noreen, please? She'd dying..."

Eithne looked towards the wagon. Rhoyd could see by her expression that the *need* was pulling her that way.

"Are you certain?" she said, her fingers tracing the track of blood that slipped into the corner of his mouth now.

He managed a weak grin. "Yeah," he said. "Just help me up."

She reluctantly took off her over tunic and wrapped it about his shoulders as she helped him to his feet. Rhoyd clutched the bones to his chest and stumbled over to the wagon. He barely managed to clamber back up on it, get the lid open and put the bones back inside.

Horns, he hoped Michan wouldn't be mad when he saw they were broken.

He sighed and worked on repairing the latch; calling the demon essence the bones had left inside him to reshape it. Little bits of him felt aware of Noreen's pain...of the dark that sank deeper and deeper. The miasma that had filled the shadows was little more than the hunger of the beast with the tentacles, and it seemed none too eager to come out of those shadows just now.

And then, he heard a familiar shout. The thunder of many feet.

"Rhoyd!"

Rhoyd ceased his spell and turned.

Conor was running at the head of a small party. Michan and another followed, and the essence of demon swelled the taste of cinnamon on Rhoyd's tongue.

In spite of that, Rhoyd scrambled off the broken carriage and stumbled across the broken floor. Arms surrounded him, lifting him, holding him close. He smelled the woolen plaidie, the musk of a man, old leather and sweat.

And he loved every reek of it for the comfort it offered.

FORTY-ONE

Eithne knew from the wretched position the cook lay twisted into that Noreen might have broken her back. She knelt beside the large woman, only slightly aware of all the commotion behind her.

"Well, Mistress," Noreen said with a gasp. "Will I die?"

Eithne stilled her expression as she let her hands wander up and down the great breadth of the woman whose skin was discolored. "Not if I can help it," she whispered.

"Will I get up, then?"

Eithne sighed. "We shall see."

She turned and looked at the small knot of men surrounding one small lad. Conor looked like he was ready to take both of them apart.

"No," he said. "I'll hear nothing of this!"

"Conor?" Eithne said. "Michan...come here, please. I will need your strong arms."

Her gentle admonishment stopped whatever argument they were pursuing. Swiftly, they raced over to the broken remains of the carriage and paused. She noticed both Michan and the newcomer peered at the chest as though assessing its condition before they looked down at Noreen. Michan quickly knelt on the far side of the cook and took her hand.

"Noreen," he said. "Are you...?" He bit off the rest of the words as though realizing the folly of the question. His gaze rose to meet Eithne's. "What must we do?" he asked.

"We need some boards," she said. "And rope, if there is any, though I would prefer soft strips of linen."

"The shroud," the stranger said. Eithne looked at him inquiringly. As if knowing her thoughts, he smiled. "You knew me as Bowen, Mistress Mahanan," he said. "But I am called Alaric Braidwine, and I am at your service."

She saw Conor quirk one eyebrow before he walked over to the remains of the carriage and began to tear off long boards. Michan leapt up to assist him. Only Alaric remained, regarding her with eyes that seemed to look inside her.

"Then find this shroud," she said.

Alaric bowed and clambered up onto the cart with a grace that belied his mortal frame. Within moments, he was back, tearing long strips of a white cloth embroidered around the edges in runes.

"But the wards..." Michan said.

"All will be well," Alaric said in such a calming manner, Eithne could not help but wonder.

Now is not the time to ask.

Eithne spurred herself into working on stitching the wound on Noreen's head and checking for possible broken limbs. Alas, no one had a flagon of ale, and Eithne's potions for stilling pain were still up with the wagons with her pack. Noreen was grey around the mouth now, and her breathing was ragged with pain. Sweat rolled from her face. Eithne cooed each time the cook flinched. "Concentrate on Rhoyd," she said. She wryly noted that the lad was standing quietly at the edge of all the activity, wisely keeping out of the way, but obviously wanting to watch. The streak of blood was drying on his face and the faintest hint of *need* tried to tug Eithne's attention from Noreen. Eithne ignored it. The lad was standing. This *need* was clearly greater than his.

In short order, they had the boards and the strips ready, and Eithne cautiously bound Noreen's limbs to them and tightly cross-beamed them above her head and below her back. Then she sighed and looked at both Michan and Alaric. "Is there some way either of you can ease her pain? Perhaps like the mind thing you did to me, Michan?"

Michan blanched at the memory. But Alaric merely took Noreen's hand. "I will do this," he said.

She watched as he whispered words and closed his eyes, and Noreen seemed to relax as though no feeling came to her. Satisfied, Eithne looked at Conor and Michan. They took hold of the ends of the braces and gently levered Noreen over on her side.

Eithne quickly worked fingers up and down Noreen's spine. She could not find evidence of a break. Still, the *need* felt strongest just at Noreen's waist, and there Eithne could feel a swelling. She closed her eyes and pressed her hands there and whispered, "Blessed Brother, hear my plea..."

Her prayer swelled in the dark, and all grew quiet as her power shifted and shimmered and filled the air around her with warm golden light. Diancecht answered Eithne's prayers, sending a strong healing into her hands, and she in turn willed that power into the cook. Then the power faded, and Eithne let her hands slide away. She nodded as she sat back on her heels. Conor and Michan lowered the boards once more so that Noreen now rested on her back.

The cook did not move as she was unbound from her braces. Then she opened her eyes and took a deep breath and stretched just a bit. Surprise washed her face, followed by tears.

"I can feel again," she said.

They helped her to sit up.

"You should rest," Eithne said, "but not here."

"It's best we all get out of here," Michan agreed. "But not until we make a decision."

Eithne frowned.

"What decision?" she asked.

"Rhoyd cannot be left in your care. He must come to Caer Keltora and seek the protection of the Council of Mageborn..."

"Over my dead carcass!" Conor snapped.

Oh, dear, Eithne thought. This did not bode well at all.

Noreen had seen Michan having fits before, but never one quite like the one he was having now.

"Be reasonable, Conor," Michan said. "Rhoyd *must* go to Caer Keltora and Dun Gealach. They will protect him."

"If yer protection is any example, Michan," Conor barked back, "then I'll not let yer bloody council near my lad..."

"Look, Conor, I did what I had to do."

"Oh, aye. You lied to me. You nearly drove Eithne insane, and ye nearly got my lad killed!"

For a moment, Michan and Conor stood almost toe-to-toe. Noreen felt like she had been flattened by a tree, but for a moment, she thought she might be forced to stand and wedge herself between them. Assuming she could stand without falling flat on her arse. She wriggled her legs to make certain she could move them, but Eithne put a hand on her arm as though admonishing her.

"Gentlemen," Alaric said. "There is no reason to cast these accusations about. What has been done is already done, and the Venomous Dark knows that Rhoyd exists. It is true that this demon will likely report all to his master and the Mother of Darkness, but I suspect that finding Rhoyd will not be as easy as you think, Michan."

"But..." Michan said.

"I know your heart is in the right place, Michan, but I set you to another task. To take these bones to Caer Keltora, not to tear this family apart."

Michan looked as though he had been struck. Noreen bit her lower lip to stave off a smile.

"But we must take him with us. What if Nimheil Dubh comes after him now?"

Alaric looked at Rhoyd and smiled. "I suspect that Venomous Dark will get another ding in the old head—whatever head he wears. This lad's welfare is not our concern—not yet. And he has all the protection he needs."

His gaze shifted to Noreen. "Are you well?" Alaric asked.

Noreen carefully pulled herself to her feet. Her legs felt wobbly, and a strange warmth tingled down her back, but she was able to stay upright, and was amused to see Eithne hovering close. *As though she could stop me from falling.*

"Good," Alaric said. "How well do you know Ard-Taebh?"

Noreen shrugged. "I've seen it from the Ranges to the sea."

"Then I will relieve you of your duties concerning the bones, and I will charge you with taking this family wherever they wish. And advise you to leave no discernable trail."

"And then?" Noreen asked.

"Go your own way," Alaric said. "I will find you when I need you again. You've earned a rest." He smiled. "Michan and I will deliver the bones to Caer Keltora. As for this caravan, we will pay these men well and release them, but with no memory of what has happened here. Come, Michan. We have work to do."

Alaric gestured, and the chest rose into the air. He left with Michan trailing after, looking none too pleased.

"So," Noreen said. "Where shall I gate you folks? Did you have any place in mind?"

"As a matter of fact," Conor said. "There is a place I know of. But first, we need our horses and our gear."

"Then let's get out of this stinking hole," Noreen said.

"First sensible thing I've heard in a sen'night," Conor said.

Eithne was looking at Rhoyd now. "And as soon as we leave this place, I need to look to that wound in your head,"

Rhoyd didn't look too happy.

FORTY-TWO

The stitches hurt for a bit. Rhoyd gritted his teeth each time he felt the needle enter his flesh and scrape against his skull. Eithne had given him a bit of poppy wine to ease the pain. Didn't stop him from wanting to push her away. Alas, Conor was holding him steady, so there was no escape. So he sat under the tree where Conor had left Battlebrute. Somehow they had managed not to lose Moonface or Maudie either. Both horses were still at Noreen's wagon outside the walls.

Noreen kept watch. She was still pale, but she walked with more confidence now. He was glad that Eithne had been able to help her, because he rather liked Noreen. For one thing, she had said nothing to Michan or Alaric about Rhoyd breaking the latch or the bone.

He couldn't help but wonder why and longed to ask her about it. But there were the stitches to sew a tear in his scalp. He vaguely remembered something glancing off his head when Venomous Dark loosed the black lightning.

Now all he wanted was to get away from here. He didn't tell Conor, but he was still afraid that Michan would convince Alaric to change his mind. That he would come after them and Rhoyd would be forced to go to Dun Gealach. Besides, his left hand was throbbing again, and as he shifted just a bit, he thought it felt wrong.

So why had Eithne not noticed? Her *need* usually felt such things. But here she was, wiping his face and telling him he was a good lad for not moving much, then putting her needle aside, she called the healing power of her Blessed Brother. Warmth shot through Rhoyd's scalp, and the burn of the stitches vanished.

He sighed and leaned into Conor.

"Can we go now?" he asked.

"Just say where," Noreen said and stepped under the tree.

"I know a place," Conor said.

Noreen held out her hand. Conor looked dubious, but he

took it. Noreen closed her eyes and said, "Think about the place, then."

Conor quirked an eyebrow in amusement, but he took a deep breath and said, "It's an auld croft near where I trained..."

Within moments, Noreen was opening a gate spell. She made it large enough that they could lead the horses through, and then she followed them.

Her gate closed, and they were standing on a high rocky moor. Just a short ways off was a small croft.

"Well, this is where I will leave you, then," Noreen said.

Rhoyd pulled free of Conor and rushed over to her. "You have to go now?" he asked.

"I'm afraid so, lad." Noreen crouched a bit. "I can't leave Bellow and Brawny to that lot. And besides, I'm going to gate back and leave an obvious trail back to Elenthorn in case anyone is following. But maybe one day our paths will cross again. Now give us a hug, and promise to be good."

Rhoyd nodded and threw arms around her—at least as far as he was able. She clutched him fiercely, then let him go and stepped back. Conor shook her hand. Eithne hugged her as well and told her to be careful and get some rest.

Then she opened her gate spell once more and was gone.

And the tingle in his hand was briefly out-shadowed by the ache of already missing her.

But then there was Conor, coaxing him towards the remains of the croft.

Inside, it was cold. Conor tented the wood and said, "All right, lad, do yer glamorie..."

Rhoyd crouched at the hearth and whispered, *"Loisg,"* as he stretched his right hand towards the wood. To his amazement, it sparked whiter and hotter than he expected, and he gasped, nearly tumbling back. Cinnamon and cloves burned his tongue.

Demon essence!

How?

He looked at his left hand. The tingling was stronger. And the sight of it vexed him. The palm was red and puffy, and there appeared to be something protruding from the middle.

"Rhoyd, what's wrong with your hand?" Eithne asked.

"I'm not sure," he said as he held it out for her to see.

Eithne gasped and Conor swore.

"Blessed Brother, it's swollen and there's a fragment of

something stuck in the middle of the wound," she said. "Why didn't you tell me you were injured there as well?"

"It's not broken," Rhoyd said. "It happened when the lightning struck the bone and shattered it. Besides, I wanted you to help Noreen and..."

"Yes, well never mind that," she said. "You should have said something before now." She crossed the room to kneel beside him bear the fire. "This will have to come out. Conor, can you hold him steady?"

"As a rock," Conor said and smiled.

He slipped arms around Rhoyd and pulled him close. Rhoyd stiffened as Eithne took hold of the sliver and pulled it free. She frowned at it then turned to toss it aside.

"No!" Rhoyd cried. "It must not touch the ground!"

Eithne hesitated, looking at the fragment. "Then what should I do with it?" she asked.

"Give it back to me," Rhoyd said, holding out his good hand. "Please."

Eithne looked at Conor. He shrugged. She shook her head and handed it back, then set about cleaning his left hand. She packed it with comfrey and bandaged it in place before calling on her god to heal him.

Rhoyd continued to stare at the fragment as she worked her healing. The essence in it sang to him, making him shiver. He looked up and saw the worried frown that converged Conor's brows into a single line. *He can feel the demon, too.*

"We'll make you a little pouch so ye can wear it around yer neck, and in years to come ye can show it off to yer descendants and brag about how you stopped the Venomous Dark," Conor suggested as he took the fragment from Rhoyd's hand and slipped it into his sporran. "But for now, I'll keep it off the ground for ye."

Rhoyd nodded. Exhaustion was finally creeping into him. Eithne's chanting was having such a soothing effect. He closed his eyes, leaning against Conor, feeling safe for the first time in days.

Conor eased Rhoyd into his bedding once Eithne was finished. The lad felt a bit warm and even feverish, and Conor worried that it was one of those "mage fevers" he had heard about. But then he remembered what the lad's Aunt Genna said about mage fever. Sleep, according to her, was a good thing for a young mageborn so afflicted to do. So he placed Rhoyd in his bed and drew the blankets to his chin. Eithne crouched on the other side, checking her handiwork, as she was wont to do.

"His color is not good," Eithne said and touched the place on his head where he had bled so profusely after the events in that dreadful place. She frowned.

"What?" Conor asked.

"Look at his hair," she said.

Conor looked, and there where the wound had been stitched and healed, was a patch of pure white hair.

"I'll be. The lad's getting grey before his time."

"I wonder how that happened?" Eithne asked.

Conor shrugged. "He told us that something hit him in the head when Fergus threw lightning at him, remember? Might be the spell caused it."

Fergus, nothing—that was a dead man carrying the soul of a demon in his flesh.

"Well, let us hope that is all it did," Eithne said with a sigh. "By the Brother, I am tired."

"Go on, sleep woman," Conor said and leaned over to kiss her. "I'll keep watch."

She smiled. "Well, first, I am going to make myself some tea," she said. "I'll sleep better for it."

Conor watched until she poured the last of the water from her water skin and set the kettle pot on to boil. He smiled and wandered over to the doorway. The moon was rising, bathing the moor white. And the rough stones looked like scattered bones under the light. He frowned and reached into his sporran to draw out the bit of bone pulled from Rhoyd's hand. It had looked just like an arrowhead, but he had never seen bone so white and bright. It almost glowed in the dark.

With a sigh, Conor returned it to his sporran. He would hang it above the hearth tonight. Tomorrow, he would see about stringing it for the lad, or making a small pouch. The demon essence that whispered across his nerves like a faint breeze brought the taste of cinnamon to his mouth.

He was about to turn back to the room when movement startled him. Rhoyd was standing back a safe ways, guilt flushing his face. Eithne had her back to him and had not seen him crawl out of the bed. Now the lad stood, watching Conor speculatively.

"What's wrong, lad?" Conor asked.

"Sorry," Rhoyd said. "The bone...it called to me. Can I have it back, please? I think it needs to stay with me."

Conor made a face, but he fetched the bone out of his sporran again and handed it to the lad. Rhoyd gingerly took the piece of bone and turned it back and forth. He yawned.

"I don't think all demons are bad," he said.

Conor tried not to frown. "What makes ye say that?" he asked.

"The Demon-Bound is not evil," the lad said in a sleepy voice. "This one wasn't evil either, not at first, but it could have been used for evil."

"Yer speaking in riddles, and I'm too tired to figure them out, lad," Conor said, and carefully brushed Rhoyd's hair back from his eyes. There were circles under them. "Besides, you need to sleep."

"Will you stay with me until I'm asleep?" Rhoyd asked.

"What makes ye think I am going anywhere without ye?" Conor asked.

Rhoyd shook his head and managed a weak smile before he returned to his bed. Conor sat down beside the lad just as his eyes closed and he slipped back into slumber, still clutching that fragment of bone to his chest.

"Poor lamb," Eithne said as she finished boiling water for tea and settled down beside Conor. "After all he's been through, do you really think we shouldn't take him to Caer Keltora?"

Conor shook his head.

"We'll pass on Caer Keltora," he said, "Though I would like to show him the highlands where I trained...and you."

Eithne smiled. "And I should like to see them," she said.

"Would ye now, woman?" Conor said, reaching out and tugging at the neck of her tunic. "Because at the moment, I know some highlands and lowlands I would like to be exploring under the light of this moon."

"Really?" Eithne said.

"Really," he replied with a smile and leaned to kiss her.

And let nature take over.

EPILOGUE

"So this is what all the fuss was over?" Etienne Savala, Lady High Mage of the Council of Mageborn, said as she leaned over and peered at the chest of white wood.

She wore that secretive smile that always left Alaric wondering what she really thought. Her black tresses, pulled back in that severe style he remembered from years ago, were showing white streaks at the temples now, and some new age lines were faintly visible around her eyes. Still, she was as beautiful and exotic as she had been the day he first met her. In spite of the strain of the position she held, the years had been kind.

He and Michan stood on the other side of the chest that now sat on a pedestal of white marble etched with powerful runes and watched as Etienne studied the markings. The whole chamber was white, stark and almost blinding to him. Inside him, Vagner lay quiet, for even protected within Alaric as he was, the Youngerkin still had an aversion to such brilliance.

At last, Etienne reared back and fixed Alaric and Michan with her most prudent stare. "May I see them now?" she asked.

Alaric nodded and stepped up to the chest. He whispered as he brushed his hand up and down the length of the lid to break the magical seals. Once he was satisfied that they were gone, he carefully raised the lid and let it hang off the back of the chest by its hinges.

The bones in the depths of the chest gleamed so white they made the wood seem dull. A full skeleton it was, thought it had been taken apart to allow it to fit in a smaller, more secretive grave. The White One told him she had done so to make it easier to conceal the bones when she buried them. One looking for a long barrow would not notice a short cairn of stones in a cavern. Indeed, when Alaric had gone to fetch them, the grave reminded him of those Dvergar built.

"So these are the bones of the first demon," Etienne said

and sighed. "They look like any other set of bones, if you ask me. I do hope they were worth all the effort—and the expense—they required, Magister Braidwine."

"I can assure you, they were worth everything they cost," he said.

He tried not to think about the lives that were included in the expense.

The Lady High Mage nodded and smiled a little more. "It is good to see you again, Alaric. When you are done here, please come have dinner with me."

He bowed. Etienne glanced once more at the chest and shook her head.

"Just bones, what a pity," she said and turned on her heel and left the chamber, escorted by the battle mages who were her constant companions these days.

"Just bones," Michan repeated with a frown once she was gone. "Sometimes, I believe our Lady High Mage does not always fully appreciate the work that we do on her behalf."

Alaric shook his head. "Who can blame her?" he said. "Fenelon's behavior—his very obsession—did make him seem mad at times. And then, with the war and all."

With a sigh, Alaric stared at the depths of the box...and frowned.

"What's wrong?" Michan asked, looking inside.

Carefully, Alaric reached into the box and shifted some of the bones. What he had assumed was a scattering of sawdust now proved to be something far more frightening.

"One of the bones has been shattered in two," he said.

Michan blinked. "Perhaps it happened when the carriage fell?" he suggested.

"No," Alaric said. "That's not possible. These bones are as strong as steel—stronger. Only a great magic could have shattered one. This is not good."

"What do you mean?"

Alaric took a deep breath. *Vagner, I know this is not going to be pleasant, but I fear this requires your skill.*

He felt the Youngerkin stir within him, and was aware of demon senses now spreading through the air. Alaric felt it as well when Michan stepped back in awe, for Vagner's form took over, shifting human flesh to demon hide and scales. It was Vagner who stretched a hand over the box and with demon magic, drew the broken bones out of the box. They hovered, shimmering and catching light and reflecting it back even greater, forcing Vagner to squint. Then like a puzzle, the halves shifted around, fitting themselves together until they were made whole once more.

"By the horns of Cernunnos," Michan muttered.

The demon magic brightened, fusing the broken ends into solid form again. Then softly, it slid away, retreating back into the hidden corners of Alaric's being, returning his awareness to that of a mageborn man. The bone, heavy as a Keltoran longsword, came to rest in his hand.

Thank you, old friend, he thought.

"Oh, you're welcome as always," the demon replied.

Alaric opened his eyes. He could tell by Michan's relaxing expression that his countenance was normal again. *After all these years, why are you are still frightened of Vagner?* he pondered.

"Well?" Michan said.

Alaric studied the bone. It was a humerus, much longer than that of a man. He turned it over when his gaze fell on a fracture in the shaft. Frowning, Alaric rubbed it with his fingers. A fragment about the size of an arrowhead was missing.

"A piece is missing," he said and peered back into the box, but there was nothing left in the bottom.

"More than one from the looks of it," Michan said as he pointed at the knobby joint end.

Alaric shifted the bone around to look at the joint. There was indeed and small chunk, no bigger than the end of his thumb, missing from the bone. It left a notch where one should not have been.

"This is terrible," he said.

"What does it mean?"

Alaric frowned. "It means that we must go back to the keep and search for the missing fragments before *Nimhiel Dubh* gains enough strength to rise again," he said as he placed the bone in the chest and closed the lid. And we must pray that we found both shards first. Else wise, all hope for the world could be lost."

And if that were true, he did not want to contemplate what it would mean.

The beast had remained hidden in the shadows until it felt certain that it was safe to return to its domain. Once the last of the light faded from the carriage spells, the creature oozed back out, slithering along the ground, tendrils always searching. It probed the remains of the dark carriage, seeking to feed its never-ending hunger.

There were bits of human remains, those dropped by the Venomous Dark when it could no longer hide within long dead flesh. The creature oozed into the body. It was rotten, for it had died long ago, but it was food and the beast did not care.

But as it pushed the bits around, sucking the ichor from them, one of its tendrils brushed a bit of bone. The fragment burned cold, and the tendril hesitated to touch it at all, probing around it instead.

Until it felt a familiar call from the depths of the world.

Yes...yes...bring that to me...

The tendril reluctantly wrapped itself around the bit of bone and sank into the ground to answer the command of the Venomous Dark.

THE END

ABOUT THE AUTHOR

Laura J. Underwood has been writing as far back as she can remember. Her fantasy stories have appeared in a variety of magazines and anthologies, including the *Sword & Sorceress* anthologies and the *Bubbas of the Apocalypse* anthologies. Her novels include *Ard Magister, Dragon's Tongue, Wandering Lark* and the soon to be released *Demon in the Bones*. When not writing, she is a librarian who enjoys corrupting small minds with words and stories so they will hopefully grow up to be avid readers. In her spare time, she likes to play with beads, draw and paint, practice harp and sew clothing for her growing collection of ball-jointed dolls (many of which are designed to look like the characters in her stories). Her webpage is located at www.sff,net/people/keltora.

ABOUT THE COVER ARTIST

Artist **Mitchell Davidson Bentley** spent the last 20 years moving physically from place to place and artistically from traditional oils to cyber compositions. Trained in the traditional medium of oil by his mother, and inspired by his grandfather's love of science fiction, Bentley began his career as a full-time science fiction artist in 1989 from his home base in Tulsa. While actively involved in the science fiction art world, Bentley also moved from Tulsa to Austin to Central Pennsylvania where his search for knowledge earned him bachelor's and master's degrees from Penn State University. Over the same period of time, Bentley shifted from the more traditional oil painting to airbrushed acrylics, and since 2004 has been working exclusively in electronic media.

As the Creative Consultant of Atomic Fly Studios, Bentley produces cover art, marketing materials and Web sites while he continues to produce quality 2D artwork marketed through the AFS Web site and at science fiction conventions across the United States.

Bentley has lectured at universities, worked in film (also as a part-time actor), edited publications and served as Artist Guest of Honor at more than a dozen science fiction conventions. He has also earned over 35 awards, and is a lifetime member of the Association of Science Fiction and Fantasy Artists.

He currently resides in Harrisburg, PA with his partner Cathie McCormick and their spoiled cats, Mr. Spike, Zöe and Drucilla. Bentley's Web address is: www.atomicflystudios.com.

Yard Dog Press Titles As Of This Print Date

The Geometries of Love: Poetry by Robin Wayne Bailey
The Golems Of Laramie County, Ken Rand
The Green Women, Laura J. Underwood
The Guardians, Lynn Abbey
Hammer Town, Selina Rosen
The Happiness Box, Beverly A. Hale
The Host Series: The Host, Fright Eater, Gang Approval, Selina
    Rosen
Houston, We've Got Bubbas!, Edited by Selina Rosen
How I Spent the Apocolypse, Selina Rosen
I Didn't Quite Make It To Oz, Edited by Selina Rosen
I Should Have Stayed In Oz, Edited by Selina Rosen
In the Shadows, Bradley H. Sinor
International House of Bubbas, Edited by Selina Rosen
It's the Great Bumpkin, Cletus Brown!, Katherine A. Turski
The Killswitch Review, Steven-Elliot Altman & Diane DeKelb-
    Rittenhouse
The Leopard's Daughter, Lee Killough
The Lightning Horse, John Moore
The Logic of Departure, Mark W. Tiedemann
The Long, Cold Walk To Mars, Jeffrey Turner
Marking the Signs and Other Tales Of Mischief, Laura J.
    Underwood
Material Things, Selina Rosen
Medieval Misfits: Renaissance Rejects, Tracy S. Morris
Mirror Images, Susan Satterfield
Mirror, Mirror and Other Reflections, James K. Burk
More Stories That Won't Make Your Parents Hurl, Edited by
    Selina Rosen
Music for Four Hands, Louis Antonelli & Edward Morris
My Life with Geeks and Freaks, Claudia Christian
The Necronomicrap: A Guide To Your Horoooscope, Tim Frayser
Playing With Secrets, Bradley H & Sue P. Sinor
Redheads In Love, Linda L. Donahue, Rhonda Eudaly, Julia S.
    Mandala, & Dusty Rainbolt
Reruns, Selina Rosen
Rock 'n' Roll Universe, Ken Rand
Shadows In Green, Richard Dansky
Stories That Won't Make Your Parents Hurl, Edited by Selina
    Rosen
Tales from Keltora, Laura J. Underwood
*Tales Of the Lucky Nickel Saloon, Second Ave., Laramie,
    Wyoming, U S of A,* Ken Rand
Tarbox Station, Rhonda Eudaly
Texistani: Indo-Pak Food From A Texas Kitchen, Beverly A. Hale
That's All Folks, J. F. Gonzalez

Through Wyoming Eyes, Ken Rand
Turn Left to Tomorrow, Robin Wayne Bailey
The Twins, Selina Rosen
Wandering Lark, Laura J. Underwood
Wings of Morning, Katharine Eliska Kimbriel
Zombies In Oz and Other Undead Musings, Robin Wayne Bailey

Double Dog (A YDP Imprint):

#1:
Of Stars & Shadows, Mark W. Tiedemann
This Instance Of Me, Jeffrey Turner

#2:
Gods and Other Children, Bill D. Allen
Tranquility, Tracy Morris

#3:
Home Is the Hunter, James K. Burk
Farstep Station, Lazette Gifford

#4:
Sabre Dance, Melanie Fletcher
The Lunari Mask, Laura J. Underwood

#5:
House of Doors, Julia Mandala
Jaguar Moon, Linda A. Donahue

Just Cause (A YDP Imprint):

The Bitter End
Selina Rosen

Death Under the Crescent Moon
Dusty Rainbolt

The Ghost Writer
Selina Rosen

It's Not Rocket Science: Spirituality for the Working-Class Soul
Selina Rosen

Meditations of a Hoarder
Melinda LaFevers

Not My Life
Selina Rosen

The Pit
Selina Rosen

Plots and Protagonists: A Reference Guide for Writers
Mel. White

Vanishing Fame
Selina Rosen

Non-YDP titles we distribute:

Chains of Freedom
Chains of Destruction
Jabone's Sword
Queen of Denial
Recycled
Strange Robby
Sword Masters
Selina Rosen

Three Ways to Order:

1. Write us a letter telling us what you want, then send it along with your check or money order (made payable to Yard Dog Press) to: Yard Dog Press, 710 W. Redbud Lane, Alma, AR 72921-7247

2. Use selinarosen@cox.net or lynnstran@cox.net to contact us and place your order. Then send your check or money order to the address above. *This has the advantage of allowing you to check on the availability of short-stock items such as T-shirts and back-issues of Yard Dog Comics.*

3. Contact us as in #1 or #2 above and pay with a credit card or by debit from your checking account. Either give us the credit card information in your letter/Email/phone call, or go to our website and use our shopping carts. If you send us your information, please include your name as it appears on the card, your credit card number, the expiration date, and the 3 or 4-digit security code after your signature on the back (CVV). Please remember that we will include media rate (minimum $3.00) S/H for mailing in the lower 48 states.

Watch our website at
www.yarddogpress.com
for news of upcoming projects
and new titles!!

A Note to Our Readers

We at Yard Dog Press understand that many people buy used books because they simply can't afford new ones. That said, and understanding that not everyone is made of money, we'd like you to know something that you may not have realized. Writers only make money on new books that sell. At the big houses a writer's entire future can hinge on the number of books they sell. While this isn't the case at Yard Dog Press, the honest truth is that when you sell or trade your book or let many people read it, the writer and the publishing house aren't making any money.

As much as we'd all like to believe that we can exist on love and sweet potato pie, the truth is we all need money to buy the things essential to our daily lives. Writers and publishers are no different.

We realize that these "freebies" and cheap books often turn people on to new writers and books that they wouldn't otherwise read. However we hope that you will reconsider selling your copy, and that if you trade it or let your friends borrow it, you also pass on the information that if they really like the author's work they should consider buying one of their books at full price sometime so that the writer can afford to continue to write work that entertains you.

We appreciate all our readers and *depend* upon their support.

Thanks,
The Editorial Staff
Yard Dog Press

PS – Please note that "used" books without covers have, in most cases, been stolen. Neither the author nor the publisher has made any money on these books because they were supposed to be pulped for lack of sales.

Please do not purchase books without covers.

www.ingramcontent.com/pod-product-compliance
Lightning Source LLC
Chambersburg PA
CBHW030646260626

47157CB00007B/2514